P9-CEZ-089

He felt the magic field strengthen, and for a moment his hopes soared. Then the counterforce hit like a hammer blow, scattering the magic field like water exploding out of a shattered bottle. Matt stood, stunned, pain pounding through his head, the world blurring around him. He sagged against the concrete wall, and couldn't tell if the roaring in his ears was the freight train or the effect of an inner concussion.

It faded, and Matt heard the traffic whirring on Main Street. Shaken, he took a deep breath, and wondered what had happened. It was almost as though the enemy sorcerer had been watching Matt in person, had known he was about to try another spell, had stood waiting, ready to hit with everything he had. But how? How could he have known?

By Christopher Stasheff
Published by Ballantine Books:

A Wizard in Rhyme:
HER MAJESTY'S WIZARD
THE OATHBOUND WIZARD
THE WITCH DOCTOR
THE SECULAR WIZARD
MY SON, THE WIZARD

Starship Troupers:
A COMPANY OF STARS
WE OPEN ON VENUS
A SLIGHT DETOUR

The Star Stone:
THE SHAMAN
THE SAGE

Books published by The Ballantine Publishing Group
are available at quantity discounts on bulk purchases
for premium, educational, fund-raising, and special
sales use. For details, please call 1-800-733-3000.

MY SON,
THE WIZARD

Book V of *A Wizard in Rhyme*

Christopher Stasheff

A Del Rey® Book
THE BALLANTINE PUBLISHING GROUP • NEW YORK

Sale of this book without a front cover may be unauthorized. If this book is coverless, it may have been reported to the publisher as "unsold or destroyed" and neither the publisher nor the author may have received payment for it.

A Del Rey® Book
Published by The Ballantine Publishing Group
Copyright © 1997 by Christopher Stasheff

All rights reserved under International and Pan-American Copyright Conventions. Published in the United States by The Ballantine Publishing Group, a division of Random House, Inc., New York, and simultaneously in Canada by Random House of Canada Limited, Toronto.

Del Rey and colophon are registered trademarks of Random House, Inc.

www.randomhouse.com/delrey/

Library of Congress Catalog Card Number: 99-94749

ISBN 0-345-42480-8

Printed in Canada

First Hardcover Edition: November 1997
First Mass Market Edition: July 1999

10 9 8 7 6 5

With thanks to Isobel-Marie for suggesting
an appearance by the old knight

CHAPTER 1

The air over the broad table shimmered and thickened, coalescing into a pint-sized gryphon who took one look at the man who had conjured it up, screamed, and shot toward him with talons reaching out.

" 'But the haunch and the hump and the hide of the law is: Obey!' " Saul intoned. "Land on my shoulder—and don't pinch!"

The gryphon changed course on the instant, wheeling about Saul's head to land on his shoulder—gently. It furled its wings and glowered at Saul resentfully, but it obeyed.

"Amazing," Matt said, staring. "And it'll work on any kind of monster you conjure up?"

"Any kind I conjure up, yes," Saul said. "How it will work on something an enemy calls up, I don't know." He snapped out a quick verse, and the gryphon disappeared.

"Very impressive," Matt said.

Saul shrugged irritably. "I don't do magic just to show off."

"No, you do it to share your research with an ally who might need it—and I very easily might. Thanks a lot." Matt smiled. "I thought you didn't do magic at all—or do you still think this is all one massive hallucination?"

"No, I've admitted to myself that it's real, at least in this fantasy universe," Saul sighed, "and that I can actually make strange things happen by reciting poetry. I still don't buy that idea about the magical power coming from either God or the Devil, though, with no gray source in between."

1

"How do you explain the difference between white and black, then?"

"How do you explain the difference between white and black on an old-fashioned TV screen?" Saul countered.

Matt shrugged. "White is where there're a lot of electrons hitting the back of the screen, black is where there are none—if you absolutely have to call it 'black'; it's all really shades of blue."

Saul nodded. "Same thing. Whether it's good magic or bad magic depends on what it's used for—which is to say, it depends on the person who does the using."

"You think it's a talent, then? Not something everybody can learn to do, like physics and chemistry?"

"I'm not all that sure that everybody can learn physics and chemistry," Saul countered. "I think there's definitely a matter of talent involved in being a good engineer. And I *know* it takes talent to be a good magician—we've both seen people try, reciting enough poetry to burn down a forest but only lighting a campfire."

"So everybody can do it, but not everybody can do it well." Matt nodded. "Yeah, I'd have to agree. But how come a poet like Frisson just happens to have such vast power?"

"Because the same talent that makes a poet, also makes a magician—at least, in this universe," Saul said. "I'm not sure yet, but I think there really isn't any distinction between them."

"So I'm a powerful wizard because I have enough of the poet's talent to love literature, and get a body-rush from it—but not enough to make up any real poetry."

Saul nodded. "But Frisson, who makes up good verses the way he breathes—sheer instinct, can't help himself . . ."

"And emits great poetry at least once a week, without realizing it." Matt felt the bite of envy.

"Right. He also happens to be such a powerful magician that he was a walking hazard, until I taught him how to write down the poetry instead of chanting it aloud whenever the Muse hit him."

"Like lightning to a lightning rod." Matt nodded with a wry smile. "Yeah, I'd have to say it's a matter of talent."

"Sure." Saul shrugged. "Otherwise, every peasant would be memorizing spells from birth, and everybody would be shooting magic around so often that a whole village would burn down every time somebody got a little irritated with somebody else."

Matt stared. "You mean magical talent could be a counter-survival trait?"

"Unless it happens to be linked to genes for unusually good judgment and amazingly good self-restraint, yes." Saul gave Matt a bitter smile. "Now do you see why I don't like to work magic if I don't have to?"

"Yeah." Privately, Matt didn't—he thought Saul was one of the most levelheaded people he knew, and his massive self-restraint was only partially disguised by the hippie ways that he tried so hard to live out.

Matt turned and looked out the window. "There's the other reason why you don't like to work magic."

Saul came to stand at the tall clerestory window, looking down into Queen Alisande's private garden, where the queen and Lady Angelique were comparing babies. "Oh, how right you are," Saul said softly. "You never know when a spell might backfire and hurt them. That's why, when I do have to do some chanting, I go off by myself, at least a hundred yards from the house—and I'm *very* careful."

He always had been, actually, where other people were concerned, though he tried to seem indifferent. "Glad you could come visit," Matt said. "There aren't too many women that Alisande can relax and gossip with."

"Well, our ladies aren't god-sibs, but I get the point," Saul replied. "Sir Guy and Lady Yverne don't stop by too often, then?"

"Christmas and Easter. Other than that, Sir Guy only shows up when there's trouble. We'd like to invite them to dinner, but we don't know where they live."

"You mean he doesn't even tell *you*?"

Matt shook his head. "Security nut. Mind you, I probably

would be, too, if I had a wife and babies and was heir to a broken-up empire—especially if I didn't want to *be* emperor, and thought the individual kingdoms were doing just fine the way they were."

"Well, when you put it that way, it does sound like *justified* paranoia," Saul admitted. "It would kind of make him liable to be a political pawn."

"Yes, and with people he loves as hostages, he could be very vulnerable indeed," Matt agreed. "Easier to stay hidden—and safer for everybody concerned."

"Suppose so," Saul allowed. "Does kind of make me feel sorry for Yverne, though."

"She knew it going in," Matt sighed, "and knew she could have been queen of Ibile, too. She doesn't seem to have any regrets, but I notice she does a lot of talking whenever she's here."

"High energy level, no doubt," Saul agreed. "One more who thinks of this castle as a home away from home."

"Yeah . . . home." Uneasiness prickled Matt's conscience. "Be nice to be able to visit the folks again."

"No it wouldn't." Saul's voice had an edge to it. "Me, I had a pompous autocrat for a father and a phony pill-popper for a mother. I like your world just fine, Matt."

"My world, yes." Matt felt a glow as he looked out over the wall of the private garden to the courtyard, and the castle towers beyond. "My world, my home . . ." He glanced down at his wife and son again and felt the glow spread. "Be nice if the kid could meet his grandparents, though."

"Yeah," Saul answered with a mirthless smile. "How do you think they'll feel about having a prince for a grandson?"

"Fine, considering who the queen is." But conscience pricked harder. "Kind of too bad we had to get married without their blessing, though . . ."

"What were you going to do? Send a limo to bring them to the church?"

Matt looked up with a sudden glint in his eye. "Maybe. Just maybe I could have!"

Saul stared at his face and shuddered. "I know that look.

The last time you had it, you got hung up on translating an indecipherable parchment, and look where that got you!"

"Yeah, with the perfect wife, a prince for a baby, and the highest position in the land next to hers! If all my ideas work out that well—"

"If," Saul said, interrupting. "You have a knack of developing dangerous projects, lad."

"Dangerous? Me, A.B.D. in comparative literature? How dangerous can poetry be?"

"Plenty, in a universe in which magic works by rhyme, and literary criticism is equivalent to theoretical physics. What bomb are you planning to explode *this* time?"

"Hey, if I could travel here, I should be able to travel back, shouldn't I?"

"Forgive him, St. Moncaire," Saul called toward the heavens.

"Wouldn't the saint want me to pay attention to my mother and father? I mean, Saul, five years! Five years since they heard anything from me! They'll be frantic!" This time conscience stabbed, and deeply.

"Not so long as that," Saul reminded him. "Remember, you'd only been gone a few days when I started hunting you, but it was two years here."

"Time moves faster in this universe, huh? But that means it's been a week there!"

"Yeah, a week, and you a hundred miles away in college! Tell me they're worried sick."

"Yeah, there is that." Matt turned to watch Alisande again, calming a little. "Probably not worried at all."

"Didn't sound like it, when I talked to them. Your mother just told me to look for you on campus. Hey, you never told me she was an immigrant."

"Yeah, came from Cuba when Castro—" Matt's head snapped up. "You talked to her!"

"I wouldn't say that. My Spanish is only a little worse than her English, and—"

"You phoned them!"

"Sure." Saul frowned. "You'd disappeared without leaving any word. Of course I thought of trying you at home!"

"But you got them worried! Now they *know* I'm missing!"

"Hey, I just asked for you," Saul protested. "I didn't say where I was calling from—and I sure didn't tell them you'd gone missing!"

"You don't know my mother! If some people have worry warts, she's got an anxiety aneurysm! She'll start wondering, she'll call the college and check!"

"Hey, man, don't freak out on me! How's she gonna check up if she can't speak English?"

"She'll pester them until they find somebody who speaks Spanish! That woman is *smart*!"

Saul lifted his head. "Dr. Korbinsky!"

"Right! *She* speaks Spanish—and she's on my doctoral committee! All I need is to have two overprotective mothers putting their heads together and working up a panic! Saul, I've *got* to get home!"

"Right, sure, I gotcha, man." Saul was actually trying to sound soothing. "But where's the bus?"

"I'll ask the Spider King! *He'll* know!"

"Sure." Saul's lip twisted. "All you have to do is find him."

"Oh, I have a notion he's keeping an eye on me—on all of us, now that you mention it."

"I didn't."

"Doesn't matter. He's thorough—attention to detail and all that."

"Oh, and I'm a detail, am I?"

"Saul." Matt put a hand on his friend's shoulder. "In the cosmic scheme of things . . ."

". . . we're all details, yeah, sure! What do you think, all you have to do is tell the nearest spider, 'Connect me to the Big Boy'?"

"Wouldn't be surprised." Matt frowned, looking directly into Saul's eyes. "You do understand how this is really important, don't you?"

"Why ask me?" Saul jerked his head toward Alisande. "*She's* your sovereign."

Matt asked his sovereign that evening. His sovereign said yes. His wife went all teary and told him he was a heartless beast for ignoring his mother for so long. He reassured her that only a week had passed for his mother, which mollified her somewhat—but she still thought he was a stony, calloused monster not to have thought of them sooner.

Privately, Matt agreed.

The next morning, he dug out the clothes he'd worn when he arrived in Merovence. He'd gone back to rescue them from the ruins of Sayeesa's castle when some hint of packrat caution had made him feel he might need them again, though Heaven knew why. He checked the pockets to make sure his wallet, key, and pocket change were all there, then put on the white shirt, dress slacks, loafers, and sport coat. It was amazing that Saul had ever been willing to talk to him—Saul, for whom the height of fashion had always been a chambray shirt, blue jeans, and boots. Of course, Saul had always paid more attention to what people held inside their heads than to what they wore on their bodies, and although the inner fashions usually went with the outer, occasionlly he found, and respected, the individual who didn't really pay much attention to either. Matt had always been a lousy dresser.

He went out while the dew still lingered on the spider silk, found the biggest web in the garden, and told the resident arachnid, "I'd like to talk to the Spider King, if he's free. It's about going home to visit—my original home, that is."

A sunbeam struck the dewdrops, glittering, making the whole web a spangled wonder; it caught Matt's attention, fascinating him, seeming to expand to surround him. The sunlight winked and dazzled and shot rays from each drop. Matt found himself overwhelmed by the beauty of it, reeled at the spectacle, felt his breath pressed from him by the impact of such glory.

Then the moment passed, the web seemed to dwindle

again, and the spider still sat in the center, oblivious of it all. With a sigh of regret, Matt straightened, lifting his gaze . . .

And stared.

He froze in shock. The corner store looked the same as it always had. Whenever he had come home to visit, it had always looked the same, only the brands on the shelves changing the styles of their labels.

Home to visit? Yes, he was, wasn't he? The Spider King, whose web of forces and personas stretched across the dimensions to catch all the Earths in all the alternate universes, had acted with amazing speed. Matt couldn't help feeling that it had been too easy, much too easy, especially considering how much effort he had expended for weeks, even months, before he'd finally been able to make sense of the arcane verse he'd found, and been transported to Merovence. Suddenly, Matt began to feel an old and highly unpleasant sensation, as if there were invisible strings tied to his ankles, wrists, and temples. He was being manipulated again. He began to wonder if it was really Saul who had put the idea of going home into his mind.

Something roared behind him. Matt whirled, adrenaline pumping. What kind of supernatural monster . . . ?

The Route 34 bus pulled up to the curb.

Matt stared. He was so used to seeing dragons and manticores that the bus did seem supernatural—and the stink of exhaust, which he'd scarcely noticed before, was a veritable stench. He'd been spoiled by clean air.

The doors folded open, and the driver said, "You gettin' on, mac, or just lookin'?"

Matt couldn't help the foolish grin that spread over his face. "Just saying hello, Mr. Joe."

The driver stared, then grinned. "Hey, it's you, Matt! Day off from school, huh?"

Matt gave a half shrug and a sheepish grin.

"Day off, but they didn't know about it." Joe chuckled. "Well, good to see you, boy. Take care."

"You, too, Mr. Joe." Matt raised a hand.

"Just 'Joe' now, Matt," the driver said. "You're old

enough, and I been telling you that for eight years. So long, now!"

The doors closed, and the bus rumbled away, turning the corner. Matt followed it with his gaze, taking in the rest of the intersection. The apartment building on the northwest corner still looked the same, except that the landlord had finally had the stoop fixed. The little meat market across the street still looked as busy as ever. As he watched, Mrs. Picorelli bustled up to put some more cans on the shelf, then bustled away back out of the light—seventy-five, and still going strong. He hoped her husband was still okay—at eighty, he should have been taking his ease in a rocking chair, not still cutting meat. But who was going to make him retire? He owned the store.

Then he remembered that he'd seen them just last Easter, and it couldn't be later than early June. If it had been, the schoolkids would have been out playing in the street, ducking out of the way when a car came along. No reason to think the old couple were in any worse shape than when he'd last seen them. Of course, that had been five years ago for him—but not for them.

He turned, strolling down the street. The Spider King's aim had been nearly perfect—not quite at his parents' doorstep but only half a block away. Not bad, from another universe. He noticed that Mr. Gussenhoven's garden was as neat and tidy as ever, his lawn still rich and luxuriant. The corner of the garden wall was broken again, and the heavy piece of angle iron tilted over, making the whole fence lean. Some drunken idiot must have crashed into it with his car, trying to make a K-turn at night. He must have been drunk, or he would have realized that the heavy steel would dent his fender nicely. He might not pay Mr. Gussenhoven for the damage, but he'd pay his body shop.

Matt turned to look down the length of the street, still not quite believing he was home. Only a few minutes ago, he'd been inside the walls of a castle; his wife had been holding court in a real, genuine throne room where the suits of armor standing in the corners had real live guards inside them—

and now he was here, on a quiet blue-collar street in suburban New Jersey! It was definitely unbelievable.

But as the gloss wore off, claustrophobia suddenly hit. The houses were so close together, the front yards so small! Had he really grown up here, and thought it was perfectly normal? It seemed so hard to believe now—not just compared to his wife's castle, but even to the university town where he'd gone to college!

Of course, it used to look a lot better. The Daleys' garden had shrunk, flower by flower, even after they'd put the chain-link fence up. "Those darn kids, while they're waiting for the bus!" Mrs. Daley had told him. "They get into fights and knock each other into my bushes! They play tag and trample all over my petunias!" But she'd kept replanting—for a while. "The police said I couldn't complain if I didn't have a fence," she said, "so I put up the chain-link. The kids climb it to pick flowers for their girls. The police tell me they've got too much real trouble to worry about a few posies."

So year by year, the neighborhood had lost its flowers. Mr. Gussenhoven had patched up the corner of his retaining wall the first time a car had crumbled it while making a K-turn. Then he'd patched it again, when he'd come out and found it broken again, only this time, he'd reinforced it with the angle iron. Apparently that had made the kids mad, when they damaged their cars on the K-turns, because they must have come back with sledgehammers and broken ten feet of wall. Mr. Gussenhoven had fixed that, too, but not anymore. The corner was broken now, and looked as if it was going to stay that way.

Matt looked up and down the street, noticing all the signs of disrepair and decay. Some of those gardener couples had died; others had moved to retirement villages. He wondered what kind of people had moved in. What were his parents doing here, his educated, cultured mother and father?

He knew the answer to that. Sure, his father had a graduate degree in literature, but he had chosen to teach college. His mother had taken her M.A. and started her doctoral coursework after Matt started school, but by the time she hit the job market, the colleges were trying to get rid of faculty, not hire new. Papa had been passed over for tenure again and again, which meant no promotions, which meant there had never been money for her to finish her degree. For a minute, Matt felt a surge of second-generation hatred for Castro, for driving his mother out of the comfortable house and life-style her father had worked so hard to keep up. They had also lost the money he had saved for her education, so she had needed to work her way through, taking two years longer.

He swallowed the anger, reminding himself that if she had stayed in Cuba, she never would have met Papa, and Matt himself never would have been born—not as he knew him-self, anyway. Different parents, different body, different per-sonality, probably—but the same soul?

He shrugged the question off, irritated. He was back in the USA now, not in Merovence! Those kinds of questions had no meaning here—did they?

"Well, if it ain't the college boy."

Matt's head snapped up. Lost in his thoughts and memories—he should have known better! Liam, Choy, and Luco had stepped out from under some rock to block his way.

"Playin' hooky, chicken boy?"

The "chicken" struck home; old fears raised their grin-ning heads inside Matt. These three had taken every chance to torment him since they'd hit junior high, even though he'd been two years ahead—along with their half-dozen buddies. The fear hollowed Matt's stomach; dread climbed up into his chest, his arms . . .

. . . and faded away. It disappeared as quickly as it had come. Iron determination took its place. Matt stood mute and staring, amazed at himself.

Luco laughed. "Too scared to talk, huh? Think I'm the truant officer?"

He guffawed at his own wit. Choy and Liam echoed him.

The jeering raised Matt's anger. He let it build, glad of it, but held it at its proper level. "Truant officer? Well, I sup-pose you know all about playing hooky, Luco."

Luco's grin turned nasty. "Permanent hooky, dum-dum. We got smart."

"That's why you've got such good jobs, huh?"

Liam swung a short, vicious jab to the ribs. Matt blocked by reflex, and for a second Liam's eyes went wide. Then they narrowed again, and he snarled, "So the college finally taught you something, huh? Let's see how they did on street fighting!"

He swung again, but Matt jumped back, knowing what was coming—Luco's fists, from the right, in a quick combination. Matt danced away, reciting,

"His nose should pant and his lip should curl,
    His cheeks should flame, and his brow should furl,
His foot should trip, for he is my foe,
    And his chin receive a hammer of a knockdown blow!"

Luco stumbled and flinched—nothing more. Of course. This was the USA, in the universe of science and reason, where poetry could only work wonders in people's hearts. Fear started again.

"Very pretty," Choy snarled, and lashed a kick at Matt's belly.

He caught Choy's foot. He actually caught it. He stared at the sneaker for a second in amazement. He'd never been able to move that fast before.

At least, not in *this* universe. He grinned up at Choy, twisting, then shoving the foot away. "Slowed down, Choy. Too many drugs, huh?"

Choy hopped backward, cursing, face darkening with anger. Liam and Luco both struck, red-faced and outraged.

"Think they really taught you something, college boy?"

"Think you're better'n we are, huh?"

Matt blocked with his left as if he held a dagger, struck with his right fist as if it were a sword. A punch rocked his head, one that would have laid him out the last time he was home. Now he counterpunched, turned to block a kick, swung a vicious jab, then stepped in to finish off Luco with three blows to the belly and one to the jaw. As the man folded, he pivoted to push Choy's punch aside, then caught his wrist and swung him, hard, into Liam. The two of them went down in a tangle of legs and shouted curses. Liam's head struck the concrete; he went limp. Choy scrambled to his feet, catching up a fallen stick, and swung it at Matt's head with all his might.

It was the worst mistake he could have made, against a belted knight. Matt ducked under the blow and came up with a left jab into the belly, as hard as if he were driving in a dagger. Choy folded over in sudden intense pain, gagging and dropping the stick.

Matt caught it and broke it over his knee. He stood a moment, panting, then reached out and shoved on Choy's shoulder, hard. The thug staggered to the side, tripped on Luco's legs, and fell.

Matt stood staring down at them, feeling the thrill of victory coursing through him. Victory over his childhood tormentors! He could scarcely believe it.

Then he fingered his own biceps, flexing the arm. The muscles Sayeesa the lust-witch had given him by her magic were still there. Sir Guy had taught him swordplay and quarterstaff play, and the knowledge he had gained in Merovence's universe was still in his mind and neurons! Magic might not work here, but the fencing Sir Guy had taught him and the martial arts Saul had made him practice stayed in his brain and nerves. He grinned down at his old enemies, letting the excitement crest and begin to slacken. Then, working hard to scoff, not gloat, he said, "Too much booze, guys—and you'd better quit smoking. Oh, and you might want to give up tobacco."

Choy glared up at him, still struggling for breath.

"Don't be here when I get back," Matt advised, and turned to stroll away down the block, looking about him and reveling in the softness of the air, the scents of home—acrid though they might have become—and the vividness of the sky. It certainly was a fine day.

But something nagged at the back of his mind—magic. It

shouldn't work at all in this universe, but it had worked a little. He had called for Luco to trip, then be punched out, or at least down—and he had stumbled, then flinched as if somebody had slapped him.

Coincidence. Matt put it out of his mind and went back to enjoying the day. He looked around him at the neighborhood—and found he was standing in front of his own house. His parents' house, he amended; he didn't live here anymore. But it was the house he had grown up in, and Merovence began to recede, to seem awfully far away, just a fairy tale . . .

Until he noticed the two-foot-wide spiderweb between the porch roof and a pillar.

Matt smiled, feeling oddly reassured. He didn't remember seeing webs like that very often around this neighborhood. The Spider King had a strand in every universe, a magical connection of some sort. Matt's magic might not work here, but somebody's did.

Of course, it might be a perfectly normal spider, completely natural.

Sure.

He smiled, feeling very nostalgic as he gazed at the house. It was three windows wide on the second story, a door and two windows wide on the ground floor. Plain wooden steps ran up to the porch, with latticework between the brick pillars that held it up. Inside, there was a narrow entry hall that turned into an even narrower stairway about four feet from the door, narrower so that an eighteen-inch-wide passageway could lead back to the kitchen—about ten feet wide and twelve feet long. To the left of the entry hall was the doorway into the living room, which opened onto the dining room with its windows at the back and side of the house. Upstairs there were two decent-sized bedrooms, a small bedroom, and a bathroom just long enough to hold a short bathtub and just wide enough for everything else. It was old, it needed a coat of paint, the front-yard garden was down to two rosebushes— and it was wonderful. Boyhood memories swirled around it, nostalgia tugged him toward the door . . .

Then it opened, and a dainty woman in a housedress, with

her black hair in a knot, came out with a broom, straight toward the spiderweb.

"No, Mama!" Matt cried in panic.

The woman looked up in surprise, and in the split second that she stared at him, Matt was shocked to see a few gray hairs in the thick, luxuriant mass. Then she dropped the broom and ran down the steps to throw her arms around his neck with a glad cry.

CHAPTER 2

"Mateo!" Mama cried in Spanish. "I was so frightened when your friend called to ask if you were home! It is so great a relief to see you!" She pushed Matt away, holding him at arm's length, her face radiant. Matt looked back at the trim, petite woman with the large eyes and full lips, carefully made-up even at home, and was stricken with the sudden realization that his mother was a beautiful woman. He managed to set the thought aside and say, "Yeah, I really should have told Saul I was leaving town."

"Now I see why—you were only coming home to visit! Still, I think you worried him, *muchacho*." Then Mama frowned, mood changing to concern on the instant. "But why have you come home before the end of the semester, eh? Are you in trouble?"

"Oh, no! Everything's fine, just fine!" Matt said quickly. "But, uh, I have some news that I thought I needed to tell you and Papa face-to-face. Can he come home for lunch?"

"Yes, at one o'clock he will lock the store." Mama turned to lead the way into the house. "The security gate is still enough."

Matt felt a cold chill. He knew she was just talking in general terms—but if folding steel gates hadn't been enough to keep burglars from breaking into other stores, how long would it be before they weren't enough here? He remembered how the owner at the Laundromat had covered up his plate-glass windows with stucco, after the third time somebody had lobbed a brick through one. He'd only been ten at

16

the time and hadn't understood why Mr. Pikovsky had wanted to keep out the sunlight.

They came indoors, and Matt looked around at the little living room that had seemed so big to him when he'd been a boy, savoring its neatness and the tastefulness of the decoration, how well the wallpaper went with the furniture, enjoying the feeling of warmth that seemed to radiate from the floor-to-ceiling bookshelves. "This isn't a bad neighborhood, Mama," he said, as if to reassure himself.

"No, of course not! It was a fine neighborhood to bring up a boy," Mama said staunchly.

Well, it had been that. The older couples had been friendly and kind, and the young families' children hadn't been all that rough. But that had started changing when Matt hit junior high. "How are the Archers?"

"They moved, I don't know, to the Poconos, I think. You sit. I will make coffee." Mama bustled out to the kitchen, moving quickly to escape the memory of the Archers, the swaggering divorcee, her taunting, insulting children, and the friend she had invited in to live with them, another divorcee with three boys—eight people in a house built to hold five at the most. The mothers had gone out to dinner together and left the kids home to fend for themselves, or spent the evening sitting on a neighbor's porch drinking beer and leaving the kids to do as they pleased. After all, if they got bored, they could always torment Matt. The boys had made his life even more miserable than the girls had. Papa had started taking the bus to work at the college, so Mama could drive Matt to school and pick him up.

That left only Liam, Choy, Luco, and the would-be thugs who had gathered around them. They'd been no threat to the grownups even when Matt had gone off to college, but he hadn't looked forward to his trips home. Matt had hoped his parents would move when he went away to grad school and had been sure they would when Papa was laid off at the college, though they didn't call it that with professors—just that he'd failed to get tenure again. But a man purporting to be from a government bureau had talked Papa into going into business for himself, using all his savings and taking out a government loan to buy the old corner grocery store. Admittedly, Papa hadn't needed much persuading—at forty-eight, he'd become rather fed up with insolent students and overbearing college administrators. Besides, running a corner store looked as if it would pay better—and it had, for a while.

Still, it was all Matt had needed to make him bound and determined to put research first, and worry about the students later.

Mama brought the coffee in a demitasse, steaming and strong. "You still drink it black, no?"

"Coffee!" Matt hadn't had a drop in four years. He sipped it and let the drops roll back over his tongue, closing his eyes in ecstasy.

Mama stared. "You don't have coffee at the university?"

"Not like yours, Mama." Matt took another sip, closed his eyes again to savor it, then opened them to say, "I've, uh, been trying to quit." Well, he hadn't been trying, but he had quit.

Mama nodded, looking wise. "Two months is just long enough to make you crave it, Mateo. Let this be the only cup for today then, eh?"

Two months? Matt was amazed. He'd been well into the semester before he'd been translated to Merovence, which meant that only a few days had passed here. But five years had passed in the world of Merovence! Apparently Saul was right about time flowing at different rates in the two universes—or at the intersection points, anyway.

The door opened, and Papa came in. Matt looked quickly enough to see the haggardness before Papa saw him. His face lit up, and he crossed the room in two strides to catch Matt to him just as he was standing up. "Matt! What a great surprise!" He held his son away and looked him up and down, grinning. "You've never looked better."

"You, too, Papa." Matt couldn't help admiring his father. At fifty, he was still lean, still moved with the grace of a man of thirty. The black hair was touched with silver at the temples now, but the mustache was still black. He looked very distinguished, and still very handsome. Matt began to realize why he had always thought of himself as homely. He was glad Alisande hadn't.

"So to what do we owe this good fortune?" Papa's brow creased with sudden anxiety. "Not trouble, I hope."

"No, Papa—good luck. But I've had to make a very big decision, and I wanted to tell you about it in person."

"Tell later," Mama said firmly. "Dinner now."

The men bowed to her will, and her menu. Dinner was chicken and rice, every bit as good as Matt remembered it, and better because he'd been so long away from it. The talk was light and gossipy, for them—but it ranged from the gaffes of the neighbors to the blunders of the government, then off into the greater blunders of the Merovingian kings, and what would have happened if the Moors had never conquered Spain. For a scholar's home, it was light but pleasant talk.

When the dinner was done, Papa sat back with coffee and said quietly, "Okay, son. Tell."

Suddenly Matt wondered if it had been such a good idea to come home, after all. His stomach tightened with the apprehension of having to tell his parents something they weren't going to like; a child's fear enveloped him . . .

And he realized how silly it was. He was a man, not a child, and a very successful one, too! Not that he could give his parents the details . . .

So he put it into the terms of their world. "You know I've been stalled on my dissertation, right?"

"Over a scrap of parchment you couldn't translate." Papa shook his head, the professor coming to the fore in him. "A few lines are not enough to build a vocabulary, my son. I know I should not tell you again, but one verse does not a dissertation make."

"Well . . . I did manage to translate it," Matt said, trying to ease into it.

Mama exclaimed with surprise, and Papa's eyebrows rose. "So? Then you're moving on your dissertation again?"

"Not exactly. The parchment turned out to be a plant."

"A plant?" Papa frowned.

"Someone planted it for you to find?" Mama exclaimed angrily. "And made you go off on a useless tangent for months? How cruel!"

"Not useless," Matt said. "It was kind of a . . . test."

"A test?" Papa's frown deepened. "You mean it told you a direction?"

"Sort of," Matt said, trying to be his ambiguous best. "It led me to . . . well, I suppose you would call it a government bureau."

"Government?" Mama leaned forward in sudden fear. "Are you in trouble after all, Mateo?"

She had been a teenager when Castro took over. No wonder "government" meant trouble.

"No, Mama." Matt smiled. "It seems I . . . well, I've qualified for a . . . government job." He supposed that was a fair description of being Her Majesty's Wizard.

"What kind of government job?" Papa was very tense.

"Research," Matt ad-libbed. It was true, in its way—he'd had to figure out magic every step of the way, in his new universe.

"Research?" Papa sat forward with hope. "Then you will finish your Ph.D.?"

"I suppose I could," Matt said slowly, "but I don't think the research can be made public for a long time."

Mama made a little mourning sound, and Papa frowned again. "You only have seven years to finish, Mateo. Surely you will not give up when you have come so close!"

Inspiration struck. If it mattered to them, why not finish it? If five years in Merovence only equaled five days in New Jersey, surely Matt could find time to finish his research by visiting from time to time!

Then he remembered that a day here would take up a year there. Even if he did everything else by correspondence, he'd still have to take a year away from Merovence, just to defend his thesis in oral examination. Still, he might found a university there . . .

"You take so long in answering!" Mama protested. "I am

proud that you try to spare my feelings, my son—but do not lie to me! You will not finish the degree, will you?"

"Probably not," Matt admitted. "It's not completely impossible, mind you, but there really isn't going to be a lot of time."

Time! A full year, if he stayed here twenty-four hours! Suddenly he was very anxious to get back to Alisande and the baby.

"You will work long hours at this job, then?" Papa asked, frowning. "What kind of work is it, Mateo?"

"Using the magic of words, Papa, " Matt said carefully.

"Propaganda?" Papa frowned. "What is it? The Voice of America? The USIA?"

"It has to be secret," Matt said lamely. "I can tell you it involves a lot of translation, though." He did have to translate a great deal of verse from his own universe, to work his spells in Merovence.

"Translation! So! This parchment was an artificial language, then? No, no, I know you can't tell me!" Papa waved a flat palm, as if wiping a blackboard. "Something international, like Esperanto, but more Germanic probably. Well, I know you would not willingly work for an evil cause, my son. But be careful—the USIA may not be the CIA, but corrupted men can use good things for evil causes."

Matt remembered that Papa had grown up in the shadow of World War II, and had the sense not to argue. "I'm working for a worthy cause, Papa, and for good people. I'm sure of it."

"Test everything, son. I agree with Plato with this much, at least—that the unexamined life is not worth living." Papa scowled. "In this day of ideologies, that is more true than ever."

"I hope it pays well," Mama said faintly.

"Oh, very well, Mama." Matt turned to her. "Better even than a full professor's pay—in the sciences."

"Well." Papa seemed a little comforted. "It is worth doing for some years, then. You can always come back to scholarship when you have saved enough. But what of job security?"

"It's as secure as the government," Matt assured him, "and I'll have the best doctors in the country." He didn't mention that he wouldn't trust one of Alisande's physicians within a mile of the castle.

"What about retirement?" Mama asked anxiously. "I know you are young to be thinking of such things, Mateo, but it will be important sooner than you think!"

"Retirement benefits are spectacular." After all, Matt expected to die before Alisande, and as long as she was queen, he certainly wouldn't have to worry about room and board. He braced himself for the worst. "There's one real drawback, though."

"Which is?" Papa braced himself, too, and Mama's knuckles whitened.

"I can't visit home very much. Maybe once a year, for half a day."

Mama keened.

"That is hard indeed." Papa scowled again. "Perhaps we could come visit you."

"I'm afraid not," Matt said slowly. "It's in a, um, secret location." At least, in this universe, Alisande's castle wasn't very well known.

"That will be . . . unpleasant," Mama said. "But if it is so fine a job in every other way . . ."

"It is, Mama," Matt said, with feeling.

"Well, if it is what you wish, you must do it," Papa said briskly.

Mama nodded, tears in her eyes, and took Matt's hand. "Yes, you must. But write far more often than you have, Mateo."

"I will, Mama." It was a safe promise, considering that Matt had averaged maybe one letter a month. He ought to be able to figure out some way to transport a letter to their house. He reminded himself to take a souvenir home—maybe a spell of contagion would work. He wondered if he could manage a telephone call.

"But if this place is so secret we cannot even visit, how shall we write you?" Papa asked.

"I'll send you an address that will get your letters to me."

Inspiration struck, and Matt suddenly knew how he was going to manage it.

"He must go his own way, after all," Mama reminded Papa.

"He must," Papa agreed heavily. "May it bring you success, son." He smiled with irony. "After all, the academic life hasn't done all that well for me."

"If you say so," Matt said slowly, "but that was because you were more interested in teaching your students than in doing research."

"Yes, or playing academic politics," Papa said wryly. "If your chosen field doesn't require those, my son, I cannot complain against it. Well, I know you cannot tell me any details about your work, but surely you can tell me what you have learned about the nature of language."

With that, talk shifted to safe topics—poetry and mythology. Poetry was really Papa's field, mythology was Mama's, and both were fascinated by the tales Matt brought them with the verse forms of Merovence, or as closely as he could manage in translation. All too soon, the clock on the mantel chimed three times.

"Three o'clock!" Matt leaped out of his chair. "My gosh! I'm late!"

"I didn't know you had a time limit." Papa rose with him.

"I've got to, um, make my travel connections." Matt had arrived about noon. He'd already been gone from Merovence for a month and a half. "Sorry. The time just slipped away."

"Well, I'm glad you still enjoy our company," Papa said.

"Of course!" Matt embraced his father. "Too much—I can't keep track of time around you." He turned to give his mother a hug. "Uh—Mama . . . could I have a lock of your hair?"

"To remember me?" Mama took the scissors from her sewing box and clipped off a few dark inches with a tearful smile. She pressed it into Matt's hand. "Take it and keep us in your prayers, my son."

"He doesn't ask for a lock of my hair?" Papa said, pretending to be huffy.

"You're not as pretty as she is," Matt said with a grin.

"He most certainly is!" Mama said, with asperity.

"As long as you think so, all is well with me." Papa gathered her into his arm with a broad smile.

Matt hesitated on the threshold. "You sure about that?"

"That all is well with us? Yes, of course!" Papa said heartily. "That does not excuse us from working, of course. But don't worry about us. Go with God, my son, and conquer your new world!"

As he closed the door behind him, Matt reflected that his father had, as usual, said more than he realized.

At the corner, he turned back to wave. Mama and Papa waved, too, arm in arm on the stoop, watching after him. Matt turned away, turned the corner . . .

"Took ya long enough, Matty boy," Liam said, and swung a roundhouse punch.

CHAPTER 3

Matt ducked and came up with his fists trip-hammering. Three punches in the belly, one in the chin, and Liam fell back. Luco caught him, and Matt saw the other three toughs Liam and Luco had called in for backup. Matt only recognized Herm; he guessed the rest of the old neighborhood gang had grown up and moved away. These six were obviously still trying to be juvenile delinquents.

Then one of the strangers shot a flat-knuckled punch fast, too fast for Matt to duck. He tried to lean aside, but it caught him on the side of the head, a glancing blow, and he staggered backward, seeing stars, shaking his head to try to clear it, because he heard the roar of the mini-mob as they piled in. Matt felt something hard and rough behind his back—a tree trunk!—set himself against it, and called,

> "Let the ground shake
> Under these boys!
> Let them all fall stumbling down!
> Let branches fall
> Onto their heads,
> 'Cause the wizard is
> Back in town!"

Choy and one of the strangers shouted as they tripped over something invisible. Matt heard something boom not far away, like a truck backfiring, and the tree branches suddenly dipped above him. He felt a slight vibration in his legs, and a dead branch came clattering out of the tree, but that was all. Well, he was surprised the verse had worked at all, here. Liam, Luco, and the other two strangers came at him, shouting.

Matt knew what to do when there were too many to fight. He turned and ran.

The boys yelled and came pelting after.

The sidewalk tilted crazily where tree roots had bulged it, but Matt knew every crack in the concrete—he ran as surely footed as a mountain goat. He glanced back and realized he was in better shape than the gang—they were far behind, though Liam was five yards out in front, yelling, red in the face. Matt swerved right down the Gussenhovens' driveway and ducked between their garage and their house. There he flattened himself against the wall, breathing deeply. He heard Liam yelling, pelting closer and closer . . .

Matt stuck out a foot. Liam tripped and went sprawling. He scrambled to his feet and turned on Matt, saying, "Bad idea, stu . . ."

Matt ducked as he swung, grunted as a fist struck his chest. He gripped and turned, then let go. Liam flew ten feet and landed hard, howling with the pain.

Baby. He'd landed on dirt, not concrete. But the gang was catching up, yelling and puffing. Matt took off again, past the garage and up old Mrs. Matelot's driveway. He glanced back, saw Choy out in front, and took a chance. He whirled back just as Choy came up, ducked a high kick—Choy had been watching too many ninja movies and listening to too few senseis—caught the leg, and twisted. Choy yelped in pain and surprise as he spun to the ground.

Matt took off running again with the pack behind him, still yelling, still furious. He swung around the corner and sprinted. The others howled, angrier than ever as they realized Matt had only led them back to his father's store.

He kept going till he was past the plate-glass windows and on the all-brick side of the store, then skidded to a halt, back to the tree again. The four remaining punks came huffing up and charged him, throwing punches. Matt ducked and shoved, caught a fist in the ribs and held his breath, kicked someone else's feet out from under him, then turned to face the last two.

But Luco and Herm pulled switchblades, flicked them open, and stepped in, grinning.

Suddenly it wasn't just bullying anymore. Matt stepped away from the tree and out into the street. His ears told him there were no cars to worry about, but he heard the bus coming. Hope quickened.

Luco thrust, cat-quick, but Matt was quicker. He caught the wrist and twisted as he turned, throwing Luco against the wall of the store. Luco shouted with pain, but Herm lunged even as Matt turned back. The knife ripped his shirt, but he stepped aside and kicked the kid's feet out from under him, then saw the dead branch that had fallen with his minor earth tremor and snatched it up. He whirled it *moulinet* style, glaring at Choy and Liam as they came panting up. They drew back, hesitating as they saw the two switchblades on the ground. Matt could see them wondering what he could do with that stick . . .

A diesel horn brayed. Matt jumped back. The boys scattered away, and the bus pulled up, slowing for the corner. The door hissed open. Matt dropped the stick and jumped aboard.

Luco and his gang realized what was happening and shouted, running toward the bus, but the door closed as the driver started moving to turn the corner. A couple of thuds clattered on the side of the bus, and the three other passengers made disapproving noises. "Kids today!" one grandfather grunted. "Ought to take the strap to every one of them!"

"Thanks, Mr. Joe," Matt panted.

"Hey, you ain't been around in months, I got to give you a ride."

"Really good to be on your bus again," Matt said fervently. "Sorry about the excitement back there."

"Them!" Joe said with scorn. "I won't let them ride my bus no more. Last time I did, one of them lit up a joint, and I sat at the curb for fifteen minutes before he gave up and threw it away. I caught hell from the checker, too."

Matt nodded. "They're not much to worry about, as gangs go."

Actually, he was surprised to find that they weren't. They had terrorized him through junior high and high school, but now he found out that they couldn't really fight all that well. They hadn't been trained, of course, but even as street fighters went, they weren't much to worry about—clumsy and slow, and they didn't know very many moves. What had he ever been afraid of?

Well, even the last time he'd been home, they'd been a lot better fighters than he had been, and there had never been fewer than three of them to his one. Now he'd had Sir Guy's lessons, and Saul's—and had the muscles Sayeesa had wished on him for her own purposes. And he'd been knighted. In Merovence, that carried a lot of benefits: authority, understanding of military strategy, fighting ability—and courage.

So *that* was why he hadn't been swamped by the surge of boyhood fears! Apparently the enchantment of the knighting ceremony stayed with him, even in a nonmagical universe. It made sense—the knowledge and skills were in his brain, no matter how they'd come to be there.

Nonetheless, Matt reminded himself, he still wasn't any world-class street fighter. It wasn't just his own improvements that made the neighborhood gang look inept. They really were—and maybe it wasn't just that he was better, maybe it was that they were worse. Six years of drugs, alcohol, and tobacco could do that. There were a lot worse than them around, and not all that far away, either.

"The neighborhood isn't what it used to be, Joe," he said.

"Used to look a lot better," Joe agreed. "Used to be some nice kids in it, too. Not now, though. Drugs and TV, that's what it is."

So it wasn't just the contrast of the cramped, working-class neighborhood with the fields of Merovence or the luxury of Alisande's castle. The neighborhood really had gone downhill, and badly. Matt found himself wishing there were some way he could get his parents out of it.

Matt changed buses across from the supermarket. It was a shock to see it closed, but it was a bigger shock to see the chain-link fence around the whole property, even the parking lot. Of course, he hadn't been down this way in a year or more—six, in his own time—since the last time he'd had to take the bus into Bloomfield, but it was still a shock.

"Six months closed, an' no sign of anyone startin' it up again," said a woman waiting nearby. "Why'd they have to close it down, anyway?"

"Said there was too much shopliftin'," the other woman answered. "Where they think us poor folks gonna go shoppin' now?"

Come to think of it, Matt did remember a lot of signs warning people not to shoplift.

Matt caught the bus to Main Street, handed the driver his transfer, and watched the familiar neighborhoods roll by. It still looked awfully run-down compared to Merovence, but at least the urban-renewal project in the shopping district had been very successful. The plastic canopies all along the central blocks made it look much nicer, anyway.

He got off at the post office and enjoyed the feeling of stepping back into a more affluent era as he came into the lobby of the 1930s Federal-Classic building. The ceiling was high, the wainscoting was real wood, and so were the windows. Matt rented a post-office box, wrote the number down on a piece of scrap paper, then also wrote down the longitude and latitude—he still had them memorized from a grade-school assignment. It had been twenty years, but things drummed into young brains tend to stay there. He bought a hundred stamps, then wrote down the exact wording above the slots for outgoing mail—"local" and "out of town." After all, he wanted to be able to send Christmas cards, didn't he? He picked up a couple of the "moving" booklets, with their forms for letting people know his new address, filled out two of them, mailing one to his parents and the other to Mrs. Vogel, the next-door neighbor who had been so kind to him when he was little. When he was a teenager, too, in fact. Then he went out for a stroll.

He went quite a bit faster than strolling, of course. Time was wasting—a week in Merovence for every half hour here.

Around behind the train station he went, through the bridge under the tracks to the far side. He glanced around before he entered—it was an ideal place for an ambush, but also for a tramp to hide out from the rain. It was empty at the moment, though, aside from some stale smells that he didn't like to think about. He took up a stance right in the middle, out of sight of anybody but some nosy kid who might happen to be wandering by, and began to recite the words of the parchment that had originally brought him to Merovence.

"Lalinga wogreus marwold reiger
Athelstrigen marx alupta
Harleng krimorg barlow steiger . . ."

They were nonsense syllables.

Matt tried again, beginning to sweat. He'd been speaking this language for five years now! He should know it as thoroughly as he knew English! But the words remained stubbornly opaque, devoid of meaning. If they would just start making sense, his mind would be in tune with the universe in which the language was spoken; if he could let the beauty of the words sink in, begin to feel the body-rush that came with that beauty, he would find himself in Alisande's castle.

He took a deep breath and reminded himself that it had taken two months and more of reciting those syllables, of digging into the origins of those words, before their meaning had come beating through. Surely he couldn't expect the magic to work on the first try!

Could he?

He tried again. Better this time—he began to feel magical force gather around him, but only its fringes. It didn't build.

He tried a third time, felt the magic field gather again, felt it starting to build . . .

Abruptly, it was gone, like an electrical motor starting up then jerking to a halt as a fuse blew. Matt stood, devastated and aghast, feeling as though a rug had been yanked out from under him and the floor with it, leaving him trying to stand on thin air. Such a complete and sudden cancellation of the magic field had nothing to do with how many times Matt recited the verse, nothing to do with the nonmagical nature of his home universe. If the magic had worked at all, it would have continued to build, stronger and stronger with each time he recited the verse, finally transferring him, exhausted but whole, to Merovence. But it had cut off as though someone had thrown a switch—and Matt was sure that someone somehow had. Some enemy had canceled his magic account and left him stranded at home.

He sat down on his heels, rested his back against the wall, put his head in his hands, and thought. Now that he remembered it, he'd been surprised how easy it was to come back to this universe. Could that have been because he'd been born here, and was part of its physical structure? He shuddered at the thought that he might belong here, where he'd always been a loser.

No, he corrected himself—*felt* like a loser. But the boyhood "winners" had been Liam, Luco, Choy, and Herm, who'd let themselves get addicted to drugs and were now eking out livings with minimum-wage jobs and mugging. They would die in the same part of town they'd been born in, or one very much like it—except that the neighborhood would get worse as they grew older. Matt, whom they had kicked around and bullied and insulted, had graduated from high school, then college, and had finished the coursework for his doctorate. Even if he'd stayed in this universe, he would have had a better life than the neighborhood toughs, who saw themselves as winners.

Or did they? Was that just his teenage perceptions talking? Sure, the neighborhood girls had scorned him and cooed over Liam and Luco—but whom would they gravitate toward now?

Not that it mattered. Matt was married, and to a woman finer by far than any of them—a real princess who had become a real queen, in a universe in which his talents and knowledge made him a winner.

He had to get back to it.

His head snapped up; he looked around, suddenly aware that he was very vulnerable—but the tunnel was still empty with no one in sight, though he did hear footsteps back toward the station. He lowered his head again, but didn't let his mind wander as it just had. He'd been so deeply sunk in the trance of thought that he wouldn't have heard any muggers coming up on him. Shame to have to think that way, but there it was.

"Is something wrong, young man?"

Matt looked up. A middle-aged man stood by him, dapper in a gray pin-striped three-piece suit and silk tie. He was lean, with kindly eyes, a straight nose, mustache and goatee. He gazed down at Matt with concern.

Matt pushed himself to his feet, forcing a smile. "Nothing, really. Just kinda tired."

"No, I can see something is troubling you," the stranger said, frowning. "Surely there is some way in which I can help."

Matt shrugged, feeling awkward. He knew the older man meant well, but was really butting in. Still, he was only trying to help, so Matt forced himself to be civil. "I'm just having trouble figuring out how to get home, that's all."

"Oh!" The stranger's face relaxed, even smiling a little as he reached inside his suit coat. "Well, if that's all . . ."

"No, no, I'm afraid money won't help!" Matt held up a palm to keep him from pulling out his wallet. "I can't get home with a train ticket."

"Not by train? But . . ." The stranger glanced back at the station.

"Why am I under the tracks?" Matt forced a smile. "Good place to be alone to think."

"Sometimes thinking is more easily done by talking." The old gent looked sympathetic again. "How *can* you get home?"

"That's what I'm trying to figure out." Matt searched for a generality that would satisfy the old busybody. "I'm from far away, you see, and it's a matter of working the system."

"Oh, bureaucracy!" The stranger smiled. "I'm expert in that. Nirobus, at your service." He held out a gloved hand.

"Matt Mantrell." Matt shook the hand, warming to the old chap in spite of himself.

"What is your situation, Mr. Mantrell? A lost passport?"

"More like a refused visa," Matt said slowly.

Nirobus frowned. "Can you be more specific?"

"Only hypothetically." Matt felt drawn to the old guy, drawn to talk. "You're right, maybe talking it out would help. But I'd have to try to explain it to you by metaphor—the real situation is just too hard to believe."

"Try me." Nirobus smiled, gesturing back toward the station. "But why don't we sit down while we chat? This tunnel is certainly not conducive to thought."

"You've got a point," Matt admitted, and fell in beside him, going back to the station. "I don't want you to miss your train, though."

"Plenty of time—I came early. Proceed with your metaphor, young man. Was it as difficult for you to come here as it is to go home?"

"No, it was very easy." Matt halted, frowning. "Maybe too easy."

"Indeed!" Nirobus sat on a bench, gesturing to the place beside him. "It would seem that you had no reason to expect difficulty."

Matt sat, gazing out unseeing over the tracks and the weathered concrete bridge. "I didn't think anything of it at the time, just that it was a sort of inertia."

"Inertia?" Nirobus frowned.

"Yes, inertia." Matt took a deep breath. "Okay, here comes the metaphor—magic. Let's say I'm transported to a foreign country by a spell."

"Magical transportation?" Nirobus smiled. "How convenient! No passports, no customs—yes, I think the idea could catch on. I rather like your metaphor, young man."

Matt grinned at the old guy, feeling a chime of rapport. If Nirobus could let his imagination wander, he was a kindred spirit. "All right, so some enchanter waves a magic wand and transports me to France in the blink of an eye—but he has to expend a lot of magical energy to do it, because I'm part of America and belong here."

"So you have magical inertia!" Nirobus clapped his gloved hands in delight. "A tendency to stay in the universe in which you were born! Magical physics—what a fascinating notion! So when you came back, it didn't surprise you that it required very little effort—inertia was helping to pull you."

"Like a rubber band, sort of." Matt grinned.

"But now you think your return was too easy," Nirobus remembered. "What do you suspect—an enemy sorcerer, not magical inertia?"

Matt felt a chill inside. "That's the obvious guess, yes."

"But couldn't this enemy sorcerer have used your inertia against you?"

Matt lifted his head, eyes widening. "Yes, he could! Our hypothetical sorcerer could just increase my magical inertia, and the spell that transported me to Merovence before, wouldn't be strong enough now!"

"Merovence?" Nirobus frowned.

"France," Matt amended.

"By any other name." Nirobus smiled. "Yes, I see—a contraction of 'Merovingian province.' But why inertia? Why not simply imagine that your enemy magus has erected some sort of magical barrier to keep you from going back to, ah, Merovence?"

Panic started at the thought—what was this nameless evil sorcerer doing to his Alisande and her kingdom? Matt fought down the idea and concentrated fiercely on not looking like a madman. "That's an even simpler way to look at it, yes. So I have to figure out how to defeat that magical barrier."

"Or to overcome that magical inertia, if you wish to look at it the first way," Nirobus agreed. "There ought to be some way to do it, no matter which it is. Can you apply physics again?"

"Only what I learned in high school," Matt admitted, shamefaced. He remembered a diagram of opposed forces. "It should just be a matter of energy. Whether it's a wall, inertia, or an actual force pushing me away from Merovence, I only need to summon enough force to counter it—and something to push against."

"A lever long enough to move you between worlds, to paraphrase Archimedes, and a fulcrum upon which to rest it?"

"Yeah." For an instant, despair almost overwhelmed Matt. "But what kind of fulcrum? What kind of backstop? To push against something, say a piano you're trying to roll onto a truck, you need to brace your feet against the ground—but how do you brace yourself when you're trying to use magical force?"

"Perhaps you have the wrong analogy," Nirobus suggested. "Perhaps you need an anchor, not a backstop."

"Yes!" Matt lifted his head, hope rising again. "If I can throw the magical equivalent of a cable to someone in Merovence, he could pull me in—or at least anchor me so that my own efforts won't push me away."

"An excellent thought!" Nirobus nodded. "But your 'anchor' would have to be a magician himself. Who do you know who could do it?"

"Oh, that's no problem—Saul! The Witch Doctor! He's common to both universes—born in this one, same as I was, but happier in Merovence because he's better suited to it!"

"Again, the same as you are," Nirobus murmured.

"Yes! . . . What?"

"This is a very interesting metaphor you've constructed," the older man said, amused. He waved a hand in a rolling motion. "Please go on. I take it you must establish some sort of contact with this witch doctor?"

"Yes. If he knows what's going on, he can be my anchor."

Matt frowned. "*If* it's just a matter of my trying to push against magical inertia, or break through an enchanted wall."

"What else could it be?"

"Now that I think of it," Matt said slowly, "I remember the magical force gathering around me, then abruptly disappearing, as though it had been deliberately canceled."

"Do you really!"

Matt eyed the stranger warily. "You wouldn't be a psychiatrist, would you?"

Nirobus held up both gloved hands, as though reaching for the sky. "Innocent."

"Well, somebody isn't. Whatever sorcerer is trying to strand me here is keeping a magical eye on me, just waiting for me to try to get home, then countering my spells, presumably with his own."

Nirobus shook his head sadly. "If I were a psychiatrist . . ."

"Don't worry, it's all hypothetical."

"Very reassuring. But, young man, do you really think your hypothetical sorcerer could spare all his time for surveillance of you?"

Matt caught the unspoken question: Do you really think you're that important? Well, he knew he was, in Merovence, but had to admit to himself that there was a snag in the idea. "Good point. If he wants me out of the way, it's because I'd be an obstacle to some major project he's got going."

"Could he assign a minion to surveillance of you?"

"Maybe," Matt said slowly, "but why would the minion let me build up some power before he stopped me? Wouldn't he have cut me off at the first sign of trying to return?"

"Slammed the door in your face?" Nirobus frowned. "Perhaps he didn't have the power himself, but had to call his master."

"Could be." Matt nodded. "Or the minion might not have been human."

Nirobus stared, appalled. "You aren't thinking of some sort of monster, I hope!"

"No, I was shifting metaphors even worse—so far I was

grinding the gears, in fact. Think about it in terms of computer programming for a minute. If our hypothetical sorcerer left the magical equivalent of a subroutine, a sort of watchdog spell, to monitor my magical efforts and automatically counter them, that could explain why the power was able to begin to build up a little before the 'watchdog' canceled it."

"I suppose that's possible," Nirobus said slowly, "but would your hypothetical sorcerer know about computer programming?"

"Why not?" Matt said airily. "After all, he's my hypothesis—I can make him think any way I want."

Nirobus stared at him in surprise, then laughed with delight.

Matt grinned, liking the man more and more. "So the question is—am I facing a man or an enchantment?"

"Which do you prefer?"

"I'd rather have the enchantment," Matt said slowly. "A resident spell should be easier to overcome than an actual, thinking sorcerer who could switch spells if I overcame his first one."

"While he was sending for his master, to hit you with really impressive power." Nirobus nodded. "Either way, though, you would need enough force to roll over the blocking spell or the magical inertia."

"Yes, I would." Matt smiled.

Nirobus smiled quizzically. "That doesn't seem to concern you overly much."

"Not really." Matt grinned. "I know just the source for all the power I need."

"Do you really!" Nirobus stared.

"Yes: the patron saint of Merovence, provided he wants me back there—and I think he does."

"I see." A shadow crossed Nirobus' face; then he forced a smile.

Now it was Matt's turn to be amused. "Don't believe in saints? Don't worry—this is all metaphorical, anyway."

"And hypothetical." The idea seemed to cheer Nirobus

considerably. "So, then! You seem to have worked out your transportation problem admirably."

Matt stared, then gazed off into space, adding up all the factors they'd just talked about. "I have, haven't I?"

"I'm glad to hear it." Nirobus stood up and clapped him on the shoulder. "And I'm very glad to see you so cheered."

"Thanks." Matt gave him a grateful smile, wondering how he was going to get rid of the nice old guy so he could try the spell again.

Nirobus glanced at his watch. "I still have fifteen minutes before my train. If you'll excuse me, I think I had better take precautions against the ride into the city."

"Precautions?" Matt frowned, then remembered that there weren't any bathrooms on the commuter trains. "Oh. Right. You might not have much time changing to the PATH train."

"Quite so." Nirobus gave him a warm smile. "You're quite understanding, for a man so young. If you'll excuse me, I'll see you again in ten minutes or so." He started to turn away, then turned back with a twinkle in his eye. "Or perhaps I won't."

Matt grinned. "Metaphorically speaking, of course."

"Or unless you're swallowed by an allegory." Nirobus shook his hand. "Good luck, young man—or should I say, bon voyage?"

"Thanks, either way." Matt returned the handshake, then watched the older man pace swiftly around the side of the train station, off toward the nearest coffee shop. Too bad the station itself wasn't open between rush hours; Nirobus was in a rush, indeed.

Then Matt looked around him and was appalled to see how much more mellow the light had become. How many weeks had passed in Merovence while he'd been talking the problem through with Nirobus? Not that there had been much choice, but it still dismayed him.

It must be getting into rush hour now. The commuter trains would be coming in, and people would be streaming through that tunnel. Maybe he'd better find another hiding place.

But there wasn't time. Matt hurried along, hoping he could get back to Merovence before the 4:15 came roaring in to disrupt his concentration. He ducked in under the bridge, stood in the center where he should be between the sets of tracks so there was no Cold Iron right above him, and visualized Saul's face as he chanted softly,

> "Nine-one-one!
> Call begun!
> Saul, by rune!
> To me tune!
> Mocker of pomposity!
> Witches' Doctor, hark to me!"

Even as doggerel, it was pretty bad, but it contained the call phrases Saul had given Sir Guy to use in an emergency, and if this wasn't an emergency, Matt didn't know what was. But he felt the force of magic beginning to gather about him again, though faintly, so faintly! He held his breath, listening with more than his ears, hoping.

All he heard was the breeze that blew through the tunnel, and the distant noise of traffic on Main Street.

In desperation, he cupped his hands around his ears, trying to shut out even that slight sound so that he could concentrate on ones that would come from his mind, but they only concentrated the sound as a seashell does, making the white-noise hiss that children thought of as "hearing the ocean." Matt listened to it with fierce determination, trying to listen through it, to hear Saul's voice.

Then a freight train came rumbling through.

Matt groaned aloud, not that he could hear himself. If Saul did send words, he wouldn't hear them through the roar.

Then he realized that the rumbling overhead had modulated, was forming into words. The more he concentrated, the clearer they became: ". . . the hell have you *been*? She's worried as fury!"

Matt could imagine his sweet wife in a worry-induced

rage all too easily. "Bushwhacked!" he said, as loudly as he dared. "Anchor me! Hold me in mind!"

There was a second's silence, and Matt's heart dropped, afraid that Saul was gone. But the Witch Doctor's voice came again with determination firmed by anger. "Right. Holding. Go!"

"Thanks," Matt called. He hoped he *could* go. He took a deep breath, hoping the freight would keep going long enough to hide his words from anybody who might happen by. He muttered,

> "St. Moncaire, who propped a king
> And guided Merovence's course,
> Your power send, to homeward bring
> Myself. Of magic be my source!"

He felt the magic field strengthen, and for a moment his hopes soared. Then the counterforce hit like a hammer blow, scattering the magic field like water exploding out of a shattered bottle. Matt stood, stunned, pain pounding through his head, the world blurring around him. He sagged against the concrete wall, and couldn't tell if the roaring in his ears was the freight train or the effect of an inner concussion.

It faded, and Matt heard the traffic whirring on Main Street. He took a deep breath, shaken, and wondered what had happened. It was almost as though the enemy sorcerer had been watching Matt in person, had known he was about to try another spell, had stood waiting, ready to hit with everything he had. But how? How could he have known?

Nirobus.

Matt stared. That kindly, dapper, sophisticated old gent? The very picture of a twentieth-century urbanite? How could he be an agent for a medieval sorcerer? It had to be Matt's imagination!

But he had been in an awful hurry to get away. Had he been looking for a rest room, or a chance to report back to Merovence? Certainly he hadn't seemed terribly surprised by Matt's "metaphor." Matt had thought he was very understanding—but why hadn't he thought Matt was crazy?

Maybe because he knew Merovence was real!

Matt gave himself a shake. He was really getting paranoid, blaming a nice old guy like that for his own failures. He sagged against the wall again, thinking wildly, searching for a way around the magical wall . . .

A way around.

Matt straightened, fired with hope. A bypass! If he could open up a channel that went around whatever magical sentry had been trained on him, he could get all the power he needed to fight back. He might even be able to return to Merovence through that channel, a sort of magical detour! And he had one available, of course—the Spider King, who had lived in both universes and a great many others besides. With that bypass, he didn't need all that much power, certainly no more than St. Moncaire could lend across the interuniversal Void. He thought of Saul and felt an answering rapport. He was still anchored, St. Moncaire was still listening—he was almost home.

He glanced around for a spiderweb, and wasn't surprised to find one—no one exactly came through this tunnel with a dust rag. A broom, maybe, but he or she didn't look up all that often.

Matt did, though. He stared up at the small black dot in the center of the web and chanted,

> "Spider King, attend and mark!
> A channel find me through chaos!
> Help me traverse the trackless dark
> Between our separate gaias!
> Through voids outside of time and space
> Guide me to my spirit's place!"

Suddenly there was tension in the air, like the feeling of stress that comes as a thunderstorm is building. Something was working somewhere. Matt took a deep breath and began to recite again,

> "Lalinga wogreus marwold reiger
> Athelstrigen marx alupta
> Harleng krimorg barlow steiger . . ."

His heart soared as the syllables began to make sense again:

> "You, betrayed by Time and Space,
> Born without your proper grace,
> To a world befouled and base—
> Feel your proper form and case,
> Recognize your homeland's face.
> Cross the void of time and space!
> Seek and find your proper place!"

Now he felt the magical force build around him as the saint of another universe laid pull upon pull, tugging at the soul and the body that came with it. Outside that, though, Matt could feel great forces piling up, resisting—but he could sense some sort of wall pushing against them, straining, straining, as the world began to spin, and dizziness seized him.

CHAPTER 4

Matt's stomach lurched and tried to climb up through his esophagus. He fought it down, telling himself he wasn't really falling, was just in free fall in a weightless void, but it was hard to believe, for all he could see was a flux and flow of colors all about him, colors that broke into tiny particles and intermingled, swirling together until they all seemed to be a sort of dirty white, making his stomach rebel against the lurch and swing and the primordial fear of the endless plunge.

Then hardness slammed against his side and arm, pain shot through him, and the stomach-sickness vanished into that pain as the colors fell into their places, coalescing into gray stone and the blue denim of Saul's jeans as he dropped to his knees beside Matt. "Hey, man, are you all right?"

"Good . . . training," Matt managed to gasp.

"Good training?" Saul stared, then grinned. "Yeah, you fell on your side, just the way I taught you. Welcome back!"

"Th-thanks," Matt managed, then closed his eyes and started a prayer of thanks to St. Moncaire before he passed out.

He was almost feeling restored an hour later. Of course, that was probably due as much to his having changed back into doublet and hose as to the brew that Saul had prepared, standing by his elbow to be sipped every few seconds.

Saul sat across from him, eyeing him critically. "Yeah, I guess you're doing better."

Matt took another sip. "When did you become a doctor?"

"When I found out people expected me to be one," Saul retorted. "I've been studying herbs as well as trances." He turned to Alisande. "I think he's almost ready for duty."

"Praise Heaven!" Alisande still clasped Matt's hand firmly; she had scarcely let it go to help him dress. Even now, her voice sounded shaken, the more so because he had done the best he could to explain what had happened. It had come out as confusing, but harrowing. "I never dreamed into what danger I was sending you, husband, when I bade you visit your mother!"

No mention of Papa, Matt noticed. "There wasn't that much danger as long as I was there, darling. It was the time-squeeze that worried me—that, and the fact that I couldn't get back. And you know paranoid me—right away, I was worrying about conspiracies against you."

Alisande exchanged a glance with Saul, and Matt frowned. "So I was right! What's been going on while I was away?"

"It is nothing beyond our ability to cope," Alisande hastened to say, "or at least, that Saul has not . . ."

The room shook, and something boomed outside.

Matt was on his feet in an instant. "An earthquake!"

"No, not really." Saul was up too, reaching out for Matt's arm.

"I can walk," Matt said testily, and turned toward the door. "Come on! We'd better get up to the battlements and see what's going on."

Thunder slammed in bursts, and the walls shook.

Matt grabbed the nearest tapestry and held on, managing to stay on his feet. When the floor steadied, he sprinted for the door. "Let's go! Something's badly wrong!"

"Wait a minute," Saul called, running after him. "We wanted to fill you in, you know, kind of gradually . . ."

"Fill me in about what?" Matt asked, and stepped out onto the battlements—into a vast roaring that he finally recognized as laughter so huge that it shook the stone blocks under him. He fell to his knees, grasping the nearest crenel, and stared upward, paralyzed by what he saw.

At first he thought it was a hot-air balloon, a huge, tan, canvas teardrop—but as his eyes began to make sense of its scale, he realized that it was a humanoid form, a huge, turbaned, bare-chested man who rose above the battlements, reaching out to the tallest tower and shaking it as he laughed. The whole castle vibrated with it. His arms were as long as a whole team of horses, his face was as broad as a house, his beard a black hedge, and his chest expanded like the widening front of a baron's castle.

But if it expanded, it dwindled, too, in the other direction. Matt glanced down and saw that the huge torso narrowed quickly, looking like the tail of a teardrop indeed. He could make out some sort of belt, the beginning of trousers, but below that, the body narrowed quite quickly to a long, flowing tentacle that ended in a point, floating fifty feet or more above the earth.

Matt looked back up, eyes wide in awe, and breathed, "A genie!"

"Look, man, I told you to get away from here!" Saul shouted at the genie, but his anger was clearly diluted by fear.

The genie roared another laugh, but one that had an edge to it, and pointed at Saul. A fireball shot from his fingertip.

Saul leaped aside, and the fireball exploded where he had been. But he didn't even look at it, just pointed at the genie, narrowing his eyes and chanting,

> "The wind comes rushing through the air
> A-seeking for a weird,
> It stirs the forest darkness,
> The darkness of your beard.
> Let royal service be your lot,
> The service that Drake paid,
> When he took his men to raid
> Upon the Spanish main,
> Then turned about to singe the beard
> Of the King of Spain."

The genie's beard burst into flame. He howled, batting at it, roaring a verse in his own language. Matt frowned; it didn't quite sound like Arabic . . .

Then rain roared down, soaking Matt in an instant—but going around or through the genie, drowning the fire in his beard on the way. He threw back his head and roared with laughter, laughter that made the walls shake again . . .

Matt thought of the walls of Jericho and knew he had to stop that torrent of sound. The torrent of rain, too, of course, but that could wait.

> "Blow, bugles, blow,
>> set the wild echoes flying,
> Blow, bugle; answer, echoes,
>> dying, dying, dying."

The genie kept laughing, but the sound no longer rang or boomed about them; it stayed with the genie himself. The walls stopped shaking, and the genie caught his breath, staring in surprise.

Saul cried,

> "Get along with you, for you give me a pain!
> My castle never leaks without your rain!"

The rain slackened, but didn't stop. Well, Saul hadn't told it to, really.

Matt called out,

> "He is not here, but far away
> The genie's noise begins again,
> And wanly, through the glimmering rain,
> On the cropped slope slides the djinni fay."

Well, a djinni wasn't properly a fay, but the unwelcome visitor apparently didn't know that—he gave a very disconcerted howl, shooting downward as though a huge hand had just yanked him. He hit the "cropped slope" below the castle and slid straight downhill.

"I hope he doesn't hit the town wall," Saul said, craning his neck downward, "at least, not too hard."

He needn't have worried. The genie slowed, then floated back into the air, windmilling his right arm.

"Here it comes!" Saul called. "Hold tight!"

As the genie's arm swung in a circle, mass gathered in his hand until he had enough to throw. The missile shot from his hand, arcing toward the castle—a boulder four feet in diameter.

Matt realized the sense of what Saul had been saying. He hugged the crenel as though it were his wife.

His wife! He spun to look, saw Alisande hanging on to a torch sconce that was very securely bolted to the granite—but his own hold was loosened.

An earthquake hit. Matt's hold tore loose, and he went sliding toward the gap between two crenels.

"Matt!" Saul shouted, and reached out toward him—then lost his own hold and came sliding after Matt as the ramparts shook them loose like fleas when a dog scratches.

Alisande screamed and dove after them.

Matt spread his feet and braced himself against crenels to either side. Saul slammed into the left-hand crenel and wrapped an arm around it, clamping the other hand on Matt's ankle. Alisande caromed into the block on his other side, and Matt seized *her* ankle.

The ramparts stopped shaking, and Saul levered himself up to peer over the crenel. "There's more of them!" he called. "Hold tight!"

Matt saw that Alisande had a firm grip on her crenel. He let go and pulled himself up to look. Sure enough, three more genies had appeared, hurling rocks that they apparently conjured just by winding up. "Can't throw worth beans!" he called to Saul. "Satchel Paige would have smeared us over the stones by this time!"

"I know!" Saul called back. "But I gotta time this just right!"

A boulder whirled loose from one of the middle genies. Saul chanted quickly,

> "The sneer is gone from Casey's lips,
> His teeth are clenched in hate.
> He pounds with cruel violence
> His bat upon the plate.
> And now the genie's winding up,
> And now he's letting go,
> And now his missile's shattered by
> The force of Casey's blow!"

The boulder exploded in midair. The biggest piece shot back at the genie who had thrown it. He squalled and disappeared. The shard struck the slope where he'd been and started rolling down toward the plain—but as it rolled, it faded as its master had.

"Keep reciting that verse!" Saul called. "If we can spout it fast enough, over and over again, none of their boulders will ever hit home!"

"Will do!" Matt had never thought he'd actually like "Casey at the Bat," but he loved it right now. He started chanting the words, one line behind Saul, and each boulder exploded, its largest fragment heading back toward its genie almost as soon as he threw it. Saul chanted, Matt chanted, Alisande chanted, and Casey piled up more strikes than any batter in living memory.

Finally Matt realized that there were three other people reciting: his assistant sorcerer, Ortho the Frank; the Captain of the Guard; and a knight whose surcoat identified him as a member of the Order of St. Moncaire. Fleetingly, Matt thought it was odd for him to be there, then recognized Sir Gilbert, but turned the thought aside—what really mattered was that he himself could stop chanting and work on making all the djinn disappear.

> "I dream of genies all with jewel-toned turbans,
> Born like bubbles in my summer bourbon.

I see them floating where the wild zephyrs play,
Happy as the daisies, then all blown away!"

A huge gust of wind blew up out of nowhere and tossed the genies turning and whirling with appalled shouts, out over the town, off to the horizon, and out of sight.

Saul stared. Then he said, "Yes." Then, "Well, I guess." Then, finally, he turned to Matt and said, "How the blazes did you do that, man?"

"Just comes from knowing a few poems," Matt said, abashed—especially in view of what he'd done to Stephen Foster. It occurred to him to hope that none of the poets whose works he mangled ever showed up in this universe.

"Husband, you are amazing!" Alisande clung to him, her voice shaking.

"So are you," Matt said, turning to stare into her eyes.

She stared in surprise, then lowered her gaze, blushing faintly, but smiling.

Matt was amazed—he'd just managed to remind the queen that she was a woman, and at the end of a battle, at that! Of course, for her, it had been months since she'd seen him . . .

But he had been at least as frantic, worried that he'd never see her again. Suddenly desire crashed through him, so violently that he had to brace himself against it.

Alisande felt his trembling, and her smile widened as her eyes seemed to swallow him. "Master Saul," she called, "can you stay the watch here? I wish to acquaint my husband with events that have happened in his absence."

Saul looked up in surprise, then saw the looks on their faces and managed to suppress a grin of his own. "Yeah, sure, Your Majesty. Just remember, he ought to be in bed."

"Indeed," Alisande agreed, and led Matt back indoors.

It occurred to Matt that this ought to weaken his magic. Then he remembered that, within the bonds of marriage, it wasn't a sin, but a virtue.

* * *

Two hours later, she laughed, softly and deeply, at one last compliment, then grew serious. "I must tell you what has happened indeed, my love."

"Well, if we must, we must," Matt sighed. He slipped out of bed and pulled on his robe. He turned to find his wife similarly robed, and turning to sit in an hourglass-shaped chair.

"It is wrong of us to delight in one another while our people are under attack." But the rosiness of her face, the glow of her smile, denied her words.

"I wouldn't go feeling guilty about it." Matt sat on the edge of the bed and took her hand, again struck by the impossibility that a loser like himself should have won the love of so beautiful a woman. "After all, the harmony of the land depends on the harmony within the monarch, and I certainly hope I'm contributing to that."

Alisande frowned. "What wizard's talk is this?"

"I suppose it is," Matt said thoughtfully. "Wizard's talk, I mean. Look at it this way—a happy queen will make a happy country, and I hope I'm doing my part to keep you happy."

"More than any other living being," Alisande said fervently, and kissed his fingers.

The touch of her lips sent desire thrilling through him, astonishing him that it could recur so soon. "You're distracting me again."

Alisande looked up in surprise, then gave him a wicked grin. "Should I not delight in being a success as a woman, sir, in addition to being a success as a queen?"

"Oh, you certainly are," Matt breathed, and lowered his face for a kiss.

Alisande interposed her hand, then turned to straighten her robe, looking prim. "Still, there is some question as to whether or not the people may continue to be happy if we cannot banish these spirits for once and for all."

"I think I recognize them," Matt said slowly. "They're called 'djinn.' That's the plural—one male is called a 'djinni,' and a female is called a 'djinna.' "

Alisande looked up, startled. "They have females?"

"Of course," Matt answered. "How do you suppose they

make more djinn? Some of them are relatively good, but some are very, very bad."

"I did not know you knew so much about them," Alisande said, frowning. "How is it Saul did not?"

"Well, he was a philosophy major—wouldn't recognize a genie unless it came out of a bottle, preferably wearing a bolero jacket and harem pants."

"Oh, he did recognize them as genies—but he said nothing of there being males and females."

"Odd, for somebody who grew up watching TV," Matt mused. "Well, it's not his field of study—though I suspect he read the highlights of the *Arabian Nights*."

"They are Arabs, then?" Alisande asked, wide-eyed. "Mohammedans?"

So the Prophet had been born in this universe, too. Matt nodded. "Some of them, yes, though I understand many djinn haven't converted. But I'm not sure this batch are all that Arabic. They look different somehow, and they don't quite sound like the few Arabs I've known."

"Have you met a genie before?"

"Well, no," Matt admitted. "How long have they been coming?"

"Since the night you left." Alisande turned grim. "In their first attack, they managed to breach the wall; the masons are still rebuilding it. Then the Witch Doctor found the spell you heard him use and chased them away. But they came back near dawn, and for every one Saul chased, another took its place. The people of the town showed great courage; they climbed the walls and hurled stones at them, but the genies only laughed and began to appear inside the city to collapse houses and pluck horses and people kicking and shouting into the air. Saul and Ortho the Frank had to work frantically to drive them off. They disappeared an hour after sunrise, as though to say that they did not fear daylight, and were going of their own free choice."

"Did they kill anybody?"

"Not that we can tell, though there have been several aged folk who died during this siege."

"There always are, though." Matt frowned. "So they're just trying to scare you, not really hurt you—but Saul was tougher than they thought. Pretty good, for a philosopher—but something tells me they could get a lot worse if they wanted to. How frequently have they showed up?"

"Once or twice a week. The priests and monks are praying to strengthen Saul and his wizards—he has taught the verse to several students—and many of the people are praying, too."

That was no idle gesture, in this universe in which magic worked by rhyme, song, and gesture, but drew its strength from either good or evil, God or the Devil. The power of prayer was more obvious here than in his own universe. Matt was surprised to hear that Saul had taken on students, and wondered if they were really doing any good. He'd noticed that virtually anybody could do some magic just by reciting a verse, but that it just didn't have much punch coming from the average citizen. Powerful magic seemed to require talent, a certain twist of the mind, and there weren't all that many people who could do it—or who had the determination to learn the rules and all the spells. To a few, like Matt and Saul, it came naturally. It had to, or they wouldn't have been able to come to Merovence.

"Well, any help is better than none," Matt said. "Does Saul have any ideas about how to keep the djinn away more or less permanently?"

"He tells me he is trying to set a magical, unseen shield around the city, as King Boncorro has set his Wall of Octroi along the border of Latruria."

"It keeps out flying magical critters but lets anything slower-moving, like horses or people, walk across," Matt said, nodding. "Might work on flying djinn, too, though I suspect they can transport themselves in here without flying. Still, it's certainly worth a try. I'll have to see if I can help any."

"Even if he succeeds, that is only a temporary measure," Alisande said, with the certainty of Divine Right; sometimes Matt wondered if she could ever have an attack of Divine Wrong. "We must seek the source of these—djinn, did you call them?"

"The source is probably an evil sorcerer who has set them on us," Matt told her. "At least, that's the way it always is in the stories. I suppose there are some djinn who are still free agents, not drafted by any sorcerer anywhere, but they wouldn't have any reason to come here."

"Unless someone in the city has angered them?"

"Possible, but not probable—and it's just too much of a coincidence that they should show up right after I left, especially since it was so easy for me to go, and so hard to come back." Matt frowned. "Easy go, hard to come back, djinn besieging the city while I was gone—that makes three events. I suspect enemy action. Just how bad has this siege become?"

"Not truly yet a siege," Alisande said slowly. "Courageous merchants and farmers still bring in foodstuffs, and folk from the town go out to forage."

"Sort of warning us," Matt guessed, "letting us know they could cut us off pretty thoroughly if they wanted to."

"The djinn, you mean? But why?"

"Interesting question, dear," Matt said. "Now that I think of it, I'm kind of surprised that Fadecourt's—I mean King Rinaldo's—people hold all of Ibile. Who lives in North Africa? The land right across the strait from Ibile?"

"Across the Middle Sea, you mean?"

Matt started to describe Gibraltar, then realized that Alisande's knowledge of geography didn't have that much detail. Besides, for all he knew, the Rock wasn't there in this universe. "That's right."

"We call them 'Moors,' " Alisande said slowly, "though I have heard that is not what they call themselves."

Matt nodded. "That much is like my home universe, anyway. And they're Muslims?"

Alisande frowned. "What are 'Muslims'?"

"Mohammedans," Matt translated.

"Ah!" Alisande nodded. "Yes, they are paynim."

With a mental wrench, Matt remembered that the medieval Christians had thought of the Muslims as pagans—and the Muslims, of course, had returned the compliment, referring to the "Franks" as "unbelievers." No reason to think it should be different here. Sometimes he found it hard to believe that both religions believed in the God of Abraham.

"Sounds like the ones I had in mind," he said. "Have they conquered any part of Ibile?"

"Aye—they hold the far south, and have for hundreds of years."

Matt frowned. "Funny I didn't see any sign of them when I was wandering across their countryside."

"They hold *only* the far south, husband—scarcely more than what would be a count's holdings, in Merovence. There is a Moorish nobleman in the city of Aldocer who calls himself an emir, and rules that countryside."

There spoke the queen—didn't know about Gibraltar, but knew the political situation thoroughly. Matt frowned. "What kept them from advancing farther?" In his universe, the Moors had conquered most of Spain, except for the northern kingdoms.

"Emperor Hardishane's grandfather," Alisande answered. "The paynim made a sortie through the mountains and struck at the folk in Merovence. Then they began to pour through the passes in their thousands. Cortshank the Hardy raised an army here in Bordestang and marched south to meet the Moors. Peasants who fled north from the burnings and bloodshed joined his army, and as it swelled, folk who feared the paynim might reach their own villages came to join him, too. They marched all day, then rested in the evenings, when Cortshank's sergeants trained them in fighting. Many knights came, too, to protect their homesteads and wives by preventing the paynim from coming near.

"They met the Moors at a bridge and fought, but the Hardy mowed down all before him and took the bridge. His army poured across it and arrayed themselves against the heathen host. Then, with a mighty shout, the two armies clashed together—but the Moors fought only for conquest and the forced spread of their religion, whereas the knights and peasants fought for their homes, wives, and children. Cortshank the Hardy carried the day, and the Moors fled. The Hardy marched after, but the Moors sped before him.

"They made their stand in a mountain pass, where a dozen men might stop an army, so long as there were men to take their places when they fell. But Cortshank's men fought with zeal as great as that of the fanatic Moors, and their armor was far heavier."

"Not such a great advantage, since the Moors could ride circles around them," Matt said, frowning.

"True, but there was no room to maneuver in that mountain pass. The knights charged and broke the line by sheer weight, then proved the keenness of their swords on the Moors. While they did, the mountaineers threw rocks down upon the paynim. Some did strike the knights, aye, but as I've said, their armor was stronger, their helmets above all. The Moors fled, their numbers sorely depleted, and some of the mountaineers, fearing their revenge, joined with Cortshank. As they rode down into Ibile, more knights and peasants joined them, so that with every battle, the Moors' army grew smaller, while the Hardy's army grew greater."

"So Cortshank didn't see any reason to stop chasing them?"

"None at all, till they came within sight of Aldocer. There, more Moors came riding to join in the battle—they had been coming up from Africa as soon as word of Cortshank's victories reached them. There they fought the army of Merovence to a standstill. The Hardy stayed in that country six more months, fighting many more battles, but for each he won, he lost another. While he fought, though, the knights of Ibile built strongholds and gathered armies of their own, so that, when Cortshank and his men grew weary and yearned for home, they were able to retreat, leaving the holding of the line to the men whose land it was. Thus they marched back through the mountains in triumph, and the mountaineers among them saw that they were honored."

"Meaning nobody threw rocks down on *them*." Matt pursed his lips. "This wouldn't have had anything to do with Hardishane becoming emperor, would it?"

"Everything! For when the people of Merovence realized who had saved them, they rose in a body to demand that the last weak king of the decadent line abdicate his throne and yield it to the Hardy. Cortshank was nothing loath, and thereby became king."

Quite a bit faster than Charles Martel and his son Pepin had managed it, but with the same result—though Charles Martel had never done so well in Spain. Matt nodded slowly. The parallels between the universes were unmistakable. The same historical forces seemed to open the way for the same kind of man to come riding in to greatness—and dominion. "Did Hardishane ever have to go into Ibile and help beat the Moors back inside their own borders?"

Alisande frowned. "Why should he? The knights of Ibile proved equal to the task. That first great surge of conquest was the worst the Moors ever tried. After that, they settled down to farm the lands they'd conquered, and study the arts of peace."

More effectively than the Merovencians had, if Matt's own Middle Ages were any guide. The Moors of his own universe had built universities and developed a far-ranging, cosmopolitan commerce while the Franks were still clearing forests and fighting each other at every chance. "The Moors never tried to conquer again?"

"Oh, there were raids," Alisande said, "but the knights of Ibile held the border, and raided in revenge—so the Moors held their places until the first Gordogrosso came to power."

"The first and only, as we know now," Matt said, with a wry smile. "I take it they attacked the king?"

"No—he attacked them. The Moors were hard put to hold their province against him, and certainly never invaded Ibile again."

"Ironic!" Matt said. "The evil that held Ibile in abasement was so bad that it kept the Moors from attacking!"

"Even so," Alisande agreed. "They wanted no part of Gordogrosso or his wickedness."

"Well, there's your evidence that they were godly men, in their own way," Matt told her, "if a devil-pawn like Gordo-grosso was as much an enemy to them as he was to your own ancestors."

"Godly!" Alisande cried, scandalized. "But they do not pray to the Christ!"

"True. But they worship God . . ."

"But their god is Allah!"

"That is their word for 'God,'" Matt acknowledged. "They worship Him, and abhor Satan, whom they call 'Shaitan,' but it's basically the same word. If Shaitan was their sworn enemy, so was Gordogrosso."

"Do you say they were our unwitting allies?" Alisande asked slowly.

"Only by accident, dear." Matt stood up and began to pace. "We had a common enemy. Now that Gordogrosso is gone, though, I think they've decided to get back to what they think was their true mission all along—conquering Europe so that everyone would have to worship Allah."

"We cannot permit that!" Alisande was on her feet and, dressing gown or no, gave the impression of having a sword in her hand.

"I don't think we should," Matt agreed. "Personally, I have a very dim view of anybody conquering anybody else. It always involves killing people and making the survivors miserable, and I can't believe God wants that."

Alisande frowned. "But you have yourself slain men in war."

"Yes, but I've left the civilians alone, which is more than I can say for the monarchs I've fought. They were true agents of evil, killing and torturing their own people even in peacetime, and generally doing their best to make everybody miserable. The only people they tried to make happy were themselves, so of course they failed."

"But succeeded in bringing agony to everyone about them," Alisande said bitterly. "Do you say that the Moors themselves are good, but whoever leads them in conquest is evil?"

"I wouldn't even go that far," Matt said. "It's more likely that their leader is a good man who has been tricked into doing evil things."

Alisande frowned. "But who has tricked him?"

"Ah!" Matt held up a forefinger. "*That* is what we have to find out." He reached for his clothes. "Let's go discuss this with the Witch Doctor."

CHAPTER 5

"Let me get this straight," Saul said, frowning. "You think some sorcerer has managed to con the emir of Aldocer into trying to conquer Ibile, then striking though the Pyrenees to conquer us, and that the same sorcerer has sent these genies to try to distract us?"

"Djinn, Saul, not genies."

"Genies," Saul said firmly. "I'll take my djinn in a bottle, thank you."

"Well, they are safer that way . . ."

"All right already! I don't cotton to that 'djinn,' okay? Personally, I thought the genies were threatening to bring Bordestang and the castle down around our heads."

"A threat as well as a distraction." Matt nodded. "Comes to the same thing—keep Alisande from marching to help King Rinaldo, and soften up Merovence for invasion."

Alisande looked surprised for a second, then nodded slowly. "That is quite true, husband. I must keep my army here to defend while my capital is under attack."

"Not a bad strategy," Saul said, "except that it warns us ahead of time."

"Well, yes, but how could they know we knew about the Moorish Conquest?"

"You mean that King Rinaldo might well be under attack even now," Alisande said, frowning. "Would not he have sent word?"

"Not if all his messengers were ambushed, and killed or captured," Saul said grimly. "Rinaldo isn't much of a wizard, from what you tell me."

"No, more of a man of action," Matt agreed. His heart was heavy for his friend. He turned to Alisande. "We'll send a magical messenger."

"And a party of riders," Alisande said grimly. "Might not these djinn waylay a magical messenger as easily as a mortal courier?"

"They might at that," Matt said. "I really ought to go myself . . ."

"No!" Saul and Alisande snapped together, and Saul went on, "You really gotta do something about this martyr complex, man."

"I cannot spare *you*, most of all." Alisande took firm hold of his arm. "But tell me—what spells *can* we use to conquer this evil magic?"

"Hey, the Moors aren't evil," Saul objected. "They worship the same god as Merovence does, just in a different way."

Alisande looked doubtful, but Matt said, "True, but if some sorcerer has conned them into attacking, there's a very good chance that *he's* evil. Certainly he's using magic that predates Islam by at least a thousand years, if he's compelling djinn and afrits to do his dirty work."

"We haven't seen any afrits yet," Saul objected.

"No, and we don't want to," Matt assured him.

"What is an 'afrit'?" Alisande asked.

One of the things Matt loved about her—if she didn't know something, she asked straight out, instead of trying to pretend she knew already. A lot of monarchs would have found that beneath their dignity. "They're sort of superdjinn—more powerful, and mean, very mean," he summarized. "Some say they're also very ugly, with features like fangs and boar's tusks."

"And I thought we only had to worry about Berber animism." Saul hurried to explain before Alisande could look puzzled. "The Berbers are the people who lived in Morocco before the Arabs conquered them."

"In Barbary," Alisande corrected. "Yes, it makes sense that those who live there would be Berbers."

"Sure, what's a vowel shift between peoples?" Saul said airily.

"But what is 'animism'?"

"Very primitive religion," Matt explained, "where people believe that everything around them has a spirit—every rock, every tree, every brook."

"Ah." Alisande nodded. "Like the dwarves in the mountains, the dryads in the trees, and the nixies in the rivers."

"Yes, organized religion is such a huge advance," Saul said dryly.

Matt shot him a warning look and defused the remark by saying, "Right. Really primitive animism doesn't have any gods—just local spirits. After a while, people invent gods, too, and after a longer while, they realize that their inventions are really only aspects of one universal God." His look dared Saul to argue.

Saul chose the better part of valor for the moment. "Of course, in Merovence, you have all the creatures magic can support—and we'd have trouble enough if our enemies were just raising those kinds of spirits against us."

"Would not our own creatures of magic defend us from these djinn?" Alisande asked, frowning.

"They might, if we asked them," Saul said, "but I gather that's what Matt has done for you before, and some of the elementals needed a lot of persuading."

Alisande turned thoughtful. "An interesting way to describe a wizard's role."

"Well, part of it, anyway," Matt amended. "Yes, that's what I was braced for, mobilizing the dwarves in the mountains to help fight off the Berber spirits—but if we have sophisticated Arabic magic on top of that, we're going to have even more trouble."

"Trouble that you might be borrowing," Saul pointed out. "We're just guessing."

"Yeah. We don't really *know* anything." Matt scowled. "We need some good, capable wizard-spies."

"NO!" Alisande and Saul said together.

"Well, it doesn't *have* to be me," Matt said, disgruntled. "I just hate to ask anybody to do something dangerous for me if I'm not willing to do it myself."

"I think I liked you better when you were a coward," Saul commented.

"You did not," Alisande countered, "but you did like the notion that he would live longer. Why must you always seek to thrust yourself into the midst of peril, my husband?" She softened, touching his face. "Am I so loathsome that you must constantly flee me?"

"You know that's not true!" Matt said fervently, and took her in his arms. He tried to reassure her with a long kiss.

"Watch the tonsils," Saul muttered.

They broke apart, laughing and blushing, and Matt told his wife, "Sometimes it's my yearning for you that manages to pull me out of a magical morass. But I won't try to shift my responsibility onto somebody else just because I don't want to suffer the pain."

"Ah, but we know you are willing to undergo the trials," Alisande countered. "Therefore may you send another with a clear conscience, for you do *not* send him to do what you shirk."

There spoke the executive, expert on delegating authority. "Well, maybe we won't have to send a living being," Matt said. "We can start with crystal-gazing—but I don't expect much luck. Anybody who can command genies can shield himself from magical spying."

"Until you can learn, we must plan in darkness," Alisande summarized. "I ask again: What spells can you use to send these djinn packing? What enchantments to shield us from a Moorish army, if one indeed marches upon us?"

"Something involving lamps, bottles, rings, and the Seal of Solomon," Matt said. "I'll have to give it some thought."

"I'll start by writing down as much of *The Rubáiyát* as I can remember," Saul offered.

"Might help. Please do."

"Then there are verses from Chesterton and Ariosto," Saul said. "Chesterton had a poem about the battle of Lepanto, and . . ."

"Ariosto!" Matt's head snapped up. "*The Madness of Roland!* It didn't happen in our universe, but it might happen here!"

Wife and friend both turned to him, puzzled.

"The Siege of Paris," Matt explained. "The Moors are going to strike into Merovence so far that they'll besiege Bordestang, if we don't stop them in Ibile!"

"What is Paris?" Alisande asked, bewildered.

"Our universe's analogue to Bordestang," Saul explained, and Matt clarified, "The capital of France, the country that takes up the same territory in our world that Merovence takes in this."

"Is it not then Merovence by another name?" Alisande asked.

"No, there's a host of cultural differences," Matt told her, "not to mention historical facts happening in different order."

Saul frowned. "You don't suppose poets can see into universes besides their own, do you?"

"Only in their inner visions," Matt said, "and if they can, what they see is so jumbled and unclear that they mix it in with what they know of their own world—so Ariosto had our universe's Hardishane defending Paris from the Moors, instead of one of his descendants."

"Of course," Saul pointed out, "there might be a universe in which it *did* happen."

"This multiplicity of universes is most confusing," Alisande protested.

"Tell me about it! I'm just glad I don't have to worry about more than two!"

"I rejoice that I only need worry about one," Alisande countered. "What do you advise I do, to prevent the Moors from streaming into Merovence while my capital is under siege by these djinn?"

"Make alliances with the mountaineers in the Pyrenees," Matt said, "then fortify the passes."

"We could get Stegoman and Gnarlh to fly in a squad of relatives to help out," Saul suggested.

"A clan of dragons can be very persuasive." Matt nodded.

"Good idea, especially since we're probably going to have to cobble up a defense without any of the royal army."

"I shall send straightaway to the lords of Anjou," Alisande said. "They shall ready themselves to withstand an army."

"They'll be outnumbered," Matt warned, remembering his history courses.

"Tell them to avoid pitched battles," Saul suggested, "just nibble away at the army's flanks. Hit 'em hard and fast, then fade back into the woods and swamps."

"I have heard of bands who fought thus," Alisande said slowly. "It goes against chivalry, but it is the wiser course. However, I shall also bid them reinforce their strongholds."

"They'll need it," Matt agreed.

"Anything we can do instead of wait for the next magical surprise?" Saul asked.

Matt shrugged. "Ransack the library, I guess. Maybe somebody wrote something about Moorish magic."

"Each to his own station, then," Alisande said. She gave Matt a quick kiss that left him wanting more, then stepped away. "I shall see you at supper. Let it be done!"

"Don't I wish," Matt muttered as he watched her sweep out of the room.

"Maybe we oughta check out your laboratory first," Saul suggested, "not that I can think of anything you can brew to chase a genie."

Matt lifted his head slowly. "I can send a servant out for some juniper berries and brew some gin. Maybe what you said about bottles could really do some good."

"It might at that!" Saul said, grinning. "Maybe we can cobble up some oil lamps."

"Can't hurt," Matt said. "Let's go."

They hurried up to the tower room Matt had commandeered. He unlocked the door, opened it, and stared, taken aback.

"Well, we couldn't let anybody in to sweep or anything," Saul said defensively.

"I *was* gone awhile, wasn't I?" Matt looked around at the

layer of dust. "Nothing's even out of place, though. I take it the djinn left this tower alone?"

"We lucked out, yeah." Then Saul frowned. "You don't suppose that wasn't just coincidence?"

"They might not like my kind of magic," Matt said. He looked out the window. "I chose better than I knew. I should have a fine view of them getting up to tricks from here."

"Where's the dust rag?"

"Hook on the wall." Matt felt a stab of conscience—housework reminded him of his mother. "Unfinished business first, though."

"Unfinished? You haven't even started anything!"

"Yeah, but I'd better check my mail."

"Oh, yeah? You know a carrier who goes between universes?"

"No, but I think I can take advantage of a space-time anomaly."

"That would be singular," Saul admitted, "or would it be a singularity?"

"The magical equivalent, anyway," Matt said. "You know, someday we're going to have to work out how closely the laws of magic parallel the laws of physics."

"Some day you're going to have to learn physics," Saul grumbled.

"Why, when I've got you? You know, you never did explain to me why a philosopher took so many physics courses."

"I was trying not to graduate," Saul retorted. "Besides, once you get far enough into mathematics, the relationships between the three fields get to be too strong to ignore."

"You'll have to explain that to me, too."

"I'll try," Saul sighed, "but it seems ridiculous, when you have such a great intuitive grasp of it yourself."

"All right, so you'll have to explain *me* to me. Besides, how can you have an intuitive grasp of physics and math?"

"How were you going to get your mail?" Saul retorted.

"Like this." Matt frowned, concentrating, then folded a piece of parchment and tucked it into a jar, reciting,

"Neither snow, nor sleet, nor gloom of night
Stays these couriers from old Persia's clime
In completion swift of rounds appointed,
Mailbags in hand for quick relay.
Let those relays trip fantastic light
Sending all that's in Box 409
'Twixt universes quite disjointed,
To this workbench here without delay."

Saul said, "Not the world's best . . ."

An envelope appeared in midair and floated down to land on the workbench.

"Okay, so it was good enough," Saul grumbled.

"Well! That was fast! Mama and Papa must have started writing the second I left the house!" Matt picked up the envelope—and stared, his face blanking.

"It's not from your folks?" Saul guessed.

"No, it's not." Matt yanked out his dagger and slit the envelope. "It's from Mrs. Gussenhoven—a neighbor. *She* must have started writing the second I stepped out the door. But how did she get my address?"

"Asked your mother?" Saul guessed.

"Yeah, over the back fence." Matt unfolded the page of stationery and started reading. Silence stretched.

"Good job of face camouflage," Saul said, "if you were in a snowbank. Share!"

" 'Dear Matthew,' " Matt read, " 'I got your address from your mother because I think you ought to know.' "

"Uh-oh."

"Yeah." Matt's face finished blanching to maximum paleness and started reddening with anger. " 'I don't think they let you know how bad things are. They're proud, God bless them, but maybe too proud. Your papa's store doesn't have any business anymore, except he delivers for some of us old folks himself. The bad boys won't let anybody else deliver. They scare the customers away so they go to the supermarket. They don't dare try to stop your papa yet, but they're getting bolder. They're mad at your papa because he won't let them turn his store into their hangout and-crack drop. He will have to close for good pretty soon, and he doesn't have unemployment, because he is in business for himself. The bank is going to foreclose on their house.

" 'I do not know what you can do, but please do it anyway. Send them some money somehow. I know that is hard, because your papa won't take it, but find an excuse.

" 'It was good to see you walk by again, and I hope your new job makes you happy.' Then the 'Yours truly,' and that's it." Matt slammed the letter down on the desktop. "She's right—the state doesn't pay unemployment benefits if you're self-employed."

Saul nodded. "Even if you go broke and have to shut down."

"And neither of them is old enough to apply for Social Security yet. Damn! What the hell can I do?"

"Same as people have been doing for centuries," Saul said. "Invite them to move in with you."

"Of course!" Matt looked up, eyes alight. "Why didn't I think of that?"

"Because you're not a genius, like me."

"Right! Thanks!" Matt was gone out the door in a whirl, pounding away down the stairs.

Saul stared, blinking, then ran after him, calling, "Hey, wait a minute! What about the genies?"

"A room in our castle? Your parents? Of course!" Alisande glared. "They may have a suite! Fetch them at once!"

"Thanks, dear, uh, Your Majesty, uh . . ." Matt caught his breath. "Why are you angry?"

"Your own parents, and you did not discover they were in need before this? Why, what an undutiful son you are! Get you hence, Lord Wizard, and bring them home at once!"

"You're so beautiful when I'm wrong." Matt darted a loud kiss onto her cheek. "And you're right, I was a louse." Then he stepped back, smile vanishing, becoming formal. "My liege, may I have leave to leave and bring back my parents?"

"Of course you may! I command you to be off at once, to

save your mother and father!" But the wife's anxiety shone through the cracks in the queen's emotional armor. "Yet I will insist you take with you at least one knight, for from what you have told me, there is danger in your world. Now be off with you!"

"Yes, Majesty! See you in a week or so!" He spun on his heel and strode back to his tower.

He slammed into the laboratory, fuming, "Blast and fusion! How am I going to manage anything in twentieth-century America with a medieval knight hanging around my neck?"

"I think I know just the man," Saul said slowly.

CHAPTER 6

The mercury vapor lamps lit the train station well enough for any late commuters to be as safe as they were going to be, but those same streetlights cast deep shadows under the tunnel to the far tracks. There, the air thickened suddenly, gelling into two human forms—and Matt lurched and stumbled, then turned to catch Sir Gilbert as he wobbled. He thrust himself away from Matt, protesting, "I did not faint!"

"Of course not," Matt assured him. "You just went dizzy for a few minutes. It always happens when you travel by magic."

"Oh. It does?"

"Can't be helped," Matt assured him. He looked the knight up and down and sighed. The castle tailors had worked frantically, and Matt supposed Gilbert could get away with it. His trousers were just tubes of cloth tacked on to the hip section of a pair of tights. His "jacket" was a doublet cut down the front and equipped with buttons. He had been adamant about the emblem of his order, so Matt had asked the tailors to sew it onto the back of the loose linen shirt that hid Sir Gilbert's chain mail—well, he wouldn't be the first person to wear a vest like that in this part of the world. All in all, Matt supposed, Gilbert wouldn't attract too much attention until Matt could get him into a department store and put some modern clothes on his back, assuming the clerks could find a sport coat big enough for that pair of shoulders.

A roar sounded overhead, shaking the concrete about them. Gilbert nearly jumped into the abutment, looking about him wildly. "What . . . ? Where . . . ?"

"It's just, um, a string of wagons." Matt decided he didn't need to have Gilbert bracing himself against the unknown for the rest of the trip. "Come on, I'll show you."

He beckoned, leading the bemused young knight out to look up at the string of boxcars going past. Gilbert saw and went rigid. "A dragon!" His hand leaped to the sword that was no longer there.

"None of that." Matt caught his hand and slapped the head of a walking stick into Gilbert's hand. "We don't use swords here. Saul said you knew how to use this."

"Of course—I am a peasant's son!"

"How'd you get to be a knight?" Matt frowned, then remembered. "Oh, that's right—you're in a religious order." The Knights of St. Moncaire were like the Knights Templar, only nowhere nearly as rich—or corrupt.

"How can I fight that dragon with a stick?" Gilbert wailed.

"You won't. It's not a dragon." Matt took a deep breath and tried to explain. "You can tell it's just a string of wagons. See how they're joined together?"

"Why, so they are!" Gilbert's fear transmuted into awe. "But what huge wagons, and how fast they move! And so very many! What manner of beasts draw this train?"

"A magical monster," Matt ad libbed. "We call it a 'locomotive.' Don't worry, though, they're all tame—well, almost all."

"Is there no end to them?" Gilbert stared back along the tracks, where car after car was rounding the bend. "How wealthy your people must be, to build so many—and all with iron wheels!"

That jolted Matt. He'd never particularly thought of his civilization as being rich, but when Gilbert put it that way . . . "I suppose we are," he said slowly, "at least in things people can make."

"But not in their spirits?" The fire of religious zeal lit the eye of the martial monk. "We must bring the wealth of grace to their impoverished souls!"

"We have plenty of people trying to do that already." But

Matt felt a touch of guilt, remembering the shrinking number of Catholic priests and nuns. "What we need is some way to make the people listen to them."

"Alas! That can never be done, my friend." Gilbert's face was almost lugubrious with sudden tragedy. "None can force a soul to open itself to God. Indeed, none can open it save the soul itself."

"And God," Matt said softly.

"God can, but He will not," Gilbert reminded him sadly. "He has given us free will, and will not take it away."

"So that we're free to send ourselves to Hell if we wish," Matt said grimly. "Sometimes I wonder if it was God who gave that gift, or humanity who demanded it."

"Sundering themselves from God by their arrogance?" Gilbert nodded. "I fear so, my friend."

"Then let's go find some prime examples of arrogance," Matt said. "Out into the night of the city, Sir Gilbert."

They climbed the steps to the station, Matt wondering what could have possessed Saul to saddle him with this great overgrown boy. Knighted or not, Gilbert was still an idealistic innocent who had only two values for evaluating experience— the wrong way, and his way.

Gilbert halted to stare at the station. "Who lives within? Some wealthy burgher?"

"Uh, no one, really," Matt said, shamefaced. "It's just a place for people to wait for the next train to come, the one that carries them to where they want to go."

"So grand a place, merely for waiting?" Gilbert stared. "Wealthy your folk are indeed, Sir Matthew!" Then he noticed the graffiti scrawled on the walls. "What amazing, glowing colors! But what do the words say?"

"Nothing important," Matt said quickly. "Come on, we've got work waiting!"

He tried to hurry Gilbert around the corner, but the knight dug in his heels. "Nay! I must see what wondrous words are written in . . . " He broke off, staring at the graffiti.

Matt held his breath and hoped that Gilbert wouldn't have learned English, or how to read script, just by being transferred from universe to universe. But he'd made him read that Shakespeare verse in English again and again, under the Spider King's magic, until it began to make sense to him . . .

"Those are most rude words." Gilbert's voice shook.

"I'm afraid so." Suddenly, Matt felt ashamed for his whole culture. Defensively, he said, "But there are an awful lot of things here that are really good." Matt wondered how he was ever going to manage with a medieval warrior from a religious order, a man who was both a monk and a knight, when he wandered down Main Street and saw what was going on after dark in a Newark suburb.

"I can see your paintings are most amazing." Gilbert looked from one poster to another. "There is nothing religious in them, though . . . Ah! The word 'Revival' . . . " Then he saw what was being revived.

Matt's stomach sank. The poster advertised a revival of *Oh, Calcutta!* and the picture featured some very artistic nudes.

Gilbert tore his eyes away, turning pale. "Would men and women truly pose for such paintings willingly?"

"They don't see anything wrong in it." Matt hoped he was right.

"Nor see any peril to their senses of who and what they are?" Gilbert shuddered. "How can your people be so rich in buildings and wagons while starving in their souls?"

"I met a man once who told me he could see no further than this world," Matt said slowly.

"Why?" Gilbert cried, anguished, but Matt had no answer for him. Instead, he said, "Let's do what we have to do, and quickly. We need to get back to Merovence."

"Can we not stay to fight the Devil, and save this world?"

"Let's save our own first." Matt heard his own words, and felt a wrenching within him. He'd spoken truly; Merovence was his home now. He remembered the Uruguayan man down the street, who'd gone to visit his village after ten years in New Jersey, and come back saying that it wasn't home anymore.

He led Gilbert out around the station and down the walk

toward the side street that led to Main. Gilbert stopped, staring. "What manner of lamps are these?"

"Huh?" Matt followed his gaze. "Oh, just ordinary streetlights."

"To spend so much fuel on lighting an empty street? Amazing!"

Matt thought of telling him that the lights didn't burn oil, but thought of the smokestack at the powerhouse and bit his lip. "It helps keep people safe," he said, "so it's worth it. Come on."

They walked on down the street, with Gilbert exclaiming softly. "So much pavement! Such huge blocks! So little sewage!"

And here Matt had been getting angry at the litterbugs. He remembered how downtown Bordestang looked at night—dark as an eight ball, stinking with open sewers. Maybe, when they got the genies under control, he ought to tell Alisande about streetlights, storm drains, and sanitation services.

They turned the corner onto Main Street, and Gilbert halted, staring in amazement. "How wondrous!"

"What?" Matt looked down the street, frowning. "Just because people are out late shopping?"

"It is as brightly lit as day! And those canopies, they might house an army!"

"Well, they *are* hoping that sheltering people from rain between stores might attract customers away from the shopping malls . . ."

"And all paved, all stone, even the buildings! Are they palaces? They must be, for they're ablaze with light, and all of stone, as tall as a castle keep!"

Matt turned back, viewing the scene as it must appear to Gilbert, and was forced to admit he had overlooked some of the more amazing aspects of his own world. What made it worse was that this Main Street was nothing special, as towns went.

"They're just shops," he said, feeling very lame.

"Shops! If these are shops, what are your churches like?"

Gilbert turned on him, eager as a puppy. "Can we not find one, Sir Matthew?"

"I'm afraid we don't really have time." Matt had needed the reminder that he'd been knighted. "For every hour here, a week passes in Merovence—don't ask me to explain the magic of it. Just take my word for it, we have to hurry."

"Can the church really be so far away?"

Matt tried to remember where the nearest Catholic church was, but no, it was Our Lady of Fatima. "It's two miles, Gilbert. Come on, we've got to go." He turned to cross the street, then stopped as the light turned red.

Gilbert kept on going.

"Hold on!" Matt squawked, and dove for him. He caught the knight's shoulder and pulled, which was about the same as lassoing a steamship and hauling. Gilbert slowed just a tiny bit—but he did turn, frowning. "What troubles you, Sir . . ."

The car horn blared down on them, the headlights blinding. Gilbert froze, and Matt yanked. The knight stumbled back two feet, enough so that the car shot by without running over his toes—or any other part of him, either. It went howling away, but other cars came roaring past. Gilbert stared at them, turning ashen, and started to shake. "What monsters are these?"

"Human, believe it or not," Matt told him. "Look inside each one, and you'll see a man or a woman."

"Witchcraft!"

"No, just our country's kind of carriages."

"But what pulls them? Where are the horses?"

"Under the hood." Matt didn't feel like trying to explain internal combustion. "They're very small, but there are a lot of them."

It turned out not to be the smartest thing to say. Every time they passed a parked car, Gilbert stooped, looking underneath to see the hooves. Matt finally had to tell him, "They pull their legs up when they're standing still. When they're running, they move so fast you can't see them." He felt bad lying to the kid, but it would have taken a couple of hours to explain, and four more to convince him it was true.

Matt saw what was coming up, and pointed down. "Watch the pavement as you go by."

Gilbert did, protesting, "I have already seen how amazingly huge are these slabs of rock, and for a mere footpath!" He lifted his head. "But why do you . . . " He broke off, seeing the neon sign over the tavern door with the glowing pink line drawing of a woman wearing only the shortest of skirts. The sign flashed, making her appear to gyrate above a sign that read, EXOTIC TOPLESS DANCERS.

Gilbert almost passed out. Matt hauled on his arm and made sure he passed on instead. Unfortunately, that meant the monk had a half second's look through the open door at the exotic dancer herself, pushing forty and very tired of it all. The young knight forced his gaze away and shuddered. "Do all your people think of nothing but the flesh?"

"No," Matt said. "They spend a lot of time thinking about money, too."

"Covetousness!" Gilbert muttered. "Greed and lust! A void within the soul giving rise to an aching hunger that they seek to fill with the things of the flesh, and are doomed to despair thereby!" He turned back to Matt. "I can see why you were not fitted for this world, Sir Matthew."

Matt was silent, staring at the street in front of him for a few paces, wondering if Gilbert was really as perceptive as he sounded, or if he was just spouting memorized doctrine. Offhand, Matt didn't remember hearing that explanation before. "You surprise me, Sir Gilbert," he said honestly, then pulled the young knight into the nearest discount store before he could ask.

Gilbert halted, stunned all over again. "Are these truly garments?"

"Sure are."

"So *many* of them?"

Matt tried a new tack. "What do you think you'd see if you went inside a merchant's warehouse?"

"Perhaps . . . " Gilbert admitted, and let Matt pull him over to a rack that held long, loose "duster" coats.

"You're not going to be here that long." Matt pulled the largest size off the rack and held it up by the shoulders. "Maybe we can get away with just covering you up. Here, slip your arms into the sleeves."

Gilbert managed it without letting go of his walking stick, shoving one hand through to take the cane while he slipped in the other. He shrugged the coat into place and Matt stepped back to look him over, frowning. "A little long, but it fits okay in the shoulders. Swing your arms and see it if binds."

Gilbert windmilled each arm, then nodded. "There is no binding."

"That'll do, then." Matt led him back toward the door. "Who knows? It might scare away muggers . . . uh, footpads."

"Why should a mere coat do that?"

" 'Cause they'll maybe think you're hiding a sword under it."

"Would that I were! But why should they think that?"

" 'Cause it's big enough." TV and movies were another set of things Matt didn't feel like explaining. He was glad he was only going to be here with Gilbert for an hour or two.

He paid with his credit card—that was another good thing about so little time having elapsed in this universe. He reminded himself to send a payment in from Bordestang.

Then they went out into the night again—and a woman with a tired, weary voice called to Gilbert. "Hey, fella."

"Yes, damsel?" Gilbert turned to look—and froze.

Matt groaned.

The garment she wore might have been called a dress, though it was about five yards short of fabric by Merovence's standards. It fit her like a second skin, a fabric that sheened softly in the streetlights, fairly begging to be touched. The hemline was a foot above her knees, and her heels were so high that Matt felt they should have had a warning to stay away from the edge. Her hair was bobbed in the latest mode from cheap salons—it wasn't her fault that it made her look like a Merovencian boy. But no juvenile male ever had such a voluptuous figure, or troweled on so much makeup.

The weary voice recited mechanically, "You wanna have a nice time?"

Gilbert turned red in the face and started making choking noises.

"He's a lay preacher," Matt explained, and hurried Gilbert away from the harsh, mocking laugh behind him before the woman could make the obvious pun.

A block farther on, Matt pulled him to a halt under a sign that said *bus*. Gilbert managed to stop gurgling long enough to draw in a deep, shuddering breath. He used it to intone, "That painted Jezebel!"

"Not that bad," Matt said. "She doesn't kill people, or try to convert them to a pagan religion. In fact, if she doesn't do what she does, her, uh, 'master' will beat her and, uh, starve her." Once again, he didn't feel like explaining—about drugs.

Gilbert stared at him, appalled. "She does not choose this immorality?"

"It beats starving," Matt said.

"Surely the Church would have given her bread!"

"Bread wasn't enough. Her 'master' probably told her she'd be rich if she did what she's doing. Now she's found out that he's the one who gets rich, and she only keeps the smallest part of the money men give her."

"The poor creature!" Gilbert was trembling, though whether with horror or anger, Matt couldn't tell. Luckily, the bus pulled up just then.

The doors hissed open, and Gilbert shrank back, eyes wide.

"It's only one of those carriages I was telling you about," Matt said, "though this is our form of coach. There's no danger."

"If you say so, Sir Matthew." Gilbert forced himself up the steps and into the bus.

"Hold it, mac!" The driver put out a hand. "Fare!"

"I'm paying for both of us." Matt dropped quarters in the meter. It clucked contentedly to itself, and he nudged Gilbert on.

They were halfway down to their seats when the bus started up, shoving the young knight down. That much, though, horses could do. He only pushed himself square in the seat, looking about. "As bright as day! So many benches, so wide, and all cushioned! Silver poles and rails! What are they for, Sir Matthew?"

"If the bus—excuse me, coach—is really full, people have to stand while it's moving, so they hold on to the poles and rails—and they're not really silver, just very highly polished."

"The amount of time that must have taken!"

Matt almost told Gilbert they had machines to do the polishing, but caught himself in time. He didn't want to have to explain what his civilization meant by a machine.

Matt didn't know the night driver—old Frank must have finally retired—so there was no need to make conversation while the bus ran. That was just as well, since he had to explain to Gilbert that the "coach" wasn't really going much faster than a team of horses could gallop, and that the signs up high on the walls were telling people about things they could buy and people who could help them if they needed it. Gilbert wasn't very much impressed by the things, but was by the number of people willing to help. He did ask, though, why the signs were in two languages, and when Matt told him one of them was Spanish, the language spoken in his world's Ibile, Gilbert asked "Are they Moors?" and several of the darker-skinned passengers looked up, ready to take offense. Fortunately, Matt was able to say "There's our stop!" and press the yellow strip. The chime rang, and the STOP REQUESTED sign lit at the front of the bus. By the time Matt was done explaining bell and glowing signboard, they were standing on the sidewalk, watching the bus's taillights go away, and Matt switched to explaining how they could afford the fuel for lights at the back of the coach, and why they were necessary. He started walking as he talked, and Gilbert kept pace with him.

A raucous laugh sounded from a front porch, and Matt's stomach clenched. "You might want to take a firm hold on that stick, Sir Gilbert."

"As you say." Gilbert grinned, his confusion and horror falling away in the anticipation of battle. Matt glanced at him, realized he was about to take out all his inner turmoil in good clean action, and felt a surge of thankfulness that he wasn't going to be in front of the young knight's stick.

"Hey, look there!" a callow young voice called out, and several other young men hopped down off the stoop. They swayed as they came toward the pair.

"What ails them?" Gilbert asked.

"They're drunk," Matt explained. He didn't mention drugs.

"Well, it's little Matty boy again!" Luco's lip lifted in a sneer. "Went back for reinforcements, huh?"

"You could say that, Luco." Matt let the boyhood fears wash over him and pass. "Having fun?"

"No, but we will now! Gonna run out on us again, Matty boy?"

"Only if it's the only way I can keep from killing you, Luco."

Gilbert said nothing, only grinned, teeth bright in the dusk.

"You talk big, Matty," said a voice from behind, mocking.

Gilbert turned, but Matt kept his gaze locked with Luco's. "How many of them are there?"

"Only five," Gilbert told him.

"And I've only got four up here. What's the matter, Luco? The rest of your buddies go to jail?"

Luco snarled and swung.

CHAPTER 7

Matt blocked Luco's swing and drove a fist into his belly. Luco grunted, folding, but pumped his fists at Matt's abdomen anyway. Matt hunched, blocking some of the blows. Several got through, and they hurt, but his own fists had taken enough punch out of them to keep them from doing any damage. Choy and Liam closed in from the sides, and Luco shouted a curse as he swung a fist back for a hammer blow.

Matt chopped a short, vicious uppercut into Luco's face.

As he fell back, Matt ducked a swing from Choy, lashed a kick at Liam, then came up pivoting to slam a punch at Choy, who blocked and counterpunched. Matt dodged enough to take it on his chest. The pain woke anger, but he caught Choy's wrist and turned, catching his shirtfront, and bowed as he stuck his hip out. Choy knew the move, though, and leaped over, turning as he did—and slammed right into Liam.

Behind them, Gilbert shouted with delight, and Matt heard some very solid cracks as the cane did its work. The punks shouted in outrage.

Then Luco pushed himself to his feet, but he and Choy stepped back as Liam stepped in, grinning, numchuks whirling.

Matt leaped away, pulling a little stick of his own out from under his jacket—fourteen inches of polished, seasoned ash, an inch and a half thick.

Liam laughed and lashed out with the numchuks—but clumsily; it was clear he hadn't taken lessons. Matt swung his own stick, and the numchuks tangled around it. Matt pulled and kicked, and Liam stumbled past, then fell.

Someone hit his back, hard. He lurched forward, almost

unable to breathe because of the pain, and swung about into Herm's pumping fists. Matt ducked over, fists close to his face, blocking the punches, trying to time his countermove, if he could just pay attention through the pain as fists landed on his shoulders, his arms . . .

But the other four punks whooped and waded in. Pain exploded on the side of Matt's head, in his kidneys, in his other side . . .

Then somebody roared, he heard a series of hollow knocks, and only Herm was there in front of him, staring over Matt's head openmouthed. Matt uncoiled and slammed an uppercut into his jaw. Without a word, Herm fell.

Matt turned in time to see Gilbert flicking his cane against the side of Luco's head, then whirling it to jab Choy in the stomach. Choy doubled over, and Gilbert swung the stick overhand. The hollow knock sounded again, and Choy slumped.

Matt stared at the wanna-be thugs. They were all on the ground, groaning or still. "They aren't . . . ?"

"Dead? No. That is the virtue of a stick—it is harder to slay a man with it."

Liam inched forward, reaching out for his fallen switchblade. Disdainfully, Gilbert kicked it away. Then he bent, picked it up, jabbed it in the crack between two slabs of concrete, and broke it off short. Liam pushed himself up to his elbows with a shout of protest that died as he saw the coldness in Gilbert's eyes. He shrank back down, speechless.

"Let us leave this heap of offal, Sir Matthew," Gilbert said. "I do not think they shall trouble us again this night."

"No, thanks to you. Let's go." Matt knew Liam was wondering what offal was.

"We'll . . . we'll call the cops on you!" Liam called.

"What are 'cops'?" Gilbert asked.

"The Watch," Matt told him.

Gilbert stared. "Footpads will call the *Watch*?"

"He's carrying a lethal weapon!" Liam blustered.

Matt shook his head and turned away.

"The switchblade!" Liam shouted. "It's got his finger-prints now!"

"It's got yours, too," Matt called back. "Go ahead and call the police."

They went on down the block, ignoring Liam's curses. "Well, Her Majesty was right again," Matt admitted. "I did need help. Thanks, Sir Gilbert."

"It was my pleasure."

Matt would have felt a bit better if Gilbert hadn't sounded quite so sincere.

They climbed the steps to the porch. Matt started to ring the doorbell, but remembered the problems of explaining to Gilbert and knocked instead.

The knight looked about him. "Truly a grand house, Sir Matthew! You are nobly born indeed!"

"Uh, nobody in this neighborhood is very rich, Gilbert," Matt said sheepishly.

Gilbert stared.

"At least, they don't think so," Matt explained. "There are a lot of people who're richer."

The door opened, and Mama stood there in her apron, hair tied up in a kerchief, eyes red. Over her head, Matt saw Papa hefting boxes into a stack, his face grim. Matt's heart sank.

Then Mama realized who was there. Her eyes went wide, and the gloom lifted. "Mateo!" She threw her arms around his neck and hugged. "So soon! What, did you forget something?"

"Yeah—you and Papa." Matt grinned, hugging her, and carried her into the little hallway where he set her down.

Papa looked up in surprise. Then his grimness vanished and he came toward his son with his arms wide. "So you couldn't stay away, hey? Too late, though—dinner is over." He embraced Matt, then held him away and looked up at Gilbert inquiringly.

"Uh, Mama and Papa, this is my friend, Gilbert," Matt explained. "Gilbert, my mother and father, Jimena and Ramón Mantrell."

"A pleasure, goodfolk." Gilbert gave a little bow.

"As is ours," Papa said, reaching out to shake Gilbert's hand. The knight went along with the gesture, albeit awkwardly. "Jimena," said Papa, "can't we take something out of the refrigerator?"

"Uh, I'm afraid we don't have time, Papa." At his father's frown, Matt explained, "We had a little run-in with the neighborhood gang, and they might call the cops."

"Call the cops! Them?"

"Surely you did nothing wrong, Mateo," his mother said anxiously.

"Just self-defense, but it'll take an hour or two to prove it, and we don't have that much leeway." Matt bit his lip; his parents were proud people, and he had to phrase this just right. "Uh, Mama, Papa—I didn't tell you all the news this afternoon."

"Oh?" Papa frowned, braced for the bad stuff. "What else?"

"Good news," Matt said, "but, uh—we were so locked away in our own little world that I didn't know I *could* tell you about it."

Gilbert frowned at him, puzzled. Well, Matt could explain it all to them later.

"I found the right girl," he said in a rush.

"Oh, Mateo!" Mama cried with delight, and reached up to kiss him soundly on the cheek.

Papa's eyes shone. He embraced his son, then held him at arm's length, grinning. "I'm glad, I'm so glad! I was afraid she'd never come along! When is the wedding?"

"Well, we already have a house." Matt was getting good at sidestepping questions. "We'd like you to come visit us."

"We will, we will." Papa's smile slipped. "But first we have to . . . " He waved at the stack of boxes and the stripped bookshelves.

"It looks like you're moving out. Well, take it all along."

"Oh?" Papa forced a weary smile. "Have you brought a moving van?"

"Isn't one coming?"

Papa gestured with futility, tried to answer, then turned away.

"Even if we had money for the van, Mateo, we have no place to take the furniture," Mama said softly. "We can take only what will fit in the rental van, and keep at the motel."

Matt turned somber. "You could declare bankruptcy."

"We could have," Mama agreed, "and Papa said to, but I knew it hurt him not to be able to pay his debts. We sold the house, and tomorrow we will rent the van and drive away with what we can. The Goodwill will come to take what we leave."

Matt frowned, looking out over the pile of boxes. "How much more do you have to pack?"

Now it was Mama who gestured with futility. "It is all here in the boxes, all that we cannot bear to leave—but the house, the garden, the memories . . . "

Tears filled her eyes. Matt said quickly, "Memories you can always take with you, Mama. I know it's hard, but if you really have to go, then let's go now."

Papa looked up, frowning. "You brought a van?" Then he looked at Matt more closely. "You're not surprised at any of this."

"A neighbor told me," Matt admitted.

Papa swore.

"What did she tell you?" Mama, at least, had no doubt about who.

"That the boys have harassed the store so badly your business went broke," Matt said. Then he realized that he could take the offensive. He gave his father a look of hurt. "You should have told me, Papa."

"It was not your fight," Papa said stiffly.

"*All* your fights are my fights," Matt retorted. "You taught me it should be that way with my friends. How much more with my parents?"

"I was being medieval," Papa muttered.

"Yes, the medieval notion of keeping faith! How bad is it?"

Papa glanced at Mama; her look implored him, and he relented. "When I came home for lunch today, I had just finished closing up the store for good."

"You *knew* that!" Matt accused his mother.

"We did not want you to worry," she explained, then turned stubborn. "You might have dropped out of school!"

"But your visit was the perfect note to raise our spirits from defeat," Papa said gently.

Matt wilted. "Okay, I'm an undutiful son not to have been checking up on you!" At least they didn't know just how neglectful he had been.

"That doesn't matter, Matt," his father said softly. "Our problems are our own. You go build *your* life."

"I will, but problems are for sharing—that's another thing you taught me," Matt said. "What does matter is that we can get you out of here."

A siren wailed in the distance.

Gilbert looked up, tensed to fight. "What spirit is that?"

"No spirit, only an alarm," Matt said quickly. "It's the police coming—Liam did call them, the idiot! And I'm sorry, Papa, Mama, but I can't afford the delay!" He didn't want to add that he might have a little trouble explaining Gilbert's lack of identity cards. "Please, I'm going to have to ask you to take me on faith, no matter how crazy it may seem."

Papa glanced at Mama. Their gaze held for a moment or two; then they turned back, nodding. "What harm can it do?" Mama asked.

"None," Matt assured her. "Here, stand around your boxes and hold hands—Gilbert, you too!"

Frowning, Mama and Papa linked hands with them. Gilbert, of course, obeyed the Lord Wizard without an instant's hesitation.

The siren wailed closer.

"Now, repeat after me," Matt said. *"Lalinga wogreus marwold reiger."*

Mama and Papa frowned, but repeated obediently, *"Lalinga wogreus marwold reiger."*

"Athelstrigen marx alupta," Matt intoned.

Mama and Papa repeated, *"Athelstrigen marx alupta . . ."*

"Harleng krimorg barlow steiger," Matt chanted.

"Harleng krimorg barlow steiger."

Matt went on, repeating the words line by line until he'd finished the verse, then told them, "Again!"

He lined the verse out for them to repeat time after time, until they could recite it all the way through without him—giving him odd looks, but reciting.

The siren came closer and closer.

"Say it over and over, no matter what I say!" Matt told them. "Just keep chanting!"

They did as he asked, saying the words over and over. Then Mama's eyes widened, and Matt knew the words were beginning to make sense to her.

Outside, the siren wailed to a stop. Orange and blue lights flickered through the windows. A car door slammed, and footsteps thudded on the outdoor stairs.

Matt threw back his head and called,

> "St. Moncaire, lend us your strength!
> Spider King, throw us a length,
> A strand to serve us as a path,
> Sheltered from the foeman's wrath!
> Lend an ear, Witch Doctor Saul!
> With physics, math, and heart, now HAUL!"

Then he called out, "All together, now!" and chanted the verse again, only this time, they all understood the words:

> "You, betrayed by Time and Space,
> Born without your proper grace,
> To a world befouled and base—
> Feel your proper form and case,
> Recognize your homeland's face.
> Cross the void of time and space!
> Seek and find your proper place!"

A fist pounded on the door.

"The words make sense!" Papa cried in delight—but he spoke in the language of Merovence, not America, and the world suddenly went crazy, tilting and spinning around them.

When it stilled, Mama slumped against Matt. He held her up, saying, "It'll pass, it's just disorientation . . . Gilbert, how're you doing?"

"Well enough," the knight called back. "Come now, Goodman Mantrell, it is a sickening feeling, but bear up and it will pass . . . there!"

Matt glanced over and saw Papa still leaning on Gilbert's shoulder, but straightening. "Thank you for your arm, Master Gilbert."

"My honor." But Gilbert looked a little nonplussed.

"He's a knight, Papa," Matt began, but Mama looked about her at the sun-filled space and let out a cry of amazement. *"El Morro!"*

Papa looked around, too. Matt took a quick glance, enough to be sure they were in the courtyard, Mama with him, Papa with Gilbert, their huge pile of boxes in between. A couple of knights and a dozen footmen were running toward them.

"I see the resemblance," Papa told Mama, "but I do not think this is El Morro. It is a castle, though."

"Not even a Spanish one, now that I look at the architecture," Mama said, "but still, a real castle! How did we come here?"

"Magic, Mama."

"Mateo, I have told you not to be superstitious!" Mama scolded.

"No, really—magic works here!" Matt opened his mouth to explain further, but Mama rushed on. "Why are those men dressed as knights, Mateo?"

"Because they *are* knights, Mama." That was as much as Matt got out before the first of the guardsmen reached them. "Lord Wizard!" he panted, bowing. "Is anything amiss?"

His parents turned to him, eyes wide. "Lord Wizard?"

"That's the government job I was telling you about," Matt said lamely.

"Government job?" Papa fixed him with a gimlet stare. *"Which* government?"

"You have been wasting your time with those Renaissance Fair people again," Mama accused.

The knights came panting up. "Sir Matthew! Is all well?"

" 'Sir'?" Papa asked.

Mama clucked her tongue in criticism.

"Just fine, Sir Norton, thank you—now that we're back," Matt said. "Uh, could you detail a few men to guard this heap of luggage? I'd like to take my parents to meet their hostess."

"Parents!" Sir Norton bowed, and Sir Cran followed suit. "We are honored to meet the illustrious parents of Her Majesty's Wizard!"

"How gracious of you," Mama said, with a warm smile. "We are honored to meet such gallant knights—are we not, Ramón?"

"Indeed we are." Papa bowed, then said to Matt out of the corner of his mouth, "Definitely too much time on Renaissance festivals."

Sir Cran said, "It will be our honor to guard your belongings." He gestured to the footmen, who formed a circle around the boxes.

"Thank you all," Mama said, and gave them such a radiant look that half of them caught their breaths. The other half were on the other side of the box-pile and didn't see.

"Yes, thanks," Matt said quickly, before Papa could begin to get jealous. "The mistress of the castle is this way, Mama, Papa."

They went in through the doors at the base of the keep. The guards at the inner door gave them cold stares until they recognized the Lord Wizard. Then they leaped to open the panel.

As they climbed the broad winding stairs set against the outer wall, Matt said softly to his father, "You know, I'd never realized it before, but Mama really is a beautiful woman, isn't she?"

Papa grinned, looking very smug. "She is indeed, my son, and she grows more beautiful every day."

"You were lucky."

"I was," Papa admitted, "though there was quite a bit of hard work in winning her."

Matt didn't doubt that Mama had made him sweat. He also didn't doubt that she'd been in love with him from the moment she saw him. He might never have realized his mother was beautiful, but he had always known he would never be as handsome as his father.

They came out into the broad, carpeted upper hall, the grimness of its stone walls softened by glowing tapestries. Mama stared, but Matt didn't give her time to think—he went straight to the solar. The guards looked up, then smiled as they saw him. One reached for the door, but Matt was there before him. He opened it and stepped in, ushering his parents with him.

Mama cried out in delight. "How lovely!"

"She certainly is," Papa said.

Alisande looked up at them from a table strewn with parchment rolls. The sunlight through the tall windows turned her hair to gold, and the maroon gown set off her complexion perfectly. The simple golden band about her temples could have been a mere decoration.

Mama gave Papa a sharp elbow in the ribs. "I spoke of the room, husband!"

Papa looked around at the beamed ceiling, paneled walls, and tapestries. "You're right, Jimena. It's a lovely room!"

"And what a lovely girl!" Mama said, fairly beaming at Alisande. "Mateo—who is this woman?"

"Uh—Mama, Papa . . . " Matt took a deep breath. "There's something else I haven't told you."

Mama recognized the tone and turned to him, frowning. "You've been a bad boy."

"Very bad," Matt admitted. "I didn't invite you to my wedding."

Both parents cried out in protest.

"I didn't know how," Matt explained. "I'll make it clear later, but for now, believe me—this really is a different world, and I didn't know how to call home."

Mama looked up at Alisande with dawning realization. "Why do you tell us this now?"

"Because I'd like you to meet my bride." Matt took a deep

breath. "Mama, Papa—may I introduce you to my wife, Alisande?"

"His mother?" Alisande rose, eyes huge.

"Oh, my dear!" With her arms wide, Mama stepped up. Surprised, Alisande reached out—and the two women embraced.

"I think you got away with it this time," Papa muttered to Matt, "but don't let it happen again, okay?"

"Uh, there's more," Matt admitted.

"More?" Papa stared, then frowned, and the storm clouds gathered. "How long have you been wedded to this woman, anyway?"

"Three years," Matt admitted.

"Three years?" Papa squawked, and Mama broke from Alisande to stare at Matt. "But we saw you last Easter, only a few weeks ago, and you said no word of having met her!"

"I hadn't," Matt told her. "It was only a few weeks for you, but it was . . . " He winced. " . . . four years for me."

"Four years?" Papa yelped. "How can that be?"

Mama turned, frowning. "And in all that time, you never thought to write to us?"

Matt chose the easier question. "I haven't figured it out for sure, but I think time runs at different rates in our two universes—an hour in your neighborhood is a week or so here. Or it could be that whoever moves us between universes is plugging us in at whatever time he or it chooses."

Mama let go of Alisande, frowning at her son. "You mean you didn't know you could go home?"

"Didn't know I could go, write, or call," Matt said. "I just figured that out a little while ago—in fact, only two days, for me."

"You have been gone from me for two weeks now, husband," Alisande said.

Mama turned to stare at her, then said to Matt, "You have a very understanding wife." To Alisande, she said, "You should scold him at least a little, my dear."

Alisande gave her a smile, brightening, then turned to Matt, hands on her hips, and said, "How dare you be so long gone from me, Matthew!"

"Sorry, dear," Matt said contritely. "Couldn't be helped."

"He had told me he needed to go to bring you to us," Alisande explained.

"Our house!" Mama spun to the men, then reached out for Papa's hand. "Our furniture, the neighbors, the closing!"

"We were going to walk away from it all anyway, my love," Papa said gently. He turned to Matt. "We can send the lawyer a power of attorney, can't we?"

"And some good-bye letters to the neighbors." Matt nodded. "I set up a system yesterday."

"We should do that right away," Mama said.

"No rush." Matt smiled. "A week here is an hour there."

Mama looked startled, then relaxed and turned back to Alisande with a smile. "Well, we will find a place to stay, but it is early. We can talk for at least a few minutes."

"You will stay with us," Alisande said firmly. "I have already ordered a suite to be prepared for you."

"We could not impose," Papa began.

"Indeed you could not," Alisande agreed, "even if you stayed here for the rest of your lives, as I hope you will. You are my parents too, now, and it will be my privilege to guest you."

Mama stared. "Do you *own* this castle, dear?"

"In some measure," Alisande allowed. "I have the use of it for my lifetime, at least."

Matt was glad she didn't mention the other half-dozen royal castles around the land.

A thin sound of crying came through the open door, growing louder.

Mama and Papa stared at Matt.

CHAPTER 8

Matt tried to look shamefaced, but only managed to look sickeningly proud.

A plump rosy-cheeked matron in a long dress and white cap came to the door, holding a blanket-wrapped, squalling bundle. "Majesty, do you wish . . . "

"Yes, I have leisure." Alisande smiled and crossed to the door, taking the baby from her arms. "Attend us, nurse."

The nurse stepped into the room and stood by the door, hands folded. Alisande turned back toward the window, smiling down at the little puckered face in the crook of her arm.

"A child!" Mama lit up with delight.

"You *have* been a naughty boy," Papa said.

"Oh, he has been a very good boy indeed," Alisande contradicted, giving Matt a wicked glance. "If I do half as well raising my son as you have with yours, I will be proud."

Papa looked up with surprise, then smiled with a little bow. "I thank you."

"You flatter me." Mama reached for the baby. "I know he's hungry—but may I?"

"Indeed." Alisande handed the baby to her, then stepped to a chair by the window, hidden from outside by a curtain, and began to loosen the laces of her bodice.

Papa crowded in next to Mama, beaming down at the child. "A real grandson! How blessed I am!"

"Oh, what a handsome little boy!" Mama exclaimed. "And how strong already!"

"At least in his lungs." Papa slipped an arm around her shoulders, and she nestled against him for a moment.

Matt smiled down into the little, bawling face. The feeling of the miraculous had worn off in the last three months, but the look in his parents' eyes brought it back.

"Come, Ramón, he is hungry!" Mama said, and took the baby over to Alisande. Matt allowed himself one long look at his wife nursing, smiling tenderly down at the little face. Desire stirred, so he turned away to Papa, leaving the mothers to discuss such burning topics as diapers, colic, and feeding schedules.

Papa clapped his son on the shoulder and smiled. "And to think that only last June, you thought you would be a failure!"

Matt stared, surprised, then grinned sheepishly. "Marrying a wife with a castle doesn't make me a success, Papa." After all, his father didn't know he'd helped Alisande get back that castle when it had been stolen from her—and the whole kingdom with it.

But Papa was shaking his head. "A wedding is only the first step, Mateo. Building a good marriage is a life's work. From the way she looks at you, you're succeeding so far—and a baby is a big step in the right direction."

Papa's view was old-fashioned, of course, but the problem was that Matt shared it. Maybe they did belong in the Middle Ages.

"How about getting rich, Papa? How about power?"

Papa sighed, shaking his head. "Power and wealth don't make a man happy, son. Love does—and doing a job you enjoy."

"Well, I do enjoy this one."

"Yes, that's why she looks happy—but this time, I *wasn't* speaking about marriage. You have to support them, after all. I meant this government job of yours."

"Oh, I do enjoy it, Papa, yes. It's fascinating, and very fulfilling."

"Then you are a success," Papa said, beaming proudly. "Remember, though, that success is like salvation . . . "

"I must win it all over again every day." Matt smiled. "Don't worry, Papa, I remember what you taught me."

Alisande handed Mama the baby and laced up her gown—

just in time, for the sentry at the door announced, "Your Majesty, a herald has come with urgent news."

Alisande frowned and straightened as the invisible mantle of authority, put aside for a brief rest, now settled its weight on her shoulders again. "Bid him enter."

"Your Majesty?" Papa and Mama said together, staring.

"Uh, yeah, I didn't finish the introductions," Matt said, shifting uncomfortably. "Mama, Papa, may I introduce you to Her Majesty Alisande, Queen of Merovence—and of my heart." He caught Alisande's hand. She forgot about being royal long enough to give him a dazzling smile.

Matt's parents stared. Then, together, they dropped to their knees, heads bowed. "Your Majesty!"

"Oh, none of that, none of that!" Alisande raised them up hastily and embraced them each in turn. "I am your daughter, and not your sovereign unless you choose it! Even if you do, you must never bow to me unless it is an occasion of state! What, do you think I make your son bow every time he would speak to me?"

Papa grinned as he rose. "I should hope not."

"Do you not think my marriage matters as much to me as my kingdom?" Alisande challenged. "Indeed, it is part and parcel of my reign, though your son must explain that. It somewhat passes my understanding, for I am a monarch and not a wizard. You will be my family, I hope, for you are grandparents to my son—and family do not bow to one another!"

"But must always speak to one another with respect," Mama qualified.

Papa nodded, smile glowing. "You are wise, my daughter."

Alisande stared at him for a moment, then threw herself into his arms, holding tight. Papa wrapped his arms about her, feeling her tremble. He looked up over her shoulder at Matt, amazed.

Matt held up a hand, palm out, and nodded reassurance, watching his wife with sympathy.

Alisande pushed herself away from Papa, head bowed. "Nay, I forget myself. Forgive me."

"No, I thank you," Papa said softly. "Such an embrace is a treasure, and makes me rejoice that my son chose so well."

Alisande looked up at him in surprise, then blushed and looked away. She raised her eyes to Matt. "I see where you learned your gallantry, sir."

"Has he finally learned it?" Mama exclaimed. "Thank Heaven!"

Alisande turned to her, startled, then laughed gaily and caught her hands. "I shall thank you, too, for I would not have him if it were not for you. But I must ask you to leave me now, for I must tend to affairs of state."

"Oh, of course!" Mama said, and stepped away to stand beside her son.

"If you don't mind, Your Majesty, I'll show them to their suite," Matt said.

"Of course, Lord Wizard."

Mama and Papa both turned to stare at Matt.

"There's a herald listening," Matt muttered out of the corner of his mouth. He bowed and stepped to the door, then out into the hallway. Mama and Papa followed. They passed a very weary-looking herald, still beating the dust from his clothes with his hat. Both parents glanced at him as the sentries ushered him into the solar, then turned to pounce on their son. "Is this real?" Papa demanded.

"Totally," Matt assured him, but frowned and nodded toward the guards. "Let's get you to your suite first, though, okay?"

"It is next to the nursery, Lord Wizard," the guard told him.

His parents glared a question. Matt ignored them. "Thank you, Sergeant."

The nursery—the sleeping part, anyway—was down at the end of the hallway. Matt turned to the door beside it, on the left.

"How do you know which one it is?" Mama asked.

"Because Alisande's bedroom is the door to the right," Matt explained.

"*Alisande's* bedroom?" Mama exclaimed. "You do not sleep together?"

Matt gave her a sunny smile. "More often than not, Mama—but I have the bedroom next to hers. It comes in handy for changing clothes."

Mama stared, then smiled, reassured.

Matt opened the door and bowed them in. "Welcome to your new home."

"Home!" Mama bustled in. "Well, we certainly can't stay *that* long . . . Oh!"

The center of the room was filled with a high stack of boxes.

"I see the chamberlain has been his usual efficient self," Matt said.

Papa stepped in, staring about him. The room was paneled in golden wood, with broad windows that looked out onto the courtyard. Heavy draperies hung to either side, opposite a large tapestry of a maiden and a minstrel.

"But this is luxury!" Mama protested.

"Then you're finally getting what you deserve," Matt replied.

"Where do we sleep?"

Matt pointed. "That door in the west wall."

Both parents stepped to the doorway, then stared. "A four-poster!" Mama exclaimed.

"With feather beds," Matt told them. "Even so, it's no innerspring mattress, and there's no electricity. I'm afraid the 'running water' only runs from that pitcher into the basin, and then only when you tilt it, and the sanitary arrangements are a seat with a chamber pot under it, in that little closet over there, but somebody will empty it every day. Not as nice as the home you gave me to grow up in, in some ways—but these are the Middle Ages, after all."

"Luxury indeed, by medieval standards," Papa assured him. Then he turned and commanded, "Sit down."

"Yes, sit." Mama set the example by going to one of the hourglass chairs and folding herself gracefully into it. She patted the one beside her.

Matt sat down, feeling the dread of the guilty child, and

his father sat beside Mama, looking grim. "Tell," he commanded, "and make sure it makes sense."

"That, I can't do," Matt protested. "But it's real, and I'll explain as much of it as I can understand."

"You can begin with how we came here," Papa said, leaning back in his chair.

"Magic," Matt said, and raised a hand. "No, really! I'm not fibbing! It really is magic, but it took me long enough to figure that out the first time I came here."

He launched into an account of his arrival in Merovence, triggered by studying the parchment he'd found between the pages of an old book in the university library, studying it until the alien words began to make sense—and when they did, he'd found himself on the streets of Bordestang.

He told his parents about his first misadventures, how he'd slowly figured out that magic really worked here, but that physics and chemistry didn't. Papa interrupted only long enough to say, "Well, quantum mechanics always did seem like magic to me," and later on Mama cried, "The brute had stolen her throne from her?"

"And killed her father." Matt gave Papa an apologetic look. "That's why she clung so tightly when you called her 'daughter.' "

"So she is," Papa said sternly, "and she can cling whenever she needs to."

Mama nodded firm agreement, but amended it to say, "I expect she will cling to you more often, though, Mateo."

"Hope so," Matt said, grinning, then gave them a brief account of the war to defeat the evil sorcerer Malingo and win back Alisande's throne. He threw in Stegoman the dragon, Sir Guy the Black Knight, Colmain the giant, Father Brunel the werewolf priest, and Sayeesa the lust-witch. When he'd finished, he was amazed to see that the light had changed; he'd taken at least half an hour.

"Let me understand." Mama frowned, leaning forward and holding up a palm. "You won back her throne for her?"

"Well, not alone," Matt amended, "but I do seem to have been one of the crucial elements in her success, yes."

"So you really are her chief wizard, then," Papa said, frowning.

"Yes. That's the government job I told you about."

"Lord Wizard! When did you become a nobleman?"

"When Alisande told me I was one—and that was before we married, by the way. A year or three before."

Mama smiled. "She kept you dangling awhile, then? Good for her!"

"I wouldn't have said so at the time," Matt said darkly.

Mama grinned. "More power to her, then!" Abruptly, she turned serious again. "I don't know, though, Mateo—this is so hard to believe."

"Are you speaking Spanish now?" Matt asked softly.

"Why, no, I am speaking English, and . . . " Mama heard her own words and stared, amazed. "I am not!"

"Try talking to me in Spanish."

"Why not?" Mama said. "All your life, I spoke to you in . . ." She stared again. "It still is not! It is the same language I spoke before!"

"You can recite a quotation in Spanish, if you try hard enough," Matt said, "or in English or French—but it takes a major effort."

"*Ou sont les neiges d'antan?*" Papa recited, then frowned. "I see what you mean—it takes great effort indeed."

"But what language are we speaking?" Mama asked.

"The language of the parchment scrap I found," Matt told her. "The language of Merovence. When you recited the verse I lined out for you, and the words began to make sense, your mind tuned in to this universe, which helped bring you here—but once you arrived, you were thinking in Merovencian."

"*Helped* bring us here?" Papa pounced on the word. "Who did the main work, then?"

"I'm pretty sure it was St. Moncaire," Matt told him. "He seemed to think I was the missing ingredient for putting Alisande back on the throne—and since Merovence was the only kingdom in Europe that hadn't fallen to the reign of Evil, it was worth some indirect saintly intervention."

"The reign of Evil?" Mama leaned forward, her gaze intent.

"White magic works by drawing on the power of God," Matt explained. "Black magic draws on the power of Satan. Both of them work by chanting poetry or, even better, singing it—that modulates the magical forces, causes the magical elements to fall into line, and makes things happen."

"Only Good or Evil?" Papa asked, frowning.

"It's hard for modern people to accept, I know," Matt said. "Saul still won't; he keeps trying to figure out some impersonal rules of magic. So does King Boncorro, in Latruria— Italy in our universe . . ."

"So Merovence is no longer the only good kingdom?" Mama asked.

"We've won back Ibile and Allustria," Matt told her. "Latruria is trying hard to be neutral, but at least King Boncorro has kicked out the sorcerer who was running things. We're worried about him, though."

"Yes—in medieval theology, walking the line between good and evil was impossible," Professor Papa said, frowning. "Equivocating, Shakespeare called it, and his Drunken Porter made it clear that you can't equivocate between God and the Devil—you fall into the Devil's hands eventually . . ."

"Just as Macbeth did." Matt nodded. "Saul's still trying, though. Every time he does something good, he commits a technical sin to balance it."

"A 'technical' sin?" Mama frowned.

"Yeah, something like eating meat on Friday—the Church hasn't lifted the ban on that, here. Trouble is, his heart isn't in it, and he usually winds up doing more good anyway."

Mama smiled. "You have told us much about this friend of yours."

"The kind of student every professor wishes to have!" Papa said fervently. "So he tries to work out laws of magic, like our laws of physics?"

Matt nodded. "He's made a lot of progress, actually. Trouble is, he can't find a poem that's value-neutral; every work of literature seems to have some sort of a theme, moral or immoral—even if it's pulp fiction, or straight from a greeting card."

"So that is why I felt this strangeness when I quoted Villon," Papa said, frowning.

Matt went still inside. "You did? Try it again."

"Ou sont les neiges d'antan?" Papa recited, then frowned. "Yes, I definitely feel some sort of tension growing around me."

"Like a force of some kind?"

Papa gazed off into space. "I suppose you could say that. It feels the way I've always imagined a dynamo would feel as it builds up electricity—if it could feel."

That said a lot about his father—that he was the kind of person who would try to imagine how it felt to be an electrical generator.

"Let me try," Mama said, and gazed off into space. Her eyes lost focus; her face seemed to empty, then to fill with glory as she recited. It was archaic Spanish, so Matt couldn't follow every word—but he recognized "rose" and "red," and something about water . . .

Air glimmered on the taboret between Mama's chair and Matt's. It thickened to mist, coalesced into solidity—and a rose lay there, fresh and velvety, its petals still beaded with morning dew.

Papa and Matt goggled.

Mama gasped. "Oh, my! Did *I* do *that?*"

"You did indeed, *querida,*" Papa said, his face solemn. He turned to Matt. "So. This is no mere fable you have told us."

"Did you really doubt me?"

"My heart wanted to believe you." Papa was skilled at sidestepping questions, too.

Matt frowned. "You don't seem surprised that Mama has the talent."

"Why should I be? I have known and felt her magic for every day of my life these thirty years." Papa turned and caught his wife's hand, smiling into her eyes. "I have lived under her enchantment since I met her, and it has been my support and my mainstay all my days."

Mama blushed and lowered her gaze.

Still holding her hand, Papa turned back to Matt. "Do you think that I, too, can work this magic?"

"I should think so," said Matt slowly. "It would make sense, after all—if I have the talent for magic, there's a good chance I inherited it from both of you." He didn't mention that double inheritance should have made him more powerful than either of them. "Besides, if you can feel the forces gathering, you must have the gift. Try a poem, Papa—but keep it small, okay?"

Papa frowned, thinking, then recited,

> "Soup of the evening, thick and green,
> Waiting in a deep tureen!
> Who for such dainties would not stoop?
> Soup of the evening, beautiful soup!"

The air shimmered, clouded, cleared, and a closed and steaming tureen stood on the taboret next to the rose.

All three of them stared.

Then Mama said, "It will mar the tabletop. Mateo, some sort of mat, quickly! Ramón, lift!"

Papa took the handles and lifted. Matt looked about the room, then took a glove from a chest against the wall and brought it back. Mama slipped it under the tureen and said, as Papa set it down, "So. You said you had no appetite for supper tonight, Ramón."

"I did not." Papa grinned. "But our new quarters have improved my appetite most amazingly." He lifted the lid, took out the ladle, sniffed cautiously, tasted even more cautiously, and nodded. "It's mock-turtle soup, all right! Apparently this magic even knows where the verse came from."

"You probably had it in the back of your mind when you recited," Matt said. "Mama, I thought you told me you still did the cooking."

"Well, Tuesdays and Thursdays this year, I had late classes." Mama sighed. "I do not suppose I will finish my doctorate, now."

"You won't need it here," Matt assured her. "I'd better arrange some lessons in wizardry for you, though."

"Oh, you will teach your parents now, eh?" Mama said it with a smile, but there was an edge to her voice.

Matt shook his head. "I do it, but I don't make sense out of it very well. I mean, sure, I figured out the basic rules, but anything beyond that, I leave to Saul and Friar Ignatius."

"Friar Ignatius?" Papa asked.

"He's a scholar of magic," Matt explained. "Saul met him while trying to find me, and incidentally overthrowing the sorcerer who ruled Allustria. The good friar doesn't do magic himself much—that was our first big hint that spell-casting requires talent. I'll ask him to come give you a crash course."

From outside the window came a crack like a cannon shot, and the whole room shuddered. Mama made a frantic grab and barely saved the soup tureen from shattering on the floor. As it was, green liquid leaked around its edges. "What was that?" she gasped.

"It must have been the beginning of our crash course," said Papa, smiling. "Would you like to explain that, son?"

CHAPTER 9

They climbed the winding stair inside the West Tower with the stones of the castle shuddering around them.

"Is this safe?" Papa asked with an anxious glance at Mama, between the two men.

"Yes, if the enemy hasn't come up with something new," Matt replied. "In fact, if we don't hurry, Saul may have sent them packing before we get there."

"What enemy is this?" Mama asked.

"Genies," Matt answered.

Mama and Papa exchanged a glance of surprise and picked up the pace. Matt felt a surge of affection—here was danger, and they were rushing toward it, afraid they might miss it.

"How do you know they are djinn?" Mama asked.

"I recognized them from your bedtime stories," Matt called back.

Mama and Papa exchanged another glance of a very different sort of surprise.

They came out onto the battlements, and the roaring smote their ears, the thundering laughter of four djinn punctuated by the blasting of huge boulders striking the castle wall. Mama and Papa froze, staring at the gigantic spirits who hurled huge stones as a baseball pitcher might throw a ball, laughing with delight as they did.

"They *are* djinn!" Mama exclaimed.

Papa just stared, then drew a long, ragged breath. "I didn't doubt you, Matthew—but I didn't quite believe all this, soup or no soup."

"Believe me now?"

"Yes. Now, I think even my stomach believes you."

"Dame Mantrell!" Alisande hurried over to her, all concern. "You should not be here—especially without armor! You might be injured."

But Mama was more concerned with the djinn. She pointed at them and cried, "They are Moorish!"

"Huh?" Matt stared at the huge humanoids, fascinated by her confirming his own guess. "How can you tell?"

"The patterns on the cloth of their turbans and trousers! Those are Moorish, not Arabian!"

Well. Matt wouldn't have known the difference—but he wasn't about to argue with an expert.

Mama held up a hand like a traffic cop and intoned foreign words in a stern tone.

Alisande stared, then seized Matt's arm. "What does she say?"

"It's Spanish," Matt said. Wonder flashed through his mind—was this really Spanish, or only an old dialect of Ibile? Which universe claimed her discourse? "I can't follow the words, though."

"It is an old form of the language," Papa told them, "an old song, a very beautiful one, in which an infanta, a princess, calls soldiers to her banner to fight for her."

The song certainly was calling soldiers. Every guardsman on the battlements was turning to stare at Mama—and Matt was amazed to realize how thoroughly she was really worth staring at. The old words made her seem to stand straighter, to grow larger, becoming a truly commanding presence, drawing all the men. Even Saul turned to stare, and took a few involuntary steps toward her. Her own son couldn't take his gaze from her—the flashing in her eyes, the glow in her face, compelled his total attention, binding him under her spell. She fairly glowed with beauty.

Human males weren't the only ones she held spellbound. The djinn dropped their boulders, staring at her. Their eyes glazed. They began to drift toward her, slowly at first, then faster and faster, as though a breeze pushed them, freshening to become a gale.

Then, suddenly, they all jerked, as though someone had given each of them a good, hard shake. They stared at Mama in disbelief. Then they began to drift toward her again—but their eyes narrowed with menace.

Mama changed meters; her chanting beat with a new rhythm, a different cadence, and her tone became severe, scolding.

Papa stared.

"It's too old a form of Spanish for me," Matt said, low-voiced. "What's she saying?"

"She is rebuking them for their temerity," said Papa.

Mama snapped her hands up, shouting a command.

"She's telling them to go away in shame," Papa translated.

The djinn's eyes turned glassy again. They turned about and drifted away, thinning as they went, becoming translucent, then fading from sight.

Everyone on the battlements was silent, staring in disbelief.

Then Saul uttered a long, shaky sigh. "Man," he said to Matt, "I can't understand how you ever resolved your Oedipal feelings."

Matt and Papa both stared at him; Alisande frowned, puzzled. Mama blushed.

Then Papa grinned. "No man living could ever fail to see the beauty of my Jimena—except her son."

Mama gave Papa a sly smile. "Yes, he was attracted to younger women—from the time he turned twelve."

"Twelve?" Saul asked in surprise, and started to say something more, but Matt said firmly, "We all have to wake up sometime, and realize that girls aren't nasty backbiting barnacles on the ship of life."

Alisande frowned. "Did you ever truly think so?"

"When he was eight?" Mama asked. "When he was eleven? Oh, yes. You shall see, young mother. You have a son yourself."

"Thank you for the warning," Alisande said, but her voice still sounded with doubt, and her gaze was uncertain. She turned to Mama, and became all business again. "You amaze me, Dame Mantrell! I had not known you were a woman of power."

"Neither had I," Mama confessed.

Papa shook his head. "How could you ever have failed to know it?"

Mama glanced at him with exasperation. "I did not speak of my beauty alone, Ramón."

"Neither did I."

"You mean she's always been able to command spirits?" Saul asked, his voice shaky.

Papa's gaze turned remote. "Now that I think of it, the neighbors did tell us we had bought a haunted house, but no ghosts ever disturbed us there."

"Nonsense, Ramón!" Mama said briskly. "It was all superstition!"

Papa's gaze focused on her. "Did I not say the peace and harmony of that house were your doing? It seems I spoke more truly than I knew."

Matt decided that his talent probably wasn't any stronger than his parents', after all—just differently directed.

"But now you are in peril!" Alisande stepped up to take both of Mama's hands between her own. "Whatever sorcerer commands these djinn knows now that there is one who can command them as surely as he himself. I fear that you will yourself be the object of their attacks now!"

"Or other kinds of magical attacks directed directly at you," Saul said, scowling. "She's right, Ms. Mantrell."

"Mrs., please," Mama said absently. "I am old-fashioned."

"Why debate?" Alisande drew her sword. "Kneel."

Mama stepped back in surprise, and Papa's eyes widened in shock even as he moved to step between them—but Matt touched his arm and said softly, "Don't worry. It's an honor."

Papa hesitated, but frowned at Alisande, unsure. Mama, however, squared her shoulders as she knelt.

"I create you a dame of the land of Merovence," Alisande said, touching each shoulder in turn with the blade. "All will now address you as 'Dame.' " She stepped back, sheathing her sword.

"It confers some extra abilities," Matt told his mother as he helped her up. "Extra courage, not that you need it—but a certain kind of tactical insight, and extra power in fighting." He grinned. "It also gets you a lot more respect."

Alisande turned to Papa. "I doubt not you also shall be knighted, Master Mantrell—but we must wait for your deeds, then give you both all proper ceremony." Finally she turned to her husband again. "How shall we protect them, then?"

"We're already doing everything we can," Matt told her. "Between Saul's spells and mine, this castle is so thoroughly wrapped in protective enchantments that if you could see them, it would look like a cocoon."

"That's why all the genies can do is stand back and throw stones," Saul explained, "plus the occasional shake."

Alisande nodded. "But Dame Mantrell can learn how to use her magic to even greater power. See it done immediately."

Matt nodded. "I'll send for Friar Ignatius right away."

"That is well. Let it be done." Alisande turned and inclined her head to her knights and wizards. They all gave a half bow in return; then she turned and strode into the tower.

Papa released a long, pent-up breath. "So. You have no problem in taking orders from your wife, then?"

Mama looked up at him sharply.

"From my sovereign, no," Matt corrected. "As husband and wife, we pretty much manage to talk things out between us."

"Is the separation of the two roles so clear, then?" Mama demanded.

Matt grinned. "No, not at all—but when we're alone, we can be pretty sure we're just husband and wife. Come on, Mama, Papa—advanced degrees notwithstanding, it's time for you two to go back to school."

I am Ramón Rodrigo Mantrell. My wife, being Cuban-born, prefers to keep the old form—she was Jimena Maria García y Alvarez when I met her—but I was born in Manhattan and grew up in the Bronx, so I think far more like an American than a Spaniard, and write my name as a man of New York.

I was born in America, but my father, Joachim, was born in Spain, not far from Cadiz. He was twenty when Franco began to build his power. Joachim argued with his mother and father over politics and left home. He saw what was coming and left Spain too, emigrating to France. There he made a life for himself working for a baker in Provence, and fell in love with a French woman. They married, but in less than a year the news from Spain began to trouble him badly, endangering his marriage. At last, when the Civil War was in full swing, his wife sadly agreed that he must return to Spain and fight for his principles. Thus he came to fight against Franco at last, as a guerrilla.

The war went badly, of course, because Franco had endless supplies of weapons and tactics from Hitler. Papa made friends among the Americans in the Abraham Lincoln Brigade. When the war ended, he escaped back into France, but saw that Hitler would conquer that land, too, and realized that America would be safer than his wife's homeland, especially for a Spanish partisan and his wife. She agreed, and they came to America.

Even there, Joachim chafed as Hitler conquered nation after nation. When the Japanese attacked Pearl Harbor, his wife, no doubt strained to the breaking point, packed him off to the army. He could not fight Franco, who, with his own war won, was wise enough to stay neutral—but he could help to defeat Mussolini and, at last, Hitler himself. He came back to his new home limping, his body wounded, but his soul at peace at last. A year later, I was born.

I grew up in the Bronx, speaking both French and Spanish at home, and English in the neighborhood and at school. My mother sang to me in French, then later taught me the old songs, of Roland and the knights of Charlemagne; my father taught me *The Song of El Cid* and told me tales of Don Quixote. They were both determined to give me a better life than they had had, and sent me to college. Then, since I did well, they encouraged me to go on to graduate school—and what should I study, with their songs ringing in my head, but comparative literature?

In that I found joy, but at Rutgers College I found more, for I met Jimena and, by some miracle, she loved me as I loved her. She was a Cuban exile whose family had barely escaped as Castro took over, and they lost everything, all their money and property. She learned English after they came to New Jersey and still speaks with a heavy accent, but thank Heaven, it is from Havana, not New Brunswick. She can make herself understood in English—but she is an absolute spellbinder when she recites poetry in Spanish. I can attest to that, because listening to her chanting of poems and seeing the excitement they raised in her eyes, I fell under her spell for all my life.

We made plans to marry once I received my doctorate, so I attacked my dissertation with zeal. I spent my evenings in the library researching criticism and my days in my office and classrooms, for once I passed my comprehensive examinations, I found a position and began to teach, first as an instructor, then moving to another college as an assistant professor.

I finished my dissertation, was awarded my doctorate, and applied for tenure. Six months later, I married Jimena, knowing I had secured a comfortable future for both of us.

My Jimena bore our first—and, sadly, our only—child, so we bought a house where we could afford to: in a neighborhood where everyone else worked in factories, and looked at me oddly because I wore a suit to work and carried a briefcase. I did not mind, knowing that it would only be a few years until we could move to a neighborhood in which there would be people who wished to discuss Voltaire and Proust as often as diapers and plumbing. Still, I did my best to be a good neighbor, winning most of those good working people as friends.

But fate played a cruel joke on us all, for the neighborhood went downhill slowly but steadily, and the recession and inflation of the seventies ate away my earning power. Since I was more skilled at teaching than at currying favor, and cared more for the students than for research, I was never given tenure, and therefore never promoted, but remained an assistant professor for twenty-one years.

No, let us not make excuses. I failed as an academic. However, I succeeded as a husband and father, which was far more important to me.

Not having tenure, though, I had to move to a new college every seven years—fortunately, there were several within commuting range. It was well that I had made friends of our neighbors, for we stayed in that neighborhood for a quarter of a century.

In my last college, my department elected a Marxist as chairman. He tried to make me teach the plays of Molière as documents of class struggle, and Malory's *Le Morte d'Arthur* as an indictment of the bourgeoisie, which scarcely existed in Malory's time. I refused, of course, and was denied tenure again—of course. Disgusted, I looked for another means of making a living. A man came to my office and told me he was from the Taxpayers' Organization for Reduction in the Cost of Education; one of their goals was to persuade faculty members to leave teaching, now that the Baby Boom had passed the colleges, and go into more profitable kinds of self-employment. He offered me a modest grant to buy my own business, explained how to arrange a small-business loan, and offered to enroll me in a correspondence course in bookkeeping. I was so exasperated with being exploited as a professor that I accepted his help and went looking for a profitable business. We did not need so much money anymore, since Matthew had graduated from college and was working his way through graduate school as a teaching assistant. My neighbor told me he was ready to sell his store and retire, so I discussed it with Jimena. It was not as though I was planning to quit a job—with no tenure, I would be out of a job in May, and being fifty and only an assistant professor, there would be little chance of employment in a time when colleges were trying to reduce faculty. In fact, we realized we had little choice, though Jimena might still be able to find a position. I took out a small-business loan and bought.

I worked hard, and at first we prospered, earning a little

more than I had as a professor. Then, though, a pusher hooked the neighborhood boys on a new drug, and before long, they would do whatever he told them. They had always been rowdy, but now they became a plague. I think it was actual malice, that they meant to close my store. With their brains riddled with that drug, I am surprised they could form the intention and hold to it. It was almost as though someone else did their thinking for them, told them what to do and how. Perhaps one of them was not so sodden as he seemed.

However that may be, they scared away the customers, and even tried to frighten me from delivering orders to my senior citizens. They failed in that, of course, partly because I know how to fight well enough myself, and they knew it—but more because they all remembered me from their boyhoods, and were still somewhat in awe. I never had to lay a hand on any of them, of course, not even now when they acted against me, though I did have to speak sharply to them once or twice.

Still, I feared I might have to declare bankruptcy, for no one wished to buy the store. We sold our house to have money to live until one of us could find a new job. I don't think the bank had any idea what to do with the store, and I suspect it will stay closed. A nice young couple bought the house—and though they seem good-humored and easygoing, there is something of the trained fighter about both of them. I hope many others like them will buy into the neighborhood and make the boys behave.

So I planned to close the door and walk away from the house, telling myself I would begin a new life even though I was past fifty. I never dreamed it would be so splendid a life as our son Matthew gave us. After all, what more could a professor of comparative literature ask, than to live in a medieval epic?

Even Papa couldn't tell if the room at the top of the south tower was a classroom or a laboratory—at a guess the magical equivalent of a physics teaching lab. One wall was solid shelves, crowded with bottles and arcane hardware and glassware. Before it stood a chest of drawers four feet high and eight feet long, with a top made of slate—a laboratory bench if ever there was one. Another wall was covered with a thinner slab of slate, already having geometric designs chalked on it. Before it stood a table strewn with parchment around a large open book, obviously being used as a desk. The far wall held a chart of the heavens, with rather fanciful zodiacal symbols.

Most of the room's floor was clear space, but with sand sunken four inches into it, twelve feet square. Beyond that, the windows were casements filled with glass, instead of the usual arrowslits, but with heavy curtains to either side of each—just the kind you would need to darken the room completely, keep drafts out, but also keep light in at night. Several lampstands stood about, with two more lamps on the worktable and one on the desk.

It was a very businesslike room, but the business to which it was devoted was magic.

Friar Ignatius, lean, tonsured, and robed, watched as Papa recited a poem, and a phoenix appeared, burst into flame, then faded from sight. The friar nodded. "An excellent demonstration of illusion for one who has had no training for his Gift, Señor Mantrell—but perhaps your education in poetry has made you something of a wizard already."

"Then that would be true of Jimena, too," Papa said.

"It would indeed, as I can see from the formidable concentration with which she recites. In fact, she brings the verse to life so intensely that I hesitate to call it reciting." Friar Ignatius faced the two of them. "You both have great powers, but I see already a difference in your talents."

"Difference?" Mama looked from Papa to the friar, wide-eyed. "What difference? We are both magicians, are we not?"

"Yes, but there are differences between magic-workers, in emphasis and sometimes even in powers. One is more skilled in healing, another more in the making of wondrous objects, a third in bringing living creatures to him out of thin air.

Even in wizards whose power is war, one may be better suited to defense, and another to offense."

"You mean not all wizards can do all magics?" Papa asked.

"That is true, but is not what I meant. Most magicians can do most magics; it is a question of each one's greatest strength, of what each does best."

"Then what is my talent?" Mama asked.

"Your talent is to bind spells that others cast, bind them so fast that they cannot hurt you or any whom you protect—and to bind others by spells of your own," Friar Ignatius answered.

Papa frowned. "Do you say that she can compel others to obey her?"

"No." Ignatius turned to him. "It is more subtle than that. Her spell binds folk to wish to do those things that make her happy."

"Well, that is true, certainly." Papa slid an arm around Mama's shoulders and smiled down into her eyes. "I have known it since I met her—but do you say it is *in fact* magic, not merely metaphorically?"

"Fact! Metaphor!" Friar Ignatius threw up his hands in exasperation. "What use are such words when you speak of magic? She has the power—what else do you need to know?"

"Nothing," Papa admitted, gazing deeply into Mama's eyes.

She smiled up at him and pressed more closely against him. "But there is more to it than metaphor here, Ramón. What I did in New Jersey, I did without knowing. Here, I can do what I intend—and by nothing more than reciting verse!"

Friar Ignatius nodded. "And the verse puts your wishes into harmony with the forces of this world, so that they can manifest as action. Remember, though, that you must always end your verse with a command for the action you desire."

Mama still smiled up at Papa. "Can I compel even you, then?"

"Me most of all," Papa answered. "You always have."

"Ah, but that was by asking, or telling you what I desired. I did not command."

"Nor could you here in Merovence either, Dame Mantrell," said Friar Ignatius, "for your husband is a wizard as powerful as yourself, though not in the same fashion."

Papa looked up, frowning at the interruption of their little idyll. "What is the manner of my power, then?"

"Would it surprise you to know that your aptitude was for the magics of war?"

Papa gazed at the friar, then abruptly smiled. "No, not really."

"Attempt it," said Friar Ignatius. "Recite a verse that would light a fireball for you to hurl." He took Papa's arm, stretched it out, and cupped the palm. "Make it appear right there, but floating above the skin, and tell it to burn everything but you. Remember, when you 'throw' it, you only direct it— propel it by thought expressed as spoken words, not by the force of your arm."

Papa frowned for a moment, then chanted,

"Let a ball grow all compact of fire,
Not gross to sink, but light to aspire
To strike at my foe. Let it not burn my skin,
But my foe scald and singe!"

A ball of fire exploded into life above his palm. Even though it was a very small sphere, perhaps the size of a bon-bon, Mama and Papa both flinched.

Friar Ignatius did a little, too. "Does it hurt?"

"No, not at all," Papa said. "I must have done correctly when I specified that it not burn me."

"Well done, Master Mantrell! Indeed, you scarcely seem a novice at all!" Then the friar frowned. "But why have you made it so small—and how?"

"Well, this is just an experiment," Papa said. "I don't want to risk any more damage than I must. But do you not know 'how' yourself?"

"No." The friar smiled sadly. "I have the interest, but not

the talent. You did not state its size in words. How did you do it?"

Papa shrugged. "This is as I pictured it in my mind when I chanted the verse."

"Ah! So your intention manifests, even though it is not stated." Friar Ignatius nodded. "Yes, you do have the talent indeed."

"Thank you, Father. Now that I have the fireball, what do I do with it?"

"Hurl it at that spot of damp on the wall." The friar pointed toward a block next to the window. "It needs drying anyway. But remember, even though you make the motions of throwing, you must tell it where to go."

"Don't tempt me," Papa muttered, then wound up like a Yankees pitcher, chanting,

> "Damp upon the granite wall,
> I target you who darken granite.
> I hold here a flaming ball
> In my hand, O Spot of Damp.
> When I hurl it overhand,
> It shall strike and on you fall.
> Then shall you dry, mildew and all,
> And all shall see what service flame is."

"Will Tennyson forgive you?" Mama murmured.

Papa hurled the fireball anyway—overhand. It arced away, homed unerringly on the damp spot, and struck the wall, exploding in a shower of sparks. Mama and Papa ducked. The sparks landed on the wooden workbench, a heap of parchment on the desk, a leather-bound grimoire—and Friar Ignatius' robe.

The friar yelped as flame blossomed on his arms and chest. Mama caught up a pitcher of wine and poured it on each of his burns while Papa started swatting out little blazes all over the laboratory. Somehow, they got them under control and put them all out.

"Are you all right, Father?" Mama asked anxiously.

"This one here!" Friar Ignatius said through tight lips, pointing at a burn hole over his elbow.

Mama frowned down at the raw, ugly flesh beneath and chanted in a soothing tone. Before their eyes, the burn faded into pink and healthy flesh.

Friar Ignatius stared, then drew a deep breath. "Yes. It seems that you have more talents than one, Dame Mantrell."

Mama shrugged off the compliment. "Every mother learns something of healing, Father."

"Then you must teach me," Papa said, frowning, "for I shall have to heal men wounded in battle."

Mama smiled up at him. "You have learned a little already, Ramón, when Mateo was ill."

"Well, yes," Papa admitted, "but I do not think we will find aspirin or thermometers here."

"Why not?" Friar Ignatius asked.

They both stared at him. Then Mama said, "You have such things?"

"No, but why should that stop you?"

Mama smiled slowly, then nodded to Papa. "Even as he says. You should be able to conjure up penicillin, if you need it."

"True," Papa said doubtfully, "but we cannot make it out of nothing, can we? From where will we steal it?"

"Your magic can duplicate anything you have seen and know," Friar Ignatius explained. "How it takes materials and assembles them, I have no idea—but I have seen wizards make all manner of things appear from thin air."

"Thin air, eh?" Papa gazed off into space. "Yes, the molecules of air could be combined to form heavier compounds."

"But why might your spells not gather molecules from earth and trees too?" Mama asked. "We do not need to see them rise for them to be there."

Friar Ignatius nodded. "Even as you gathered fire, Señor Mantrell. Did you think where it must come from?"

"No, I did not," Papa admitted. "It seems the magical forces themselves seek out the raw materials."

"Your mind supplies the pattern," Friar Ignatius explained. "The magic constructs the artifact as that pattern directs. You could supply arms and armor for a legion, though I suspect it would be exhausting."

"So this is the magic of war," Papa said slowly.

"Some of it," Friar Ignatius allowed, "though you will find there are many more spells to learn and, I am sure, even more that you shall invent. But when last comes to last, Señor Mantrell, you will find that the greatest war magic of all is the ability to inspire men to fight, and make them want to follow you and obey your commands."

"Perhaps that is why the boys obeyed you," Mama said.

CHAPTER 10

Friar Ignatius pounced on it. "What boys?"

So they told him about Liam and his buddies. The friar heard them out, frowning, then nodded. "It would seem, then, that some quality in you overawed them."

Papa shrugged it off. "It is as I have said—to them, I will always be as overpowering as I was when they were little boys."

"And as kind?"

"He was," Mama said instantly. "When their own papas ignored them, Ramón talked with them and counseled them and listened to their tales of woe."

"Yes, and for thanks, they bedeviled my son," Ramón said darkly. "I cannot say we were any longer friends when they strove to shut down my store."

"Grown boys seek to defy the men they knew in childhood," Friar Ignatius told him. "There must have been some quality in you that wakened their old feelings of awe and reverence."

Papa frowned. "Do you say that 'quality' was magical?"

"There is an old word for it in our world," Mama told him. "It is 'charisma.'"

"And in this universe, that 'charisma' manifests itself as magic. Yes." Friar Ignatius nodded. "But that quality only gathers magical force; you must direct it with your verses."

"If that were so," Papa argued, "why would they have continued to bully my customers and tried to drive them away?"

"Because that charisma is *not* magic, in your universe," Friar Ignatius told him. "It only works within the minds and hearts of people, not within the very forces that constitute the matter of your world. They obeyed you only so long as you were there in person; away from you, the magic faded, for in your universe, it *was* metaphorical, and a matter of metaphor only."

"I do not believe that Good and Evil are only metaphors in *any* universe," Papa said flatly.

"Nor are they." Friar Ignatius' eyes gleamed. "You do not mean to tell me that people in your world think they are!"

"Some do, and highly intelligent, educated people among them," Papa told him. "Myself, I believe that actions may be evil, but that no people are really, truly evil by nature—only confused or sick in their souls."

"But they can turn to doing only evil works," Friar Ignatius reminded him, then smiled with gentle sadness. "Are you so heartsick, then, that your own goodness could not overcome the evil that sought to draw these boys into its grip?"

"I do not think of myself as a very good man," Papa muttered, and Mama clasped his arm, as though trying to lend him strength.

"But you do think there is goodness in the rules by which you try to live," the friar pointed out. "Are you disillusioned to discover that such goodness could not triumph in your own neighborhood?"

"I suppose I am," Papa admitted.

"You should not be," Ignatius said. "You were only one man, Señor Mantrell. How many were arrayed against you, to twist the souls of those boys?"

Papa stiffened, staring off into space, astonished. "Why . . . the drug dealers . . . the older boys who had taught them that the Law only oppressed them, and did not need to be obeyed unless it could punish them . . . the businessmen who saw them only as a source of profit, and were willing to tell them anything, sell them anything, so long as it would coax money from them . . . the singers to whom they listened, who urged them to distrust the police and be brutal toward others, especially women . . . "

"And the list goes on." Friar Ignatius nodded. "I doubt that you could tell me all who unknowingly conspired to twist the souls of the young. I doubt that you *know* of them all." He shook his head. "How can you blame yourself for losing against such odds? You should honor yourself as a hero for fighting alone against them, still striving to lead the boys to Right!"

"He grew up listening to tales of Don Quixote," Mama said, beaming up at Papa. "As a man, he studied those tales in depth."

"I do not know this don of whom you speak, but if he strove for goodness when no one else did, and against odds so great as those that faced your husband, he must have been a hero indeed."

"He was to our century, though the man who wrote of him meant to ridicule his romanticism." Papa frowned. "But surely it was only self-interest that made me rebuke the boys! Surely it was only the desire to save my store! You cannot mean it was goodness!"

"Was it self-interest that made you kind to them when their own fathers were not?"

"Of a sort, yes," Papa said, frowning. "I enjoyed their company, enjoyed seeing them relax into innocent boyhood games when I took them sledding with my Matthew."

Friar Ignatius turned to Mama in exasperation. "Is he always so unwilling to admit his own goodness?"

"Yes," Mama said, smiling. "He tries too hard to exercise humility. But in his heart, he knows it is goodness that moves him."

Papa spoke quickly, to avoid having to admit she was right. He allowed his twentieth-century skepticism to show, telling Friar Ignatius, "But in this universe, surely the power of magic doesn't really come from Good or Evil! Isn't it only that our goals clash, that what we believe to be right is opposed to what they believe to be right?"

"He is reluctant to admit his own virtues," the friar told Mama. "Remember, Señor Mantrell, that there comes a point at which too much humility ceases to be a virtue and becomes false humility, a form of bragging."

"Do you say that the good in this universe are truly of Good, and the evil truly of Evil?"

" 'By their works you shall know them,' " Friar Ignatius quoted. "I could give you many examples, but look at the worst—the first man who brought down holy Reme: Tatali the Nomad, leading a vast barbarian army whose soldiers had been enslaved by evil magic. They exploded out of Central Asia on horseback, galloping around the Caucasus Mountains, looting, raping, and pillaging as they went, leaving heaps of corpses behind them, making torture and raping a sort of sport to be enjoyed as much by watching as by partaking, delighting in the agony of those they conquered and dedicating the pain of all their victims to their evil god, whose description is strangely like Satan's."

Papa shuddered, but remembered the Huns of his own world and protested, "They were deluded. They followed a leader who persuaded them that victory was everything, and that their gods loved brutality."

"Exactly!" Friar Ignatius cried. "You have seen the core of it! Satan seduces a few humans to his worship by lying and pretending to be their defender, then helps them to seduce and compel hundreds of thousands to follow them— but he could not do so if there were no desire for evil in human hearts."

" 'You can't cheat an honest man,' " Papa quoted with a wry smile.

Friar Ignatius' eyes gleamed. "That has the sound of a saying invented by one who made a living by cheating."

"It does indeed," Mama said, with indignation. "One might as well say that a man cannot seduce a woman by lying that he loves her, if she does not want to be loved."

Friar Ignatius frowned. "Isn't that true, Dame Mantrell?"

"As far as it goes," Mama said, "but the man lies that he loves the woman and wants to marry her, and the woman wants to believe that she has found true love. Is this dishonest?"

"In him, yes," Papa said, affronted.

"But in her, no," Mama said. "Surely there is no sin in desiring love!"

"Surely not," Friar Ignatius agreed. "But if she held to her principles and refused to make love till they had married, she would not have been seduced by the man's lies."

"There is truth in that. Believing in goodness and God can give a woman belief in herself."

"I do not doubt it," the friar said.

"So you say that goodness, and holding fast to the principles goodness teaches, can be a source of strength even in our own world."

"That is so, Dame Mantrell—but in this world of Merovence, it is the *only* source of magic that nurtures and builds. All others will, sooner or later, destroy and kill."

Mama's fierceness faded, and she reached out to touch Papa's hand. "Then it is doubly my good fortune that the first man I believed, spoke truly."

It is that charisma of which I told the good friar that drew me to Ramón—though truly, it was his handsomeness that first attracted my notice. I was reluctant to credit that he was so wonderful to behold, because all the other girls told me that the beauty of his face nearly made them swoon. But when I saw him, I believed them—and it was not just his face, for even though he wore his shirts loose, you could see the breadth of his shoulders and the play of his muscles beneath the cloth. I was even more reluctant, though, to admit to the attraction, and it was not until I heard him reciting the poetry of Calderón that I could no longer deny my infatuation. Indeed, I had to confess to myself that I had fallen in love with him.

This was in a coffeehouse, for this was the early sixties, and we both played at being beatniks—at least, I think we were playing. When it came my turn to recite, I read the poetry of Lope de Vega and saw the fire ignite in Ramón; I think he tried to devour me with his eyes then and there. I refused to go out with him at first, for I was afraid to be alone with him, which is to say that I was afraid of my own desires—but I need not have worried, for his machismo was balanced by his gallantry and, I think, by the Catholic upbringing he tried so hard to deny. He never tried to do more than kiss me, though he did that so constantly and so well that both of us nearly fainted with the desires it kindled in us. We waited years until we had money enough to wed. He finished his doctorate while I began mine, and it was a blessing that we were in separate cities, though it is amazing that our letters did not ignite fires in the mailboxes into which we dropped them. But it was worth the wait—it was a most memorable honeymoon.

Now the young folk come back early from their wedding trips; they tell us they were bored. I pity them deeply.

I went back to my graduate classes in cultural anthropology as soon as Mateo began high school. I finished my coursework as he entered college, and passed my preliminary examinations in the spring of his freshman year. Then I took a teaching post in the nearest junior college and began the research for my dissertation on the mythic roots of Spanish literature. The research is finished now, but the writing is only begun. I was not awarded tenure—there are not so many students pounding on the doors of the colleges as there were when Ramón and I began our studies—so I was out of work and seeking another position when we lost our house.

Since Papa taught literature and I taught Spanish, we really could not complain too loudly when our son wanted to major in comparative literature. We are only disappointed that he did not become a teacher. We *were* looking forward to his gaining a Ph.D. of his own, and teaching college. But I console myself with the thought that he is, at least, engaged in research, although magic is more my field than his, at least in terms of academic study. We are delighted that he has married a nice girl, even if she is an Anglo. Well, I know, of course, that Merovence should be more French than English, but she seems more like a Briton than anything else. Friar Ignatius has told me that there is no English Channel in this universe, and never was—that Hardishane, their great emperor who is equivalent to our Charlemagne, conquered

England too, and made them very much a part of his empire. The two cultures have clearly melded, and at least the English and French do not hate one another here.

I have always been a devout Catholic, so I have been delighted to make the acquaintance of Friar Ignatius. Perhaps he is right, perhaps it was the morality of a strong religion that kept me from letting young men exploit me—but I would rather think that it was simply believing that I would know true love when I felt it, and would not be deceived by my own sexuality, and the lies of handsome and charming young men. Not that my Ramón is not handsome and charming— he is both. However, he was the only one who asked nothing but a kiss of me, and the only one with whom I fell in love because of poetry—but then, Ramón too took his religion rather seriously.

Still, the friar is right in many things, and I will not deny that a young woman must have some firm beliefs to which she can cling, to give her the strength to say no. As to his discourse about powers stemming from good and from evil, he speaks of something that every mother knows, once they begin to fear for these bold little ones who are given to them to protect. The difficulty is to tell the good people from the evil ones. The good may sometimes appear rather forbidding at first, for they pay little attention to appearances, and the evil are very skilled at disguise.

I told this to the friar, and he explained it.

Friar Ignatius nodded. "That is true, Dame Mantrell. In this world of enchantment, though, you can look into a man's heart with your magic." He went to the window and pointed down into the courtyard. "That guard who stands at the left side of the door to this very castle, for example—craft me a spell that will let you see him as he truly is."

Mama frowned. "I am not sure that I understand you, but let me see what I can achieve. Do I dare attempt a verse of my own making?"

"You do," Friar Ignatius assured her, "as long as you are

careful to say that you wish to see his true nature, not to have him change his appearance to all the world."

"Ah!" Mama nodded. "Subjective, not objective. This I can do."

"You see? You have words that I do not, and ideas that I have never heard to match them." Friar Ignatius bowed her toward the window. "You, too, are trained in poetry, good dame. Let us see what verse you can render."

"That? It is simple; I have only to remember one English sentence and craft another to match it." Mama frowned down at the sentry.

Both men suddenly felt the tension in the room, the ferocious concentration she bent to the task.

Then Mama intoned,

> "Ah, would Good Power the grand gift give me,
> To see you as you truly be.
> It would from many an error free me,
> To see you as you are."

"Must she not say to whom she directs that?" Papa asked in an undertone.

"Not as intensely as she is concentrating on him," Friar Ignatius told him. "You or I would, yes, but not she."

Mama gasped, and there was no delight in the sound. In fact, there was horror.

Friar Ignatius was beside her in an instant. "What do you see?"

"A snake!" Mama said. "His head has turned into a snake's head, and a forked tongue flickers between his lips!"

Friar Ignatius frowned down at the sentry. "You have seen his true nature, Dame Mantrell. In his heart, he is a traitor—perhaps a spy."

The sentry suddenly looked up, darting quick glances around the courtyard.

"He senses that someone is studying him," the friar said. "Withdraw!"

But before they could, thunder rocked the castle, overwhelming their ears so that they staggered. Then their hearing adjusted, and the booming became laughter, gargantuan laughter. Staring out the window, they saw three vast djinn looming above the castle, each swinging a huge boulder. They loosed, and the missiles shot toward the wall.

Mama recovered from her surprise and threw up her hands, chanting, but she was too late. One of the boulders smashed into the tower, and the room shook. The three people seized one another and managed to stay on their feet by bracing against each other. The shaking passed, and Friar Ignatius snapped, "That was no coincidence! Down to the battlements, quickly!"

Another crash sounded near them as they ran down the stairs, and the building shook, toppling both Mantrells—but below them, Friar Ignatius braced arms and legs against the sides of the stairwell. They struck against his back, jolting him, but he managed to hold firm. They scrambled to their feet, saying, "Thank you, Father."

"My pleasure." Friar Ignatius was already in motion again, running down to the battlements. "Let us go!"

They came out of the tower door, and the genie who had been targeting them saw and changed the direction of his swing at the last moment, hooking the stone to hurl at them.

But Mama was ready now. She threw up her hands, shouting a verse in Spanish, and the boulder suddenly dropped to bury itself in the hillside below the castle.

The genie bellowed in anger, swinging his hand in a circle, and as he did, another boulder materialized in his grasp.

Farther along the battlements, Saul and Matt, hands joined with two junior sorcerers, finally finished shouting a choral verse. The boulder, and the latest missiles from the other two djinn, suddenly slowed, stopped, then fell.

The djinn roared in rage and dove at the castle. They slowed suddenly and drastically, then rebounded. They screamed imprecations in Arabic, pounding at the unseen barrier with their fists. One of them soared high, then dove down. He bounced back up as if he had hit a trampoline.

Mama stared, then ran to her son. "What is it?"

"Saul's." Matt pointed.

"It's a Wall of Octroi," Saul explained, "like the one the French Revolution accused Lavoisier of trying to erect around Paris. I got the idea from King Boncorro in Italy. Best border fence you ever saw—if you wanted to keep out things that flew."

"Only ones that flew?" Papa frowned.

"It's like the barrier dividing Maxwell's demon-box," Matt explained.

"I remember that the hypothetical demon had to decide whether or not to let individual molecules through."

Matt nodded. "Maxwell was trying to get around the Laws of Thermodynamics. He imagined a box of lukewarm air with a wall down the middle, and a little door only wide enough to admit one molecule. His doorkeeper was a hypothetical miniature demon, who would only open the door if a slow-moving molecule came by. After a long enough time, all the fast molecules would be on one side of the wall, and all the slow molecules on the other. Fast-moving molecules are hot, so he would be getting more energy out of the box than he put into it."

"If he didn't count the energy of the demon opening the door," Papa qualified.

Matt nodded. "And didn't mind the fact that as a whole, the box still averaged out to the same temperature. So he failed in trying to outsmart the Laws of Thermodynamics, but he did invent a supernatural being that's stood me in good stead, one time and another."

"Even if a neighboring king borrowed an idea from him?"

"Right. Boncorro's Wall kept out flying monsters, such as dragons, but anyone moving at a walking pace could get through without even noticing there was a barrier."

"I don't think you should have said that out loud," Saul said, pointing at the djinn.

One of them was sinking down to the ground of the talus slope. As he fell, he shrank, and by the time he hit the ground, he was no bigger than an ordinary mortal. He strode up toward the castle—and passed through the Wall of Octroi as though it didn't exist.

With a whoop of glee, the other two djinn swooped down to the ground, dwindling.

As they did, the one who had crossed the Wall stepped up to the drawbridge, raised his arms, and chanted a spell. The drawbridge came crashing down, and the genie waved his hands.

"What is he doing?" Mama wondered.

She saw her answer quickly enough. Their tower stood far enough out from the wall so that they could see the portcullis begin to dissolve.

"How impertinent!" Mama said severely, and held up her hands as she began to chant in Spanish.

"She has remembered her talent," Friar Ignatius told Matt in glee.

"Uh—which one did you have in mind?"

"She is a spellbinder!"

Mama snapped her arms down, speaking her last phrase as a command. The portcullis froze half-faded, then slowly gained more and more substance until it was solid again.

The djinni howled in rage as his spell was canceled.

Mama pointed at him, snapping out another short Spanish verse, and suddenly they could all understand the genie's words. "Cursed be the sorcerer who has frustrated my spells! Cursed also be the sorcerer who has brought me here!"

"Brought him?" Matt stared. "Not sent?"

"Even so," Mama said. "That sorcerer must be nearby, then."

CHAPTER 11

Now it was Papa who held up his arms and spoke in tones of command.

> "None can take without exaction.
> For every gift is payment made.
> None can act without reaction.
> Djinn, your masters may be paid!"

The genie whirled away from the drawbridge and leaped back to the invisible Wall, then stepped through it. As one, all the djinn shot into the air, then dove, roaring, to converge upon a low hill that rose at the edge of the castle's plain.

"Have I passed the final examination?" Papa asked.

"Only the first problem," Friar Ignatius answered.

Three multicolored dots appeared on the side of the slope, darting and dashing every which way.

"Water!" Matt called. "In a bowl!"

A soldier stepped up, pouring water into a broad goblet. Matt waved his hand over it, muttering a verse, and the fluid darkened. The others gathered around in time to see it clear, and saw the hillside in much closer view.

Mama and Papa stared in surprise, then relaxed into fond smiles. Papa whispered, "It is good to see him practicing his profession, isn't it?"

Mama nodded. "And with such assurance, and others so confident in him!"

They beamed proudly in unison.

In the goblet-view, the multicolored dots turned out to be

robed and turbaned men, shouting furiously up toward the djinn. One was rubbing a lamp, another a ring, the third a bottle.

The djinn swooped back up, howling in frustration, then turned to dive again. The sorcerers chanted, still rubbing, and the djinn seemed to be pushed aside. They swooped up high in the air again, darted together, and hovered.

"War conference," Saul interpreted.

But in the goblet, one sorcerer suddenly looked up, then pointed straight at Matt, calling to his colleagues in excitement and anger.

Matt dashed the water to the ground and held the goblet upside down. Even so, the miniature bolt of lightning lanced out of it and struck the stones of the battlements, leaving a smoking charred spot.

"I think they're onto us," Saul said.

"Then we must fight them on their own ground!" Papa dashed for the stairwell.

"Ramón, no!" Mama cried, but too late—her husband was already out of sight.

Matt shot off after him.

"No!" Alisande cried in frustration. "Dame Mantrell, can you do nothing?"

"With such headstrong mules as these? No," Mama said, exasperated. "But I can protect them." She turned back to the battlements and began to gesture, chanting.

A dot of light sprang from the sorcerers' hill, swelling into a fireball—but Mama finished her verse, snapping her hands out as though she were tightening a cord, and the fireball's flames dwindled, then vanished, leaving only a charred and smoking lump that bounced off the Wall of Octroi and plummeted to earth.

All three enemy sorcerers bunched together, just as the three djinn dove toward them, welding themselves into a single mass, a giant spear aimed at the sorcerous target. But the sorcerers chanted so loudly and in such perfect unison that their voices came faintly even to the battlements, and the spear burst apart into the three djinn, who fell to the ground around the trio, kneeling and salaaming to them.

Then one of the sorcerers whirled and pointed toward the castle.

Saul shouted with pain, shaking his hands as though he'd touched something hot. "The Wall!" he cried. "He tore down my Wall of Octroi—don't ask me how!"

The djinn rose into the air, ballooning into giants again, arms windmilling to gather the missiles that began to materialize in their hands.

Mama intoned a Spanish verse, fingers outspread like antennae to direct her spell toward the djinn. The vague gray forms in their palms stayed dim and misty, then began to fade.

"You have canceled their spell!" Alisande cried, amazed. "They cannot make boulders anymore! Well done, Dame Mantrell!"

"At least I have given some return for your hospitality," Mama said, pleased. Then she turned her antenna-fingers toward the sorcerers and began to chant again.

Sharp reports sounded, and cracks began to appear in the stone of the battlements.

Mama intensified her chanting.

The cracks healed and disappeared.

Alisande stared at Mama.

But Mama's voice shifted rhythm and emotion, becoming even more stern, more compelling—and the sorcerers began to run erratically around their hillside. Above, the djinn gave a shout of triumph and dove toward their masters again.

One of the sorcerers stopped. A few seconds later, one genie sheered off with a cry of anger.

"The sorcerers have lost their lamps and rings!" Alisande cried. "One has found his talisman, though, and has regained command over his genie!"

Again Mama chanted, and again the third genie stooped with a cry of vindication.

"Once more you have hidden his lamp!" Alisande cried in delight.

The other two sorcerers stopped their frantic scurrying,

and their djinn sheered off with howls of rage. The third sorcerer dashed madly about the hillside, searching. He stopped, snatching something up; his genie swerved to the side and plowed into the hill. Well, not "plowed," really—he disappeared into the dirt and grass.

Then the father-and-son team reached the foot of the hill with a squadron of knights right behind them. They all charged up the hillside, chanting in unison.

"What poem are they reciting?" Saul asked.

Mama shook her head. "They are too distant to say with any certainty, but I think I hear something about San Juan Hill."

The two remaining djinn stopped dead in the air, a yard short of their masters. The third genie shot out of the hillside straight toward the charging squadron. The other two veered aside and arrowed after him.

The three sorcerers turned and ran.

Suddenly there were two charging squadrons, one a mirror image of the other. Then each of them doubled, and four identical bunches of horsemen charged after the sorcerers.

The djinn roared confusion, darting from one squadron to another, unsure which to strike. Half a dozen horsemen veered off with Papa at their head, swinging wide around the djinn to follow the sorcerers.

The djinn decided on a process of elimination, and started eliminating. They faced the four squadrons, shooting lightning bolts from their fingertips.

Mama shouted an infuriated verse.

Bolts struck two of the squadrons; they disappeared. The lightning froze in midair over the third, then hovered sparking and flashing.

One of the sorcerers fell.

His genie swooped toward him with a shout, but Papa was faster and closer; he leaped down beside the fallen man, caught something up from the ground, then swung an uppercut into the sorcerer's chin. The genie slowed, dropped to earth, and salaamed to Papa.

Mama clapped her hands. "Ramón has found the sorcerer's lamp! He commands the genie now!"

Matt was gesturing at the two other djinn. They started gesturing too, but didn't see the huge sheet, like a blown-away ship's sail, that swung down upon them out of the sky. They didn't even notice it until it struck. Then they whirled, howling, to jerk free of it—and couldn't. Every gyration made it cling more tightly to one portion of their anatomies or another. Finally, in frustration, they disappeared.

"Flypaper," Mama said with satisfaction. "A giant sheet of flypaper. And to think I was worried that my son might forget the practicalities of life."

"It will not work again," Alisande told her. "They will be watching for it now." Then she smiled at a happy thought. "But that will keep one of them from attacking while he watches."

"Or handicap all three, by distracting them continually." Mama nodded. "Well thought, Your Majesty."

Alisande stared at her, startled, then bit her lip.

Mama gave her a warm smile, stepping close enough to speak in an undertone. "When we are alone with family, we shall use family names—but in public, I should address you formally, no?"

"Of course." Alisande smiled with relief.

Mama looked out over the field. "They are riding back now, and I think they have taken a prisoner. Saul, have you tried conjuring up modern gadgets?"

"No, I haven't," Saul said, startled at the thought. "I assumed they wouldn't work, so I cobbled up magical equivalents."

"It would not hurt to be sure." Mama held her hands in front of her eyes, cupping fingers and thumbs and looking through the closer hand to the farther, chanting in Spanish. A spyglass appeared in her hands.

Saul stared.

But Mama shook her head and lowered the telescope. "No, you were right. It does not make things look bigger. We shall have to employ magic after all. How did you craft your enchanted gadgets, Saul?"

Saul shrugged. "I made them look like the real thing from our universe, then told them what to do."

"Told objects what to do?" Mama raised her eyebrows. "Well, well!" She turned and spoke a stern verse to the spyglass, then held it up to her eye again. "Yes, now it works indeed."

Alisande glanced at Saul in surprise. He shrugged and spread his hands.

"The prisoner is one of the sorcerers." Mama collapsed the telescope with a snap and pointed at the war party, intoning a verse in dire tones. Then she lowered her arm with a nod of satisfaction. "That should hold him."

"What did you do?" Alisande asked, wide-eyed.

"Bound his spells, of course. If that sorcerer attempts any magic, he will find it recoils upon him." She held up the spyglass again, then smiled. "I do not know what he tried, but he jerked most unpleasantly in his saddle." A minute later, she said, "He tried again."

"I would like something left of him to question," Alisande said.

"Then let us hope he is not too trying," Mama told her.

Alisande eyed her warily. "Do you not mean, 'Does not try too hard'?"

"Is that how you say it in your language?" Mama asked, all innocence. "Well, I shall remember."

Alisande was sure she would. Somehow she was very glad the older woman was on her side—and likely to stay so, because of family ties. The queen resolved to treat her husband more kindly.

The horses trotted into the courtyard, and Matt dismounted, grinning up at Alisande. Her eyes glowed as she smiled down at him, and Mama, watching, smiled, too, behind her hand.

Papa was more open about it. He raced up the stairs to catch Mama in his arms, whirling her about and laughing. "See the trophy I have brought you, *mi corazón*! But what did you do to him?"

"Only made his own spells rebound upon him," Mama

said, laughing. "Put me down, Ramón! The children are watching!"

Alisande and Matt were watching indeed, then shared a glance as Papa put Mama down.

She tucked her hair back into place, smiling and saying, "If your sorcerer had tried to do anything to favor himself, he might have managed it—but since he only sought to hurt you, he hurt himself instead."

Papa looked up in surprise, then called down to Matt, "Block his magic!"

Matt turned to find the sorcerer had become transparent. He sang,

> "Will ye no' come back again?
> Will ye no' come back again?
> Nay, ye will come back again,
> Whether ye wish or no!"

The sorcerer grew more opaque, then cursed. "What foul magic made you able to keep me here?"

Matt lifted his head slowly. "So. You speak our language."

The sorcerer's eyes became hooded, wary. "And a most barbarous dialect it is, that flows like water and seeps through the understanding!"

"Yes, not a single guttural to recommend it," Matt said with irony. "But if you can converse, Master Sorcerer, you can answer questions."

Fear showed in the sorcerer's eyes, but he blustered, "I shall never answer one single demand!"

"I can't go on calling you 'sorcerer' or 'prisoner,' " Matt said. "What's your name, anyway?" Then, as the shadow of dread passed over the Muslim's face, "Your public name, not your secret one."

"Achmed," the sorcerer said warily.

"See? You answered one of my questions already."

Achmed went red with anger. "I shall answer not one single other, pork-fattened unbeliever!"

"Hey, pork isn't bad if it's cooked hot enough," Matt objected. He called to a soldier, "Guard! Run to the kitchens and bring a slice of that ham we had for supper last night, will you?"

"At once, my lord," the soldier said, grinning. He turned and ran.

Sweat sprang out on the sorcerer's brow. "You wouldn't!"

"Why not?" Matt said. "We must be hospitable, after all—couldn't see a guest go hungry."

"You swine!"

"Careful, there," Matt cautioned. "You might be advocating cannibalism."

"I shall never touch a morsel of that foul meat!"

"No," Matt said softly, "it will touch you."

Papa frowned. "My son, I had never thought to see such ruthlessness in you."

"I'm a knight now, Papa," Matt said simply. "I can do what I have to do."

"But such disrespect for another man's religion!"

"It's kinder than torture, isn't it?"

"You could visit no worse pain on me than forcing me to sin!" the sorcerer accused.

"Don't be so sure." Matt turned back to his father. "What do you suppose would happen if you rubbed your lamp and told the genie he could do whatever he wanted to his former master?"

"You could not be so barbarous!" the sorcerer gasped.

"No, you could not," Papa said, and it was a command.

"See?" Matt asked the sorcerer. "Sinning is much less painful—but it's even kinder to let you decide to commit the sin of your own free will."

"I could never so oppose my own conscience!"

"I suppose your conscience doesn't trouble you when it comes to enslaving djinn and conquering Christians?"

"What is done for the Faith is no sin!"

Matt looked up at his father. "Seems to me that every time I've heard a religious man say that, he's coming up with an excuse for breaking the most fundamental doctrines of his own faith."

Papa nodded grimly. "Murder and looting. I trust you will not try to tell me that the ends justify the means?"

"Sometimes they do." But Matt winked with the eye the sorcerer couldn't see.

The soldier came pounding up with a ham bone that had quite a bit of meat left on it. "I thought you might wish to threaten him with this club, my lord."

"Not a bad thought." Matt took the ham bone and held it out to the sorcerer. "Have a bite."

"Never!" the sorcerer snapped.

" 'Never' is such an absolute term," Matt sighed. He brandished the ham, chanting,

> "The southern end of a northbound sow
> Will delight your tastebuds now.
> You'll crave it, rave it, cry for more,
> Once you've scented our roast boar!"

The sorcerer's mouth began to water. "What corrupted magic do you seek to practice on me?" he wailed.

"Only the transformations any good cook can bring about," Matt answered. "Never knew pig meat could be so good, did you?"

The aroma of the meat drew Achmed into lifting his head closer to the ham bone. "This is most immoral of you! To make me lust after forbidden food!"

"Hey, it's not a sin in my religion." Matt turned to the guard and called, "Light a little fire. Let's warm this roast up a little and let Achmed get a whiff of its full aroma."

The soldier grinned and called to a groom, "Bring some hay and some sticks!"

"You are the cruelest torturer of all!" Achmed groaned. "Others twist a man's limbs—but you would distort my soul!"

"Would you like some wine with that ham?" Matt gestured to the soldier who was lighting the fire. The man nodded to the groom, who ran off toward the kitchens.

"You know it is forbidden! I shall never drink of the fruit of the vine, unbeliever!"

"But there are Muslims who do," Matt pointed out. "I don't know if you've heard of Omar Khayyám, but his verses go like this:

> "And lately, by the Tavern Door agape
> Came shining through the Dusk an Angel Shape
> Bearing a Vessel on his Shoulder; and
> Bid me taste of it; and 'twas—the Grape!
>
> Then said another with a long-drawn Sigh,
> My Clay with long oblivion is gone dry,
> But fill me with the old familiar Juice,
> Methinks I might recover by and by.
>
> And much as Wine has played the Infidel,
> And robb'd me of my Robe of Honour—Well,
> I often wonder what the Vintners buy
> One-half so precious as the stuff they sell!"

"How can this be?" Achmed cried. "I lust for this wine you speak of now—and I have never tasted of it!"

"Probably won't be as good as you're imagining," Matt consoled him. "But then, what ever is?"

The soldier held the ham bone over the little fire, and the first trace of a delightful aroma filtered through the air.

"You shall regret this corruption of one of the Faithful, minion of Shaitan!" Achmed cried. "You may doom my soul, but Nirobus shall give my colleagues enough magical power to set you aflame like the Hell to which you would send me!"

Matt went very still. "Nirobus? I think I've heard that name before. But he's very far away—too far to send you any reinforcements."

"He can and he will! Already he has given us the power to strengthen the arms and the swords of the Moors!"

"Really?" Matt said, bright with sarcasm. "And what piffling little service does he expect you to perform for this power? Conjuring demons? A little contract in blood, maybe?"

"Only what any good Muslim would do if he could—inspire a jihad, a holy war to spread the faith of Islam to enlighten the whole world!"

"Light a fire that will sweep through all of Europe, huh? Won't work, Achmed. You can inspire men to fight, but all you'll have then is a mob. You have to have a general if you want to make them into an army."

"Do you think me a fool?" Achmed said, his voice acid with contempt. "We have such a Mahdi, a young man of devout faith and burning zeal, a veritable genius at stratagems and battles! He needed only a little persuasion to make him see that he could conquer all Europe for Allah, and the Moors needed even less to acclaim him as their Mahdi!"

"Sounds like the only power Nirobus needed to give you was finding that military genius and starting rumors of invincibility," Matt commented. "How old is this Mahdi, anyway?"

"Perhaps twenty-five. Soon all the world shall know his excellence!"

"Twenty-five," Matt repeated, deadpan. "A really tried and proven soldier, huh?"

The sarcasm went right by Achmed. "He has fought five great battles already, and has driven the Christian knights into a strip of land along the northern coast of Ibile! His arm is strong with the might of Allah, his sorcerers bold with the power of Nirobus!"

"Oh," Matt said. "The armies win by magic, huh?"

"The armies triumph over the cumbersome, bulky knights of Christendom as his sorcerers defeat the weak magic of the Christian wizards! You cannot stand against him! Yield, and he will treat you with kindness!"

"As long as we convert to Islam, that is."

"Nay! He will not force you, only encourage you to see the benefits of Islam, of surrender to the will of Allah!"

"Only encourage us," Matt said, nodding. "Of course,

Christians will have to pay heavier taxes than Muslims, and Christian dukes and earls will have to give up their castles and lands to Muslim aristocrats, and the Muslim judges will tend to decide in favor of Muslims who are suing Christians— but that's just the fortunes of war, right?"

"Even those mild punishments need not be yours, if you surrender to Allah."

"So you're not just promising your soldiers victory— you're promising them loot from Christians who won't convert. Tell me, just how did you manage to defeat King Rinaldo's wizards?"

Achmed seemed to expand with pride, his eyes burning with arrogance. "Nirobus does indeed send us power from his distant land, unbeliever—a new sort of power, that strikes deep into a sorcerer's soul and swells him with strength. There is no feeling like it! When I draw on Nirobus, I feel as though I were more intensely alive than ever before, filled with the strength of three, four, five lives, even more!"

"Matthew," Papa said, "the new drug in the neighborhood— while they are under its influence, the boys go limp, with foolish grins. Indeed, some must stand guard while the others are under its influence. And even when they are sober, they seem to be weaker, slower, less vital . . . "

"So that's why they weren't fighting as well as they used to!" It was galling for Matt to realize that his victories might not all have been due to his new strength and skill. "How do you think the addiction will end, Papa? With each of them completely drained of his life force, dying as a shriveled husk of his former self?"

Achmed frowned. "Of what do you speak? Nirobus would never leach the souls of the living!"

"Not their souls, maybe, but their vitality." Matt held up a hand to forestall the sorcerer's protest. "Don't misunderstand me, I don't doubt that your Mahdi is a good man, or even that you and your fellows aren't sorcerers at all, but good and virtuous men by the tenets of your Faith, wizards who mean only to draw on the powers of Goodness."

"Then what is this talk of weakening young men?"

"I think Nirobus has pulled off the world's biggest con," Matt said, his face somber. "That means a cheat, a fraud. I think he's managed to persuade you all that he's a holy and righteous man who's only trying to advance the cause of your Faith."

"Assuredly he is!"

Matt shook his head. "Afraid not. At best, I think your Nirobus might be out to advance the cause of himself, to let your Mahdi conquer the world for you, then kill him off and Nirobus himself become emperor of all."

"It cannot be!" But doubt shadowed Achmed's eyes.

"Oh," Matt said. "You don't want to know the worst, then?"

"I do not!"

"I'll tell you anyway," Matt said softly. "Who is the Father of Lies, Achmed? Who is the Sultan of Fraud? The worst of it might be that Nirobus isn't trying to conquer for himself at all. He might have a master, a very evil master."

Achmed writhed and gyrated, trying to shrug off his bonds. "Free my hands to cover my ears! I shall not hear your blasphemy!"

"It's not blasphemy to say that you and your fellow sorcerers are credulous fools who have let an amoral predator convince you of what you want to believe," Matt said, "that you have let yourselves be convinced that Nirobus wants to bring all the world to Allah . . ."

Achmed began to scream, thrashing about in his bonds.

"But he doesn't want the world for Allah!" Matt shouted. "The master he really serves is Satan, and he really wants to put us all into the power of Hell!"

"I did not hear you!" Achmed cried. "I did not hear the words of blasphemy!"

But they both knew he had, and knew that it wasn't God that Matt was indicting.

CHAPTER 12

"He is so ruthless now, Ramón!" Mama huddled within the circle of her husband's arms, head against his chest, both taking and giving comfort. "When he tortured that Moor, I scarcely knew him for my own gentle son!"

"I know, I know, *mi corazón,*" Papa soothed. "But remember that he did not actually torture the man, only subjected him to the pain of temptation, which relied on the man's having pleasure."

"I know, I know, but he was straining the man's soul! Could my little boy have been so careless of another man's beliefs?"

They sat on the bed in their suite, it being the only piece of furniture wide enough for two people side by side. The sunshine of late afternoon turned the paneling and the tapestries to gold.

"He honored the Muslim's faith, in his way," Papa said. "He did not force a morsel of pork between Achmed's teeth, after all, nor even sustain the temptation to the man's breaking— only used it to upset Achmed to the point at which his anger and pride impelled him to speak."

Mama's shivering stilled.

Papa took note, and pressed his consolation. "He has remembered our teachings, Jimena, and is slow to give hurt and quick to give help."

"Yes, but, Ramón!" Mama looked up into his eyes. "He would have hurt that man if he had to, I know it!"

"Certainly he would have, if the man had struck at him."

141

Papa smiled sadly down at her. "He would have struck faster and harder, if the sorcerer had offered harm to his Alisande."

"Well ... I can understand that, certainly ... " Mama lowered her gaze.

Papa felt a knot of concern loosen in his breast. He rested his cheek against her hair and mourned, "He has become a man, *mi corazón.*" But fierce pride glowed in him, too, pride in this man who had been his boy.

In the queen's solar, Matt sat at the table with Alisande, his hand covering hers. "Achmed didn't tell us all of it, dear—and oh, was he furious when he realized how much he *had* said!"

"He let slip one or two more bits of knowledge, then, when you led him to his, ah, chamber?"

"Your most comfortable dungeon," Matt assured her, "the one you put me in when I tried to leave for Allustria by myself. It even has a writing desk and a real bed."

Alisande shuddered at the memory of the event, if not the space. "What more did he say?"

"Only that this 'Mahdi's' name is Tafas bin Daoud, and that he knows about the sorcerers but ignores them. Apparently he's convinced that his victories are a matter of destiny and the will of Allah, so whatever the sorcerers are doing doesn't matter to him."

"But that leaves the sorcerers free to use him by talking people into fighting for him, then making sure of victory with their magic!"

"Which is fueled by the new magical power that Nirobus is channeling in. Yes." Matt nodded.

"Did you truly speak with this man Nirobus?" Alisande asked.

"Yes—and in my home universe, too!" The words tasted badly on Matt's tongue. "He's a smooth operator, no question. He pretended sympathy, pretended to want to help me out, even coaxed me into telling him who I was and how I was trying to get home. Then he blocked my transportation spell." He simmered in embarrassment.

"You could not have known." Alisande caressed his hand with hers now. "Did he not resemble a man of your world completely?"

"Down to the last detail," Matt assured her. "He's been there awhile, that's for sure. So he's managed to convince the sorcerers that they're using the power he gives them without having to do anything they didn't want to do anyway."

"And they, in their turn, are certain they can use this Mahdi as their figurehead to conquer Europe for them, while they use their magics to gain the true victories."

"Yes, and that's what Achmed *didn't* say," Matt said grimly. "They may be real genuine religious fanatics, or they may be a bunch of greedy, self-serving powermongers—but whatever they are, they're sure they can manipulate their Mahdi when he's won Europe for them."

"And believe they can thus carve up Europe between them, becoming the Mahdi's governors and ruling as they will. Yes." Alisande glowed with anger. "Do they not see that this Nirobus intends to serve them as they would serve the Mahdi?"

"Oh, once he proves he can kill them in agony, I think they'll be quick enough to accept whatever administrative posts he gives them," Matt said. "After all, Governor of Ibile wouldn't be a bad settlement."

"No, it would not," Alisande said grimly, "nor would Governor of Merovence. Husband, I think we must settle their ambitions before they seek to settle us."

"They're already seeking," Matt said dryly. "Achmed didn't deny that their genie attack was intended to soften us up for the Mahdi's conquest. What he didn't say was that it's also supposed to keep us from going to help King Rinaldo."

"Let us disappoint him, then," Alisande said. "How shall we begin our campaign?"

"That's for you to say—you're the military genius. But for the larger picture, I think it might be a good idea if I had a little talk with this Mahdi—show him how he's being used, maybe even persuade him that Allah doesn't want his servants fighting, and definitely doesn't want us trying to convert each other by the sword. Not easy, considering that's what Emperor Hardishane did, but that was five hundred years ago."

"To do that, though, you would have to go to this young Mahdi yourself!"

"Yes." Matt nodded grimly. "I would. We know where he is, though—Achmed said he's in the southern capital, Avordoca, consolidating his forces and training them for the big offensive to push Rinaldo and his army into the sea."

"But Avordoca is a hundred miles and more past the mountains! To speak with Tafas bin Daoud, you would have to travel through all that distance of hostile countryside!"

"Sure." Matt gave her a sardonic smile. "I've done it before, haven't I?"

"Not when a whole countryside was up in arms against you! I cannot hear of it!" Alisande cried.

"Oh, they were all against me then, too, everyone who was loyal to King Gordogrosso or feared him. They just didn't know I was coming."

"But they will know now! You must not go this time! Think, husband—someone else can travel in your place!"

Something hardened inside Matt. "You know I can't think like that—that I'll never send someone to face dangers that should be mine."

"They need not be yours! You rob other men of their chance for glory!"

"Who else is qualified?" Matt asked. "I'm the only knight who also happens to be a wizard. No one else stands as good a chance of coming back alive."

"Then I shall send two men, a wizard and a knight to guard him! Oh, husband!" She clasped his hand with both of hers, eyes suddenly brimming with tears. "Do not leave me again!"

Shaken, Matt returned the clasp and gazed into her eyes. "You know I can't bear the thought of an enemy king throwing you into his dungeon."

"Then stay and guard me! But if you will not stay for me, then stay for our son!"

Her words conjured a vision of enemy soldiers beating

down the nursery door and slashing at the baby with scimitars. Matt shuddered and said, "No! I can't let them get that close to you! I'll leave Saul and my parents and Ortho! Between them all, you'll be at least as safe as though I were with you—and I actually might be able to keep the enemy from invading!"

"Your parents are no substitute for . . . "

The knock at the door was very heavy, emphatic.

"We must have been louder than we thought—they're trying to stop us." Matt kept hold of Alisande's hand, but stood up to face the door.

Alisande dashed the tears from her eyes, squeezed his hand, then let it go as she sat up straight, leaning a little against the back of her chair, the invisible mantle of authority settling over her once again. "Enter!"

The door opened and a guard stepped in to bow. "Majesty, there is a courier come hot from King Rinaldo."

"From the king!" Alisande was on her feet. "Show him in on the instant!"

The guard stepped aside and a small man stepped into the room, dressed like a caravan guard, still covered with the dust of the road. His whole body seemed to droop with fatigue; his face was gray with weariness, but he fought to hold himself erect. He pulled a scroll from a pouch at his side and presented it to Her Majesty with a bow—and almost fell over. Matt stepped forward, straightening him with a clap on the shoulder. "You're a brave man, to bring word through, against such odds."

Alisande looked up from the scroll. "There is nothing here but what I already knew—that the Moors have broken out from their enclave in the south and marched against the king and his armies."

"Yes, Majesty," the courier said, every word weighted by weariness. His accent was thick enough to make him hard to understand. "The scroll was only for men to read, if I was captured. The true message is on my tongue."

"Speak, then!" the queen ordered.

"Tafas bin Daoud has launched a lightning attack on the

North," the courier said. "His men charged out from every direction, numberless as the blades of grass on the plain. He has conquered half the province of Vellese in one day, with five battles twenty leagues apart. His horsemen are lightly armored, but they came against the king's knights five to one and worried at them like hounds at a bear until they brought the knight down." His voice broke; he dropped to one knee. "Oh, Majesty, ride quickly! For if you do not come straight to the king's aid, all of Ibile will be lost!" He tottered and nearly fell, but Matt reached out and caught him in time. One of the guards stepped forward and pulled the man to his feet.

Alisande turned to Matt with the determined, absolute certainty of the monarch. "There is no longer room to talk of a personal mission, Lord Wizard. The war has come to Merovence. We must march."

Mama was incensed. "Why must I stay to guard the castle, Ramón?" Fear shadowed her eyes. "O my beloved, what shall I do if you never return to me?"

Papa took her into his arms, murmuring, "Be sure I shall come back, beloved. With so fair a lady waiting for me, how could I let armies stand in my way?"

"Then why should I not go, and you stay!"

"Because in the Middle Ages, the office of women was to stay and hold the castle—and that because their men cannot bear to risk them in battle."

"But we are expected to risk our men, whom we love as our lives? Why does not Mateo's wife have to stay, then?" But Mama knew the reason very well.

So did Papa. "Because she is the queen, and by the magic of this universe, only the sovereign can know with certainty which terrain to choose and how to manage the battle. From what they say, I believe she will do as a modern commander should, watching the battle from high ground and directing the movements of the troops in relative safety."

"Why must she wear armor, then?"

"Because none can be sure she will not have to fight, herself—on a hilltop or not, she may be attacked, or ambushed as her army travels. You must stay here with Saul, my love, to be sure there is a castle to which our daughter-in-law may return when her war is won."

"It is still most unfair," Mama grumbled, but she let Papa's caresses soothe her anyway.

The soldiers milled about in the courtyard, knights and courtiers riding through them, bawling orders. Against the range of kitchens, provision wagons were loading their last stocks of food and ale. Another set of wagons loaded extra weapons from the smithies. There were no camp followers, especially no prostitutes—yet. Alisande would not have them, maintaining that her soldiers would not exploit women. It galled her to know that the prostitutes would materialize every night they marched, as if from thin air.

She sat astride her mount by the gatehouse with her dukes, gazing out over the courtyard, impassive face hiding the warring of emotions within her—sadness at leaving her home, eagerness for the journey and for action. Matt stood nearby, arguing with Saul.

"Look," the Witch Doctor said, "how about we make a deal? *You* stay home, and *I'll* go with the army."

Matt shook his head. "Your wife doesn't have to march with the soldiers. Mine does."

"Yeah, but it's not fair to leave you to take on all the danger by yourself! At least you could let your dad stay home as resident magician, and let me go!"

"Angelique would never forgive me." Saul's wife was Matt's trump card, and he played her unmercifully.

"How about your mother? Why should she have to risk her husband when Angelique doesn't?"

"Because she's related to the queen, and Angelique isn't—and because her baby is grown up now."

Saul took a deep breath, striving for composure. "Look, let's try to be reasonable about this. If your parents hadn't dropped by, who would have had to stay to defend the castle?"

Matt started to answer, but Saul said quickly, "Never mind. Don't answer. Dumb question."

Matt relaxed with a smile of amusement. Saul growled a

good-bye and turned away. He knew very well that if Mama and Papa Mantrell hadn't appeared on the scene, he would have been stuck with being castellan without any hope of debate.

Then he turned back, holding out a small gray sphere pierced with holes. "At least take one of my communicators! That way, if you get into too much trouble, you can call for help and I can at least send a spell!"

"Thanks, but I'm supposed to be incognito." Matt smiled even as he held up a palm to ward off the talisman. "If I'm wearing a bauble that suddenly starts talking, it might make peasants and soldiers a little wary of me."

Saul didn't say anything, just glowered. He hated having to admit the other guy was right.

"As long as I don't look like a wizard," Matt explained, "people *may* trust me. If I look magical, nobody will tell me anything."

"Okay, okay! At least take a good long look every time you pass a puddle, though, will you? I can send a message that way if all else fails."

"Deal." Matt held out a hand. "I always did like to take a little time for reflection."

Saul winced, but shook his hand anyway.

So the army rode out across the drawbridge with the queen at their head and her Lord Wizard right behind her with his father beside him, and with Saul, Angelique, and Mama waving from the battlements atop the gatehouse.

The army's campfires made a very orderly galaxy, a spiral that lapped into five separate circles with the queen's pavilion at its center. Inside that tent, she forced herself to submit to her own intuition born of the magical link between monarch and people, queen and country.

"I hate the thought of it," she told Matt, "but the certainty grows within me that I must needs have a vanguard, a small party going before the army to prepare the way—and that it must be you, that none other stands even a chance of success."

Matt held himself very still, though his eyes widened. He

wasn't used to Alisande saying someone else was right when she was in monarch mode. Of course, she hadn't said she was wrong, and hadn't *quite* said that he was right—but it was enough. "I'll sneak out while nobody notices," he promised.

"I would go myself, but . . . "

"I know," Matt assured her. "You're the monarch, and the army probably wouldn't follow anyone else. Certainly they wouldn't be as strong without you."

"I have sent word to Allustria and Latruria to help. Surely Frisson will send troops, and even King Boncorro may, though I cannot be sure." Then the queen weakened, and the woman shone through, tears glinting from her eyes. "But O my love, take care! If I should lose you, I do not know what I would do!" She lifted her arms, and he came around the table to lift her into his.

It was several hours later that he slipped out of her pavilion. The sentries spun, halberds raised, but Matt raised a palm in greeting, and they relaxed. As he stepped away into the night, he hoped they would be as alert to people trying to get into the tent as they were to people trying to get out.

The moon rode high, its dim light most of what there was; the campfires had burned to embers and been banked, the ground was clear, the soldiers asleep in their tents. Matt stopped by a provisions wagon to take a pack and fill it—but a hand came out of the darkness holding one already stuffed.

Matt froze, every nerve on edge, hand on his sword. Then he saw the grin beneath the mustache, and relaxed. "Papa! You nearly scared five years off me!"

"I could wish you no greater delight than eternal youth," Papa returned. "Did you think you could creep from this camp without me?"

"So how did you know?" Matt said, chagrined.

"Because you did the same thing when you were fifteen— sneaked out of the house when you should have been doing your homework."

Matt remembered. "Yeah. I forced myself to go to the carnival when nobody else would be there, because I was afraid of riding the Round-Up and determined to prove I wasn't a *total* coward."

"So you told me, afterward." Papa nodded. "Besides, I have seen some tension between your sweet wife and yourself, and knew you would do what you thought you must to defend her."

"Well, as it turns out, she put on her crown instead of her wife-hat, and ordered me to go." Matt decided he had to set the record straight. "But I don't doubt my courage anymore, Papa. I've been knighted, and the ceremony's magical."

"Literally, I am sure—though even in our world, ceremonies have metaphorical magic, and that is what they are for. I lived through three months of torture at Parris Island and wondered why, but it ended with the Trooping of the Colors, and I knew I was a Marine. Even more, I knew I was a man." Papa clapped him on the shoulder, then held up the pack for him to slip into. "Just as you know you are a man, for you have been knighted. Come, let us be off."

"We always have been," Matt muttered, but he slipped his arms through the straps, then followed his father through the tents, sneaked past the pickets, and went off into the night.

They had gone about five hundred yards down what passed for a road when a huge dark shape rose up before them to block the way. Red jewels glowed for eyes, and the top of the shape was serrated.

"Beware!" Papa fell into a crouch, a spear appearing in his hand.

"Who is this uncouth fellow, Lord Matthew?" a deep voice rumbled. "Why does he seek to prick me with that pin?"

"He's just trying to protect his hatchling—me," Matt said quickly.

The glowing eyes stared. "Him? Yes, now I see some resemblance. Your paternal progenitor, truly?"

"Very truly. Stegoman, meet my father, Ramón Mantrell. Papa, my friend Stegoman. He's a dragon."

"I never would have guessed." Papa bowed to Stegoman. "I am pleased to make your acquaintance."

"And I am pleased to meet you," the dragon replied. "Your son does you credit, Master Mantrell. He is a true nobleman. You have reared him well."

"Why, thank you," Papa said, pleased, "though the credit is at least as much his mother's as mine. You have known my son long, then?"

"Some years—since his first day in Merovence, in fact. He has mended my wings, and I have carried him on my shoulders." The dragon swiveled his head toward Matt. "As I mean to do again. How discourteous of you, Matthew, to go adventuring without informing me!"

"Thought I could sneak off without you," Matt said, smiling. "How'd you know?"

"The Witch Doctor called to me by magic, of course, as soon as you had left the castle! Surely you will not insist on walking when you have such a distance to traverse, and so much of it through hostile territory!"

"Of course I'd rather ride," Matt said, amused. "Are you offering?"

"Certainly—at the price of being included in your exploits."

"Just remember, you might be the one who does the paying. Not much chance of keeping you out, if we're riding on you." Matt turned to his father. "What do you say, Papa? You always did like flying."

Matt glanced back to see his father hanging on to the huge dorsal plates, thin-lipped and pale-faced. Matt smiled. "I know it's a bit more scary than being inside a jet, Papa, but you get used to it."

"I'm sure that I shall." Papa's voice sounded only a little strained. "I do wish we had seat belts, though."

"I know the feeling," Matt agreed, "but even if we did fall, Stegoman would loop back and catch us. Besides, with these plates to hang on to and break the wind, there isn't much that could knock us off."

A huge impact jolted Stegoman, and a voice thundered around them as they all plummeted toward the ground.

CHAPTER 13

"What mortals dare to challenge the djinn by venturing in the element of air!" the voice bellowed.

"Good question," Matt called to Stegoman. "Head for the ground!"

The dragon had already begun to pull out of his dive. "Art thou afraid?" he demanded in disbelief.

"Damn straight I'm scared! But more to the point, why fight this spirit in his own element? On the ground, we can call up a few forces he might not know!"

"I might have known 'twas strategy, not cowardice!" Stegoman exulted, and dove again. The huge voice shouted angrily behind him.

"Still there?" Matt called over his shoulder.

"Of course, as you know well," his father snapped. "It was a hair-raising experience, though."

"There are lots of bad moments like this," Matt said apologetically.

"I always yearned to be a part of the epics I read," Papa told him. "At last I have my wish!" He sounded more resigned than overjoyed, though.

Stegoman pulled up sharply, and they jarred to a stop on the ground. Papa winced. "More like a fighter plane than a passenger liner."

"Look out!" Matt scrambled down and ducked under Stegoman. His father stared a second, then followed.

The dragon spread his wings and roared defiance at the huge being who swooped down upon them—roared fire, and the genie's clothing burst into flame. Away the spirit sprang, with a shriek that echoed off the hillsides.

Matt stared out from under Stegoman's belly plates. "It can't be!"

"Why not?" Papa squirmed up beside him, then stared up. His eyes widened. "It is!"

"I didn't really believe they came in both genders," Matt said.

"You should have," Papa reminded him. "You watched that TV show enough when you were little."

"Yeah, but not even Barbara Eden was built like *that*!"

The spirit came storming back, smoldering clothing reknitting itself into bolero jacket and gauzy harem pants even as she swooped down on them. Her face was oval, her eyes slanted and furious, her lips full and cherry red, her hair a lustrous black waterfall. "For that, you shall roast in your own flame, dragon!" She drew back a hand to throw a whammy.

Matt chanted quickly.

> "She walks in beauty, like the night
>   Of cloudless climes and starry skies;
> And all that's best of dark and bright
>   Meet in her aspect and her eyes:
> Thus mellow'd to that tender light
>   Which heaven to gaudy day denies.
>
> One shade the more, one ray the less,
>   Had half impaired the nameless grace
> Which waves in every raven tress,
>   Or softly lightens o'er her face,
> Where thoughts serenely sweet express
>   How pure, how dear their dwelling place.
>
> And on that cheek, and o'er that brow,
>   So soft, so calm, so eloquent,
> The smiles that win, the tints that glow,

But tell of days in goodness spent,
A mind at peace with all below,
A heart whose love is innocent!"

The whammy hand stayed poised. The slanted eyes narrowed and lost some of their fury. "What nonsense is this you speak?"

"No nonsense at all," Matt said smoothly. "You are indeed a most fair damsel, of perfect proportion and radiant features, lovely to behold in every way."

"Of course I know that, but why would you waste breath saying it?" Even so, the whammy hand lowered, and she tossed her head. "Nevertheless, say it again." Suddenly, she shrank, and when she stepped down to the ground, she was a half-head shorter than Matt. "If you still wish to."

Matt caught his breath; so did Papa. At normal human size, her proportions seemed even more spectacular, her face even more perfect in its beauty.

Stegoman watched with a cold reptilian eye, his lip curving in silent laughter. *He* didn't have to worry about his hormones—it wasn't a female of *his* kind.

"Can you not speak, now that I am of your own size?" the spirit demanded. "Do I only appear attractive to you when I am gigantic?"

"Not at all," Matt said quickly.

"She was a phantom of delight
When first she gleamed upon my sight;
A lovely apparition, sent
To be a moment's ornament;
Her eyes as stars of twilight fair;
Like twilight's, too, her dusky hair;
But all things else about her drawn
From Maytime and the cheerful dawn;
A dancing shape, an image gay,
To haunt, to startle, and waylay."

The spirit woman's eyes became slumberous; her lips curved in a sensuous smile. "You have great audacity, mortal, to so address a woman of the djinn."

"I'm not telling you anything you don't already know," Matt pointed out.

"True," she agreed, "but I enjoy the extravagance of your terms."

"Surely you must be the most beautiful of genies!"

Her laughter chimed like finger cymbals. "I should think so, for a djinni is a male, and though some may be handsome, none have any great beauty. I am Lakshmi, a djinna, ignorant mortal, and there are many of my kind more beautiful than I."

"Then your kind must be amazingly attractive indeed," Matt said, pitching his voice low and throaty.

The djinna tilted her head to the side, considering him. "You are a flatterer," she decided, "but you may prove all the more amusing for it." She stepped closer, swiveling her hips and moistening her lips. "Do you frolic as well as you flatter?"

Matt caught his breath; the djinna exuded raw sexuality, her movements so lithe and sensuous as to be a declaration. "No man alive could help but dream of such a frolic with so amazing a female—but if he had a wife, he really shouldn't do anything more than dream."

The djinna swayed closer yet, tongue-tip flicking out to pass over her lips. "You have a wife? What a shame! Still, we are here and she is there, and need never know what transpires between us. This companion of yours will surely not tell her."

"I am his father," Papa said, almost apologetically.

The djinna stilled, then turned to Papa with a slight frown, as though trying to solve a puzzle. If anything, her sensuality increased. "You should rejoice to see him so bedded."

"Ah, but I have a grandchild now," Papa said, "*his* child."

"Is this so great a matter among your kind?"

Well, actually, no—it was the marriage that mattered; the baby just made the relationship between Matt and Alisande that much deeper. Somehow, though, he knew he couldn't say that, especially not to a woman who could cause an earthquake if she thought she was being scorned.

Papa thought so, too. "Among our kind, sweet lady, those who fall in love feel deeply betrayed if their partners sleep with other companions."

"Have *you* a wife?" the djinna asked, advancing.

"Yes, and she is my greatest reason for wishing to live," Papa answered.

"But she, too, need not know."

"She would." Papa shook his head, smiling. "Don't ask me how, but she would. What matters more, though, is that *I* would know."

A trace of contempt showed in the djinna's smile. "Are you so enfeebled by these things you mortals call 'consciences'?"

" 'Conscience doth make cowards of us all,' " Papa quoted.

Matt agreed. "Conscience is part of it, but most of it is that I would be betraying myself."

The djinna turned, frowning. "I do not understand."

"I'm not sure I do, myself," Matt confessed. "I only know it's true. If I betrayed Alisande, I would betray the strongest, truest impulse inside me, and be maimed in spirit forever after."

"What strange creatures you are!" the djinna exclaimed, but her smile stayed broad and inviting. "Why should *I* not try to maim *you*, though?"

Matt swallowed hard, thinking fast, then said,

> "To each his suff'rings; all are men,
>   Condemn'd alike to groan,
> The tender for another's pain,
>   Th' unfeeling for his own.
>
> All souls self-aware are one,
>   Lives linking in a web,
> Expanding, weaving, never done.
>   One's flow's another's ebb.

Every other's loss, you own.
So lady, care for all!
Each pain you'll feel, so none condone,
Hearken ever to love's call."

A shadow of concern crossed Papa's face. "That last line . . . "

"What have you done, mortal?" The djinna's eyes had misted over. "You have taught my heart to weep!"

Matt breathed silent thanks. Aloud, he said, "It is only growth, fair lady, for if you have never wept, your soul is incomplete."

"Weeping for myself, I can understand—but to weep for another? And for harms he has not even suffered yet?"

"Ah, but to think of the harm he might suffer because of your actions is to care for him," Matt said.

Papa looked up with surprised approval.

The djinna frowned, head tilted. "I think that you have infected me with one of these consciences of yours, mortal man."

"People with consciences do less harm," Matt told her, "and more good."

"Why should I care about your puling race, for good or for ill?"

"Why," Matt said, "because magicians of our feeble kind can enslave and compel you by their spells."

Lakshmi stilled, eyes narrowing, and Matt could feel her anger rising.

"Who enslaved you," he asked her softly, "and by what token? I may be able to free you from his compulsions."

She stared. "Are you a wizard, then?"

"I am," Matt confessed.

"So that is why your flattery lit the fires of desire within me!"

"Uh, sorry 'bout that," Matt said, shamefaced. "I was just trying to keep you from wiping us out."

Her stare turned into disbelief. "Can you really feel sorrow for inflaming a woman with desire?"

"Well, if she didn't want it—yes."

"Most strange indeed!" she marveled. "Such human males as I have dealt with before would never have scrupled so!"

"My son is a rare man indeed," Papa said proudly.

"Rare and strange," Lakshmi agreed. "Dare you truly free me from the bonds of these Moorish magicians, mortal man?"

"Of course I dare! Do you expect me to believe you're going to turn on me the minute I liberate you?" In fact, Matt would have believed exactly that, if he hadn't just given her a conscience.

"A mortal might well believe that of a djinna, yes." Her eyes were calculating now, evaluating him. "You would trust me, then?"

"I would. Is that so foolish?"

"Perhaps," Lakshmi allowed, "but your flattery was most persuasive." She came to a decision. "Well enough, then. He who enslaved me was a Persian magus, one Haziz al Iskander, and the token in which he bound me was a bracelet with a moonstone inset."

"Persian?" Matt stared. "How long ago was this, anyway?"

The djinna shrugged. "I have slept long and often since then, within the prison of the gem—but from what free djinn have told me when I have been awake and done with whatever task my new master set for me, it has been perhaps three hundred of your years. Is Kaprin still King of Merovence?"

"I'm afraid not," Matt said, then remembered that she might not have meant Alisande's father. "Which Kaprin? There have been four of them."

"Four?" The djinna stared. "I only know of one! How much time has been stolen from me? How long since the first Kaprin died?"

"About two centuries." Matt braced himself for hysterics.

They didn't come, but Lakshmi began to look very angry. "Five hundred years since Haziz enslaved me, then. I have slept through much of my life, mortal man. If you can free me, I shall be as grateful as a djinna can be." For a moment, her sensuality gleamed its promise again.

Matt forced his mind back to the problem. "So you were

bound into the moonstone by a Persian? Well, let me think."
He bowed his head.

The djinna's eyes flashed with anger. She started to speak, but Papa forestalled her with a raised palm. "Peace, milady. He makes magic."

The djinna stared and bit off her rebuke.

Matt raised his head, eyes unfocused, and recited,

> "When Beauty with unconfined wings
>   Hovers within my sight,
> And an airy lady brings
>   To outshine every light,
> When I lie tangled in her hair
>   And fettered to her eye,
> The birds that wanton in the air
>   Know no such liberty."

Lakshmi fairly glowed with allure, and stepped forward, hips swaying.

Matt shot the next verse in quickly:

> "Brightest in dungeons, Liberty! thou art,
> For there thy habitation is the heart—
> The heart which love of thee alone can bind,
> And when thy child to fetters is consigned—
> To slumber, and the moonstone's opal gloom,
> Then Freedom's fame finds wings on every wind."

He ended, looking up at the djinna expectantly.

She frowned, gazing off into space, and moved her arms experimentally, then shook her head. "The ties still bind me. They are weakened, but still there."

"I was afraid of that," Matt sighed. "I can't do anything more without knowing your name."

"My name?" The djinna stared. "I told you—it is Lakshmi!"

"No, no! Not your public name—your true name, your secret name, the one that only your mother knew until you came of age, and she told it to you!"

Warily, Lakshmi demanded, "How did you know of secret names among the djinn?"

Matt could have answered that most primitive peoples had such names, and kept them secret specifically so that sorcerers couldn't use them to cast hurtful spells over the people—but it was more tactful to say, "Because your people have been around for a very long time."

"What need have you of my secret name?"

"The magus used it to bind you to the moonstone, didn't he?"

Fear touched the djinna's eyes. "How did you know that?"

"It's not your body that's bound, really," Matt explained, "it's your inner self. There's nothing outside of you that forces you to return to the moonstone or obey the wishes of the one who carries it—it's a compulsion laid in your heart of hearts. The magus used your true name to bind you, and I can't free you without it."

"But if you know my true name, you will be able to work foul magics upon me, and will have power over me in any way you choose!"

"I know," Matt said apologetically, "but that's how it works. He bound you by your secret name, so I can't free you without saying it. You'll have to trust me."

The djinna's eyes hardened. "Can I trust you to forget the name as soon as you have said it?"

"Good thought!" Matt said, and chanted,

> "I shall serenade sweet Lakshmi
> With a verse that frees her past;
> Her name I'll speak but once
> While spellcasting shall last,
> The slaver's spell I'll best,
> Then her name will sink
> And be forgotten with the rest."

Papa nodded, eyes bright with understanding. "You may tell him your name now, sweet lady. He cannot remember it after he has spoken it once."

She still looked doubtful, but she snapped at Papa, "Cover your ears and turn away your eyes."

Papa did.

Lakshmi stepped very close to Matt, all business now—but the sheer impact of her sensuality still hit him like a hammer. Dazed and tingling with desire, he forced himself to focus on the single word she spoke, then nodded and snapped, "Step away."

Anger lit in her eyes, but she stepped back anyway.

Matt drew a ragged breath as her effect diminished enough for him to remember his verse. He recited the song of separation again, but included the name she had given instead of the pronoun. Then he looked up, startled.

"What troubles you?" she snapped.

"Something's missing," Matt said. "From my memory, I mean."

"Of course—my name!"

"Is that all?" Matt frowned, attention turned inward. "Yes, I can remember reciting the verse that told me to forget your name as soon as I used it, I can remember using it—but I can't remember what it was!"

"That is good." The djinna smiled. "You are a man of your word." Then she frowned. "If you speak truly, that is."

"Hey, you gotta trust me *some*," Matt said, affronted. "How're you feeling? Any strings attached?"

Lakshmi lifted her arms again, gazing off into space. Then her face lit with delight. "They are gone! The constraints and compulsions are gone! You have freed me indeed! I am no longer bound to the mission on which he sent me!"

"Great!" Matt smiled, elated. "What was your mission, by the way?"

"To slay a wizard named Matthew Mantrell."

Matt stared. So did Papa. Then as one, they drew a deep breath.

The djinna frowned. "This troubles you?"

"You might say that," Matt agreed. "You see, my name is Matthew Mantrell—and for once, I'm very, very glad I was willing to help out a stranger!"

"Are you truly he?" Lakshmi swayed closer again, hitting Matt with a sensual blast twice as strong as anything she'd dealt before. "Of course I shall not kill you—but perhaps I can remove you from this conflict by other means. What say you, mortal—will you spend a month or so with a djinna? I promise you pleasures of which you can barely dream, ecstasy so intense as to make you think you have died."

Matt swallowed hard, wondering how his spells had backfired. "Look, you don't really have to show that you're grateful . . . "

"I do not," she breathed, lips only inches from his own. "I am entirely selfish in this. I seek my own pleasure, but I assure you it shall result in your own. Do not fear this conscience of yours; you shall die to remorse, only to come alive again to delights only spirits can know."

"Exactly—only the spirit can know true ecstasy." Matt clung to the idea, like Ulysses lashed to the mast. "That means that the real thing, the fullest intensity of it, is only for those in love."

"Perhaps among your kind," she said, "not mine." Her breasts brushed his chest.

Matt fought the urge to step back, knowing how that would end. He had to convince her, not avoid her—and had to do it with his body screaming at him to stop being an idiot and take what was offered. "You wouldn't want to take your pleasure knowing I wasn't really enjoying it as much as I could, would you?"

The djinna stilled. "If that is true of you, mortal man, you are the only male of such persuasion that I have ever met."

"No, the others just don't admit it, even to themselves," Matt told her. "That, or they've never known what it is to be really in love with someone who's in love with them." For a moment, a wave of sorrow swept him, pity for all the poor people who had never known the intoxication of being in love. He remembered what Saul had told him once, and said it again now: "If you're not in love, it's nothing. It's a long, tantalizing climb, but when you get to the top, there's nothing but ashes."

Lakshmi stepped back an inch, tears on her lashes. "What is this heaviness that drags at my heart of a sudden? O wicked magician, you have made me sad again!"

Matt realized that his pity for the untold millions had engulfed her. "It's just the sorrow that comes over me when I realize that so many people have never really been in love. It happens whenever I remember how lucky I am, to love and be loved."

Even as he said it, joy flooded through him. The djinna felt it, too; astonishment swept her face. "What an amazing feeling! Can mortals truly know such bliss?"

"The lucky ones, yes."

"I could almost begin to believe that some things may be sacred." Lakshmi stepped farther away, face becoming stern with the effort of pulling her allure back in. "I could not intrude on something so precious. No, Wizard Matthew, I'll not beguile you with dalliance. How, then, may I thank you for freeing me from the sorcerer's bonds?"

Matt heaved a silent sigh of relief. "You could tell me some more about the sorcerer who sent you after me, and the army he's helping conquer Ibile. Where did they come from? How did they get this far into Merovence?"

"As to how they came in, your border guards made no effort to keep them out," she said, surprised. "They admit all who claim to have business here."

"Yes, the disadvantage of an open border." Matt had recommended the policy himself. "On the other hand, why bother closing the roads when they could walk in through the fields so easily?"

"As thousands of folk from Ibile do even now," Lakshmi told him. "I have seen them from the air, when I have gone about the errands on which my master sent me." She grinned. "My *former* master, now."

For a second, Matt imagined he saw pointed teeth. He hid a shudder and wondered what kind of spirit he had loosed on the world. "I hadn't realized we were absorbing a flood of refugees. I'll have to send word to the queen so she can have support services ready." He wondered why they hadn't had any word from her reeves in the provinces. "How long has this been going on?"

"Perhaps a week."

Allow a few days for the reeves to realize something big was afoot, another day for them to decide they should report it, three more days for the messengers to arrive—yes, Matt could see why word hadn't arrived till Alisande had left the castle. "So the Mahdi's big offensive only started a couple of weeks ago?"

"It did," the djinna confirmed. "Of course, for half a year he has been biting off one province at a time, but the folk who fled that war only needed to go to a province he had not yet conquered. There have been some coming through the mountains for several months, but the steady outpouring did not come till the Mahdi made his rule among the borderlands completely sure, then struck north against King Rinaldo."

"And Christians were told to convert or get out?"

"Not forced," she said slowly, "but encouraged."

"So he's not killing or torturing unbelievers, only taxing them and keeping them out of the big-money industries." Matt nodded. "Well, I can accept that. Even the early Christians had to place their faith above worldly success. Doesn't mean I'm willing to let him keep doing it, but at least I don't have to think of *him* as being evil."

Lakshmi frowned. "How is this? Would you rather fight a good man than a bad?"

"No, but if my enemy deserves respect, I'd like to know it. It has something to do with whether or not I pull my punches."

"Pull your punches?" the djinna frowned.

"How much mercy he shows," Papa clarified.

"You mortals worry about such silly things!"

"Yes, I'm sure." Matt felt a chill down his spine. "Where do they come from, this Mahdi and his men?"

"From Morocco, across the strait by the great rock. Many are Arab, but most are Berbers or Rifs."

"What started them moving?"

"Holy men arose among the hill folk, the Rif, and preached

that they had found a sheikh who could lead the faithful to victory—that the time had come for a jihad to conquer Ibile."

"Holy men." Matt frowned. "They didn't work magic, did they?"

"No, but my master and those like him were the ones who persuaded the holy men that the time had come, that they were seers who had seen the birth of a general who could bring Islam to Europe."

So the sorcerers had fired up the holy men, and Nirobus had started the sorcerers. "That pretty much confirms what we guessed, and tells us a bit more."

"What?" She frowned.

"Who we're *really* fighting," Matt said, "and where to hit them. Thanks, Lakshmi. You've been a big help."

"I would be an even greater aid." For a minute, allure blazed forth again, and she took a step closer to Matt. "Are you sure there is no other way in which I can serve you?"

"Not right now, thanks," Matt said quickly. "In fact, you can go anywhere you want. You're free."

"I thank you." She didn't sound as though she meant it. Then the other side of her freedom must have occurred to her, because her lips curved into a secret smile. All she said, though, was "If you ride your dragon again, you will seek to fly, will you not?"

"We will," Stegoman replied.

But Matt was finally picking up on hints. "Any reason we shouldn't?"

"There is," the djinna told him. "The sorcerers have set other djinn about the queen's army, and between her and the mountains, to watch for Matthew Mantrell and smite him down if they can, chase him away from Ibile if they cannot."

CHAPTER 14

"Yes," Matt said slowly, "I'd say that was a good reason not to start flying again. Stegoman, do you mind a hike?"

"It is not my favorite form of travel," the dragon grumped.

"Maybe we can get by if we scrunch down on your back and fly low," Matt suggested. "They're looking for me, but they're not looking for a dragon." He turned back to the djinna. "Either way, we stand a lot better chance of survival, now that we're warned. Thanks."

"It is my pleasure, though not pleasure enough." Her eyelids drooped, her smile became lazy and inviting, and she radiated allure again. "Are you certain there is no other service you wish from your handmaid?"

Matt didn't want to see the hand that had made her. "Not at the moment, thanks—but I'm sure we'll meet again."

"Oh, be very sure," Lakshmi said with a sultry smile. "We shall meet again indeed. Until then, farewell, O most considerate of wizards."

But her words had a sarcastic tone to them, and as she faded from sight, Matt didn't know whether to sigh with relief or moan with disappointment. He compromised with a shudder. "I tell you, Papa, I've had a lot of run-ins with a lot of strange spirits and creatures here, but in some ways, I think that was the most dangerous!"

"She may have been indeed," Papa agreed. "Son, have you begun to find amusement in dancing with tigers?"

"Well, I didn't want to hurt her felines. Seems I remember a certain party telling me I should always be polite to strange women," Matt said, with a pointed glance.

"Well, yes, but I didn't mean *that* strange," Papa said. "Still, I am quite proud of you, my son—I had not known that you had developed such a way with the ladies."

Matt frowned. "Just being polite, the way you taught me."

"Yes, but I did not teach you to win their hearts as a matter of course."

"Oh, come on now! All I did was throttle her most murderous intentions!"

"You don't know?" Papa said with surprise. "Your spells did considerably more than that, my son."

"Oh?" Matt felt a very nasty sensation of foreboding creeping over him. "What else?"

"That line I had doubts about, where you told her to 'Hearken ever to love's call'? That, plus verse after verse praising her beauty and allure? They made her fall in love with you, at least as much as her kind seem able to do!"

"Which means fall in lust." Matt shivered. "Help, Papa! I just got myself in deep trouble!"

"Courage, my son." Papa clapped a hand on his shoulder. "Maybe the spells didn't include a compulsion."

"Yeah, but maybe they did." Matt frowned. "Come to think of it, though, I did follow them with a spell that liberated her from compulsions."

"Yes, and told her she was free to go where she wished."

"Yeah," Matt said with relief, then frowned again. "Let's just hope she doesn't wish to go where I go."

"That could be a problem," Papa admitted.

Matt remembered that Solomon had originally imprisoned djinn in bottles and lamps because they were so dangerous. He hoped he hadn't made a very bad mistake.

"You are on the side of the angels," Papa said by way of reassurance. "Surely they will protect you from your enemies."

"Enemies I can deal with," Matt said. "Who's going to protect me from my new friend?"

Saul and Mama began their acquaintance with a strategy conference. She was very patient with his prickliness, and he came out of the meeting with a high respect for her as a person, a strategist, and a diplomat. She didn't seem to be the slightest bit paranoid, but she did manage to think of every conceivable enemy who might come against them and how those enemies might attack, even though she claimed to know nothing about matters military.

"I have read the old epics," she explained, "the Songs of El Cid and of Roland, of *The Madness of Roland* and *The Death of Arthur*. I have learned from them which enemies came, and how they attacked."

It made fine sense to Saul. He had learned from his association with Matt that a literary education in his birth-universe was an excellent preparation for life in this one.

So they set out their sentries, established patrols, and took turns walking the battlements, making the rounds with a word of cheer for each sentry and the occasional brief conversation that let them come to know every soldier as a human being. So it happened that Saul was on the ramparts when he saw a rider raising a dust cloud fifty feet long, streaking flat-out toward the castle gate.

"What man is that?" he asked the nearest sentry.

The man shaded his eyes and peered. "I cannot see clearly, Witches' Doctor, but he wears our livery."

"Hoist the portcullis and let him in!" Then Saul ran for the nearest steps, heading down to the courtyard.

The rider pounded into the bailey and reined in his horse. Saul ran up. "What's the news, man?"

"Moors!" the rider gasped. "Ships with triangular sails! Our squadron was riding patrol and saw them sailing up the river toward Bordestang! Fifty at least, perhaps a hundred! The fleet went on as far as we could see!"

Saul stared. His first thought was, Where did *they* come from? His second thought was how to stop them, but his third thought was that he couldn't tell without more information. "The rest of your squadron still scouting?"

The man gulped air and nodded. "They ride behind the cover of the trees atop the ridge that runs beside the river, to learn what they may of this sudden enemy. They sent me to bear word. By your leave, my lord, I should ride to rejoin them."

"Sure." Saul was oddly touched by the man's devotion to his buddies. "But rest for an hour and take a little food and ale first, okay?"

The man nodded his thanks, still gasping, and Saul turned away, heading for the solar. "I think Lady Mantrell needs to be told about this right away." He didn't even realize that he had promoted Mama—she hadn't officially been ennobled yet. But what else do you call the queen's mother-in-law?

The solar door was open. Saul nodded to the guards and went in. "Mrs. Mantrell, a little problem has just come up."

Mama looked up from a huge leather-bound geography book. "What kind, Saul?"

"A hundred ships full of Moors. Maybe more. A lot more."

Mama stared. Then she said, "Where did *they* come from?"

"Just what *I* said," Saul answered. "I think the answer is 'Morocco.' "

"Yes, of course," Mama said impatiently, "but how?"

"Nice question, now that you mention it. I never knew the Moors were sailors." Saul frowned, thinking.

"The Rifs and Berbers were not, but the Arabs had excellent fleets," Mama reminded him.

Saul lifted his head, wide-eyed. "The Moors could have borrowed them!"

"They had sources for a fleet, surely," Mama agreed, "and they did have a small colony on the European side of Gibraltar, no?"

"Yes," Saul said, surprised at her knowledge—but why shouldn't she know Spanish history as well as he knew English?

"In fact, 'Gibraltar' is the English form of an Arabic name," Mama went on, "Tariq, the general who conquered that first European province. Since the Moors hold both sides of the Strait, Algerian ships could pass with ease."

"And around the Spanish coast to the mouth of the Seine!" Saul nodded. "Now that I think of it, Alisande has built an excellent army, but I've never heard anyone say much about

a navy! They just sailed right on up the river without anybody so much as asking to see a passport!"

"We must send a courier to the queen." Mama rose. "Let us
hope that courier reaches her—there will be many Moors, and
many agents of their sorcerers, between Her Majesty and our
rider."

"I can do a backup on that," Saul told her. "I can send
word to your son—*if* he looks into puddles now and then,
the way I told him."

"Excellent." Mama nodded. "Since they are together, if
one receives the message, both will. Come, let us go up to
the battlements. These Moors may anchor near Bordestang
before the day is out. We should prepare a few surprises for
them."

On the way up, Mama told the Captain of the Guard to
dispatch three couriers by three different routes. Saul was
amazed at her air of authority and at how easily she had
taken to running the castle.

By evening, the Moorish ships were anchoring in Bordestang's harbor. They found empty docks, and a waterfront
so silent that its only longshoremen were ghosts.

Mama and Saul looked out over the city with Sir Gilbert,
Captain of the Guard under protest—he had protested not
being able to ride with the queen and her army. The castle
stood atop a talus slope, kept bare of all trees and bushes,
sheep-cropped to smooth lawn. A road wound down its sides
from the drawbridge to the first houses, a hundred yards
away. There it turned into a broad avenue that ran straight
downhill, between half-timbered houses, inns, and stores, to
the gate in the city wall.

Outside that wall lay a ring of more modest houses and
commercial buildings. The boulevard ran on from the gate,
all the way down to the river. There, the buildings were all
warehouses and chandlers' shops, with a generous sprin-
kling of taverns with upstairs rooms for sailors between
ships—all dark now, emptied of valuables and people.

Sir Gilbert chafed under restraint. "We could have fought

them on the docks, Lady Mantrell! We could have prevented them from coming ashore!"

"You could not, Sir Gilbert, and you know it," she said gently. "They would have poured in more soldiers than we have in the castle, hundreds more, perhaps thousands. Your men would have died to no purpose."

Saul nodded. "Even if you had fought them off, they would have just landed someplace else. No, better to clear the docks and let them come ashore where we can keep an eye on them."

"But the city!"

"Your men-at-arms have already evacuated most of the civilians," Mama said. "They found shelter in the parts of the city away from the river, did they not?"

"Yes, and the movement out of the city has begun. With any luck, most of the common folk will be safe in the hills before the Moors draw their siege lines tight."

"And you sent the merchant ships out upstream in a timely manner," Mama said. "I think the citizens who have fortified their houses along the streets will prove all the defense Bordestang needs."

"The Moors could overcome them in a day!"

"Yes, but it is the castle they seek, not the port or the suburbs, and staying to overcome the civilian defenders would cost the Moors lives they need for their siege. No, they shall secure the boulevard that leads up to our walls and be content with that. Then your militia may slip away unnoticed, if it is necessary."

"It will be, if the siege lasts longer than a week!"

"Then we must see it does not," Mama said calmly.

The Moorish ships were able to sail right up to the docks, tie up, and unload their cargoes of men and horses without having to ferry them ashore in longboats. Then, to Saul's and Mama's astonishment, the ships not only shoved off and made room for the next to unload—they sailed back down the river and out of sight!

"They are leaving their men!" Mama exclaimed. "Are

they so sure of victory that they do not even feel the need to secure their line of retreat?"

"No, milady," Sir Gilbert said, his face somber. "They disdain retreat. Those ships are returning to Morocco for more soldiers. The Moors will have to conquer Bordestang, or die."

Papa finished the last bite of beef jerky stew and wiped his bowl with a sigh. "Well, that was filling."

"But nothing more?" Matt shrugged apologetically. "Sorry about the menu. Too bad there isn't a little game in this woodlot."

"Too many refugees, even this far from the border?"

"More likely the hazards of traveling with a dragon," Matt told him. "Just think how much slower we'd be going without him."

"Think how much more quickly you would go if I did not need to land every time you did see a heat-flickering in the air or even the smallest whirlwind," Stegoman huffed.

"Yeah, but who knows how many djinn we've avoided this way?" Matt pointed out. "Besides, we're halfway to the Pyrenees—not bad, for one day's travel."

"If you must say so," Stegoman grumped.

"I do," Matt told him. "What's the matter? Still hungry?"

"Nay. The roebuck that I seized from the air was ample."

"Look, I told you it would taste better if you'd let me cook it a little," Matt said. "Just a few turns over a hot fire . . ."

"And it would be inedible," the dragon huffed. "Seared roebuck? Disgusting!"

"I must agree." Papa looked up from rinsing his bowl. "I prefer my steaks rare, too."

"Not as rare as he likes 'em," Matt retorted. "I know what I tell the waitress when I'm ordering well done, but he takes it literally."

"Perhaps, but deer don't moo," Papa said.

"Yeah, I know the lowdown, and I know he isn't really grouchy because of his dinner," Matt sighed. "He's just impatient because of the delay."

"Impatient? From what little I know of medieval travel, he has taken us much faster than any horse could!"

"And the Mahdi will wait." Matt finished washing his bowl and put it back in his pack. "That is, unless he's marching our way. Got a blanket, Papa? The spring's still early enough to have chilly nights."

"A blanket? I have none," said a husky contralto that made every male hormone stand up and take notice. "May I share yours?"

Matt jumped to his feet—this was one antagonist he didn't want to catch him lying down—and turned slowly, forcing a smile. "Why, Lakshmi! Nice of you to stop by!"

"When night fell, I thought of you." The djinna was in her human-size form, fairly glowing with desire. She stepped very close to Matt, murmuring, "When the nights are chill, beings nestle against one another to stay warm."

"Oh, it's not too cold for more than a blanket," Matt assured her. He held up his poncho on display—right between them. "See? Nice, tight weave."

"I can weave tightly, too," Lakshmi breathed, leaning closer. "Allow me to demonstrate."

Matt swallowed through a suddenly tight throat. "Look, I told you that you were free to go where you wanted!"

"I did," she said.

Her sensuous aura was so strong that it bypassed Matt's mind and heart completely, going straight to his glands. No matter how much he was in love with Alisande, this female spirit had a very commanding presence—and he was all too present to her commands.

Still, the thought of Alisande was a defense in itself. "I hate to say no—you don't know how much I hate to!—but I'm very thoroughly married."

"Thoroughly?" The djinna frowned. "One is married or one is not! How can one be more thoroughly so, or less?"

"Uhhhh . . ." Matt thought fast, trying to put words to what he meant. "By how deeply one is in love, and whether or not one has children."

"Are the small ones so great a seal upon union as that?"

"They are," Papa said, "when a man loves them. The more souls he loves, the more deeply he wishes to stay where they are."

"And you?" Lakshmi turned to him, her allure suddenly blazing at him—and leaving Matt shaking with relief. "Your child is grown," the djinna said. "He has left your house. You should be less thoroughly married now."

Papa didn't even look tense; he only smiled, a gleam appearing in his eye. "Ah, but twenty years sharing the pain and the burden and the joy of his upbringing—the bond that grew between us in that time is far deeper and far, far stronger than it was when we married. Even then, it was so powerful we could not imagine it being any stronger."

"Ah, but has that bond ever been tested?" Lakshmi asked, hips rolling as she stepped closer to Papa.

"Several times." Now it was Papa who stepped closer, the gleam growing more intense. "It has always held."

"But there have been times when you wished it had not?" Lakshmi breathed, swaying very close indeed.

Matt stared, scandalized. Papa had been tempted? While he was *Papa*?

"I have never wished for that bond to be broken, or even loosened," Papa said firmly, though his eyes said otherwise.

"But you have lusted after other women," Lakshmi insisted.

"Lust is not love, beauteous lady," Papa sighed, "and gives rise to no bond. Rather, once it is satisfied, it loses what little bond it had."

Lakshmi recoiled, revolted. "What strange creatures you humans are! If a djinni desires a djinna, he will desire her whenever he sees her!"

"We do not speak of desire," Papa said. The gleam was still there, but his smile turned sad. "We speak of a bond, an invisible tie that holds two people together for a lifetime, a tie that is like a growing vine and must be nourished and watered and given sunlight, but which thus grows stronger and stronger with every month that passes."

Lakshmi eyed him warily, turning pensive. "I could almost wish my soul was such that it could know the delights of which you speak."

"Almost?" Papa asked, still sadly smiling.

"Almost," Lakshmi confirmed. "To a djinna who has only now regained her freedom, a bond smacks too much of bondage. Does it not chafe you? Do you not long for freedom?"

"There was a year or two when I did," Papa admitted, "but even then, I wished even more to be with my Jimena. For all the rest of my married years, I have scarcely missed my freedom at all, for I have treasured my love far more."

Lakshmi shivered. "Yes, I wish I could know such a feeling," she said slowly, "but not for long. Still, that is not possible, is it?"

Papa shook his head, eyes glowing. "If it is only for a short time, it cannot give the warmth and closeness and delight of which I speak. Do not misunderstand me—there is great pleasure in falling in love for a few months, even a few years—but it is a different sort of delight entirely."

"Oh, a pox upon it!" Lakshmi jammed her fists on her hips, stamping her foot.

Matt had to catch his breath all over again at the vividness her anger gave her.

"It is disgusting, it is outrageous, and I must be done with it!" Lakshmi threw an arm around Papa, growing as she did, so that it only took her one step to seize Matt in her other arm. She continued to grow, swelling into a giant again, the men clasped to her bosom like toddlers as she sprang into the air. Her contralto deepened to basso, almost too deep to hear. "I shall take you to the Mahdi, and be done with you for once and for all! When you have come to your goal, you shall have no need to travel where I may see you!"

Behind them, a roar of outrage split the night with flickering flame.

"Follow, dragon!" the djinna called. "But do not land within the ranks of the Moors, for they are desert folk, and may take a fancy to reptile's flesh!"

Somehow, her expansion in size killed off Matt's lust completely; she no longer seemed human. He glanced down past the huge curve of her bosom to the ground far below and swallowed heavily. He hoped she was still enough enamored of him to hold tightly.

CHAPTER 15

"Go with God, and good luck ride with you!" Sir Gilbert clapped each man on the shoulder.

"Thank you, sir," each said. Then the postern gate opened, and Marl, Hode, and Doman led their horses out into the night, mounted, and sped away under the stars, with Bordestang and its castle between themselves and the Moors.

At the foot of the slope they came to a crossroads. Hode rode to the left, to join the river upstream, following it away from the Moorish army. Doman turned to the right, riding toward the distant bulk of the forest, and Marl rode straight ahead, down a road that would curve east, then south toward the mountains.

Marl rode through the night, rested in the morning, then rode through the afternoon. He slept that night, then rode out again at sunrise. The Pyrenees were a dark line on the horizon ahead when he came to the fork in the road, and the Moorish patrol emerged from behind a roadside thicket to surround and imprison him.

Hode rode along the river through the night, kept riding after dawn, then dismounted, hid, ate, and slept in the afternoon. He began his ride again in the evening, and came to the forest as the day was breaking. He slept in a thicket at the edge of the trees and woke at sunset. He came out of the thicket, leading his horse, and found the boat waiting. He froze in surprise, and the soldiers stepped out from behind trees to surround him. One look at their conical helmets, and he knew he had failed.

Doman rode through the night but, when the sky lightened, drew off to find a hiding place, chewing hardtack as he searched. He slept in a barn and woke at dusk, saddled his horse, and rode on through the night, munching his hard biscuits on horseback whenever he grew hungry. He rode around the forest in the dark until he came to a road that led east, and followed it till dawn, when he hid and slept again. When he woke, he heard hooves approaching, and had just time enough to soothe his horse Bubaru and hold its mouth shut while voices spoke in foreign words outside the cave in which they'd hidden. When the hoofbeats faded into the distance, he came out and rode again.

The third night found him in the mountains. He was climbing a mountain path scarcely four feet wide when a giant rat came scuttling out of the rocks ahead. Bubaru shied from the creature, and only hauling savagely on the reins and kicking with the off-side spur kept him from going over the edge. Then the horrible rodent ran at them, baring long, slimy teeth, reaching high to bite the horse's side, Doman's leg, whatever it could reach. Again Doman spurred frantically to keep from going over the edge while he drew his sword and plunged it down the rat's throat. The beast screamed, scrambling, but was dead as it fell over the cliff, almost dragging Doman with it—but he had the presence of mind to let go of the sword at the last moment. He felt horribly vulnerable without it, but he was alive. Bubaru took a deal of calming, but finally they went on their way. Doman still trembled. Were such rats native to the mountains? He'd never heard of any. Or had a Moorish sorcerer set it to guard the passes? If so, did that sorcerer now know where Doman was?

"You're borrowing trouble," he scolded himself, and tried to shut off his thoughts as he rode on up the pathway through the night—but he couldn't help thinking that he might switch to daytime riding now.

By the end of the week, an army of thirty thousand Moors was camped around Bordestang, with more arriving every day. Gilbert and Mama stood with Saul on the castle battlements, looking down over the capital at the new city of tents that had grown up past the frame houses beyond the wall. To their right, a dozen ships lay moored, having just disgorged their cargoes of men and horses. They would sail with the morning tide.

"They will stage their assault soon," the young monkknight said, "perhaps even tomorrow."

"It's a wonder they haven't attacked already," Saul said.

"They were wary," Gilbert told him, "because we did not resist their coming ashore."

"Yes, that makes sense," Mama said. "They fear a trap, do they not?"

"When they come and find the docks deserted, and all the houses outside the walls too? When they find their moorings ready and their quarters swept and waiting? Yes, I would be wary, too."

"Which explains why they set up their tents instead of moving into the empty houses." Saul nodded. "Too bad—we had some nice booby traps planted. So what makes you think they're going to attack tomorrow?"

"It is in the air. Can you not feel it?"

"I can," Mama said. "Their fear has faded. They know now that we cannot meet them in the open field, but must wait upon their siege."

"And their scouts can find nothing to fear, no traps or spirit-weirs," Gilbert agreed.

"Spirit-weir?" Saul looked up, interested. "What's that?"

"A sort of trap for men's enthusiasm." Gilbert sounded surprised. "There is also a trap that gathers in ghosts, to loose them upon an enemy. I am astonished you did not know of these, Master Saul."

"Hey, I'm always willing to learn." Saul turned to watch the last fingernail of sun slip below the horizon. "You sure they're going to attack tomorrow?"

Trumpets sounded in the distance. Deep-voiced drums rolled. The Moorish soldiers came riding to assemble in the plaza where the boulevard debouched onto the docks.

"I was mistaken," Gilbert said. "They attack tonight! Beware sorcery, Master Saul. Why else would they charge at dusk?"

The first riders trotted into the boulevard as others were coming up from the plaza, while a steady stream of riders poured into it from the camp. The army rode up toward the town wall, four abreast.

As Doman rode down to the foothills, dirt and dust suddenly boiled in front of him. Bubaru shied, whinnying fear, and Doman clutched at his empty scabbard, heart racing. Then the dust cleared, and a huge man floated there before him, bare-chested, bearded, and turbaned, with legs tapering into a wisp. "Queen's man, where do you go?"

"To—to join my queen," Doman stammered.

"What message have you for her?"

Doman thought fast. "That I am well at last, and able to fight with her troops!"

The genie drifted closer, looming over him with menace, glowering, and Bubaru shied again. The genie put out a huge hand that grew and grew on an arm that stretched around the horse's rump to hold the horse in place as he demanded, "Empty your pouch!"

Doman stretched his arms wide, heart thumping, overwhelmingly glad that Lady Mantrell had entrusted the word's to Doman's memory and not to paper. "I bear none!"

"Your saddlebags, then!"

Doman took out journeybread and cheese, then turned the pouches upside down to show there was nothing more.

"Even so, why should I take a chance?" The genie scowled like a thundercloud. "Each soldier less is one more who cannot slay a Moor!"

Doman raised a hand to ward off any blow that might come and cried out the verse Lady Mantrell had given him, though the words made no sense to him.

> "Whatever spirits aid Mantrell,
> Come to me, and grief dispel!

Rescue me from hateful shades!
Ward me now from spells and blades!"

The chant had its effect, though—the genie halted and stared. "What good can the Queen's Wizard do you? He is far from here!"

A gust of wind blew past Doman's ear, and a huge but somehow feminine voice commanded, "Leave the boy, djinni!"

The genie stared up, awed. So did Doman, for he found himself gazing up and up past gauzy trousers that grew from a point to hint at perfectly tapering thighs swelling into the alluring curves of hips. He stared, astounded, past a magnificent bosom to a face that awed him with its beauty—and with its anger.

He wondered why he felt not the slightest ounce of desire.

"As you command, my princess!" The genie bowed and, bowing, disappeared.

The huge djinna glared down at little Doman. "Who bade you summon me with that verse?"

"The—the Lady Mantrell!" Doman stammered.

"His wife?" The djinna stared—then frowned. "Perhaps she knows more than a Christian should." The huge face turned brooding for a moment. "Or a Muslim, for that matter—especially a spouse." Then her eyes snapped as they focused on Doman again. "Begone, wretch! Do not recite that verse again—and tell no one that you have seen me!"

Gilbert grinned. "Their mounts will do them no good, in a narrow street facing a city wall. What do they think to do—stand on their saddles and leap to the top of a thirty-foot wall?"

All along the city ramparts, archers nocked arrows to their bowstrings. Other soldiers readied small catapults, while still others stood by with forked sticks to push away scaling ladders. Spears lay ready to hand in case some Moors actually managed to reach the battlements.

"A snake of fire!" Gilbert pointed toward the river.

Mama and Saul spun to look. A trail of flame ran along the surface of the water, blossoming into a fence of fire.

"It cannot be!" Gilbert cried. "Water cannot burn!"

A moan of fear went up from the soldiers on the battlements. Men crossed themselves.

"Water can't burn, but something floating on that water can!" Saul grabbed the knight's shoulder, pointing. "Can't you see where it's going?"

Gilbert gave a shout of delight, fear forgotten. "Toward the Moorish ships!"

The trail of fire expanded, mushrooming into a blazing lake that swallowed all the anchored ships. The few that were moored at the docks stood unscathed—until each exploded into flame.

"The Moors are burning their only escape!" Gilbert cried.

The sound reached them, and the town shook with the soft basso roar of the explosion. A cry of fear went up from the Moorish army, and the advance stalled as all men turned to watch the fire.

"No, it was not their doing," Mama said. "They will blame us!"

"Hey, cool." Saul grinned. "Let 'em think we're that much more powerful, and that much more ruthless. The truth would just make them cocky."

"There is truth in what you say," Gilbert said, frowning, "but who *did* set that blaze?"

The Moors poured onto the docks. Buckets appeared, and they formed chains to try to drown the fire; each charred ship meant fewer reinforcements.

A brisk breeze sprang up, fairly sopping with humidity. Mama and Saul stared in surprise as storm clouds gathered over the burning ships. Then Mama cried, "The Moorish sorcerers! They seek to drown the blaze with rain!"

"Son of a gun!" Saul exclaimed in admiration. "Would I ever love to have those boys handy in a Nebraska summer!"

Mama frowned, concentrating, making shooing motions while she chanted. The clouds stopped moving together, hanging motionless. They darkened, and the rain-breeze freshened, sharpened. The first drops began to fall.

Mama scolded them sternly in Spanish, waving her hands, palms up.

The raindrops froze in midair. More and more fell, but held firm at an invisible line.

"Witch Doctor!" Gilbert caught Saul's shoulder with one hand and pointed with the other. "Look! At the edge of the crowd, there in the plaza!"

Saul looked, and saw, here and there, a Moor clutching his chest and falling from his horse. Their friends didn't seem to notice—everyone was too busy trying to save the ships. "Who're the snipers on our side, Gilbert?"

"None of our folk are down there, unless it be some householders who seek to protect their dwellings!"

But the Battle of the Fireships claimed Saul's attention. He saw Mama clenching her fists, arms curved as though she were holding up a barbell. Drops of perspiration began to appear on her forehead.

Saul realized what she was doing. "You can't hold a ton of water all by yourself, Lady Mantrell. We'd better slope the line, make it a roof." He propped his fingers together like a rooftop and tried to think of a verse.

But Mama beat him to it. Her voice turned sonorous as she chanted in Spanish. Saul managed to pick out the words for "forbidding" and for "rain." It gave him an idea.

"Get busy on a day that's fair and bright,
And patch the old roof till it's good and tight!
Then you'll never have to worry, and you'll never have
   a pain—
Your roof will never leak no matter how much rain!"

The water began to flow down, running at an angle until it splashed into the river—fifty feet to each side of the ships.

The flames started to die down anyway.

"They are quenching the blaze by commands alone!" Mama cried.

"Well, we'll just have to see about that," Saul said, grinning, and recited,

> "Fire answers fire, and through their pale flames
> Each pyrotic sees the other's umbered face:
> Steel rasps on flint, and sparks dry wood ablaze.
> Piercing the night's dull ear, infernoes race."

The fire billowed higher. For a split second, Saul saw a face in the flames, a familiar face whose eyes widened in amazement as it recognized Saul; then it was gone. The Witch Doctor cried out, then muttered to himself, "No, can't be! He's not a magus!"

The Moors seemed to have forgotten that the ships weren't going to take them back; they churned into a shouting mob, pouring bucketful after bucketful onto the wharfside ships.

Saul grinned and chanted,

> "Pour it on, invincible!
> But let it be immiscible.
> Oil in water, though unseen—
> Each bucket now pours kerosene!"

The ships exploded into flame, and the Moors staggered back with cries of distress, certainly never noticing that more and more of their mates lay dead on the fringe of the crowd with crossbow bolts in their chests.

"That's not just a few outraged citizens, Gilbert," Saul said, frowning. "I think we have some unexpected allies."

"Yes, but can we afford allies we do not know?" Gilbert asked nervously.

"I know what you mean," Saul said grimly. "I've had people pitch into a fight to help me out, but I wouldn't have wanted to know them if I hadn't been distracted at the time." Then he noticed that the ship fires were starting to gutter. "I think you can let the rain come down now, Lady Mantrell. The ships have burned down to the waterline."

Mama dropped her hands, trembling with relief, and gasped for air. "That was a heavy burden indeed!"

"Heavy, but very effective," Saul assured her. "I just hope we like the guy who started those fires." He frowned. "Can't be who I think it is . . ."

A moan swept the Moorish ranks as they saw that their transportation was charcoal. They began to mill about, and the sound rising from their ranks was angry.

"Here we go." Saul tensed. "Payback time."

A howl of rage went up, and the mob surged toward the boulevard.

"They've found the dead bodies," Saul said, leaning on a crenel to look, every muscle tense. "They're chasing somebody!"

Shouting, the mob streamed into the boulevard, most of them on foot. The few horsemen couldn't make much headway among all the infantry. Light gleamed off scimitars and spears, but the Moorish footmen could only come twelve abreast in the boulevard, and the whole front rank suddenly fell with crossbow bolts in their chests. The second rank tripped over them and went sprawling, then the third rank and the fourth. The mob stalled, milling and trying to sort themselves out with angry cries at one another.

A black horse burst from an alleyway and galloped up-hill. A score of dark-clad men burst from the alleys and ran after it.

The Moors howled and scrambled over their fallen comrades. The second-rankers struggled frantically to their feet. Finally the whole mob was charging again.

By that time, though, the black horse was almost to the gates. The dark-clad rider waved and shouted. The officer on the wall shouted back, raising his arm.

"It is him!" Saul cried.

"Who?" Mama demanded.

The gates groaned open, and the rider reined in, dancing his horse to the side of the road. His sword flashed in the light of the fires as his men streamed past him.

The mob saw the open gate and belled like hounds sighting a fox. They actually crowded aside to let a few riders pass, and half a dozen horsemen charged uphill. Arrows flashed, but fell short of the dark-clad men.

On the wall, the officer shouted and swung his arm down. Catapults snapped, and fireballs arced through the air.

The Moorish horsemen shouted and pulled up sharply. The fireballs crashed into the street before them, breaking apart into shards of blazing tow. The Moors hurdled them, rode between them, and charged uphill again. The footmen streamed after.

The officer on the wall bawled again, raising his arm and chopping down. A flight of arrows sprang out, arcing toward the Moors. They saw in time and tried to back away, but the men pushing behind them prevented retreat, and half a dozen fell. So did two horsemen; the others bellowed in rage and charged at full gallop, hanging their bows on saddle hooks and drawing scimitars.

The last of the dark-clad men ran through the gate, and the huge portals began to swing shut. The officer shouted and chopped with his arm again. Another flight of arrows sprang out. The Moors reined in, cursing, and the arrows fell short. They waited for the rest of their army to catch up— and another flight of arrows shot up. The Moors retreated beyond bowshot, but the dark-clad men scrambled up to the wall and loosed a hail of crossbow bolts. Two more Moorish horsemen fell; the others retreated farther, commanding the mob to halt. Reluctantly, they did, milling about, shaking their fists at the defenders, and cursing in Arabic and Berber.

The black horse trotted up toward the castle, two knights of the guard escorting him.

"Now we will learn who our unexpected ally is," Mama said. "Can he really be the one who burned the ships?"

"Only if he knows about Greek fire," Saul answered.

"I have heard of it," Sir Gilbert said, "and if he is a knight, he may have, too. He may even know the making of it. He could be our firestarter, Lady Mantrell."

"How?" Saul challenged. "The line of fire came from the breakwater, not the docks."

"He is mounted," Sir Gilbert said. "He could have set the flames, then ridden to join his men in the alleyways."

A cry of delight went up from the gatehouse, and the soldiers cheered as the black horse came riding into the bailey—a black horse with a knight in black armor.

Saul stared. "It *is* him!"

"Who?" Mama demanded. "May not I know him, when even your soldiers seem to?"

"They do indeed," Gilbert said, grinning from ear to ear. "Heaven be praised! I need no longer command this garrison! But how he knew of our plight I cannot guess."

"He knows everything that goes on in Europe, especially if it's dangerous," Saul said. Then, as the rider came trotting up below them, he told Mama, "Let's go downstairs—I want to introduce you. This is Sir Guy Toutarien, the Black Knight, and one of your son's strongest allies." He started down the stairs, calling, "Hail, Sir Guy! Come on and meet the family!"

The Pyrenees loomed high in front of the army by the time Doman caught up with them. One sentry ran ahead to tell the queen of his coming; two others escorted him in.

"Well done, faithful servant!" she said, and the soldier glowed with praise from his sovereign. She asked, "Was your passage dangerous?"

"I went as secretly as I could, Majesty," he answered, "but by sunset of my first day, they were on my trail—how, I do not know."

"A rider coming from Bordestang and following my army would be cause enough for their concern." But her brow creased with concern of her own. "What manner of hounds did they set on your trail?"

What could Doman say? A giant rat wasn't a hound. Of course, there had been hounds of a sort, and Doman shuddered at the thought of the huge things, heads tall as his horse's shoulder, with eyes glowing red as fire—but with dark green scales instead of fur, and beaks instead of muzzles. They had run on all fours like dogs, but huge leathery wings had unfolded from their backs as they had sprung into the air to search for him. He had taken cover at the first sound of their strange cries, half bay and half crow, and lay huddled in a thicket holding Bubaru's nose desperately closed. The horse kept trying to tug its head free, eyes wide and rolling with fear, but Doman hung on with a death grip. He was very glad that he had waded a hundred feet down every stream he'd come to.

Bubaru jerked its head, frightened by the strange creatures— Doman wondered if it could smell them, or if it was taking fright from sight alone. Certainly that was horrifying enough. If the horse whinnied, they were lost . . .

But Doman kept firm hold over its muzzle, and the horse gave only a grunt or two. The lizard-hounds didn't hear; they banked away and flew off into the night, their strange cries dwindling behind them.

And, of course, Doman remembered the beauiful spirit and her command to tell no one of their encounter—so when the queen seemed concerned about his journey, all Doman could say was "It had its worrying moments, Your Majesty, but I am come safely to bring you the message that Lady Mantrell sends."

Alisande frowned at the title—it reminded her of an oversight—but said, "Speak."

"Your castle stands," Doman recited, "but hundreds of Moorish ships have come sailing into Bordestang's harbor, bringing thousands of soldiers to besiege your city. More come every day."

"A siege!" Alisande stared, thunderstruck, and in an instant the strategy was clear to her. "They waited till my army and I were gone, then struck!"

She didn't ask how the ships had come so far without hindrance—she saw that clearly, too, and knew with bitter certainty that she must build a fleet, and quickly.

But if the Moors' strategy was clear, so was her own, and her obligation to her countrymen. Her heart twisted within her as she realized what she must do, and that she must leave Matt and his father to fend for themselves.

Her face became a granite mask. "Turn the army! We must march back toward Bordestang, and quickly!"

"Return to Bordestang?" Her aide, Lord Gautier, stared. "Why, Majesty? Surely the castle can hold long enough for us to put paid to these Moors!"

"They are doughtier soldiers than you know, my lord, and there are very many of them," Alisande replied. "They might occupy us for a very long time—but that is of little consequence. What matters most is that, by returning, we may catch one army of Moors between the city and our ranks."

Her aide's eyes widened. "Why, so we may! Surely King Rinaldo can wait a few days longer for our rescue!"

Again, foreboding shadowed Alisande. It was excellent strategy on the Mahdi's part, to prevent her from coming to Rinaldo's aid. She wondered if he might really manage to conquer northern Ibile while she countermarched to save her capital, and if his armies might then prove too strong for her.

Her face stayed frozen while she told Lord Gautier, "Our obligation is to Merovence first, and our more important foes are those already on our own soil. Time enough to keep other enemies from crossing the Pyrenees when we have routed those already here."

"Of course!" her aide cried. "Why did I not see it? We may strike down tens of thousands of them, and there will be that many fewer to fight in Ibile!"

"We cannot let the chance pass us by." Sudden anxiety twisted Alisande's heart again. "But O, my husband! How shall he fare?"

"The Lord Wizard?" Lord Gautier stared. "How could we help him, Majesty? He has gone to face the paynim with only his magic for his strength!"

"But he may be relying upon my army to rescue him, if he encounters magic too strong for him!"

"Magic too strong for the Lord Wizard?" Lord Gautier

exclaimed in disbelief. "Majesty, he has always been able to spell his way out of any trap into which he has fallen!"

Alisande's anxiety abated a little. "There is some truth in that . . ."

"Great truth, be sure! Lord Matthew has a knack of summoning up whatever sort of magical friend he needs, to face any given crisis." He smiled. "Rather, ask how we will manage without *his* aid!"

Alisande wished he hadn't brought up that point. "We can, at least, send a messenger to tell him what we do! See that this courier who brought the news is given meat, ale, and rest, then send him after the Lord Wizard!"

"Majesty, I shall." Her aide bowed. "I know it is useless to tell you not to be concerned for your husband, but I shall say it anyway. No matter what his danger, the Lord Wizard shall prevail."

"I hope you are right, my lord." But Alisande wondered just what kind of predicament Matt would get himself into this time. Considering that his goal was to meet the Mahdi, she was more afraid of his succeeding than of his failing.

"*That's* the Mahdi's camp?" Matt stared down, appalled at acre after acre of campfires.

"Surely you are not surprised!" Lakshmi boomed. "You knew his armies were mighty, did you not?"

"Yeah, but not so close! I mean, this is just on the other side of the Pyrenees!" Matt glanced back at the bulk of the mountains, looming huge in the darkness, black against the stars. "I didn't know they'd marched this far! Weren't they supposed to be attacking the north?"

"They did, then gave over that campaign quite suddenly, to march east to this camp. Did you not know all of Ibile is theirs, save the northeast?"

"Only the northeast, now? I thought it was the whole north! So the whole point of the attack was to secure this base, huh? But why?"

"Perhaps the Mahdi is more concerned about the Queen than the King of Ibile," Papa offered.

"Really reassuring," Matt growled. "I'm beginning to have a very bad feeling about this."

"I shall leave you and be done!" Lakshmi declared. "Where would you stand?"

"Well, facing the Mahdi, of course!" Matt said. "That's what we've come for, isn't it?"

"Perhaps just outside his tent," Papa suggested, "so that his guards may announce us."

"Announce you? They would slay you on the spot!" Lakshmi told him. "If you would meet the Mahdi, then meet him you shall!" She caught them to her and began to spin around and around, chanting a verse in Arabic, becoming translucent, then transparent, then a whirlwind. Matt shouted in protest as the wind that had been Lakshmi whirled him about and about, and the whole world became a blur of darkness streaked with orange light.

CHAPTER 16

Matt's stomach churned even faster than the whirlwind. "Somebody stop the merry-go-round!"

"Close your eyes!" Papa shouted.

Matt squeezed his eyes shut, hoping Papa was right and that it would help the motion sickness. He wished for a Dramamine, but had sense enough not to say it out loud.

Then the ground jarred up against his feet, canvas was flapping about him, and he spun one last time, then fell over. Dizzy and seasick, terrified that enemies might jump him, he tried to push himself to his feet, groping for his sword hilt.

Sure enough, rough voices shouted, and rougher hands clamped down on his own. Somebody snatched the sword hilt out from under his hand; somebody else yanked his arms up high behind his back. He bent forward, still trying to struggle up from his knees.

"No more!" a clear tenor commanded. "I must speak clearly with men who come by such magic as this!"

Finally Matt's vision cleared, and he found himself staring at a Persian carpet. Panting, he glanced around frantically and saw Papa kneeling, bent forward, arms forced up behind his back by a robed and turbaned African. Matt felt massive relief that Papa was okay, or at least no worse off than he himself. He resisted the urge to transport them both out of there with a spell. After all, he'd worked very hard to come here, hadn't he? He turned his gaze forward and stared up at the figure reclining before him in a sea of cushions.

"I am Tafas bin Daoud," the young man said. "Who are you, and how have you come here?"

Matt stared, and had to suppress an urge to call the roll. The kid looked scarcely old enough to have graduated from high school. He was slender and fine-featured, with dark skin, a high forehead, straight nose, and smooth cheeks— either he had a really excellent barber, or he had just had this week's shave. But his chin was strong, the set of his mouth was determined, and his eyes flashed with a lively and curious intelligence. Somehow, Matt felt certain he would have been an ideal student in an American university.

But he wasn't in a classroom; he was in a tent big enough to be a small house, with tapestries hanging as partitions between rooms and big, stern-faced men in turbans and robes watching him with eagle eyes over hawk noses, hands fingering the hilts of scimitars and curved knives. Some of them were very dark-skinned, some light, some every gradation between; some were clearly Africans and some equally clearly Arabs. Some wore mustaches, some were clean-shaven—but all looked ready to kill Matt on the spot. They were only waiting for the Mahdi's nod—and he was only waiting to hear what these strangers said.

Matt had better make it good.

"Good evening . . ." Matt wondered about the form of address, and settled for ". . . Lord Tafas. I am Matthew Mantrell, Lord Wizard of Merovence." He snapped a glare over his shoulder at the man holding him. The soldier stared in surprise; his hold loosened for a second, and Matt forced himself to his feet. "May I introduce my father, Ramón, Lord Mantrell."

Papa looked up, eyebrows raised at the title.

The Mahdi's eyes widened. "Ramón? You are of Ibile?" He finally seemed to notice Papa's indelicate position and waved impatiently at the guard holding him. "Let him stand— we must honor enemies of such caliber."

The guard reluctantly let Papa up, but kept hold of his hands.

"I am not of Ibile, Lord Tafas," Papa said, "but my grandfather was. He crossed the Pyrenees in his youth to escape an evil tyrant."

"Gordogrosso." Tafas nodded. "Yes, the sage could not bid us march against Ibile until that corrupted king's vicious force was gone."

Matt thought of explaining that Papa had been talking about Franco, not Gordogrosso, but decided to let it pass.

"So now you come to reclaim your father's estate," the Mahdi inferred.

"No, Lord Tafas, we come to protest servants of the same God fighting one another."

The kid on the throne stared, amazed by Papa's audacity. So did Matt, though he'd been planning to say the same thing. The guards and officers around the room muttered in anger.

Tafas turned to Matt. "Do you, too, wish to follow your father's cause?"

"Of course." This wasn't the time to explain who was following whom. "But at the moment, Lord Tafas, I'm astounded that you have come so far from Gibraltar so fast."

Tafas waved the hidden compliment away. "These cowards of Ibile do not even stay to fight—they are gone before our army so much as sees their towns."

So King Rinaldo was evacuating the towns that he knew he couldn't defend, and avoiding a pitched battle. Wise. Probably overly cautious in getting the civilians out—Tafas's troops seemed to be tightly disciplined—but soldiers on campaign had reputations for their dealings with civilians, so Rinaldo was probably wise. Besides, though most Muslims didn't convert people by the sword, there was no guarantee they wouldn't start, and there were always people hungry for martyrdom.

It also smacked of Rinaldo's gathering his forces. He wondered what the King of Ibile was planning.

Tafas' turn. "By what magic have you come here?"

"Oh, that?" Matt tried to be nonchalant. "A djinna gave us a ride."

A murmur of surprise and wariness passed through the tent, and Tafas stared, a piercing look that seemed to go right through Matt. The young man asked, "A djinna? A female of the djinn? They are rarely seen!"

"Yes," Matt agreed, "but very much worth the seeing. Seemed to be powerful enough, too."

"How did you compel one of the djinn?" the Mahdi asked, wide-eyed.

"I didn't." Matt shook his head. "Just the other way, in fact. Her mortal master sicced her on me, sent her to try to kill me, so I had to free her from his spell in self-defense."

The murmur was one of awe and fear now, and Tafas exclaimed, "*Freed* her? But a djinna must have been compelled by the Seal of Solomon!"

"Oh, I doubt that," Matt said. "I mean, once you seal a djinni in a bottle with the Seal of Solomon, he stays there—and if you let him out, he's a wild force. No, tying djinn to lamps and rings and such is another spell entirely."

The whole crowd stared. Even Tafas seemed suddenly nervous. "You are indeed a master of magic, are you not?"

For the umpteenth time, Matt felt like an absolute charlatan. He'd been studying everything he could find about the lore of magic ever since he'd come to Merovence, but still felt that he barely knew how much he didn't know, and it didn't help to remember that every brand-new Ph.D. in any field of study felt the same way. But in this universe, poetry was magic, and he did know verse. "Let's say I'm an apt student."

"Surely if you can loose the djinn from their bonds of magic, you are a master, not a student!"

"Well, yes, but we're never done learning, are we?"

"Are we not?" Tafas asked, round-eyed, and watching him, Matt could see that the so-called Mahdi had just absorbed something vital—and had suffered a major blow to his overconfidence.

Suddenly, Matt felt vastly wiser than the boy, and very, very old. "No one can make you keep learning, milord—but I've seen people who stopped. They grow stiff and narrow in their minds; they see less and less of the world around them, and never realize that it has changed since they were young, when everything was new and they delighted in each discovery. After a while, they grow so bored with life that they start wanting to die."

Tafas almost managed to keep his shudder from showing. "A horrible fate! But how can people find new things to learn? Once you have memorized the Koran, what else is there to know?"

Somehow, Matt didn't doubt this kid had memorized every letter of the holy book. "There is an ocean of commentary, just to begin with, which is what turns a man into a quadi, a judge, or a muzzein. Then, too, did you learn strategy from the Koran, or from campaigning?"

"I see your thought." Tafas carefully evaded the question. "Perhaps it is that the Koran is life, and there is always more to learn about it."

Some of the older men around the room were frowning. They had the look of clerics about them, and Matt decided to tread warily. "God is infinite, milord. We can never be done learning about Him—but we must never shirk the obligation to do so, either."

One or two of the old men nodded grudgingly, and Tafas' eyes brightened. "That is quite true. Really, for an unbeliever, you show remarkable knowledge of the Faith. Are you sure you do not wish to profess Islam?"

Time to tread warily here, but the pride in Papa's eyes boosted Matt's confidence. "Rather, milord, I wish that all men who serve God by any name should ally with one another against the forces of Evil. Instead, we fight one another; instead, you have brought fire and sword into Ibile. Why did you not strike while Gordogrosso held this land in bondage, when your swords could have been striking the agents of Satan?"

"Why, the greatest reason is that I was too young." Tafas smiled, secure on home ground again. "As soon as I was old enough to bear arms, though, I did strike."

"But not against King Gordogrosso, who served Satan and who used evil magic to make himself young time and time again, so that he might rule Ibile for hundreds of years."

Matt frowned. "Why did the armies of Islam not surge up from Morocco when he first usurped the throne? Why didn't the Moors attack him at any time during the centuries that followed?"

Tafas frowned. "I cannot answer for men who died before I was born."

They both knew the answer, of course—that Gordogrosso was ruthless and unbelievably cruel, and would have delighted in destroying any invaders in the most painful ways possible. But Rinaldo, being devoted to God and Good and Right, would show mercy to an enemy, and wait to attack until he was sure he couldn't make peace. He also wouldn't force every available man to fight for him, throwing the untrained against the Moors to die by thousands, wearing down the invaders so that the professionals could finish them off—and he wouldn't call up demons to slaughter God-fearing enemies, either, as Gordogrosso would have done.

But there was no way to say that diplomatically; no matter how you phrased it, it would still sound like, "You guys were too chicken to attack when that ruthless sadist was on the throne, but now that the good guys have kicked him out, you've got courage enough to attack the nice ones who fight by the rules."

Instead, Matt said, "Now that devout and godly people rule Ibile, it is no time for servants of God to go fighting one another, Lord Tafas."

The old men frowned, but the Mahdi replied, quite calmly, "Islam must triumph throughout all the world, Lord Wizard. Ibile must surrender to Allah, and I am born to bring that to happen. Indeed, if Allah would have seen fit to bring me to life a hundred years ago, I would have marched an army against Ibile then, too."

Matt didn't doubt it—but he was pretty sure that Nirobus, or whoever had put Tafas up to this, wouldn't have tried to talk him into it as long as the draconian Gordogrosso was on the throne. In fact, if Matt hadn't been foolish enough to volunteer for the job in an unguarded moment, and if Heaven hadn't poured as much moral support in as it could,

Gordogrosso would still be ruling Ibile, and he doubted if any sorcerers would have tried to light a fire under Tafas then.

On the other hand, since those sorcerers probably worked for the same master as Gordogrosso, they probably wouldn't have been allowed to challenge him—though Matt had noticed that Satan didn't seem to mind how many of his servants killed each other off, as long as they didn't weaken his side in the process. Seemed to encourage them, in fact.

But that did raise the question of who Nirobus was working for. Were the Moors just pawns in a Hell-sponsored countercoup? If they were, what would happen to them when they had done Nirobus' dirty work for him? More immediately, what would happen to this clean-cut young Mahdi?

This wasn't quite the time to say that, though—Tafas wasn't exactly in a mood to listen. Instead, Matt forced a smile and tried to hide his own skepticism. "I'm sure you would have attacked against any odds, my lord—if you had been born in those days."

For a moment, the Mahdi's whole face seemed to glow. "If I had been born, and if there had been a messenger from Allah to set me the task."

Papa recognized hero worship when he heard it. "You met such a messenger, then?"

"I did," Tafas answered, beaming.

"Tell us of him," Papa invited, "of this man who taught you of Islam's destiny, and your own. What manner of clergyman was he?"

"He is a sage—not a clergyman, but a holy hermit living in a cave high in the Rif hills." Tafas' eyes glowed with fervor. "I came upon him while I was herding goats. 'Why do you sit here idle, Tafas?' he asked. Do you not see? He had never laid eyes on me, but he knew my name!"

"Very impressive." Matt could think of half a dozen ways to learn a name, only two of which involved magic. Of course, the little problem of finding a boy who was a military genius, but who didn't know it, was another matter entirely. "So it was he who showed you your destiny."

"Of course." Tafas fairly glowed with serenity, with the sure knowledge of his mission.

It bordered on the kind of smugness that always made Matt angry. He fought the emotion down and asked, "What did he look like, this sage?"

"Quite simply dressed, but his robes were of a quality of cloth that I had never seen before, like silk, only thicker. They were midnight blue, and his beard and hair were gray. His eyes, though, were the arresting, magical feature of him— shining eyes they were, of silver, and made all his face seem to glow! I knew on the instant that I addressed a holy man, an emissary of Allah."

The old men murmured pious Arabic phrases. Matt, however, recognized the description of Nirobus without any difficulty, though he would have described his eyes as gray, not silver—and the cloth had to be polyester! "He showed you your destiny by quoting the Koran?"

"No. He set his fingers on my temples and brought up visions behind my eyes—visions of the siege of Aldocer, of an army of Moors marching toward Vellese, of victory after victory to claim Ibile!"

"But no mention of the Koran," Matt said, frowning.

"No. First he sent me to wizards, who imbued me with strength and taught me the use of weapons, of the strategies and tactics of all the generals who had conquered Northern Africa before me. Then, when they judged me ready, they sent me to the mosque in Casablanca, to present myself to the muzzein. He knew me for what I was at a glance and took me to the emir, who allowed me to swear allegiance to him, then made me a general over one of his armies and enjoined me to conquer Ibile."

"Oh, I'll just bet he did." Matt had a vision of a shrewd middle-aged man recognizing a talented, charismatic upstart who could gather enough of a following to strike a coup d'etat. No wonder the emir had sent him off to pick a fight with a whole country and get himself killed. How could the emir have known Tafas would win?

But he *had* won, and that, of course, made him a real

threat to the throne. Somehow Matt had a notion that if he needed allies against Tafas, the Emir of Morocco would volunteer for the head of the list.

"But it was the sage, the holy man in the hills in his wondrous robes of blue, who gave this victory into my hand!" Tafas enthused.

"But you have said yourself that he wasn't a clergyman," Matt said, frowning. "Can he really be holy if he sends you to cause pain and suffering? Can the work he wishes you to do by fire and the sword really be God's work?"

The old men stiffened, glaring, and set up a furious babble. The soldiers stiffened, too, and took firmer grips on their spears.

But Tafas only held up his hand and waited for silence. When it came, he told Matt serenely, "Suffering is only momentary, Lord Wizard."

"Tell that to the widow who must scrape out a bare living because her husband was slain in war," Matt countered.

"Hunger is illusion," Tafas told him, still serene. "All suffering is illusion."

"Mighty painful illusion."

"It is not real people who are cut or beaten," Tafas explained. "Martyrs for Islam are snatched away at the last second, and stocks put in their place. That which is hurt is not truly human—indeed, it is only a waking dream, and does not exist at all."

Matt stared. Could the poor naive kid really believe that line?

Before he could collect his wits to answer, though, Papa frowned and said, "Shame on you, young man, for regarding people as objects, not true beings! Do you think ordinary peasants slain in war will be whisked away to Heaven before any great pain is visited upon them? Do you truly believe one of these 'stocks' you mention will be set in the place of a woman about to be raped, that the screams and cries for mercy will come from the throat of some sort of magical automaton?"

"Allah would not permit such suffering!" Tafas protested.

"Yet real people suffer every day, and a thousand times

worse when war tears them apart. Their cries will rend your ears every night, young man, and their deaths will weigh heavily on your conscience."

"Human life has value only insofar as it advances the cause of Islam!" one of the old men snapped.

"Every human life is sacred to God," Papa retorted. "You hurt Him when you hurt anyone, no matter how poor or worthless they may seem."

"Blasphemy!" the imam cried. "Mahdi, you have heard the heresy for yourself. It is thus that Christians seek to make gods of men!"

"Your war is a Holy War, O Mahdi!" cried another. "Surely you cannot believe the words of your enemies! They seek only to prevent your winning Ibile for Allah!"

"We wish Moors and Christians to be friends," Matt protested.

"Yes," snapped another old man, "with the Moors in Morocco and the Christians in Ibile! Lord Tafas, can you not see how they seek to betray your goodwill?"

"I see that they seek to thwart the cause of Islam," Tafas said heavily. "Yet we cannot simply hew off the head of the Lord Wizard of Merovence."

"If you do, you shall rid yourself of one of the most powerful of your enemies!"

Matt took a deep breath, recalling a particularly gory passage from Byron.

"If I do behead him," Tafas said, "I shall bring down the full wrath of the Queen of Merovence and all her allies, and though I am ready for her alone, I am not yet strong enough to fight such a coalition. No, I must consider most carefully how to deal with this unbeliever." His voice was very sad. "It is a shame that you cannot see the truth, Lord Wizard. I would have valued your friendship."

"That friendship was offered, Lord Tafas." Fear riddled Matt—to say the least, he and Papa were outnumbered. But he kept his voice level. "It still is."

"Such friendship cannot be lightly turned away," Tafas replied, "but I must consider carefully how I am to respond, without wronging you or betraying the cause of Islam. You will be my guests for the night, and have every comfort we can provide."

"Every luxury except freedom, huh?"

"That, I fear, I cannot accord you." Tafas waved to the guards. "Raise a pavilion and escort our guests to its shelter."

The guards bowed, then turned on Matt and Papa, half a dozen of them, huge, muscular, and glaring.

Papa braced himself, frowning.

"You are very kind," Matt said quickly. "We are fortunate in your hospitality." He bowed, then turned away toward the door. "I get to try room service first, Papa."

Papa stared, taken by surprise, then smiled and followed Matt.

CHAPTER 17

The pavilion was of silk, but the guards walked the two men around it several times as it was being raised, no doubt to point out the lack of a back door, and to introduce them to the sentries who were standing, two by two, at each corner.

"It's nice to feel secure," Matt told Papa.

Papa gave him a peculiar look, but only said, "Yes, it will be pleasant to sleep in safety."

When the pavilion was up and the front flap raised to form an awning, they went in. A guard lit a lamp for them; another set out a bowl and pitcher for washing, a third placed a tray with a small brass pot and two shot-glass-sized cups. They all retreated, bowing, leaving the father-and-son team alone.

"Not bad." Matt looked around at the walls of maroon silk, letting himself enjoy the feeling of the thick Oriental carpet beneath his feet. "Certainly a lot better than some of the jails I've been in."

Papa stared. Then he frowned, stern and forbidding. "You have been in jail?"

"At least once a year, ever since I came to Merovence. Has something to do with fighting evil tyrants for the sake of the rightful queen." He smiled at Papa. "Of course, when you're in love with her, it's worth the inconvenience."

Papa stared for a moment, then gave him a smile that combined warmth, shared understanding, and pride. "As long as you weren't doing anything wrong."

"Only by the most puritanical definition. In fact, in this world, you can land in prison for doing right."

Papa grinned. "Well, if you were a respectable criminal, I cannot but approve."

"Anyway, it's the first jail I've seen here that had coffee." Matt stepped over to the low table, sank down on the cushions around it, and inhaled the strong, heady aroma from the little brass coffeepot. "In fact, it's the first coffee I've seen anywhere in this world! After we get this little misunderstanding about conquest straightened out, we'll have to see about establishing trade."

"You're not really planning to sit there and do nothing!"

"What can I do?" But Matt pointed toward the silken wall, then pointed to his ear.

Papa's eyes widened. He got the message—every word they said was going to be heard very clearly. He sank down on the cushions across from Matt, reached inside his medieval doublet, and pulled out a very modern notepad and ballpoint.

Matt grinned. "The old professor strikes again, eh?"

Papa nodded at the wall and pointed at his ear, saying, "Lifetime habits don't die just because of a change of scene."

It was true; Matt couldn't remember his father ever being without writing materials in some pocket or another. Still, he had to keep the chatter going, or the people outside would start wondering what mischief he was conjuring up.

Papa seemed to be thinking the same way. "It is my fault that we are here at all. I am sorry for my outburst, Matthew. I simply could not bear to hear such specious reasoning any longer." But he pushed the pad over to Matt.

"Don't worry—you were only ahead of me by a minute or so." Matt scribbled a note on the pad. "Mind you, I would have tried to put it nicely, but it still would have sounded like blasphemy to them. Christianity and Islam may come from the same source, but there really is a fundamental difference in the way they see the world."

He turned the pad around so Papa could read it: *We're going to break out, of course.*

"A fundamental difference, yes." Papa took the pen and scribbled a response. "But I recognize the boy's attitude. He is a typical adolescent, assuming that he is right, and that anyone older must be wrong." He passed the pad back. It bore one single word: *How?*

Matt grinned. "Mark Twain's old line about being eighteen, and realizing that his father was so stupid he was ashamed to be seen with him?" He took the pen and wrote, *I'll try a few magical probes first, to see if they've put prison spells on us. If they haven't, I'll have us ten miles away in a jiffy.*

"Yes," Papa said, to both spoken and written comments. Matt started writing again, and Papa added, "Of course, Twain went on to say that when he was twenty-two, he was amazed to discover how much the old man had learned in four years."

Matt turned the pad around for Papa to read, feeling he should say something in defense of the younger generation. "On the other hand, when the elders agree with the teenager, he's *really* sure he's right. Me, I'd put Tafas' attitude down to a good old-fashioned case of religious fanaticism."

Papa read, then wrote, *What if they have chained us with magic?* But aloud, he said, "Fanaticism, yes, and adolescents are especially subject to intense and narrow convictions." He smiled. "Convictions which experience, and greater knowledge, sometimes prove to be entirely wrong."

Matt wrote, *Then we have to outsmart their spells.* But Papa's spoken comments were making him squirm inside as he recognized himself at seventeen—and eighteen, and nineteen. "You just taught college for too long," he protested. "Me, I was only a teaching fellow for a couple of years—not long enough to become jaded."

"But long enough for a little tarnish to cloud your ideals?" Papa's eyes were gentle with sympathy—but he read the note and wrote back, *That will take time, no?*

"A little," Matt allowed, then clarified, "A little jaded. I did decide that not all college students really wanted to learn, anyway." He wrote, *It could take a while, yes. Any urgent appointments?*

"But they do expect to receive high grades." Papa wrote, *Not I, but perhaps you do.*

Good point, Matt wrote. *I'd better check.* Aloud, he said, "Just as well I washed my hands of them. In fact, might not be a bad idea to wash my hands, period. You never know, they might bring us dinner."

"That would be pleasant," Papa agreed.

Matt poured water into the bowl, then passed his hand over it, murmuring,

> "Darken, churn, and stew!
> Show another view!
> Receive what's sent from other pools!
> Answer to another's rules!"

The water darkened, even as he'd said, then began to churn about and about. Bubbles arose; then the surface stilled, became glassy, and Matt told it,

> "Now, with some reflection,
> Engage you in detection!
> Discover sights of far-off prospects,
> And make of them election."

Papa's eyes widened as he saw an image take form in the water, three-dimensional, seeming chaotic at first until he realized he was looking down from above—down at Bordestang and the countryside about it, with the river curving like an embracing arm. It was a freckled arm, though, and Matt stared. "Ships! Burned hulks! And ones that could still sail, tied up at the wharfs!"

"What is that ring around the town?" Papa asked.

"Tents!" Matt was tense in an instant. "And soldiers! They're charging the wall!"

Cavalry galloped up the boulevard to the huge town gates. Behind them rolled a wooden tower, archers ready at its windows, spearmen standing at its doors with plank bridges to drop onto the battlements.

"Here comes the artillery!" Matt cried as genies appeared to hurl huge boulders at the gates.

But the boulders slowed in midair, then dropped onto the Moorish host.

"Well done, Jimena!" Papa cried with glee. "She is a spellbinder indeed!"

"You knew that before anybody else." Matt watched with concern as the boulders faded, growing insubstantial, until they were only clouds that wreathed themselves about the soldiers. "They've got their magicians, too."

The Moors plowed through the fog anyway, but met a storm of arrows from the archers on the wall—arrows that looped in midair, turning to speed back at the men who had launched them. But they slowed abruptly as they crossed the wall, and the archers reached out to snatch them and set them to bowstrings again.

"That could have been Mama, or it could have been Saul," Matt muttered.

Then the ground exploded in front of the Moors, sending up a cloud of chicken feathers that filled the air, blinding the invaders—and, Matt was sure, making them gag and choke as well.

Then the gates swung open, and a band of horsemen charged out led by a knight in black armor.

"Sir Guy!" Matt cried with relief. "He came to join the party!"

The clash in front of the gate was brief and furious, but the defenders could see clearly, and any attacker riding against them was still half-blinded by feathers and gagging on down. The Moors retreated in chagrin. In one last punctuating action, a small catapult on the wall released a boulder that took the top off the siege tower. The scene faded as Sir Guy's sally party rode back into the city, the gates closing behind them.

Matt was livid. "The bastard! The sneak! The genius! He sent his army around by sea! As soon as we were out of sight, they came sailing up the river! No wonder he's sitting here by the Pyrenees, instead of attacking Rinaldo!"

"Why, yes," Papa said, his eyes widening. "He has only half his army, has he not? And that half must wait for the queen to come through the mountains!"

"No wonder Rinaldo's courier got through—Tafas wanted Alisande to come riding to the king's rescue! Damn! I could strangle that kid, if I wasn't awed by his strategy!" He waved a hand over the bowl. "We've got to tell Alisande—if he hasn't ambushed her, too!"

The vision of the castle dissolved, and another image grew in its place—an army on the march, filling a road that strayed between newly planted fields.

Papa frowned. "It is night here, but we see them by morning light."

"Predawn," Matt pointed out. "It's grayish, and there're no shadows. Must be some kind of time delay here." He pointed out the figure at the front, golden hair spilling around armored shoulders. "Alisande! She really does get her troops up and moving at first light."

"She is well," Papa pointed out. "They march, and are not ambushed."

"Yet," Matt said darkly. "How can I get word to them?" His brow knitted as he searched for a message spell.

"Perhaps there is no need," Papa suggested. "Do they march toward the rising sun, or away from it?"

"Good question!" Matt seized on the notion and passed his hand over the bowl again, muttering. The army shrank in the circle, the surrounding countryside filling more and more of the aperture, until golden light burst at one side.

"Sunrise!" Papa said, then remembered the listening ears. He seized the pad and wrote, *She marches away.*

"Thank Heaven," Matt breathed, as softly as he could, and took the pen to write, *Back to Bordestang. Saul must have gotten the word to her somehow.* Then he frowned and wrote, *She's going back to catch the Moorish army between her forces and the city wall. I ought to be there.*

Perhaps, Papa wrote. He watched his son for a moment, frowning. Had he realized that his wife was riding away and leaving him to his fate? If so, it didn't bother him—but this wasn't the time to talk about it.

Papa said aloud, "We must consider how much good you're doing here. You show a knack for diplomacy that I had never suspected in you, my son. It may be that you can shorten this war by thinking and talking, or even end it completely." On the pad, he wrote, *Stay.*

"I have difficulty believing I can do that much good," Matt said sourly. But he realized that his father had a point—if he could show Tafas which force really lay behind his invasion, he might sue for peace, and Alisande might not have to fight when she arrived back in Bordestang.

Guerrilla, Papa wrote, and Matt nodded grimly. If diplomacy failed, he might do better to organize a resistance movement. After all, he wouldn't be the first member of his family to be a Spanish partisan. "Of course, we can't do anything inside this tent."

"What choice have we?" Papa asked, but his eyes were gleaming again.

Matt sighed; he'd been putting it off long enough. He pushed himself to his feet and strolled around the tent, next to the walls, reciting,

> "Stone walls do not a prison make,
> Nor iron bars a cage . . ."

He reached out to touch the silken wall—and a big fat spark jumped out at his finger, making a crack as loud as a firecracker. He mouthed agony, cradling one hand in the other, bending over as he waited for the pain to pass. Papa was by his side in an instant, frowning and massaging the knuckle, but Matt shook his head—there was nothing to do but wait for it to pass.

"Static electricity," Papa offered.

Matt shook his head impatiently, but Papa pointed toward the walls, then cupped his ear, and Matt understood—any words would do, so that the guards wouldn't wonder why

they were being so quiet. "These walls are very heavily
guarded by magic, Papa."

"So." Papa nodded. "It does manifest as energy, then?"

"It can," Matt told him. The pain was receding now. "Mind
you, I don't think the sorcerer who set this spell knows about
electricity—he probably just made a simile to lightning."

" 'Fire from the sky,' eh?" Papa nodded. "I suppose you can
ground it?"

Matt had to admit this dialogue would probably be confusing the guards delightfully—presuming any of them spoke
the language of Merovence. He decided that he would indeed presume it—less chance of an unpleasant surprise that
way. "Dunno. The potential might be automatically renewed.
Even if it's not, we might get one heck of an explosion." He
held up a hand. "I know that sounds feeble, but the other
H word isn't a good one to say around here."

"Yes, I can see how that might be," Papa said thoughtfully.
He went back to the table and scrawled a question mark on the
pad and sighed, "I still have a great deal to learn about the
physics of this universe."

"Well, the Moors have algebra, so they may be ahead of us."
Matt didn't really think so, though—the forces of this universe
seemed to be best expressed in poetry, not equations. He took
the pen and wrote, *I'll try a transportation verse. Hold tight.*
He caught his father's hand and recited,

"Take me somewhere east of Suez, where the best is like
    the worst,
And they don't know the Commandments, and a man can
    raise a thirst:
For the temple bells are callin', and it's there that I
    would be,
By the old Moulmein Pagoda, lookin' lazy at the sea."

Papa looked up in alarm, but it was too late now—too late to
change the verse, and too late to explain; the world seemed to
go crazy, slipping and sliding about them . . .

Then it jarred to a halt. Matt lurched forward over the table, and Papa fell backward among the cushions. Dazed, Matt pushed himself to his feet and started toward Papa in frantic worry. Papa levered himself up, though, looking very disoriented, and Matt relaxed with a sigh.

"Let me guess," Papa grunted. "Our jailers thought of that possibility, too."

"Either that, or they're watching us closely this very minute." Matt flirted with the idea of one of the guards being a sorcerer in disguise, then wondered who was in the tent next door.

Papa nodded and took the pen. *Call Lakshmi.*

Matt stared. Then he felt a panic rise that had nothing to do with counterspells or listening sorcerers. He shook his head very emphatically.

Papa sighed and started singing.

> "Oh, Lakshmi lass, where are you roaming?
> Oh, Lakshmi lass, where are you roaming?
> Oh, stay and hear! To us be coming,
> For we shall need you high and low,
> We shall need you high and low!"

Matt kept shaking his head more and more frantically, but a tiny whirlwind sprang up in the middle of the room, growing amazingly, beginning to make a small whine as it reached five and a half feet in height, a whine that descended the scale and turned into a contralto that demanded, "Why should I come to men who have spurned me?"

"Why, to return a kindness," Papa said, all innocence.

The whirlwind began to shrink in on itself, assuming contours that would have set Matt howling at the moon if he hadn't known how much potential for mayhem they contained. "Kindness?" the contralto challenged. "I have returned your kindness twice over! I have spared your lives, I have chased away lesser djinn, and I have taken you to the Mahdi! Would you have me return your favor tenfold?"

"It was a very big favor," Papa reminded her. "However, if paying a debt is not reason enough, then I pray you do it for friendship."

"For friendship?" The whirlwind shrank in on itself even further, died down, and Lakshmi took a step closer to Papa. She glanced at Matt, looking him up and down, and he could almost hear her thoughts: *If I cannot have the son, perhaps the father will do.*

She turned back to Papa, purring, "What evidence of friendship do you offer?"

"Why, only what I ask," Papa said with a slow smile, "to help you when you are in danger, in any way that we can." But he took a step closer, too, and Matt suddenly realized that his father—*Papa!*—was exuding a testosterone glow.

"In danger?" Lakshmi's voice was more throaty than ever as she stepped even closer to Papa. "Is that the only case in which you may give me comfort?"

"Alas, I fear so," Papa said, though his body language screamed regret, "except to offer companionship if you are lonely."

"Djinn are solitary creatures," Lakshmi murmured, "but there are times when we long for closeness."

"I know such longings well." Papa's voice was heavier now, too. "But it would be wrong for me to offer what I have already pledged to another. Still, friendship is no small gift."

For a moment, Lakshmi blazed with anger—literally; small flames danced upon her brow, her shoulders, her breasts—and Matt, on the verge of panic, summoned up his most powerful anti-spirit spell.

"All men long for the companionship of beauty, great and wondrous beauty," Papa murmured.

The flames doused on the instant, and Lakshmi's glare turned into a sardonic smile. "Yes, but you already have such beauty for companionship, do you not? Nonetheless, perhaps friendship is not to be lightly refused, and I am sure your wife will befriend me as strongly as you do. Enough, then, O Promiser of Favors Not Given! What would you have me do?" She glanced at Matt, a long, lingering, speculative glance that set every hormone howling even as it rang every warning bell in his intuition.

Papa said quickly, "Why, we ask nothing but that you take us out of this silken prison to which the Mahdi has consigned us."

Lakshmi turned back to him, frowning, leaving Matt shaken with relief and racked with thwarted desire. The djinna said, "Two mighty wizards seeking escape from a mere silken pavilion? There is more to this than mortal eyes see." She turned to scan the walls, and a strange glow sprang from her eyes to shimmer about her face as she pivoted in place. Then it died, and she nodded. "Strong spells indeed have been worked into the very fabric of this tent!"

"Surely not too strong for a princess of the djinn," Papa protested.

"Surely not," Lakshmi said absently, then reached out to catch both their hands in vise grips as the tent began to rotate around them.

CHAPTER 18

Lakshmi pulled the two men in against her bosom. Either they were shrinking or Lakshmi was growing, but that couldn't have been happening or she would have ripped right through the roof of the tent, which was spinning around them, faster and faster until it was a blur and Matt was fighting to keep his stomach down. Then the blur darkened; streaks of light appeared, then began to grow fatter, and Matt's insides told him they'd begun to slow down. The djinna-tornado rotated more and more slowly as the streaks shrank into points of light swinging past, slowing and slowing until they came to a stop.

Lakshmi released the men. They staggered away stumbling and reeling. Matt caught hold of Papa; the two of them braced against each other until the world stabilized and they saw the Mahdi's camp spread out below them, thousands of campfires imitating the stars that spattered the sky above. Matt realized they stood on top of a low hill. Relief surged, and Matt fought to keep from sagging to the ground. He managed to say, "Th . . . thanks, Princess Lakshmi."

"Yes, a thousand thanks, O Gem of Djinn," Papa said. He sounded a little shaky, too.

"It was my pleasure," Lakshmi said with a sniff of contempt. "After all, what need have I to do anything that is not my pleasure? By your own spellbreaking, Wizard, I am freed to go where I will—or will not!"

Matt stared; she fairly seemed to glow against the sky. But the glow began to turn again, spinning, whirling, swirling, fading . . .

Gone.

Now Matt did let himself sag to the ground with relief. "I never knew such tantalizing feelings could be such an ordeal!"

"That's not how I remember it from your high school experiences," Papa said, but his voice trembled a little, too.

Matt took a deep breath and looked up. "Frankly, Father, you amaze me."

"Did not know that the old man still had it in him, eh?" Papa managed a grin.

"Didn't know you were a football player," Matt said, "but you sure know how to intercept a pass!"

"It is a skill which, once learned, is always easy to recall." Papa frowned, concerned. "I hope you do not think I have been unfaithful to your mother, Matthew."

"Well . . ."

"Be assured I have not," Papa said earnestly. "A man cannot help being attracted to a voluptuous woman—but he can help what he does about that attraction."

Matt nodded. "He can say no—but he could hurt the woman really easily if he did."

"Ah, I see you understand," Papa said, relieved. "A woman will accept rejection more easily, if you make it clear to her that you wish you did not have to refuse her favors, but that you must be loyal to your wife."

"Or your principles," Matt said, remembering.

Papa flashed him a smile. "Yes, you have taught undergraduates too, have you not? There are very few women who will not honor faithfulness, though, Matthew, for they wish that same fidelity in their own men, when they find them."

Matt nodded. "Must have been tougher on you before you met Mama, though."

Papa was silent long enough that Matt turned to stare at him, appalled.

"I can only speak for myself," Papa said at last, "and I have learned from some men that they have felt the opposite—but personally, I find that living with a beautiful woman makes all other women seem more wonderful, more spectacular."

"And makes you desire them more?" Matt asked, mouth dry.

"That, it does not," Papa said frankly. "It is more of an aesthetic impulse that allows me to admire other women but to desire my Jimena even more." He turned to look directly into Matt's eyes. "Does that stand to reason?"

"Only from personal experience," Matt assured him. "Sense it makes not." He grinned at his father. "But it does make me feel a lot better—less guilty about Alisande."

"There should be no guilt at all," Papa said promptly. "You cannot help physical responses, and must not distance yourself from any of your feelings, or they will leap out to overcome you when you least expect it. But you can control your actions."

"And you do a great job controlling yours," Matt said. "Must have been tough when you were a grad student teaching pretty undergrads, though."

"I have never been sorely tried since my Jimena came to protect me from them," Papa assured him.

Matt frowned. "Never?"

"Never," Papa said firmly, then relented. "From what other men tell me, though, I am exceedingly fortunate in that, and exceedingly rare in having so all-encompassing a love."

Matt was still, reflecting on his relationship with Alisande.

"It does not come fully formed in an instant, my son," Papa said softly, "not when you first see her, not when the priest pronounces you married, not even when your child is born. It grows and deepens slowly, year after year, not steadily but by highs and lows. However, if you both work at it and care for it as the most valuable treasure you will ever have, your marriage can become both the substance and joy of your life, and your proudest accomplishment."

"Yes," Matt said slowly. "I do have to remember that, don't I? That you two have been working at it for thirty-five years."

"Twenty-nine," Papa said. "You forget that time has moved more quickly for you than it has for us, these last few weeks." He pushed himself to his feet and reached down to pull Matt up. "Come, my son. Where shall we go, now that we are free?"

"Yeah, I do have to figure that out," Matt muttered. For a few seconds, he gazed down at the Mahdi's camp. Then, without turning his head, he asked Papa, "How did you know Lakshmi would come?"

"Really, son! I know women well enough to be able to see the signs of fascination. I told you that you had enchanted her in more ways than one. Did you really think she would choose to be far from you?"

"Maybe I underrate myself," Matt said. "Even so, it wasn't me she was paying attention to, it was you."

Papa shrugged. "You had made it clear that you admired her, but would do nothing because your heart was already pledged. I do not doubt that, since you were not available, she thought I would do quite well."

"Yes," Matt said, frowning. "It was your call she answered, not mine."

"Genetically, we are nearly identical," Papa said mildly.

"Now I know what Mama meant, about you being a charmer!"

Papa shrugged, looking out over the camp. "Women are wonderful creatures. You have only to treat them with gentleness, sympathy, and all possible consideration."

Well, he had certainly done that. Again, maybe his experiences in developing a relationship with a woman he really loved had given him greater understanding and appreciation of all the other women who had come into his life. He had certainly fielded the djinna's sex plays with an ease that his son found stunning. Matt glanced at his father covertly, studying the tranquil, smiling face in a new light, realizing for the first time since high school that his father was a very handsome man. He found himself speculating about Papa's past, and wondering just how spectacular Mama must have been in her youth.

Papa turned to him with a disarming smile. "Tell me, now—what would you have done if that transportation spell really had taken us to Mandalay?"

"What?" Matt stared, thrown by the change of subject.

Then he smiled. "Recited another verse to take us back to Merovence, of course! Or maybe King Rinaldo."

"I should have thought of that," Papa said judiciously. "But in the second line of that verse, didn't Kipling say . . ."

"Not here!" Matt cut him off. "Please, not here! You don't know what it would do."

"Hmm." Papa frowned at the ground, running through the verse in his head. *Where there ain't no Ten Commandments* . . . "Yes, I can see that might be a problem. I shall have to be very careful what I recite."

Alisande's army camped in a meadow. As the sun was setting, Queen Alisande told Lord Gautier, "When darkness has fallen, send half our men out in groups of six and have them bid all the peasants pack their most precious goods, then flee after sunset."

Lord Gautier stared. "Majesty! We have only come a day's ride back toward Bordestang! Are we not returning to raise the siege?"

"We are not," Alisande said, with the complete certainty of a monarch who spoke for her whole land and people. "It cuts hard, but we must trust the city to its own defenses. The opportunity to take the Moors at a disadvantage is too great to miss."

"I have missed it completely, then," Lord Gautier said, mystified. "Everyone has been talking of our return to Bordestang!"

"Yes, and the Mahdi's spies have surely heard, and taken word to him," Alisande said. "He will curse because we have turned away from his trap; he will ride after us, with all his men marching through the mountain passes and double-quick along this road, to catch us. He shall find half our army camped a mile farther on, and shall draw up his troops to do battle. Have the other half of our force evacuate the people of the countryside by night, Lord Gautier, then have them dress in peasants' clothing and busy themselves tilling the fields. It should not be difficult for them; most of them began as plowboys, after all."

Lord Gautier began to understand. "So they shall till the fields, but keep their weapons near?"

"Near indeed, hidden in furrows and under hedgerows," Alisande confirmed.

"Then when the Moors attack our army, half our men shall boil out of the fields all about them!" Lord Gautier slapped his saddlebow, grinning.

Alisande nodded. "We shall take them in both flanks and in the rear, Lord Gautier, and even if they outnumber us, they shall fall to our spears—*if* the Mahdi knows not of our ruse." She turned to her left, to Matt's assistant wizard, Ortho the Frank. "That shall be your task, Master Ortho—to confound the spells of the Moorish sorcerers, that they not espy our true positions."

"That should not be difficult," the wizard said, grinning, "for those sorcerers are not likely to scry us clearly by night, and when dawn comes, they shall see only our army encamped, and if they notice how much smaller it is, they shall put it down to men deserting because they believe they cannot win against the Mahdi."

"There is much to be said for conceit," Lord Gautier said, "at least, for an enemy's conceit."

"It is a most excellent scheme," Ortho said, his eyes glowing, then frowned. "But what of Bordestang?"

"It is a hard choice," Alisande admitted, "but the good of the whole country requires that I trust the safety of the city to its walls—and to Sir Gilbert, the Witch Doctor, and Lady Mantrell."

Privately, of course, she knew Matt's mother couldn't do much. She was too new to wizardry. But her main concern was for her infant son, and if anyone could protect him, it would be his grandmother.

Mama cried, "What are these loathsome creatures!"

Two guards, Saul, and Sir Guy came running to her on the southern side of the castle. Sir Gilbert stayed resolutely on watch on the northern side, commanding his men sternly to hold their posts, though he was aching to see what had happened. He reminded himself that his men were dying of curiosity, too. "It may be a ruse," he cried, "to draw us all away from our posts!"

The sentries held their places, renewed in resolve.

The rest of the commanders looked out over the castle wall and down on the houses and shops. The river flowed under the city wall, snaked through the town, then back out under the wall—and all along its length, great shimmering half spheres were crawling out of the water onto the banks. Citizens howled and ran from them. The creatures flailed about with tentacles. Two managed to touch people; they went rigid and fell, paralyzed too quickly to scream.

But the monsters didn't stop to eat—they crawled very purposefully through streets and alleys toward the outer wall, still streaming with water. Where they passed, the streets glistened.

"They seek to take the town wall from within!" Sir Guy cried. "What can these creatures be?"

"I don't know," Saul answered. "They look sort of like jellyfish, scaled up about a hundred times. They shouldn't be able to support their own weight on land, though—they should collapse!"

"Magic can do amazing things," Mama reminded him.

"Yonder! A citizen fights back!" Sir Guy pointed.

They all looked, and saw a spear falling from a third-floor window. It struck a jellyfish squarely in the back—and bounced off.

"The Moorish sorcerers would not send creatures that could be slain so easily," Sir Guy said grimly.

"But how did they come in?" Mama asked. "Are not the watergates barred?"

"Sure," Saul told her, "but these things are very flexible. All they had to do was stretch out thin and squeeze through—assuming they didn't tear out the iron grilles instead."

"We shall have to be sure of that, as soon as we have dealt with them," Sir Guy said grimly.

The monster oozed on up the street. A mongrel burst

from hiding behind a rain barrel. A tentacle lashed out; the dog froze in midstride, then fell. The monster crawled on over the dog. Where it had passed, only a stream of water trickled. There was no sign of the mutt.

"We must stop these creatures at once!" Mama declared. "They might slay a child as easily as they have slain that dog, and just as mindlessly absorb it!" She began to gesture, reciting in Spanish.

Sir Guy stiffened. "Their goal is the wall indeed! The Moors attack from without while their monsters attack from within!"

Saul looked up and saw a dozen wooden towers rolling toward the city. The infantry marched behind—well behind. "What's making them roll? I don't see any oxen pulling."

"And no soldiers pushing, either," Sir Guy told him. "They are self-moving."

"Auto-mobile, hm?" Saul grinned. "Well, I might know a spell or two about that."

"While you chant, I shall lead the defense in disabling those towers," Sir Guy told him. He ran down the stairs, calling, "Ho, men of mine! To horse and away!"

Saul found time to wonder what Mama was chanting. After all, she couldn't ever have seen monsters like these, could she? Maybe at the aquarium, but . . .

A jellyfish blew up. That was the only word to describe it; in a single second, its body swelled to a tight and glistening half ball, then popped like bubble gum—except that it dried up as it fell in on itself, and in another second was only a desiccated, rubbery film on the cobbles, a film that evaporated even as Saul watched. He stared, fascinated, listening to the popping sounds all over town.

When they died away, Mama nodded, satisfied. "No town should suffer such vermin."

Saul gave himself a shake. "Yes. Amazing job, Lady Mantrell."

"It is nothing." Mama waved away the compliment. "If you had ever had to clean bubble gum off a child's face, you would understand it quite quickly."

Now Saul understood why her chant had seemed familiar; even though he couldn't understand the language, he'd recognized the tune—from a television commercial.

Mama frowned out over the city. "How are those towers approaching us?"

"By magic, I think," Saul said. "Either that, or they've got people inside walking treadmills."

"They would not go so smoothly if that were all," Mama told him. "Let us spike their wheels, yes?"

"Yes," Saul agreed. He lifted his hands to start miming, then saw Sir Guy running up the steps to the ramparts of the city's wall. "Hold on—let's see what the professional is doing."

Mama turned to watch, frowning. "Why does he not wear full armor?"

"He only does that for infighting," Saul explained, "when he has to face other knights' swords and lances. He can't run around in it. All he's worried about right now is arrows, so he makes do with a mail shirt and a light helmet."

Sir Guy paced to and fro along the wall, waving at the towers, shooing archers into position. Flame blossomed on their bows, then leaped in blazing arcs toward the towers. Burning arrows fell on the thatched roofs, bit into the wooden sides—and promptly went out.

"Fireproofed!" Saul cried. "The sorcerers have found some way to make sure those towers won't burn!"

"If it is a spell, I can stop it." Mama raised her hands again, face grim, and began to recite. Spanish words ran from her tongue in a stream.

Sir Guy, obviously believing in occasional bad luck, sent another flight of flaming arrows into the siege engines. They struck, guttered—then blazed up again.

Mama lowered her hands, satisfied. "That should suffice."

The flames suddenly guttered again.

Mama threw up her hands, speaking quite angrily as she commanded the fire to grow. The flames licked up again, and the siege engines began to burn.

"I must stay on guard against their spells," Mama snapped,

"and even burning, those towers could do great damage to our wall. Stop them, Saul!"

Saul fought down irritation; he didn't like anybody bossing him around. This wasn't the time to make an issue out of it, though. "Anything you say, Lady Mantrell." He thought a moment, then took a piece of rope from his pocket and tied a knot as he chanted,

> "Under a spreading canopy
> Stands the town smith's lass.
> She's not making horseshoes—
> She's only pumping gas.
>
> For carts not pulled by horses
> Cannot run on hay.
> Whatever fuel they use to run
> Can be cut off any day,
>
> As OPEC cut the flow of oil,
> Or fuses cut the juice.
> So towers rolling by themselves
> Can't be of any use
>
> If I do crimp the pipeline
> Through which pours the flow
> Of energy from sorcery!
> Cease rolling, towers of foe!"

The burning towers ground to a halt.

> "By axle, rod, and bearing,"

Saul added,

> "By crankshaft, gear, and brake!
> Let turning parts all seize up!
> Let wheels fall off and break!"

One tower's corner suddenly jolted to the ground, then another. Slowly, the burning towers tipped and fell. Moors leaped from them as they tumbled. Saul hoped they were empty when they crashed full-length on the ground, burning merrily.

"Well done," Mama said, folding her arms with a satisfied smile. She nodded and said again, "Yes, very well done."

Saul felt an irrational rush of pleasure at her praise, and turned away, scolding himself. He should have been beyond such infantile responses.

Matt and Papa hiked a mile away from the Mahdi's force, then rolled up in their blankets for a few hours. They woke at sunrise, blew their campfire aflame, and boiled water for herbal tea to wash down journeybread and cheese.

"It was good of that young man not to take away our packs," Papa said.

"Yes, and I'll bet his sorcerers are chewing him out for it right now," Matt agreed. "They're probably sure we escaped because we had some magical gadgets."

Papa smiled. "Then they are as angry at losing our packs as they are at losing us."

"Sure." Matt poured the tea, passed a cup to Papa. "Maybe we should have left them. It would hold those sorcerers up for a year, trying to figure out what kind of spells we could work with blankets, wooden bowls, Brie, and crackers."

"Well, if they have gained no knowledge, neither have we," Papa sighed.

"Oh, I wouldn't say that," Matt mused. "We know there's a hidden persuader behind the sorcerers, and that they're the power behind the Mahdi."

"We knew that before," Papa pointed out.

"Yes, but it helps to have it verified. Besides, I like knowing I guessed right about the man behind the men behind the throne."

"About Nirobus being a sorcerer and not a clergyman?" Papa asked. "But if he is not a holy man, he could be anything."

"Yes, including a demon in disguise, or a genuine sold-his-soul necromancer." Matt shuddered. "Met one once. Don't want to do it again."

"Which means we know nothing about this Nirobus," Papa said. "He could be anything."

"He could," Matt said slowly, "but I think he's human—that, or wearing an awfully good disguise."

"What makes you think so?" Papa asked, frowning.

"Because when I met him, that first time I went back to New Jersey," Matt explained, "he acted awfully sympathetic."

"Acted," Papa reminded. "Any good con man can seem very sincere."

"True," Matt admitted, "but he wasn't just sincere, he seemed genuinely interested."

"In discovering an enemy's plans? Of course!"

"Not just that," Matt protested. "He was interested in me as a person, in finding out how my mind worked, what I was feeling, what I needed, how to help me figure out how to get it . . ."

"Like a good teacher," Papa said softly.

"Yeah."

Papa stared into the campfire, lips pursed. "A man genuinely interested in people, who can bridge the universes?"

"Why not? We can. All he had to do was follow my backtrail."

"Why bother?"

"Well, aside from the little factor of stranding me away from Merovence, where I couldn't do him any harm," Matt said, "there's the little matter of a necromancer's power source."

"It comes from slaying people, does it not?"

"It can," Matt said slowly, "and I think he may be killing a lot of New Jersey kids very slowly."

"With the new drug, yes."

Matt nodded. "Carefully structured to retain magic, to channel energy from New Jersey to this universe. It bleeds away only a little more energy than its host is producing, so that the kid who takes it goes on providing life energy for

sorcery for a few years instead of one blazing instant." He
shivered. "Talk about a designer drug!"

"You speak of it as though it were a living thing."

"Why not?" Matt shrugged. "Years ago, before the Fed-
eral Drug Administration, swindlers used to sell diet pills
that would make you skinny no matter how much you ate."

"I remember reading of it—the 'pills' contained tapeworm
eggs." Papa shuddered. "It seems incredible that people really
will do such things. Can magic manufacture some sort of
parasite that will do what you have explained?"

"I don't know why not. I've certainly seen enough magi-
cally produced monsters here—chimeras, manticores, trolls,
even a few that seem very original, like Narlh the dracogriff."

Papa shook his head, almost in despair. "So by not letting
the neighborhood boys use my store to spread this drug, I
marked myself as an enemy of this Nirobus?"

Matt nodded. "Unless he'd already pegged you because
you were related to me."

Papa looked up, staring. "I thought your description
sounded familiar! It fits the man who talked me into going
into business for myself!"

"So he did have you marked right from the beginning,"
Matt said grimly. "Sorry, Papa. I didn't mean to get you into
trouble."

"This is the sort of trouble I wish to be in," Papa said
grimly, "the defense of the innocent and young, even if I die
in the fight. No, my son, I only regret my failure to protect
them, not my defeat." He bit his lip. "Except for the anxiety
it has caused my Jimena."

"If I know Mama, she would have raced you for the box-
ing gloves if she'd known about all this," Matt told him.
"Anyway, it's working out okay for her."

"And for me also!" Papa clapped him on the shoulder. "I
thank you, Matthew, for another chance to fight!"

"Any time, Papa," Matt said, grinning.

Papa's brow furrowed. "But if the whole campaign is so
well planned, why has the Mahdi besieged Bordestang when
he should have consolidated Ibile first?"

"Nice question." Matt frowned in thought, then said, "The logical reason is that Alisande is a greater threat to Nirobus' plans than King Rinaldo is." He tensed with anger. "If they can bump her off, Rinaldo will be isolated, and be easy meat."

"Then her best protection is for this King Rinaldo to be anything but an easy victim." Papa gazed off into the distance. "There must be some way in which he can become more of a threat—able to attack the Mahdi, harry his forces, distract him from Merovence."

"Some way like teaching him modern guerrilla techniques?" Matt felt a surge of elation. "Maybe we oughta check up on my old pal Rinaldo and see if there's anything we can do to help."

"Certainly! Perhaps in helping him, we can help your wife." Papa began throwing dirt on the campfire. "I think it is time to march, Matthew."

A shadow loomed huge in the night. "Surely you will not depart without me," Stegoman rumbled.

"Only if we couldn't find you, Scale Runner!" Matt grinned. "Feel like a trip to the North Shore?"

The men hooked their packs over huge triangular plates, then climbed up among them. "Night flyers are harder to spot, right, Stegoman?" Matt asked.

"Assuredly—but I shall stay low in any case." Stegoman spread his wings, leather booming open in the quiet of the night. But he only flapped them twice before a shooting star plunged down at them and exploded.

CHAPTER 19

The ball of light exploded outward to reveal a genie who expanded even as his star had, shooting up to become twenty feet tall, brandishing a battle-ax that was three feet across, booming, "Are you the Wizard Mantrell?"

"Uh—no!" Matt stated with all the assurance he could muster. "Can't stand the man! Never even heard of him!"

Papa got the idea. "We weren't there," he protested, "and even if we were, we didn't do it!"

"You lie!" He was a very perceptive genie. He swung the battle-ax up over his head two-handed.

"Run, Stegoman! . . . Papa, no! *Wait!*"

But Papa had already jumped down, calling, "We must not drag your friend into our own dangers, Matthew! Besides, two smaller targets are harder to hit than one big one!"

Matt cursed and jumped down, then started broken-field running.

"Matthew, no!" Stegoman roared. "I can carry us all to safety!" He started chasing after Matt.

Papa caught on. He started running in zigzags, each zag taking him farther and farther away from the ax.

"Stand still, blast you!" the genie roared. "Or at least stay together!" The huge ax roared down out of the night, but Matt swerved at the last second, and it bit into dirt—way into dirt, which was just as well, because Matt collided with Stegoman. The dragon screeched to a halt, but Matt bounced ten feet.

"Prepare to die!" the genie roared, managing to wrestle his ax free.

"I forbid!" cried a contralto.

Matt scrambled up, staring toward the sky. Sure enough, Lakshmi towered over them, just as tall as the genie.

"I must do as the Master of the Lamp has bidden me, Princess!" the genie protested. "You cannot command me in defiance of its power!" He wrenched his eyes away from her and aimed another blow at Matt.

Matt scurried around to hide behind Lakshmi's kneecap.

"Son! I taught you never to hide behind a woman!" Papa called.

"You didn't mean it literally, did you?" Matt called back. "At least, not when she's this big!"

"Stand aside, Princess." But the genie lowered his ax. "You must not come between a genie and his appointed task."

Suddenly, Lakshmi seemed to blaze with feminine allure. "Come, Kamar! Are you a slave, or a free djinni?"

"I have been bonded to a lamp, as you know, Princess." Kamar swallowed hard, and Matt thought that if his eyes bulged any further, they'd hatch. "I must do as I have been commanded."

"Perhaps." Lakshmi took two steps toward him, rolling her hips—and other portions of her anatomy. "Surely, though, you can tarry a little on your way."

Matt goggled, too—he'd never known a woman could have voluntary muscular control in quite those sites.

Then he remembered himself and his predicament. He waved to Papa, jerking his thumb over his shoulder, and began to inch away from the confrontation.

Kamar was panting now. "I am a slave! I dare not do as a free djinni would!"

"If you are a slave, it is scarcely your fault," Lakshmi told him, "and the dalliance need not be great." She brushed up against him, head tilted, eyes half-closed, lips half-open. "Or is your lust for blood so great as to dull all other appetites?"

"You try me unfairly," Kamar protested, but he must have

realized this was his one and only chance at a princess of his own kind, because he lowered the ax to the ground, slid one arm around Lakshmi, and buried her lips in his beard.

Matt turned and ran as lightly as possible, glancing back at Papa, who was running flat-out—and the poor princess, who was making so great a sacrifice for him, never mind that Kamar really was fairly handsome, as genies went . . .

Conscience pricked like a loaded hypodermic, and Matt skidded to a halt. Papa hissed "Run!" as he passed, then circled back. "Don't waste this one opportunity!"

"I can't leave the poor thing to make such a huge sacrifice," Matt said, "and I can't leave an enemy behind me." He threw his arms up, gesturing the unwinding of a mummy's bonds, and recited,

> "With no throbs of fiery pain
> Nor cold gradations of decay,
> I break at once the unseen chain
> And free Kamar the nearest way
> From antique lamp and magic's might.
> Do as you will, but will what's right!"

He lowered his arms. *Then* he spun on his heel and ran.

Behind him, he heard a sucking like a huge suction cup pulled off a wall, then Kamar's voice shouting in jubilation, "I am free! The lamp no longer commands me! Princess, I worship at your feet! What magic there is in your kiss!"

"Not that sort, certainly," Lakshmi answered in surprise. "Will you befriend whoever freed you, no matter what your former master commanded?" She emphasized the "former" nicely.

"I will! Oh, thrice blessed be she who has freed me from the shame of that bondage!" cried Kamar.

"Not she but he. Come back, Lord Wizard of Merovence."

Suddenly, there was no ground beneath Matt's running feet. Pedaling air frantically, he nonetheless found himself turning and plunging back toward the djinna and her new friend.

"Kamar," said Lakshmi, "meet your liberator. Wizard, did you not free him even as you did me?"

"Well, not quite the same way." Matt had carefully left out the part about fanatical loyalty to himself. "But basically, yes."

"A thousand thanks!" Kamar plucked Matt out of the air and held him in his cupped hands. "I am your friend for life! Whatever you wish, only ask, and it is yours!"

"Thanks." Matt swallowed, then grinned, trying to put a brave face on it. "I'll save that favor, if you don't mind, until I really need it."

"Only call for Kamar of the Djinn." But the genie was staring in disbelief. He looked up at Lakshmi. "What manner of man is this, Princess? Any other would have taken the offer of a wish on the instant, and called for wealth or luxury!"

"He is a most exceptional example of his kind." Lakshmi didn't sound completely happy about it. "But since you are freed and no longer a threat to him, Kamar, fare you well."

"Farewell?" Kamar dropped Matt like a hot potato, eyes showing the misery of learning he'd guessed right the first time. "Do you not still wish me to dally, O Pearl?"

"With you? Be not absurd!" Lakshmi turned away, scooping Matt up, and called back over her shoulder, "Earn greater fame among the djinn if you would seek to speak to me again!" But she rolled her hips as she went, just to rub it in.

Behind her, Kamar groaned.

"Well, you sure know how to motivate males," Matt called up to her.

"Aye, except for the one I wish to move, or the other who would do in his place," Lakshmi said with a sardonic smile. She leaned down to set Matt on the ground next to Stegoman.

Matt felt sheepish. "I can't thank you enough, O Princess . . ."

"You can," she said, shrinking down to human size, blazing with every erg of allure she possessed. Matt staggered back, gasping, and Lakshmi's smile turned bitter. "You *can* thank me as I wish, but you *will* not."

"Well, you know the rules about interspecies dating . . ."

"I know quite well that it has been done," she answered tartly, "though rarely, and even more rarely to both partners' satisfaction. To be plain, your kind lacks endurance, Lord Wizard."

Matt fought down the urge to prove her wrong. "Well, we intellectuals are apt to be a bit absentminded . . ."

"Not at all," Lakshmi countered. "Your mind is entirely too present. Were it absent, your body would do as it wished— and as I wished." Her smile turned sardonic again. "But since your mind *is* present, and you will not act upon my desires, then find me some mate worthy of me, mortal man—one who will make me forget you quite. Now, farewell."

She disappeared suddenly and completely, and reaction made Matt sick and weak inside. He dropped to his knees, gasping for breath. "Papa . . . maybe we could find some way to break a love spell . . ."

"Better men than we have sought that cancellation, my son," Papa sighed, "and have learned that an obsession is far more easily begun than ended. Come now, let us ride." He clasped Matt's forearm and braced him as he stood up, then turned away to climb aboard Stegoman.

"They're okay, Lady Mantrell!" Saul assured her. "Believe me, Matt has done this kind of thing before—four times before, and he's still in one piece!"

"Yes, but with how much pain?" Mama countered. She looked around the royal library, at a loss. Bookshelves climbed to the ceiling, filled with huge leather-bound parchment volumes. "Certainly there must be something here that can tell us how to protect him!"

"Believe me, milady, the only things that can hurt your son are so thoroughly evil that only a saint or an angel can help him any." Saul spoke from personal experience. "And he rides under the protection of St. Moncaire, at least. I suspect, being in Ibile, that he also has St. Iago looking out for him."

"Oh, I have asked the good saint to intercede for him,

every night!" Mama said fervently. "If only I could know he is safe!"

"All right, we'll look again," Saul said, exasperated. He leaned down over the writing desk and pulled the inkpot over. It was heavy-duty, four inches wide and three high. Saul took off the cover and passed his hand over it three times, muttering,

> "By phosphor, pixel, line, and screen,
> Let Wizard Matthew here be seen!
> Ferhensehen, video, television,
> Distantly we watch his mission!
> He went, he came, he saw—we think.
> Let his image show in ink!"

Slowly, a picture appeared in the small pool.

Mama stared. "That spell works most amazingly, Saul!"

"You mean it's amazing that it works," Saul said with a grimace. "I think it's only because the magic associates pixels with pixies."

They saw a dragon gliding low under the morning sun with Matt and Papa on his back. Around them stretched a flat and dusty plain with rows of small trees marking watercourses.

"What remarkable transportation!" Mama stared.

"Transportation? That's a friend, a dragon named Stegoman. You see, Lady Mantrell? He's alive and well."

"Yes, but for how long?" Mama frowned. "There must be some aid I can send them."

Saul forced a smile. "You really don't believe those silly men can take care of themselves without a wise woman to watch over them, do you?"

"Don't be ridiculous, Saul." Mama sniffed. "I know they're not silly." She carefully didn't comment on the rest of his statement.

Saul frowned. He started to say he could see she was planning something, but caught himself in time—Mama's gaze was so intent that he felt sure she was either working magic, or thinking some up.

"That landscape around them," Mama said. "What does it look like to you?"

Saul frowned, studying the image for a minute, its flatness, emptiness, the broadness of its reach . . . "Nebraska."

Mama nodded. "I thought so, too. But this is Ibile, not America, so it must be La Mancha."

Saul gave her a leery glance.

She watched Stegoman's slow glide for a minute more—and on the horizon ahead, a windmill appeared, its sail turning lazily.

"No doubt of it," Mama said. "It is La Mancha."

Saul caught his breath, then recited, almost without thinking,

"Cervantes on his galley sets the sword back in the
    sheath
(Don John of Austria rides homeward with a wreath.)
And he sees across a weary land a straggling road in
    Spain,
Up which a lean and foolish knight forever rides in
    vain,
And he smiles, but not as Sultans smile, and settles
    back the blade . . .
(But Don John of Austria rides home from the Crusade.)"

Mama looked up, nodding, pleased. "So you know of him. Yes, Saul. I think that, in this world, that is a name to conjure by." She turned back to stare into the inkpot, intoning a brief, singsong chant, then sat back, relaxing.

Saul waved a hand over the inkpot, muttering quickly. It went dark, and he covered it. "Satisfied, Donna Mantrell?"

"I am not a donna," she said automatically, then caught herself, wide-eyed. "But I suppose I am—here, am I not? If my son is a lord."

"Not officially," Saul told her, "but I'm sure that's just an oversight Alisande will get around to fixing as soon as she's back. Think your men are safe now, Donna?"

"Oh, yes," Mama said, with a little smile. "As safe as they

can be. I have sent them what aid I can, at least." She frowned suddenly. "Pray Heaven it is enough!"

Gliding over the plain, they saw another small town appear ahead of them. Matt pointed. "Down there, Stegoman. It's bigger than the other towns we've come to. Maybe there'll be somebody left to sell us dinner."

"Or perhaps a stray cow," Stegoman grumbled. "These people seem to have been remarkably efficient in taking their beasts with them, Matthew!"

"Can't leave food behind for the enemy, you know. Besides, I think Rinaldo's planning on making the whole northern coast into one big castle, and they're going to need every calorie they can find for the siege."

"They could have left the swine," Stegoman grumbled. "The Moors will not eat pork."

"Maybe we can find you a real boar."

"Thank you, I have met too many of those." Stegoman banked, coasting around the town, then cupped his wings, braking hard, and touched down on the main street.

Papa climbed down, looking about him with a shudder. "It is so empty! In the West, they might think it a ghost town!"

"I have to admit, Rinaldo did a great job getting his people out of here," Matt agreed. He slid down off Stegoman's shoulder and strode toward an inn. "Let's see if anybody's home— or if they left anything."

"Why should they?" Papa asked. "The people in the last three towns didn't." He shook his head in amazement. "They were surprisingly efficient, these folk of Ibile. Fleeing an enemy, they would be expected to take only what was vital, or valuable—but we haven't found a single plate or cup, not a stick of silverware or a spare sandal!"

"Maybe they have so little that even everyday things like that are very dear to them," Matt suggested. "Let's see if these folk had any more in the way of priorities."

One minute proved the building was empty of life above

the cockroach level, and even the bugs were looking malnourished. Ten minutes' searching, though, turned up a bonus. Matt came staggering back into the street under a double armload. "Hey, Stegoman! What do you think of this?"

The dragon scowled down. "As firewood, it is excellent. As carving, it lacks something—perhaps skill."

"Yeah, but as meat, it should be delicious!" Matt dropped the two bulbous brown objects, careful to yank his toes out of the way. "Whaddaya think?"

The dragon stared, then caught one of the things up in his mouth. He dropped it a second later. "I could chew it if I had to, but I might break a tooth—and quickly though I regrow them, it might not be worth the while."

"Oh, they'll be edible after we've soaked them overnight," Matt told him. "Salty, but soft enough to eat."

"What *are* they, wizard?"

"Hams," Matt told him. "Salt-cured, smoked, and dried. Probably weighed too much to cart along. Just as you guessed, there was no worry about leaving them—the Moors won't eat pig meat."

There was, of course, the little problem of where to soak the hams.

"It does mean we'll have to stay here overnight," Matt pointed out. "You might be able to pack a dozen hams, but not a whole water tank."

Papa dropped his load of hams and said, "Yes, we must stay the night."

Matt frowned, looking about him. "I don't like it. Not that I'm really worried about ghosts, mind you, but I'm not keen on staying in a place that's so easy to infiltrate. No matter which house we choose, any good second-story man would have a dozen windows to choose from."

"A point," Papa admitted. "Therefore, let us sleep outside the town."

"I don't mind camping out," Matt said, "and I suppose it's an advantage to be able to see a mile in every direction—but it does feel a bit exposed, with the Mahdi's army only three days behind us, and his scouting parties all around."

Papa pointed at a structure poking up above the houses. "There. I noticed it as we came in. It is several hundred yards past the town."

"A windmill?" Matt stared. "Hey, not a bad idea! The walls should be as thick as any in this country, and no windows on the ground floor! Shouldn't be too hard to defend."

"And being outside the town, it will probably have its own well," Papa pointed out. "We shall find water for your hams."

"Let's go!" Matt said. "You climb up, Papa, and I'll start tossing them up to you!"

They loaded the dozen hams as efficiently as experienced stevedores, then secured themselves for takeoff between Stegoman's huge back plates. The dragon took a little run, a lot of flapping, and took off in time to clear the town wall by three feet. They soared out toward the windmill.

"Wait a minute!" Matt pointed down. "What's that?"

They all looked down, in time to see Stegoman's shadow glide over a man who labored along the roadway, leaning against the crossbar at the front of a wagon tongue. Behind him rolled a two-wheeled cart—but slowly, very slowly. The man was straining every muscle to keep it moving, for it was piled high with small pieces of furniture, wooden plates and spoons, pewter mugs and the occasional earthenware stein, feather beds, casks, and bottles. The stakes of the cart were hung with hams, sausages, and bulging wineskins.

"I think," Papa said, "that we have found all the personal items that were so obvious by their absence in the three towns we visited."

"Yes, and maybe half a dozen more! Either that, or he's an innkeeper who can't bear to leave his capital behind to be confiscated."

"Would he truly rather risk death at the hands of the enemy?" Papa wondered.

"I don't know, but I think we might want to ask him," Matt said. "How about landing, Stegoman?"

"As you wish," the dragon rumbled. His eye gleamed as he looked down at the hams. He banked into a tight curve.

His shadow fell over the traveler again. The man looked up in alarm.

Stegoman circled back, coming lower, and the man dropped the wagon tongue in a panic. He sprinted away from his cart—then skidded to a halt. Face a mask of agony, torn between fear and avarice, he turned back, yanking a cudgel from his belt, and set himself between Stegoman and the cart as the dragon landed.

"Foolish man!" Stegoman rumbled. "Do you truly think that puny twig could halt *me*?"

The man flinched but held his ground. "If it doesn't, I'd rather be dead!"

From the ground, Matt could see that the fellow wasn't very large—maybe five feet tall and skinny as a rail. The wizard stared in disbelief at the man's words. "You'd die rather than lose a cartful of junk that's making you labor worse than a galley slave just to keep it with you?"

"I've never had anything before!" the man whined. "Not anything, except the shirt on my back and the lice in my hair! 'No, Callio,' they told me, 'you can't have this, and you can't have that—unless you pay!' And where was I supposed to get money to buy with? 'We won't hire you, Callio,' they told me. 'You're too small to do any good.' Now all of a sudden, here's all these wonderful, useful *things*, in perfect condition, and they can't really be very important to anybody, or no one would have left them behind!"

"On the contrary." Papa slid down from the dragon's back. "They are the little things that make a household comfortable and that bring delight to a wife's heart. I think they were quite important indeed to the folk who left them."

"They couldn't be! Or they would have taken them with them *some*how!"

"Important, but not so vital as spouses or children," Papa corrected. "They took with them what they could easily carry or what was most important among their worldly goods. They left only the things that they wanted, but could do without."

Matt nodded. "It was leave the extras, or travel so slowly that the Moors might catch them and sell them as slaves—or maybe even kill them in a battle frenzy. Only a fool would think possessions were worth his life."

"All right, I'm a fool!" the little man screamed. "If the people who left all this thought they could do without them, then let them do without them now! It's *my* turn to have some nice things!"

Matt slid down now, too. "That makes you just a common thief, you know."

He was appalled when Callio burst into tears, sagging to his knees.

CHAPTER 20

"Hey, now, hold on!" Matt went up to him, reaching out to reassure.

The little man flinched away from his hand, crying, "All right, I am! Just a thief! Nothing but a thief! Been a thief since I was a boy learning how to cut purses! Is it my fault I was never any good at it? Is it my fault I was caught every time I tried something big?"

"You were caught?" Papa frowned. "But in the Middle Ages, the punishment for theft was cutting off a hand! How is it you still have them both?"

"Well," said Callio, "I may not be much as a thief, but I'm very good at escapes." His tears dried on the instant and he smiled, expanding. "Let me tell you of some of them! There was the time I lurked in a guard's shadow as he went out— I'm small enough so that no one noticed—and the time I went along to comfort a man on his way to be hanged, then in the fuss after he fell, I wiggled away into the crowd. After that, there was the bar in the window that was a little loose, and the more I wiggled it, the looser it became—how the other prisoners howled when I slipped through the hole and they could not! But by the time the guards came to see what all the shouting was about, I was away and gone into the night!"

"Amazing," Matt said, and watched the little man preen. "You don't maybe sing to yourself while you're doing these things, do you?"

Callio stared, openmouthed. "How did you know? Yes, I sing, but very, very softly, so that only I can hear."

Yes, only he could hear—and focus the back of his mind on bending forces to help him. Matt suspected the thief was a magician with a very limited, but very strong, power. "Did you ever try singing while you were pulling off a robbery?"

Callio stared. "Sing while I was robbing? And alert my targets to what I was doing? Certainly not!"

But he'd been plenty willing to sing while he was escaping, literally in a guard's shadow. Matt didn't bother pointing out the discrepancy—there was no point in telling the man until he was sure. Why raise false hopes? Especially if he was going to use his powers to steal from honest citizens.

How about dishonest citizens? Matt decided to mull that one over—but Callio probably would have been afraid to rob other criminals. He exchanged a glance with Papa and saw that the older man had grasped the same idea about the thief's powers.

Callio caught the look. He frowned, fear gone, looking from one to the other. "How is this? What have you learned about me that I don't know? What is happening?"

"War," Matt said slowly, "and the Moors may come charging over the hill at any moment."

"Don't try to scare me!"

"Why not, if it will help you? Make no mistake, Callio—if the Moors catch you, not only will they take away all your loot, they'll also take *you*! They'll sell you for a slave!"

"I'll escape!" But Callio had turned pale.

"Maybe," Matt said, "but you'll be poor again. What good will all these things do you then?"

"Do not tell me to leave them!" the poor thief wailed in agony. "They're all I have, all I've ever had! No woman would want me because I was too poor and couldn't earn money for her! No woman, no children, no home! No friends, because they all think I'm too small and weak to be worth respect! This is the first time in my life that I've ever had *any*thing, anything at all!"

Matt's heart went out to the man.

So did Papa's. All sympathy, he said, "If they catch you,

though, you'll have nothing again, and the more you collect, the slower you'll go."

"Yes," Matt agreed. "They're bound to catch you sooner or later. A cartload of miscellaneous household goods isn't worth your hands—or your life."

"Do you think I don't know that?" Callio wailed. "If I had found any gems or gold or other small things of great value, I could tear myself away from these—but I've found nothing of that sort, nothing! No jewels, no coins, no plate! The self-ish pigs took it all with them! I haven't found anything really valuable, not anything at all! Don't deny me this little bit, at least!"

"The more you have, the more you become a target for some bigger thief, or even a band of them," Matt warned.

"Don't *tell* me that!" Callio cried in an agony of appre-hension. "They'll do it, I know they'll do it! Big burly brutes! Overbearing ogres! Shambling giants! They'll take everything from me if they see I have anything! They've done it before and they'll do it again! But I can't just leave it all! You want me to give it up so nobody can steal it from me? What good will *that* do?"

"Not a whole lot," Matt admitted, "but you don't have to give it up forever—just for a little while."

Callio stared. "What? That's ridiculous! How can I give it up for a while, but have it when I want it?"

"Well, maybe not the instant you want it." Somehow, Matt's main concern for the little thief was to get him out of the bind his greed had gotten him into.

Papa nodded, catching on. "You can bury it. Haven't you ever heard of buried treasure?"

"Bury it?" Callio stared. "Well . . . yes, but . . . that's only for *real* treasure, I mean, gold and jewels and such!"

"But you just told us that if you'd found anything like that, you wouldn't need to haul all this stuff with you," Matt said patiently.

"Well . . . yes, but . . . that's because you can carry jewels with you, without hauling a whole cart!"

"Then why do you think people buried their gems?" Papa asked.

Matt nodded. "It was because they were going into country where there were a lot of robbers—or because war was coming."

Callio looked around wide-eyed. "You mean the townsfolk might have buried their treasures?"

"I doubt that," Matt said.

Papa nodded. "They wouldn't have had all that much, any of these commoners—except a few rich merchants, and I don't doubt they hired small armies to guard their goods as they moved north to join the king."

"Right." Matt nodded. "No treasure to be found here—unless you bury it."

"Me? Bury my things? But how could I do without them?" Nevertheless, Callio's gaze strayed to the loaded cart.

"You'd know where they were, and you could come back when you'd managed to stea . . . uh, *stake* yourself to a horse or two, to do your pulling for you." Matt didn't believe for a second that the petty thief would ever manage to steal a whole horse.

"But what if I forget where I buried them?" Callio wailed.

"Draw yourself a map," Papa suggested. "*Three* maps—this is too big a load to bury in a single hole."

"But the wood, the feather beds! They'll rot!"

"You won't be leaving them that long." At least, Matt hoped this whole conflict would be tidied up within the month.

"Then, too, this is the countryside of La Mancha," Papa said. "It is very dry here, not much water in the ground."

"It rains, though," Callio protested weakly. "Not very often, but it rains."

Matt shrugged. "So lay planks on top of the hole, a foot below the surface—and a second layer crosswise, to keep out the damp better."

"It could work." Callio's gaze strayed to the cart.

"Sure it could!" Matt said heartily. "Then every time your cart gets full, you just bury the load again."

"I could, I could indeed." Callio gazed at his cart, nodding, lost in thought. Suddenly he turned on Matt. "Why should you care, though? What do you expect to get out of this?"

"Me? Nothing," Matt said with contempt. "Just the satisfaction of helping a fellow creature." He started to climb up to Stegoman's back. "Come on, Papa. No point in staying where we're not appreciated."

"No, wait!" Callio called out, hand upraised.

"I have waited long enough, morsel," Stegoman rumbled. "Wizards, mount!"

But Papa turned to the thief before he boarded. "What is it, then?"

"I . . . thank you," Callio said lamely. After all, there wasn't really much more he could say.

"Glad to help." Matt settled in among Stegoman's plates.

"There is great satisfaction in having given even this small advice," Papa assured Callio.

The thief eyed him peculiarly. "You have a strange notion of pleasure."

"I must, or I would never have become a teacher," Papa told him. "Try it sometime. You may find that helping others is more rewarding than robbing them." He gave Callio a parting smile, then climbed aboard the dragon. Stegoman ran away from Callio, huge wings beating, and climbed into the air. He banked around man and cart once, gaining altitude, then arrowed away toward the windmill—but that one circling was enough for them all to see Callio pulling a shovel from his cart and beginning to dig.

The owner of the mill, as it turned out, had been ingenious; he had built over a well, and connected the sails to a windlass that pulled a chain of buckets. It took Papa only a few minutes to figure out how to put the contraption into gear, and the sails pumped him a tank full of water. They put the hams in to soak while Stegoman went hunting for stray mavericks, but it was a comfort to know that even if he didn't find any, he was assured of a full belly in the morning.

Meanwhile, Matt scrounged up a couple of sacks of meal

that the miller had apparently overlooked on his way out, lit
a fire on the hearth, found a cracked skillet that the family
hadn't thought worth taking along, and managed a reasonable facsimile of tortillas to go with their salt-beef stew.
They were just about to sit down when there was a knock at
the door. They traded glances of puzzled alarm; then Matt
stood up and slipped toward the door, drawing his sword,
while Papa called out, "Yes?"

"Shelter, gentles, I pray you!" called a voice they knew
even though it was muffled by oak.

Matt relaxed, sheathing his sword, and opened the door to
find a dirty thief, sagging with weariness. "I think there will
be rain," he said, "and I'd liefer have a better roof over me
than the bottom of my cart."

"Good thought." Matt waved him in, touching his wallet
as the thief passed. He had a notion he was going to have to
guard it closely. He barred the door and turned to find Papa
on his feet, beckoning Callio to a seat by the fire. "Welcome,
welcome indeed!"

"I—I thank you." Callio sat down on a rough wooden
chair, but his eyes and his nose turned automatically to the
fire and the cooking pot.

"Surely you must share our dinner!" Papa told him. "It is
rough fàre, but travelers cannot be epicures. Matthew, a
bowl for our friend?"

Matt pulled the spare bowl from his pack and filled it with
stew. Callio accepted it with a sigh. "You are friends indeed,
for the sky does indeed look like rain, and my things would
have been soaked if I hadn't buried them as you said!"

"No trouble finding planks, then?" Matt asked.

"None at all—I'd found some near a sawmill, solid oak,
beautifully grained, and even some sailcloth for mending
another mill. The boards were part of my treasure, and I covered them with the canvas."

"Well, that oughta do it." Matt settled on the center chair
and picked up his bowl again. "Hey, don't burn your throat!"

"I shall try not to." Callio picked a strip of meat out on the point of his knife and blew on it to cool it. "But I am so very hungry!"

"Yes—the refugees seem to have been bound and determined not to leave any food for the invading army," Matt said, frowning.

Of course, Callio couldn't bring himself to eat any of his loot.

Callio nodded. "I've never seen a countryside so stripped of anything that could be eaten." He tucked the meat into his mouth and chewed.

Matt agreed. "Good thing it's so early in spring, and the crops scarcely sprouting, or the farmers would probably have burned their fields as they retreated."

"What a waste," Callio mumbled around his meat.

"War always has a bad effect on crop yield," Papa said.

Callio swallowed heavily and asked nervously, "What of the dragon?"

"Oh, he'll be okay," Matt said. "He'll find something to eat, even if it's only a mountain goat—but if it really does rain, he'll find a cave for the night."

"He will not come back to sleep in the mill?" Callio asked, relieved.

Matt shook his head. "Can't get him through the doorway. He might try the stables back there in town, especially if they left a horse or two—but he won't come back here until morning."

"A lonely night for him," Callio sighed.

"He's used to it," Matt said. "Dragons are basically solitary creatures. Oh, they like company, but they don't feel they have to have a whole herd around them."

"Unlike people?" Papa asked, smiling.

"We do seem to be social creatures," Matt said. "Maybe that's why empty towns are so depressing."

"Places where the flock used to be, but is no longer?" Papa nodded. "There is sense to that."

Thinking of the emptiness of the land loosed a tide of melancholy. Matt laid down his empty bowl and glowered into the fire. "Haven't done much, have we? Most of Ibile is still a conquered Moorish province, its people fled to rally to their king."

"True, but the Mahdi isn't marching against that king yet," Papa protested. "He has only mounted a diversion, then turned to camp by the Pyrenees."

"Only because he's waiting to fall on my wife as she comes out of the mountains with every soldier she's got!"

Callio stared, wide-eyed and chewing, wondering what he'd wandered into.

"Meanwhile, Bordestang is besieged, and I've left my poor little mother to try to defend it!"

"Your 'poor little mother' is a holy terror, if she is angered," Papa reminded, "and this war is scarcely begun. Be of good cheer, my son—it is not that you have lost, but that you have only begun to fight." Papa clapped him on the shoulder. "You must not blame yourself when you have done nothing to deserve it."

"I know," Matt mumbled, but he stared into the fire anyway, feeling the melancholy descend further.

"There is no cause for such darkness of the heart," Papa said softly, "and this mood has come very suddenly, suspiciously so. Might it not be a spell cast by an enemy?"

"Yes, it could!" Matt sat bolt upright, staring as though he'd never seen flames before. "Try to bury *me* under depression, will he? We'll see how far he gets with that!"

They talked for half an hour longer, Matt trying very hard to be cheerful—but when he lay down, sorrow still tugged at his heart, and with it, fear. As his eyes closed, he couldn't stave off the feeling of failure. Okay, so he was up against insurmountable odds—but even so, he had to be doing awfully poorly if the only ally he could find was a thief too inept to make a peacetime living, and too insecure to bury his loot when the countryside was deserted. So it wasn't surprising that, when his eyes did close, he should dream of an empty land, bone-dry and breathless, under a lowering sky that darkened and deepened with a feeling of doom about to fall, the sun searing mercilessly in front of that purpling background. Maybe it wasn't even surprising that bare bones should begin to rise from that dead land, rise and pull themselves together, until a nightmarish horde of skeletons came plodding toward Matt, skeletons of extinct rhinoceroses, chalicotheres, giant lizards, and even a few Neanderthals. *We are the dead,* they seemed to chant. *We are what you shall become very soon. Welcome among us, for you shall never leave.*

Matt screamed denial inside his head, but he couldn't let the sound out, couldn't utter, because he didn't seem to have a body, was only a point of consciousness that the skeletons approached with a steady and inexorable tread.

Then a shout sounded behind him, hooves beat a tattoo, and an armored figure on a spavined horse sped past him. A broken, poorly mended lance dropped down.

The army of skeletons all turned their plodding gait toward the horseman, their very postures threatening to grind him beneath their hooves, their feet—but the broken lance touched the first bony mastodon, and it exploded into a shower of ivory. The horseman swerved, riding a great circle through the horde, and wherever his lance touched, bones shot into the air to fall as they had been before Matt saw them.

Then out he came at a wobbling gallop, turned his nag for another charge—and the half of the horde that was left turned and fled, bones clanking and clacking in their hurry.

One skeleton, though, somehow flew with no skin—its structure showed it to be a pterodactyl. It banked, turning back, and struck at the knight with a cawing shriek that extended into the sound of nails on glass as it flew apart, its bones raining down—but the knight swayed in the saddle.

Quicker hooves sounded, and a short, chubby man on a donkey galloped past Matt's viewpoint to pull up beside the swaybacked nag. The knight leaned and fell, his brazen wide-brimmed helmet flying away, but the chubby man caught him and somehow bore up under the weight of his armor.

With the helmet gone, Matt could see that the knight's hair was snowy white. He muttered his thanks to his squire and clambered back into the saddle. The squire turned the donkey and trotted after the helmet, and the knight turned to Matt. "You need not thank me, *señor*—it is I who must thank you, for an opportunity to strike a blow for Right and Goodness."

Now Matt could see his face clearly. He was old and wrinkled, his beard sparse and patchy, his armor dented and rusty—but his eyes were young, and alight with zeal.

"No, it is I who must thank you, milord." He tried to bow. "You have saved me when fear and self-doubt had paralyzed me."

"Never doubt yourself!" the old knight said sternly, jamming his lance into its stirrup. "If you fight for Right and Good, your arm will always be strong, your sword keen! You may be struck down, but you shall rise again! You may lose the battles, but you shall win the war!"

And in Ibile rather than Spain, Matt reflected, the old cavalier was probably right. But how had a fictitious character from his own universe come to be in this one?

He was in Matt's dream, of course. No doubt Matt had brought him along, unknowing, waiting to be needed—as he surely had been now. The idea seemed somehow wrong, but it would do for the time being.

"Never fear," the old knight counseled, "or rather, pay no attention to your fears. No man can help being afraid now and again, but he can take that fear as a blow struck against him, and parry it, block it, let it serve only to inspire him to strike back with greater strength, to bend his mind more sharply to outwitting the enemy."

"Yes, my lord." Matt felt humbled and exalted at the same time.

"You must never cease to strive," the old knight told him. "The good fight is worth fighting for itself, even if one loses." A sudden grin broke the old leathery countenance into wrinkles of delight. "Besides, one always might win."

"As I am sure you will." Inspiration struck. "Could I ask you to help me, my lord? The paynim strike against the heart of Ibile, even to the mountains, even to the rivers of the north! The rightful king gathers his people there to make one last stand. With your arm to aid us, we might yet prevail!"

"A quest!" the old knight cried joyfully, and turned to his

squire, who came riding up with the brass helmet. "Old friend, once again we ride on a quest!"

The squire grinned from ear to ear. "More misadventures!" He handed the helmet up to his knight.

The old knight clapped it on his head and turned back to Matt. "Be assured that we shall aid, *señor*—if we can only think how!"

"I am sure that you shall, my lord," Matt said, grinning. "You never fail to be inspired with new blows to strike against the enemies of Right!"

"I shall ride through men's dreams, I shall inspire women to esteem themselves!" The broken lance suddenly dipped, and Matt tried to flinch away, but its tip touched him somehow. Fear and melancholy vanished as the old knight intoned, "You, too, must believe in your own worth! The world falters, the world totters, and it is you who must brace it up! No, do not flinch away in false modesty, for I know you are equal to this task!" Then the old knight's eyes seemed to expand; everything outside them became indistinct, and the rusty voice echoed in Matt's head. "Awake now, freed from self-doubt and feelings of doom impending! Shoulder the world, and be glad of your purpose!" The slight pressure vanished, and Matt knew the lance had lifted, but the light old eyes still commanded every iota of his attention as the old knight intoned, "Awaken! Awaken in every fiber of your being; awaken in hope and in zeal!" Then the light eyes expanded still further till they were all that Matt could see; they turned blue, the pale blue of earliest dawn, a paleness that became tinged with rose at one side, tinged then swept with rays of gold, and Matt blinked, realizing that he was staring at the morning sky through the window of the mill, and that somehow the night had ended.

He levered himself up on one elbow and saw the campfire, bright and smokeless, with Papa watching a steaming bucket and toasting wheat cakes in the cracked skillet. He looked up, anxious, concerned. "Good morning, my son."

Matt blinked, then smiled. "Good morning, my father."

The concern lightened a little, and Papa asked, "Have you found a cure for your melancholy?"

Matt looked about him, and was amazed that the inside of the mill looked so bright, so golden. He was filled with elation, with a bubbling enthusiasm. He remembered the Mahdi, the towering djinn, the acres and acres of Moorish troops—but somehow he was sure that all these things would pass, that he and his family, and all the good folk of Ibile and Merovence, would still be standing and triumphant when they did. He turned back to Papa, grinning. "No. The cure found me."

Unfortunately, the world wasn't the only thing that was still with them—so was Callio. Papa generously slid pancakes onto the thief's plate—he had saved one of his own, as well as a cup and spoon, out of his loot; the three were only wooden, so their owners hadn't bothered taking them along. But when they had finished breakfast, washed their tableware, drowned the fire, and started hauling the hams out of the water trough and into the sunlight, Callio bent to help with a will. "Why do we set them outside? Ought we not to put them in my cart, so we can take them with us?"

"We're not going far," Matt told him, and they went back for a second load.

When they finished hauling, Callio was still tagging merrily along.

"I think we have gained a mascot," Papa muttered, not entirely happily.

"Don't worry," Matt muttered back out of the corner of his mouth. "He's bound to take off when he sees Stegoman again."

"I think the dragon has seen *us*." Papa nodded at the sky.

There, gilded by the morning rays, soared a creature that might have been an eagle, if it hadn't been so long-necked. Callio came up with them, following their gazes, interested. "Is it a swan?"

"A little larger than that," Matt explained. "He just looks smaller because he's so far away."

Callio's eyes widened, and dread began to show. He backed

away as the flyer banked, sliding lower and lower in a spiral, swelling into the form of a dragon, and Stegoman landed in a shower of dust.

"Good morning, High Rider," Matt said with a grin—a grin because he'd noticed that Callio was no longer beside him. "How was the hunting?"

"I found a mountain goat just before the light left the hill-tops," Stegoman grumbled. "He was small and tough. I am hungry, Matthew."

"Help yourself." Matt gestured at the hams, then stepped back. Stegoman stepped forward, lowering his head, and started gulping. Five minutes later, he sighed and nodded. "Well done. I shall be content for the day now. Will you fetch your packs and mount?"

"We'll be glad to," Matt said. "Thanks for the invitation."

They went back inside the mill, and Matt found himself suddenly wondering if their belongings would be where they'd left them—but he did Callio an injustice; everything was there. They left the mill with their packs on their backs, then realized that their footsteps had developed an odd echo.

CHAPTER 21

Matt turned around, holding out a hand. "Well, Callio, it's been nice meeting you. Have a nice trip."

"Why, thank you, Lord Wizard!" Callio seized his hand and began pumping. "It's so good of you to invite me!"

"Sarcasm is sometimes ill placed, Matthew," Papa muttered in an undertone.

Even more silently, Matt cursed his own stupidity. In desperation, he said, "Oh, how silly of me! I can't invite you—I'm not the one who'd be carrying you!" He looked up at the dragon and shook his head as he said, "Stegoman, you don't really want to carry one more, do you?"

His heart sank when the dragon didn't answer, but studied Callio long and hard.

Callio, no doubt wondering whether he'd been added to the menu, began to back away.

"There is a need to bring him," the dragon rumbled. "I sense a rightness in his joining us."

Callio looked relieved, then realized that he might have been dropped from the menu only to be put in the larder.

"Are you sure?" Matt wasn't used to Stegoman having hunches.

"I know not how or why, only that he must come with us," Stegoman said slowly. "But know, slight man, that your cart must stay here."

Callio's face twisted in agony.

"Yeah, can't be without that," Matt said quickly. "How would you carry your loot? But you can't pack a cart on top of a dragon, not with three men along. Too bad, Callio. Guess you'll have to stay here. Good meeting you, though." He turned away to Stegoman—fast.

"If I must do without it, I must," Callio cried. "I shall come, Lord Wizard!"

Matt slowed and muttered something under his breath.

"No, no, Matthew, he is only a thief," Papa said, grinning. "I am sure he will prove invaluable in helping us find dinner. Let us accept your scaly friend's invitation, and fly."

Apparently Callio hadn't really thought out the flying part. He clung to a back-plate, staring down in terror, rigid as a board the whole way. Matt's reassurance that he wouldn't let the thief fall didn't seem to console him much.

"It is better if you don't look down," Papa said helpfully.

Callio tore his eyes away from the ground and stared ahead. "I would never have dreamed that I would ride a dragon!"

"Takes a little getting used to," Matt called over the roar of the wind. "Just be glad he's flying low."

To be on the safe side, he touched his purse. Yes, it was still there. He tucked it down inside his hose and called, "Papa, how many fingers do you have?"

Saul and Mama patrolled the battlements, fidgeting. "Anyway, it's quiet, Lady Mantrell."

"Yes. That worries me." Mama frowned. "I would expect them to attack now and then from sheer boredom, if nothing else."

"Well, they've tried all the basic assaults and found that they don't work. Sooner or later, every siege boils down to sitting still and trying to wait out the defenders."

"But not so soon," Mama said. "It has scarcely been a fortnight. Perhaps we should have men stab the earth with rods, all around the inside of the wall."

"Checking for miners, you mean? Good thought." Saul frowned. "Seems as though we ought to be able to do better than that, though. Maybe a magical equivalent of sonar . . ."

"Yes, and a warding spell! You can make a magical fence, no?"

"Yes. I mean, it's fairly easy—but it's also easy to by-pass, since every magician knows about it."

"But if they are stopped by a warding spell underground, they will not be looking for your alarm system! They will bypass the wards, but we will still know they are coming!"

"Great idea." But Saul eyed Mama warily. "You have problems with home security?"

"No, I have Ramón," Mama said absently. Her brows were knit; she was still worrying over some problem.

"What's bothering you?"

"The commander of this assault," Mama said.

"You mean the guy with the big gaudy turban and the huge gaudy pavilion? What about him?"

"He is too obvious," Mama said, "and he is a general. Sorcerers began this war—does it not make sense that sorcerers would still command it?"

And Saul had thought *he* was paranoid! On second thought, maybe he was—Mama was just being rational, given the circumstances. "Why do you think there has to be a ruler behind the ruler, milady? Why won't the obvious do?"

"Because we deal with a wily enemy, one who specializes in feints and diversions," Mama said. "His drawing Alisande away from the city before the attack shows that—and his soldiers descending in force the day after she was gone. Additionally, he must know we have sent couriers after her and, even if his minions stop the riders, that we have magical means of sending. Would he not fear that she would turn back and attack him from the rear?"

"It makes sense, now that you mention it," Saul said slowly, "but I would keep on going, trusting my castellans to hold the city for me."

"You are not a general, though. We must ask Sir Guy. Before that, however, humor me, Saul—make your gazing bowl again and tell it to show us who truly commands this army."

Saul looked down at her a moment, considering. She hadn't

been wrong yet, and she was a scholar who had read virtually all the medieval literature there was, with its descriptions
of treacheries and double-dealing. Somehow, he didn't doubt
her hunches. "Right away, Lady Mantrell."

So he filled the bowl, made the passes, and chanted the
spell, then told the water,

> "Beauty is not, as fond men misdeem,
> A show of things that only seem.
> Waters, show us, let us see
> Exactly who our seemers be!
> Rich or poor, or high or low,
> Show us to whom these Moors do bow!
> No matter how rich or poor his quarters,
> Show us who really gives the orders!"

The pool clouded, then cleared, and they found themselves staring at the gorgeous pavilion, all right—but it was
to the side of the bowl. In its center stood a small, unassum-
ing tent, bigger than most, but nowhere near as big as many.
An ordinary soldier sat at its door, dressed in a camel rider's
robe and head cloth held by a braided camel-hair rope—but
he was studying a huge old book in his lap.

"Now may my spells his book engage," Saul improvised.
"Let us see and read his page."

The picture swelled until one leaf filled the bowl, but they
still couldn't read it—it was in Arabic. But they could understand the geometric symbols they saw, at least the penta-
gram and the elaborate, curlicued decahedron.

"He's thinking about warding spells, all right!" Saul said.

The book slammed shut.

Mama cried,

> "Raise the view a little space!
> Let us look upon his face!"

"Hey, that's my spell," Saul objected.

The bowl didn't seem to mind; it blurred as the view tilted up, then steadied on a face that was frowning upward, searching the sky, a very ordinary Berber face, mostly African but partly Arabic, though not as dark a brown as some, with wide brown eyes and a small, neatly trimmed mustache and beard.

"I shall remember you," Mama promised the image.

The sorcerer's frown didn't change, but he waved a hand across his face, and the bowl went cloudy. When it cleared, it was only water again.

Saul sat back with a sigh. "You were right. The real commander is a sorcerer disguised as a minor officer. He knows we're on to him now."

"Much good may that do him." Mama smiled. "But it will do far more good for us."

"Just what are you planning?" Saul asked warily.

"Female magic," Mama answered. "Good day, Saul."

Saul watched with trepidation as she went back into the castle. He watched with even more trepidation an hour later, when she came out wearing a gown that was officially demure and modest, with a high neckline, long loose sleeves, and a hem that brushed the toes of small cordovan slippers—officially demure, but clinging to her figure in ways that should have classified it as a lethal weapon.

"Lady Mantrell!" Saul exclaimed, shocked. "What are you doing?" After all, everyone knew that mothers weren't supposed to be sexually attractive, especially mothers of grown sons.

"Only what I have done every day since this siege began, Saul," she told him, "patrolling the battlements and encouraging our soldiers."

Well, she certainly raised the morale of the soldiers, even though her manner was far from alluring—but between sentry posts, she moved with a languid grace that would have made Saul feel like baying at the moon, if he hadn't had a wife of his own. In a panic, he wondered what duty he owed to Matt. Sure, he was supposed to protect Mama from the

Moors—but was he really supposed to protect the Moors from Mama?

Stegoman dropped them at sunset and went off to hunt.

Matt stretched. "At this rate, I'm going to have saddle sores."

"Yes, and you don't even have a saddle." Papa smiled. "Was it not pleasant to have so uneventful a flight?"

"Seems that's what I always said whenever I reached O'Hare Airport. But it was kinda nice not to see any genies trying to swat us out of the air."

Callio looked up from his own stretching, alarmed.

"Yes, I had expected at least one such run-in," Papa admitted. "Do you suppose Lakshmi and her associates have spread the word to leave us alone?"

"That wouldn't matter to lamp-slaves and ring-slaves. They have to do as they're told, no matter what."

"True," Papa said thoughtfully. "Perhaps the word has also run to the sorcerers who hold the lamps and the rings, and they are holding back for fear of having the genies freed."

"That could be a really well-earned fear, for some of them," Matt agreed. "There might be a genie or two wanting revenge." He shuddered at the thought of a maimed and dying sorcerer, then reminded himself sternly that one less enemy shouldn't bother him—should it?

"Are we truly apt to be attacked by a genie?" Callio quavered.

"It happened yesterday," Matt told him, "and another time before that, too. Look, you don't have to come along, you know."

"Oh, but I wish to!" Callio developed a faraway gaze. "Perhaps I am fortunate in not having met you sooner."

"I was afraid you'd say that," Matt sighed. "Well, down to practicalities. How are you at lighting a campfire?"

The thief answered with a mirthless smile. "I have done it more nights than not, Lord Wizard."

"I knew there was a reason we brought you along. How about lighting up for us, okay?"

"My delight!"

"Always like to see a man doing something he enjoys." Matt turned to Papa. "I don't suppose there's any point in hunting?"

Papa shrugged. "There is always the . . ."

Puffs of dust shot up from the ground in a semicircle around their feet. Matt stared at them. "Now, what do you suppose that could be?"

The wind brought them a sound like a string of firecrackers blowing.

"Enemy fire!" snapped Papa. "Get *down*!" To emphasize the point, he swung a leg, knocking Matt's feet out from under him, then fell beside him—just in time, for bullets kicked up dust behind them.

"What evil magic is that?" Callio asked, facedown in the dirt.

"A rapid-fire spell!" Matt shouted.

"Roll into the streambed, quickly!" Papa cried.

They did, with bullets kicking dust about them, following them, reaching them only as they fell into the little trench. Callio cried out in pain and fear.

"Let me see it." Matt crawled over to him and took his arm. The blood oozed out over Callio's homespun sleeve. "Only a flesh wound. Here." Matt tore off the bottom of the man's tunic and wrapped it around the arm. "We'll fix it when we've chased away the, ah, enemy sorcerer. How's the pain?"

"I can bear it," Callio whimpered, "but how shall I steal with only one hand?"

"Very carefully," Matt told him, and slapped him on the other shoulder. "Buck up—we all have setbacks." He squirmed over to Papa, reflecting that maybe he wouldn't have to check his wallet every fifteen minutes from now on.

He came up beside his father, who had found a stick and wadded bulrushes about it.

"What kind of gun is it?" Matt asked.

"An automatic weapon of some sort," Papa answered. The wad of bulrushes was about as big as his head now; he stuck it up above the bank. Puffs of dirt exploded all along the bank. Finally the wad blew apart. A few seconds later, they heard the chatter of the shots. "An assault rifle, from the sound of it," Papa said, "and although he's not the greatest marksman in the world, he is good enough."

"How do you define 'good enough'?"

"By whether or not I stay alive," Papa said grimly. "I did not know that gunpowder could work here."

"It can't," Matt said, then frowned. "No, come to think of it, I've never tried gunpowder itself, without a spell to help."

"But it will work with a spell?"

"Empty cartridges will work, with a spell." Matt's eyes lost focus. "Come to think of it, maybe even without cartridges . . ."

"Catch up on your research and development later," Papa told him. "For now, let's see if we can't find a way to stop the dunderhead." He started to crawl along the streambed.

"Wait." Matt reached out and touched his shoulder. "Let's figure out what we're up against first. If it's an assault rifle, how did it get here?"

"Yes, the weaponry is a little advanced for this universe," Papa said, frowning, "though as you've just pointed out, it may not be a real assault rifle—only a local imitation."

"It still means that whoever made it copied the design from our universe," Matt said. "That kind of limits the possibilities."

"Why? We know this Nirobus of yours doesn't do the actual dirty work himself—he sends others to do it for him. Why couldn't he teach some local peasant how to handle the weapon?"

"That would account for the marksmanship," Matt agreed. "Even if Nirobus imported the sniper from New Jersey, though, he'd be unfamiliar enough with the territory so that he wouldn't be sure what to shoot at."

"And would therefore shoot at anything that moved," Papa said grimly. "I shall have to go very carefully." He turned away.

Matt caught his arm. "Hold on. My universe, my risk."

"You have more of your life left to live," Papa objected.

"You have plenty, too, though, and some unborn grand-children left to see. I'm pulling rank, Papa—youth before beauty."

Papa frowned. "I don't think you have the quotation quite right."

"Good enough to get by you, though." Matt squirmed past him, then turned back to cut off his protest. "Besides, you can do a better job keeping his attention."

"I can?" Papa asked, wide-eyed. "How?"

"However you did in the Marines! Just keep him shoot-ing, if you can do it safely—the less ammunition he has, the better."

Matt left him thinking and crawled on down the streambed. He didn't know what Papa was planning, only knew that every now and then, he heard a burst of firing behind him. He hoped Papa wasn't getting reckless, and began to be afraid—the veteran seemed to be determined to take a risk. He reminded himself that his father had always been the cautious sort and crawled on.

The streambed widened out where it joined a drainage ditch coming from another field. Matt sat up on his heels, considering. He could crawl up the ditch to the hills, but that would take so long a time that the enemy might have fled, and Matt had no great desire to have a sniper following them. On the other hand, what kind of magic could bring him in behind the other man unnoticed?

A dust devil suddenly boiled up from the streambed. Matt shrank back, hissing, "Keep down!"

The tiny whirlwind fell in on itself into voluptuous, if diminutive, contours, and Lakshmi stood before him in miniature. "I thank you for your kind thoughts, wizard, but I had already realized the need for discretion."

Coming from her, that wasn't entirely reassuring. "Uh—good to see you again," Matt said lamely. "Sorry I can't talk just now, but I have to go kill off somebody before he kills me."

"So I see," Lakshmi told him. "I shall be glad to take you to him—for a price."

Somehow, Matt had a notion what the price would be. "Thanks, but my mommy told me not to talk to strange women."

"Ah, but you know me well by now."

"Yeah, but you're one of the strangest women I've ever met." Matt held up a palm. "Sorry, no offense—but you *are* the first female genie I've seen, if you don't count the one on television, and she was just an actress."

"Actress?" Lakshmi frowned. "A player, you mean?"

"Not in any game I've ever heard of, no. Sorry, but I can't afford to take on any more debts right now—I'm in up to my neck as it is."

"Perhaps I should slay this cowardly assassin for you, then."

"Nice thought," Matt said, with what he hoped was a grateful grin, "but I need him alive, at least temporarily. I have to ask him a few questions."

"He will be in more of a mood to answer them when I have done with him," Lakshmi said ominously, and turned into a whirlwind again—a small one, that died down as quickly as it had come.

Matt stared at the pattern it had left with a sinking heart. He turned and started crawling back to Papa. A flock of crows flew overhead, toward the sniper. He wondered who had sent them.

Then suddenly, there was a wild burst of machine-gun fire. The crows came shooting back, cawing frantically. Then the machine gun went silent, and Matt pushed himself to his feet and sprinted, doubled over. Somehow he suspected what had happened and wanted to be there before Lakshmi.

"Matthew! Get down!" Papa called as he came into sight. Matt shook his head, though, and came panting up just as the whirlwind careered down from the sky and dumped a black-clad bundle into the ditch before it turned into Lakshmi, ten feet tall and glowing with anger. "The fool had the audacity to strike at me!"

"They went through her!" the black-clad bundle howled,

still curled in a ball. "They went right through her, and she didn't even notice!"

"Oh, I noticed, well enough!" Lakshmi snapped. "They were quite painful, I assure you!" She turned to Matt. "You will understand, therefore, if he is not completely unharmed."

Matt frowned. "I don't see any blood."

"It is not a cut or a wound, but knots tied in certain muscles," Lakshmi said evenly. "It is well I went in your place, mortal man, for this is truly one of the *hashishim*."

"The original assassins?" Matt stared.

"The same. He is dazed with hashish, or something much like it, and sent to slay you so that he can obtain more from his master."

"Thank you," Matt said, feeling totally inadequate. "Thank you very much. I—I'm sorry I can't show my gratitude in any more tangible way."

"I am scarcely in the mood for it now! See if you cannot find better company to keep!" Then the whirlwind kicked up about her, absorbing her, and disappeared.

Matt nudged the black bundle with his toe. "She's gone. You can come out now."

"For real?" The assassin unwound enough to risk a peek. "Really gone?"

Papa stared. "Luco?!??!?"

Mama sat in her chamber, brushing her hair with long, languid strokes, singing a pensive melody, ostensibly alone.

The air shimmered, a heat-haze that slowly thickened until it disappeared with a soft explosion. Mama turned, wide-eyed, heart racing.

CHAPTER 22

The sorcerer-commander stood there in her boudoir, but he had changed his camel rider's habit for a white silken robe with a purple sleeveless surcoat, and a turban of cloth-of-gold. He bowed, touching forehead, lips, and breast. "I greet you, O Fairest of the Fair!"

"I am not fair, but dark!" Mama's voice trembled.

"Hair like a raven's wings, eyes like those of a gazelle," the sorcerer breathed. "I am Beidizam, commander of the forces at your gate—as you know."

Mama came to her feet in one lithe movement, raising a quivering hand to ward him off. "What do you in my chamber, sir?"

"What should a man of youth and vigor wish, in the chamber of a beautiful woman?" Beidizam breathed.

"Sir!" Mama cried. "You insult me!"

"I certainly did not intend to do so." But Beidizam's eyes glittered with contempt as well as lust. "I wish only to give praise where it is due, and to establish a feeling of friendliness."

"Friendliness?" Mama drew back a little more, eyes wary. "Strange words, for the man who besieges my city!"

"Ah, but though we are enemies, surely we may converse in civil tones," Beidizam protested, "for it has occurred to me that a conference between the two commanders might be of benefit to us both." The sorcerer raised a palm to forestall her objections. "Do not deny it—I felt your regard as I sat before my tent, reflecting upon the wizardry of the ancient Greeks. For my part, I have watched you on the battlements, and have seen that, although the Witch Doctor and the Black

Knight command with you, it is as often your spells that balk my army as theirs. No wonder, when they are cast by a lady of such loveliness!"

"I am only one castellan of three!" Mama objected. "I cannot answer for all of us! You must speak to us in unison, sir, or not at all!" She frowned. "But surely you know that. Why do you seek me out separately?"

"What man would not seek to be alone with such a beauty?" Beidizam stepped forward and caught her hand. "You are a woman of passions, long estranged from your man—and the ways of the Franks are well known, how they make gods of their women, and the women grow willful and wanton thereby. Oh, the attitudes of the Frankish women are famous, I assure you." He pressed her hand to his lips.

Mama snatched it away. "But you may not know of the loyalty of Frankish women, of our devotion to our husbands and to the chastity our Church so praises!"

"As you do not know of the skills of Muslim men," the sorcerer said, voice low and husky, "of how intimately we know women, of the heights of ecstasy to which we . . ."

A dull thud dammed his stream of talk. His eyes glazed for a moment before he fell.

Mama stepped away from the unconscious man, scrubbing her hand against her robe. "Thank Heaven you were here, Sir Guy! It has been many years since I met a man who so disgusted me with his contempt for women!"

"Tapestries have many uses," Sir Guy said, "and you were quite clever in drawing his attention so that his back was to me." He tucked the cudgel into his belt, looking down on Beidizam with distaste. "Much though I mislike striking a man from behind, I must admit it is the only way to capture a sorcerer. Still, considering how greatly he wished to take advantage of you, and how little chance he meant to allow you to refuse, I think I can contain my shame." He pulled a cord from his waist and knelt to tie the sorcerer's hands and feet.

Mama took a strip of muslin from her dressing table and

handed it to him. "Gag him well, Sir Guy. He must not speak until we wish him to—no, not in any language."

"Help me!" Luco howled. "I've got cramps in all five limbs!"

"Oh, for crying out softly," Matt said in disgust, and pantomimed untying a knot as he chanted,

> "Vulgar layabouts that want
> Words, and sweetness, and be scant
>   Of self-rule's measure,
> Tyrant pushers have abused
> So that they long since have refused
>   To heed folks' censure.
> She who now arrested thee
> Bade your joints tormented be,
>   Cramp'd indenture.
> Still may syllables amain
> Loose those cramps and soothe your pain,
>   But in debenture!"

Luco relaxed with a groan.

"You could say 'thank you,' " Matt said, irritated.

Luco dared to peek. "Is she gone?"

"Yes, she is gone." Papa frowned. "What are *you* doing here?"

With a yell, Luco uncoiled, yanking at the trigger.

Papa and Matt both stood, frowning darkly. "Just what in creation do you think you're doing?" Matt asked.

Luco stared down at his hands, cupped to hold a rifle that wasn't there. "It's gone!"

"You always play air assault rifle?" Matt demanded.

"But it was there just a second ago!" Luco cried, looking about him frantically.

"Wizard," asked Callio, "what is this contraption?"

"There!" Luco lunged.

Matt caught him and spun him around, tripping him. Luco went sprawling and burst into sobs.

Papa looked down at him uncertainly. "I know you have been through an ordeal of the unexpected, Luco—but to be so unmanned as to weep?"

"He's in withdrawal." Matt had other problems, though. He moved slowly toward the thief. "How about handing it to me, Callio? Very carefully."

"Is it truly dangerous?" Callio held the gun up and peered down the barrel.

Matt caught his breath before Callio could hear the gasp rattle and said, with exaggerated calmness, "Very dangerous. Put it down carefully, Callio. Just lay it flat on the ground."

The thief lowered the rifle but looked up at Matt, and the wizard could almost hear the gears turning in the thief's head. If the thing was dangerous and rare, it should have value— and it might give him some control over the wizards . . .

"You just looked at your own death," Matt explained. "If you had happened to push the wrong lever or button while you were looking into it, that gadget would have blown your head to bits."

With an oath, Callio dropped the assault rifle.

Fortunately, it didn't go off. Matt caught it up with a sigh of relief. He pointed it toward the hills, examined it quickly, and threw the lever he thought was the safety. Then he squeezed the trigger. When it wouldn't move, he finally began to relax—but kept firm hold on the stock and barrel. "It's this little lever right here, Callio. As long as you push it over to this side, the big lever—the trigger—is locked in place, and the rifle can't hurt anybody."

"There is only one magazine in his belt, and none in his pockets." But Papa held up a small flat envelope between thumb and forefinger.

Matt nodded, but only said, "Probably more of them up on that ridge. I'll have to go scout for them."

"I shall," Callio volunteered. "What are they?"

Matt was tempted—one less chore, one less delay—but decided he didn't trust the thief farther than he could see him. "Thanks, Callio, but they're dangerous, too—not as dangerous as the machine itself, but dangerous enough."

"Oh." Callio shrank back.

It was galling to realize that Matt probably owed his life to the thief's acquisitive streak—but he reminded himself that it had been an accident. Callio hadn't intended to save Matt's life—it was just that, like a magpie, he felt the need to pick up anything that caught his eye.

Papa was seeing to more immediate problems. "Tell us now, Luco—how did you come here?"

The kid snarled something unprintable about something anatomically improbable.

Papa frowned and turned away, making a gesture over the packet, muttering something under his breath.

"Luco," Matt said softly.

The kid glared up at him, then stared down the barrel of the assault rifle. For a moment he froze stiff; then he relaxed, mouth quirking into contempt. "Who are you trying to kid, Mantrell? You don't even know how to work that thing—and even if you did, you're too chicken to use it!"

"Too good, you mean," Papa said, frowning. "We are not in New Jersey now. There are no police to arrest Matthew for killing you."

Luco kept his glare locked with Matt's, but what he saw there seemed to unnerve him.

Matt nodded slowly. "There's a war on, Luco. Nobody's going to count one body more or less."

"You wouldn't do it, churchboy!"

"Not kill," Matt agreed, "but remember your debenture— the last line of the rhyme that killed your cramps, remember?"

Luco eyed him with complete suspicion. "What's debenture?"

"Well, in your case," Matt said, "it mostly means I can make the cramps come back at a moment's notice."

Luco went very still, but his glare was pure hatred. "Always so high-and-mighty! Always thinking you were better than us!"

"No," Matt said, "but you did."

With a shout, Luco shot to his feet and charged at Matt, whipping out a switchblade. Matt stepped aside and swung the rifle; the barrel clouted Luco on the back of the head. He fell and went limp, sobbing again.

"He is not that much of a coward, Matthew," Papa said before he could ask. "It has only been too long since he has taken his drug."

"Just leave me alone!"

"Yes, leave you alone for five minutes, so you can sniff your powder," Papa said, and shrugged. "Why not? Come, Matthew—let us look away for a space."

Matt stared at him as though he were crazy, but Papa took him firmly by the arm and turned him away, pointing at the hills. "As I remember, he was atop that crest that is a little lower than the two to either side of . . ."

Luco let out a wordless yell of agony, anger, and panic.

Papa turned back to him slowly. "Yes?"

"They're gone!" Luco was frantically searching every pocket.

"What—these?" Papa held up a handful of the little envelopes.

Luco stared, mouth gaping. Then with a shout of rage, he lunged at Papa.

Papa danced out of his way; Matt stuck out a foot, and Luco went sprawling. The kid thrashed around, eyes wild, gathering himself for another spring.

"I think we know why you did it now," Papa said with disgust. He tossed a packet to Luco.

Luco pounced on it, ripping it open, pouring the powder out into his palm, and licking it up.

Matt watched, shaking his head, face somber. Once, very long ago, Luco had been his friend. Then he had started listening to the older boys, and had started smoking marijuana. Not too long after that, he had started beating up Matt. His heart twisted with sorrow for the nice kid Luco had once been, the good man he might have grown up to be.

"Perhaps you can heal him here, Matthew," Papa said

softly, "but not back there, and you cannot heal our old universe. Magic does not work, there."

Matt frowned. "You mean that's what Luco's trying to get?"

Luco cursed violently.

Papa turned, raising his eyebrows. "Yes?"

"It didn't come on, you old swindler! It didn't do anything!"

"No, nothing," Papa agreed. "Magic works in this universe, Luco. I took the kick out of that packet. If you want it back, you'll tell me who brought you here, and how."

"You bastard!" Luco was trembling now. His eyes were bloodshot. "I'm getting strung out! You said you'd give it back to me—give!"

"Ah, but I'm a storekeeper now." Papa sat on his heels, just beyond Luco's reach. "I don't give anything away."

Luco bellowed and sprang at him.

Papa leaped to his feet and stepped aside. Luco went sprawling in the dirt and began sobbing again.

"No, you cannot take it from me," Papa said. "You want something, you pay for it."

Luco reached for his pocket.

"Not money, no," Papa said. "Information."

"All right, all right, anything! Just give me the packet!"

"First the answers. Question One: Where did this new drug come from?"

"From Groldor! Word is he moved in with a gang of his own, a bunch of cavemen with AK-forty-sevens, and put the drug out on the streets!"

"Groldor?" Papa frowned. "I thought the drug boss in our town was Cracker. Didn't he object?"

"Sure, man! This new stuff, Magic, makes you forget about crack and even heroin!"

"So it satisfies the old cravings and plants a new one," Papa said. "What did Cracker do?"

"Hit Groldor with everything he had. Word is it was short and hard—by the time the cops got there, only two bodies were left, and they were each holding the gun that shot the other guy. Groldor's smart and clean." He shivered, only partly from withdrawal.

"Yes, I remember reading about the 'gangland duel' in the newspaper," Papa said. "So he took the territory, and the gangs decided not to fight him."

"Why should they, when he cut them in?" Luco asked. "Gave each gang its own stash to sell—but he drew the lines, told 'em where their selling territory ended and the next gang's began. The Tics got greedy and jumped the Sangers, but Groldor's muscles showed up and beat them both into the ground." He shivered again. "Bastard knew when and where the Tics were going to jump, even though the Sangers didn't!"

"Almost as though he could read their minds," Matt said grimly.

"So nobody tried to poach anybody else's customers after that?" Papa asked.

" 'Course not, man! Two Tics died, and died hard!"

"But all the gangs did good business."

"Fantastic, man! Groldor made 'em keep the price down, said it'd sell more, and it did! Addict on one dose, just like crack. You feel great for an hour, okay for a day, but when you wake up, you gotta have more!"

"So you're in good shape long enough to steal enough to pay for tomorrow's dose," Papa interpreted. "I haven't heard of the police arresting anybody, though, Luco. Why is that?"

Luco laughed. "Stuff's not on the banned list, man! Nowhere near! I don't know what it is, but word has it the cop labs can't find anything but salt! Cops can't touch 'em! Can't touch Groldor, can't touch his muscles, can't touch the gangs, can't touch the buyers!" Luco gave them a shaky grin. "This Groldor is one smart dude."

Matt shuddered at the hero worship in his voice.

"Only salt, but it takes you to Heaven and dumps you into Hell." Papa looked up at his son.

Matt nodded grimly. "This Magic is magic, all right, or made by it."

"Yes, or my spell would not have rendered it useless," Papa said. "Does that not also mean it was made in Merovence?"

"Made in Merovence, and Nirobus found some way for this Groldor to take it to our universe and keep the magic working." Matt's eyes widened. "So the link wasn't just between universes—it was between me and my old neighborhood! That's why it was so easy for me to get home! Sorry, Papa—it looks as though I've unleashed this monstrosity on all of you!"

"Not you," Papa snapped, "but someone who exploited you."

Luco grinned. "Not hard."

Papa turned back, and for a moment, the look he gave Luco was pure poison. He had to look away for a moment to recover his composure. "If it was made in Merovence, and Nirobus is keeping a channel open, our magic should be able to affect it even in New Jersey."

Hatred still shone in Luco's eyes, but the craving was too strong. "All right! The old dude blindfolded me and started me walking. I got dizzy and almost fell down, but he held me up and kept going. When he took the blindfold off, I was up in those hills, and he was pointing at you and handing me the rifle!"

"What old dude is this?" Papa asked, voice soothing.

"The one who dishes out the dope to Groldor! The one with the two-thousand-dollar suits and the five-hundred-dollar hats!"

"What kind of beard?" Matt asked.

"Real neat! No hair on his cheeks, just mustache and jaw! Why the hell do you want to know that?"

"Does he have a name?" Papa asked.

"Nirobus!" the kid snapped.

Matt stood still, feeling a shock wave pass over him. It was one thing to guess correctly but quite another to have that guess confirmed.

"Why, Luco?" Papa asked, very softly indeed. "I was always good to you. Matthew never hurt you, though Heaven knows he had reason. Why did you scare away my customers? Why did you try to kill us?"

"Nobody puts me down on my own block!" Luco snapped.

"Envy and revenge, then. That's not enough. Why else?"

"Why? Why do you think? 'Cause this Nirobus guy told us he'd give us a lot of dope if we did it!"

Papa nodded. "And he gave you a good stiff dose before he sent you here, yes?"

"Not a lot, no! Just enough to make the shakes quit! He told me he'd kill *me* if I took any more before I killed *you*!"

"Lakshmi was right, then," Papa sighed. "You are of the *hashishim.*"

"What you talkin' about, man?" Luco shouted, on the verge of panic. "I did it, I told you what you wanted! Gimme the Magic!"

"Yes, all right." Papa sketched a design in the air and chanted in French. Luco stiffened, eyes widening—but the pupils shrank in those eyes, shrank to pinpoints. Then the eyelids closed, and Luco went limp, trembling, but sighing in bliss.

Matt turned away, revolted. Papa joined him. "He is thin, Matthew, and his face is so painfully hollow!"

Matt nodded. "The drug is letting Nirobus drain his life energy any time he wants—slowly and steadily." He shook his head, tasting bile. "Sometimes I hate being right."

"It is even as you said," Papa sighed. "The new drug showed up in the neighborhood, and suddenly the gangs were no longer fighting each other—they were terrorizing the neighbors instead, feeding on their fear and anger, so that Nirobus could feed on it through them."

"What did the news say, Papa? Was it happening all over, or just in our neighborhood?"

"All over, Matthew—in all the big cities. The police were delighted at first, because the gangs stopped fighting, and there were fewer muggings. Then the robberies began to increase again, and the police were worse off than ever, because the citizens once again began to live in fear."

"And they wonder why people move to the suburbs!" Matt shook his head.

Papa glanced at Luco. The trembling had stopped now. His stare was vacant, and his lips were parted in an idiotic grin.

"We must watch him," Papa said. "So, Matthew. This drug, you think you can neutralize it completely?"

"Sure, same as you did," Matt said, "but so can Groldor. As soon as the fix stops fixing, he'll figure out what went wrong and sing the counter-enchantment."

Papa frowned. "So you say we must immobilize this Groldor before we disenchant the drug?"

"Only sensible thing to do."

"Will not Nirobus merely send another sorcerer? Or promote one of Groldor's henchmen?"

"I think the henchmen are just local thugs, hired on," Matt said slowly, "and sure, Nirobus will send a replacement, but it will take him a while to find one. He may even have to train one. I could be wrong—he could have a dozen sorcerers waiting in reserve—but I think the only ones he has are already assigned and on duty, one in New Jersey, one with the besiegers at Bordestang, and the rest with the Mahdi and his army."

"Have you reason for thinking this?"

"Only intuition."

"And intuition is not to be lightly dismissed, even in our home universe, and even less here," Papa said. "In any case, we must go home to deal with this Groldor, must we not?"

Matt swallowed, feeling the fear rise. The thought of facing a drug lord with his private army was bad enough, but to have to do it in a universe where he didn't have his magic to protect him . . .

Then he remembered that a few spells had sort of worked in New Jersey, and that Nirobus had to keep the magic-channel open. He should be able to figure out how to draw on Merovence's natural forces to make magic work in New Jersey, and if any place ever needed it . . . "Yes, Papa. We have to go home."

Saul had to admit he could look pretty scary when he wanted, and he really wanted to now. When Beidizam awoke, he saw a bearded, long-haired, blade-nosed face hovering over him with a gloating grin, lit only by the flickering flames from a brazier below it. The sorcerer stared, frozen with fear for a moment, then turned purple with rage, gargling curses through his gag. His arms lurched and spasmed, trying to gesture—but they were tied securely behind him.

"I don't like men who harass women." But Saul's eyes gleamed with anticipation. "I love seeing them punished, though."

Beidizam froze at the leashed mayhem in Saul's eyes. The Witch Doctor lifted a poker from the brazier; it glowed cherry red. Saul spat on it, listened to the hiss, then shook his head with regret. "Not hot enough yet."

He stuck it back into the coals and turned to the appalled sorcerer, saying, "You see, we have a few questions that need answering. Not that we mean to hurt you, of course—at least, nothing permanent . . . we hope . . . unless it's absolutely necessary, of course . . ."

He slid a hand under Beidizam's robe and squeezed his leg, gently but in exactly the right place. The sorcerer went rigid, cawing with pain.

Saul let up instantly, but explained, "That was very gentle—just a demonstration. If I'd really clamped down, you would have been in agony for hours, even after I let go. The ancient Greeks and the modern Arabs have learned a lot about anatomy, but the people farther East know a lot more—at least, in some respects . . ."

Beidizam bleated incoherent protests through his gag.

"I know, that's pretty crude—just main force, no magic to it." Saul picked up a thick piece of rope. "This one's a bit more subtle." He began to recite nonsense syllables in a sonorous chant, making sure it had both meter and rhyme, as he slowly and carefully began to tie a series of knots in the length of cable.

Beidizam's eyes bulged; he knew the spell, or one much like it. He howled frightened protests through his gag, struggling furiously against his bonds.

"Oh, don't worry," Saul told him. "This won't hurt a bit—not me, anyway . . ."

The door opened, letting sunlight into the chamber, and

Mama cried, "Witch Doctor! What do you do? You are a healer, not a destroyer!"

"Well, there's some truth in that," Saul allowed, "but nobody knows how to hurt so well as a healer, so . . ."

"No!" Mama stepped up and snatched the rope from his hands. "This man may have sought to dishonor me, but he is a man, after all, not a beast!"

"You're entitled to your own opinion," Saul said stiffly.

"Leave torture to they who seek to advance the cause of evil!"

"Just a little one," Saul pleaded.

> "Let him dwell in dungeons damp!
> Let his toes seize up with cramp!"

Beidizam howled as the muscles in all ten toes suddenly knotted.

"That is unworthy of you!" Mama scolded Saul. "We persuade, we do not torture!" She pushed him aside and sat on the hard cot, yanking off Beidizam's shoes and massaging his toes while she sang in Spanish—a lullaby, a soothing tune. Beidizam groaned with relief and Saul, standing against the wall, glowered with irritation.

"I must apologize for my friend," Mama said. "He was perhaps even more incensed by your overtures than I was." After all, Beidizam didn't know who had knocked him out—let him believe it was Saul. "Do not think that I do not appreciate the compliment." Mama smiled, projecting the image of the demure maiden blushing with pleasure at flattery. "But I spoke truly in telling you of the loyalty of Frankish women, a loyalty that any Muslim would treasure in his own wives. I must remain true to my marriage vows, after all, as my religion requires—by my hope of Heaven, I must! With that Faith to strengthen me, I will keep faith with my husband through all trials. I would not betray him even if I wanted to." She smiled, letting Beidizam glimpse all the tenderness and desire that thoughts of Ramón could evoke in her. "But I do *not* want to, because I do love my husband, am more in love with him than when first we wed."

Beidizam gazed at her, spellbound—literally. He couldn't know the Spanish of her universe, couldn't know that the song she had sung while she massaged his cramps was really a spell that would transmute his lust into awe—not love, but making him look on her as though she were a statue on a pedestal.

"Come, let me free your mouth—you must be parched." Mama bent forward to untie his gag. Her nearness made him shiver, but as the gag came away, he turned on his side, coughing, working his mouth. All sympathy, Mama held out a goblet. He sipped, then remembered that he was in the house of his enemy and muttered a charm as he gazed into the wine.

"It will not change color," Mama assured him. "There is no drug in it, no poison. That would be rude treatment indeed for a guest! And our guest you shall be, for I shall see you housed and served according to your station, as soon as you are recovered from Saul's harshness." She glanced up at Saul, irritated. "It was most unkind of you, really!"

"I am covered with rue," Saul said, all repentance.

"He is overly concerned for my safety," Mama explained, "and was overcome with anger; that is why he acted so rashly." Then she frowned. "But it must be extremely wearying, coming so far to assault a town that is no threat to you! He must be quite a villain who set you to the task."

Beidizam stiffened. "Our Mahdi is no villain!"

Mama stared. "Was it the Mahdi who sent you to besiege us, then?"

"It was!" Beidizam exclaimed, then saw her skepticism and relented. "Of course, I was one of those who raised him up to be Mahdi in the first place—but it is nonetheless he who commands!"

"Commands in war," Mama qualified. "Will not the real sage govern, when the Mahdi is done conquering?"

"Sage?" Beidizam grinned, confidence restored—he knew something she didn't know after all. "Say rather, the schemer! Yes, Nirobus seeks to conquer all the world, and will use the religion of Allah to that end as easily as any other. All he cares is that all be unified under one rule."

"His?" Mama asked.

"Why not? He can be sure of his own motives, at least, and can trust himself!"

"Can you?" Mama asked.

"As long as I do his bidding, yes." Beidizam shrugged. "And why should I not? He will give me power over a fifth of the world; I will govern with only Nirobus himself above me! Why should I not do as he bids me?"

Mama frowned. "And what will you do with this fifth of the world?"

"Be sure that there is justice for all men, no matter their rank," Beidizam told her. "Be sure that there is peace—that no man raises his hand against another, or steals his wife or goods; that every merchant can go safely from Ibile to Latruria, or even Allustria, with no fear of bandits."

"Is that all?" Mama smiled as though at a shared secret. "Will there be no wealth, no luxury, no harem?"

"Well, of course." Beidizam grinned. "The ruling of a fifth of the world is a heavy burden. Will I not deserve some comforts to console me?"

Saul snorted. Mama frowned at him, but he only said, "Rank has its privileges, huh?"

"But of course." Beidizam returned the gloating grin that Saul had given him so shortly before.

"What is he like, this Nirobus?" Mama asked.

"Fair in his judgments, mild in his speech and manners, and courteous to all," Beidizam told her. "He is a sage in his way, but is far more practical than that."

"Young or old?"

"Mature," Beidizam said judiciously. "His hair and beard are gray, as are his eyes. To speak truly, he looks more like a Frank than a Moor."

"Does he indeed." Mama turned thoughtful.

"Be sure he is no traitor, though!" Beidizam said quickly. "He could not be a Frank—his Arabic is too perfect, his Berber too homely!"

But Mama had considerable experience in the learning and teaching of other languages, and knew that educated foreigners frequently spoke a language better than those born to it. She didn't say so, of course, only smiled and changed the subject. "I must go now, Lord Beidizam, but I shall send men to conduct you to chambers far more pleasant than this."

Beidizam frowned. "Must I remain your prisoner, then?"

"I would prefer to think of you as a guest," Mama said, "but yes, you must remain with us—and I must ask you to speak to no one, most especially not to recite a spell."

Beidizam gave her a sly grin. "I will not promise you that—nor should you trust me if I did!"

"As you say," Mama sighed, and sang a little song. Saul frowned, recognizing the language for Latin, but understood only one word, repeated several times.

"A pleasant ditty," Beidizam told her. "Is it your farewell for me?"

"Only until noon tomorrow." Mama rose from the cot. "I shall visit you once every day—we shall eat the midday meal together, unless I am called away. My servants shall make you comfortable. I trust your stay with us shall be a pleasant one."

"As pleasant as it can be, when I cannot be about the work for which I burn," Beidizam said sourly. "Nevertheless, it is better than the company of your bloodthirsty friend there. May I hope that you will take him with you when you leave?"

"Of course. Saul, please come with me." Mama went to the door and passed out. Saul paused for one last murderous shark-smile at Beidizam, then went after Mama.

As he closed the door, he said, "Nice work. You did a great job of charming him—literally."

"Why, thank you, Saul," Mama said, with a polite flutter of the eyelashes. "But I should take no credit for it—it is more a matter of talent than of accomplishment, you know."

"Well, yes, but you certainly had the skill to use that talent."

Behind them inside the cell, Beidizam grinned in the ruddy light of the brazier. The foolish Franks had left him bound, yes, but with his lips free! There was no gag, and did a sorcerer ever need more than words to escape a prison? Softly, he began to chant an ancient Arabic verse.

CHAPTER 23

Outside the cell, climbing the stairs up from the dungeon, Mama said, "You did your part very well, Saul. He was quite frightened when I came in."

"Why, thank you, Lady Mantrell," Saul said, with an "aw, shucks" sort of grin. "I used to watch horror movies when I was a kid."

"Educational media, no doubt—you must have learned well from them. What did you do to him?"

"*To* him, nothing. I just imitated the sadists I've met one place and another, especially since I came to this world. Of course, Beidizam couldn't know that . . ."

"You must be quite talented," Mama said, "a natural mimic."

"Why, thank you." Saul told himself he shouldn't be so pleased. "You realize, of course, that the second we walked out that door, Beidizam started chanting a verse to transport him out of that cell and back to his own tent."

"Of course, but he will not succeed," Mama said with certainty. "I have made sure of that."

"Yes, that was an odd little spell you sang him. What was it? All I could pick out was the word 'aphasia.' "

"You know of it, then?"

"Of course—it's the ultimate speech defect, usually caused by damage to the brain. Someone who suffers from it can make all the speech sounds—his tongue, vocal folds, and lips are just fine. But they're disconnected from his brain; the link between mind and mouth has been broken."

"An interesting way to put it," Mama said, frowning.

"Sure. The person with aphasia thinks she's saying, 'I'm speaking perfectly clearly,' but all that's coming out is gibberish. She can't encode her thoughts as language; no matter what she tries to say, all that comes out of her mouth is babbling non . . ." Saul stared. "You didn't!"

"I most certainly did," Mama said with asperity. "He shall have aphasia indeed, unless he talks to me—and I trust you shall always be near, to counter any spell he tries to cast at such times."

"Well, I will, of course," Saul said, frowning, "but why would you need me? You're the spellbinder!"

"Because sooner or later he will try to knock me out or gag me, to prevent my blocking his enchantments," Mama said with complete assurance. "He may not be the tiger he thinks himself, but he is most certainly a wolf. You will not let me go alone into his den, will you, Saul?"

"Not a chance," Saul said fervently, thinking of the prophet Daniel.

So no matter how hard he tried, Beidizam remained their permanent guest, and none of his underlings wanted to take the responsibility for attacking the city without magical backup. Without their sorcerer there to command, no one did anything, and the siege ground to a sit-down halt.

Matt went over and nudged Luco with his foot. The boy's head rolled, a silly grin on his face. "He's out, but good and proper. What're we going to do with him, Papa? Can't just leave him lying around cluttering up the place."

Papa shrugged. "What did I always do when I found him out too late? Send him home."

"Sure, why not?" Matt turned thoughtful. "It could be that every time somebody makes that trip, the channel becomes a little more solidly established, couldn't it?"

"Making it easier for you to go back to New Jersey? Yes, quite," Papa said, "but more importantly, making it easier for you to return."

"Good point." Matt frowned. "I don't want to close that

channel until after I'm back here, do I? But for the meantime, to help keep it open . . ."

> "Take him back to Lackawanna,
> Where the Plaza was going under,
> Till they changed the old train station to a mall!
> Back to Bus Route Thirty-Four,
> And the radon sites galore,
> Where the sunrise did surprise us one and all!"

Luco's form blurred, seemed to stretch and condense, then faded from sight.

"He was a good boy," Papa said sadly, "and would have stayed that way, if his father had paid him any attention."

"Oh, he paid attention, all right—whenever he wanted somebody to listen to him brag about him being the big hero in the Battle of the Bulge."

A squall of surprise and fear made them both whirl toward Callio. The thief was staring at a section of ground in front of him that had sunk a few inches, leaving an oblong platter-shape in the dirt. Matt frowned, stepping over. "What happened, Callio?"

"My loot!" the thief cried. "I buried it, even as you said I should—and it has sunk deeper than I dug!"

"Oh." Matt nodded sympathetically. "It didn't sink, Callio, it disappeared. That rifle is out of this world, now. Literally. Luco brought it from another land, and I just sent him back where he came from—so I guess the weapon went with him."

Callio leaped up, fists clenched, glaring up at Matt. "So this is your reason for burying things—so that you may steal them from me by your magic!"

"Only this item," Matt assured him, "and it's not the kind of thing you would have wanted to have around anyway, believe me."

Callio opened his mouth for an angry retort, then suddenly went pale with fear. "Do you say it is magical?"

"In terms of this universe," Matt said, "yes—and bad magic, too, the kind that can kill a lot of people."

Callio turned away with a shudder. "Thank you for stealing it from me, wizard!"

"But I didn't . . ." Matt broke off, too frustrated to explain.

Papa laid a sympathetic hand on his shoulder. "Don't bother to try, Matthew. Our Callio is a pleasant enough rascal, but he is also one of those who will only hear what he wants."

"Or what he understands?" Matt asked, with a sardonic smile. "I'm not sure I'm all that much better."

"Of course you are!" Papa said with a grin. "Look how much you guessed about our enemy Nirobus without any evidence!"

"Sheer hunch alone, huh?" Matt shook his head. "Hard to think of the old guy as an enemy—he seemed so nice, so gentle and sympathetic."

"Yes, but I can appear so, too, when I wish," Papa told him.

"You *are* nice and gentle and sympathetic!"

"Many people who are, try not to let it show, Matthew. Besides, I can be quite unpleasant, even hard, if there is need."

Matt remembered a few run-ins with other parents when he'd been a child, not to mention the exploits he'd been watching in the last few weeks. "True enough, Papa. So we have to figure Nirobus is the man behind all this trouble, no matter what his reasons are."

" 'There can surely be no greater treason . . .' " Papa began.

"Hey, be careful, okay?" Matt interrupted. "You don't want to go slinging rhymes around here just to make a point."

"True enough," Papa agreed, abashed, then brightened. "But since I have said other things since, it will no longer be a rhyme. '. . . To do the right thing for the wrong reason.' "

"I definitely do not agree," Matt said. "What's important is to do the right thing, period. Even so, I'd say our Nirobus may be doing the *wrong* thing for the *right* reason."

"At best," Papa agreed. "More likely, he is doing the

wrong thing for the wrong reason, but is skilled at making himself appear to be good."

"At least in the past, my enemies have all looked like villains," Matt sighed. "I suppose I was due for a bad guy who looked good. Let's just hope his deputy the drug baron doesn't look so respectable."

"Be sure that he will," Papa said grimly, "but the appearance of respectability is another matter entirely from the appearance of goodness. Surely when he talked me into leaving teaching for small business, he looked both respectable and good."

"Yes, and after you'd bought the store, he left it up to Groldor to ruin you."

Papa shrugged. "We were in his way; he killed two birds with one gang."

"Well, between them, they certainly did a good job of drawing me away from Merovence," Matt said, "and I don't doubt they would have done an even better job of keeping me from getting back, if I hadn't had the Spider King and St. Moncaire both working on my side."

Papa nodded. "But their leaching may have been their own downfall in that, for to use their drug to steal energy from our young people, they had to keep the link between the universes open."

"Good point." Matt looked up, a gleam in his eye. "In fact, that's the kind of side effect I really like—using the enemy's own schemes against him."

"You mean to find an effect that can be used as a weapon?" Papa grinned. "The justice in it appeals to my poetic soul."

"I knew there was a reason you were a good magician here."

"The soul reason?" Papa asked.

Matt winced. "That's another one, your fondness for words."

Papa shrugged. "They taste good."

"The wizard as sensualist," Matt mused. "Interesting paradox. But I hope we can find some of those side effects to use against Groldor, because no matter what else happens, I have to go back and knock him out."

"Well, I think I am ready for that fight." Papa stood up, grinning. "Shall we walk, or ride?"

Matt looked up, turning somber. "I said *I* have to go, Papa."

Papa frowned. "But he is more my enemy than yours! I cannot let you fight my battles!"

"Groldor is just a side theater of operations in my own major war," Matt reminded him, "Alisande versus Nirobus— which means Nirobus versus me."

"Yes, that is so." Papa turned somber, too. "But you must not neglect the other theater of operations, Matthew— northern Ibile, where your King Rinaldo is hard-pressed."

"Right." Matt nodded. "But all he needs is news, guerrilla training, and a resident wizard to travel with his army, if he doesn't already have one."

"All things which I can do." Papa frowned.

Matt nodded. "And the guerrilla training, you can do better than me—you were a Ranger."

"All well and good," Papa said, fighting down anger, "but why do you think you can deal with Groldor better than I?"

"Because," Matt said, "you didn't grow up in New Jersey. And believe me, there are some back alleys you don't know."

Papa's face turned thunderous. "I thought I told you to stay out of such places."

"You did," Matt said, "but I didn't always have a lot of choice, when bullies were chasing me. I know the hiding places, Papa, and the local customs."

"I could go with you!"

"I'd love it," Matt said fervently, "but there isn't time— and there's no guarantee we would be able to come back. Besides, Mama is holding off an army and needs to have someone come lift the siege, and since Alisande's tied up with the Mahdi, the only troops who can ride to the rescue are Rinaldo's."

Papa lowered his gaze, troubled; the mention of Mama in danger gave him pause.

Matt saw, and followed up his advantage. Pitching his

voice low, he said, "Besides—it's something I have to do alone, for personal reasons."

Papa looked up, startled, and locked gazes. Looking into his son's eyes, he said, "I see. You must overcome the bullies of your past by fighting their boss in New Jersey."

Matt nodded. "Merovence needs to have me go back, and *I* need to have me go back. Please, Papa. I need you in the North."

Matt watched his father walk away, pack on his back, eyes fixed on the north, and Matt felt very much alone. He hoped Papa knew the territory well enough by now to deal with whatever trouble he ran into.

Papa disappeared below the crest of the hill and Matt turned away, scolding himself. Of course Papa would be okay—he was a wizard now, and had a good deal more life experience than Matt had. If worse came to worst, he could summon Lakshmi and charm her into fighting his battles for him.

The thought relaxed him for a moment—his plot had worked. He breathed a sigh of relief, knowing Papa would be out of danger, or at least in less danger than he would have found in New Jersey. Okay, he'd be in a war, but he'd be in the middle of an army, with a lot of soldiers between himself and the Moors—and if they fought guerrilla-style, they probably wouldn't come anywhere near a pitched battle.

Matt, on the other hand, was going to be alone against a dozen merciless thugs. He felt himself turn hollow at the thought and tried to remind himself that some of the villains he'd faced in Allustria and Ibile had to be worse than anything New Jersey could produce—but he had a hard time believing that one, too.

Papa had given in kind of easily, though. Matt wondered if he should feel hurt, or suspicious.

He turned back to pack away the food and douse the campfire. Then he remembered Callio, and was surprised to discover that his backpack was still there. For that matter, he was surprised to find the campfire was still there.

Then, when he looked around, he was even more surprised, for the one thing that wasn't there was Callio.

Matt's first impulse was huge relief—the thief had been a bit of a burden, or at least a bother. He felt rather ashamed of the emotion, but there it was.

Not that it mattered—he was going to New Jersey alone, anyway. He tried to recall the tune and lyrics of the latest rock song he'd heard there, and had to work hard to think them in English instead of the language of Merovence. He succeeded, though, and began to sing. The peculiar biorhythms of the piece began to reverberate through him; he felt his heartbeat synchronizing with it, felt the English words coming with less and less effort, and the world began to go gray around him . . .

Just before the world went crazy, he felt two hands seize his arm, hard, but his trance was too deep to bother shaking them off. A vagrant thought flitted through his mind, that if anyone from Merovence wanted to come along to his native universe, they deserved what they got.

Then the world swirled around him, shapeless, formless, and the familiar dizziness swept him away.

Papa descended the trail, glanced back to make sure Matt was out of sight, then dropped his pack behind a rocky outcrop and called, softly, sweetly, and in his most enticing tone,

> "Lakshmi, most beautiful of the djinna!
> Come to the aid of this unworthy sinner!
> Assistance I beg, for I wish to live,
> And need such help as you alone can give."

A dust devil boiled up out of the ground before him, towered swirling and rumbling over him, threatening and dark. Then it pulled in on itself and became Lakshmi, pivoting in place as in a dance, slowing and halting to glare at him, defiant and truculent. "What do you wish of me now, O Unnaturally Virtuous Man?"

"Assistance that you may find enjoyable," Papa said; then,

quickly, because of the gleam in her eye, "No, not that kind. But my son has foolishly decided to go to another universe, another world, and battle an arch-sorcerer and his minions alone, with no weapons other than his magic—and spells will not work as well there as they do here."

"But a djinna's magic, even diminished, may turn the tide?" Lakshmi asked sourly. "Well, I have been to other worlds before—no, do not gawk like a peasant seeing a city for the first time! We djinn have many powers that you know not of. But what reward shall I have for my efforts, eh?" She raised a hand to forestall his answer. "I know, I know, your undying gratitude! Well, you shall die long before I, I doubt not."

"I was going to say," Papa protested, "that I shall aid you in your hour of need."

"Your son already has, and the fool would not take such reward as I wished to give! Why should you do differently? Nonetheless, I shall do the two of you this one favor more. Do not push too hard at the boundaries of my gratitude, O Man!"

"I regret that I must do so," Papa said meekly, "for I have nowhere else to turn for the kind of help that we need."

"Then do not put yourself into such straits again!" Lakshmi snapped, and wound up to start whirling again.

"And might I ask one more boon?" Papa asked quickly.

Lakshmi froze and gave him a dagger-glance. "I do not promise to grant it—but ask!"

"That you take me to my son in his hour of need," Papa said quickly.

"If I have a whole hour in which to do it, yes. If help must be given on the instant, I will help him myself and without you," Lakshmi snapped. "I say again, O Wizard, do not ask too much!"

"Forgive me," Papa said, all meekness.

"My mother told me never to trust a man with honeyed words," Lakshmi sniffed, "especially if he was in love with another! You should have summoned me before your son married, foolish mortal! Even so, I shall guard him for you. Farewell!" She spun into her whirl, too fast for him to get another word in edgewise, blurred into a howling whirlwind, and sank into the ground.

Papa smiled with fond amusement. Really, he was coming to like Lakshmi immensely. She might complain about it, but the poor thing was so blatantly in love with Matthew that all Papa had needed to do was to say that his son might be in danger. There was no chance that Lakshmi would have refused. Considering Matthew's misspelling in his freeing her of her lamp, she had no chance at all.

The huge lock ground and clanked, the door grated open, and Mama stepped into Beidizam's chamber with Saul behind her. "I trust you are comfortable, milord."

"As comfortable as I may be, in a Frankish castle," Beidizam grumbled, "but I thank you for a proper bed and windows, even if they are mere arrowslits, and barred."

"I hope to treat you as a noble guest deserves," Mama said demurely. "Is there anything you wish, that we may supply?"

"Other than guards who understand the words I speak, so that I need not pantomime my wants?"

"Other than that, yes."

"Well, a houri or two, some properly cooked food, and some Moorish sweetmeats would do nicely."

"I feared you would find our way of living too modest." Mama sat in a small, straight chair. "But surely it is better than your tent and field quarters."

"Well, it is that," Beidizam admitted. "Still, you might tell me how you have bound every spell I utter, so that it might as well never have been spoken."

"Because it has not been," Mama said simply.

Beidizam stared.

"I have tangled your tongue, milord," Mama said with gentle sympathy. "When you speak to anyone but me, your lips will not form the words your mind has chosen—they will only spout nonsense syllables."

"How is it I have not noticed this?" Beidizam demanded.

"Because you hear only the words you intended to say,"

Mama explained. "Others hear only the random noises your mouth makes instead."

"Ingenious!" Beidizam's eyes glowed with reluctant admiration. "But how is it you understand my words?"

"I made that one exception when I cast the spell, milord—that when you are in my presence, your tongue is straightened, and your lips once more do your bidding. When I am with you, your mouth speaks the words your mind intends."

"If that is truly so . . ." Beidizam said, and rubbed one hand over the other.

Saul saw, and leaped. "Stop that! Lady Mantrell, he's rubbing his . . ."

Smoke billowed out of Beidizam's hand, turning into a huge genie with bulging eyes and boar's tusks. "Who summons the Genie of the Ring?"

"I, Beidizam!" the Moor cried. "Take us from this place, O Genie! Take all in this room to my tent outside the city!"

Mama instantly chanted in Spanish.

"I hear and obey!" the genie thundered to Beidizam, then turned to Mama and Saul, gesturing.

Saul pulled a dried herb from his pocket and caught Mama's shoulder with the other hand as he chanted quickly,

> "Touch-me-not, the flower's called.
> By that flower, your magic's stalled.
> Shout and threaten as you will,
> Inviolate we stand, unmauled."

The genie finished his gesture, chanting in Berber. There was a blinding flash of light.

CHAPTER 24

Saul held tight to Mama's shoulder even as he swung his hand up to shield his eyes, staggering back against the wall. Then the glare was gone, and he lowered his hand to stare around at the cell, empty now except for its furniture, Mama, and himself—and some very large afterimages.

"How foolish of me!" Mama cried. "I should have foreseen this!"

"We didn't know how clever he was," Saul groaned, "or how quick. I should have seen it coming, too."

Mama shook her head in reluctant admiration. "He may be a sexist beast, but he is a formidable adversary. I should have wondered why he wore so many rings! I should have realized that Beidizam could work a spell in my presence!"

"You realized that last part, at least," Saul reminded her. "That's why you brought me along, remember? For backup. Turned out you were right, too."

"But I should have suspected those rings!"

"Why?" Saul shrugged. "Neither of us is a jeweler, and Beidizam was so obviously vain that he would have seemed odd if he *hadn't* had a ring on every finger. And neither of us is an expert on genie lore, either. Yeah, I remember the Slave of the Ring who got Aladdin out of the cave, but mostly you think of genies as living in lamps."

"You are good to ease my feelings, Saul," Mama said, a little less distressed, "but still I burn with anger that an enemy has outmaneuvered me. Worse, he shall now seek to outmaneuver us in war!"

She swept out the door toward the stairs, calling to the

guards, "My compliments to Sir Guy and Sir Gilbert, and I would appreciate it if they would wait on me in my solar. We must have a council of war!"

The soldiers stared, then ran.

Saul caught up with her. "That bad, huh?"

"Worse," Mama snapped. "The only question now is whether the Moors will attack tomorrow, or the next day!"

Under the railroad bridge, the air thickened, then thickened more, until it coalesced into Matt, blinking about him in surprise. He hadn't really expected to arrive at night. Good thing, though, come to think of it—the cops might not be too understanding about somebody wearing doublet and hose, especially when they were so worn and travel-stained as Matt's.

He took a step out, glancing to left and right to see if he was alone. He thought he saw movement under a streetlight, and turned back—to find Callio huddled against the wall, trembling.

Matt stared, then stepped up. "So it was you who grabbed my arm! Were you really trying to hold me back?"

"Who . . . ?" The thief looked up. "Oh no, Lord Wizard! But I made sure you would not leave without me—life has been so much more interesting since I joined you!"

"Not to say profitable, hm?" Matt shook his head. "Well, don't try lifting anything here, Callio. We have a lot of thieves, and they resent anyone poaching on their territory. The citizens are also pretty careful," he added, "and the shopkeepers are worse."

"If . . . if you say so, Lord Wizard." But Callio was clearly disappointed.

"I came here to fight a villain," Matt told him. "This could get dangerous. You'd better stay here and wait; I'll come back and get you if I can."

"If you can?" Callio stared. "What could prevent you?"

"Death," Matt snapped. "The outlaw I'm going up against is very mean, and he has some extremely tough bodyguards.

They also have magical weapons, like the one Luco tried to use on us. You're far safer staying here."

"Yes, if you live! But if you don't, I'm stranded here in a world that is foreign to me!" Callio crept out and took a quick look at the railroad station, the cobblestoned yard, the streetlights—and just then, a commuter train came roaring by. For a minute, the whole world was filled with its thunder, resounding and echoing under the bridge. Callio cried out in panic and clung to Matt.

"Okay, so you're coming along," Matt said, disgusted—but he also remembered that even if he got through this alive, he might not have time to come back to this bridge before he returned to Merovence.

"Thank you, Lord Wizard," Callio whimpered.

"But if you're going to come along, you'll have to do as I say—and do it instantly, understand? There isn't going to be time to explain."

"Surely, Lord Wizard! Yes, surely!" Callio nodded so hard Matt was afraid his head would fall off.

"Okay, wait for magic," Matt said, and stepped deeper into the shadow under the bridge, reciting,

> "Like Coleridge without his pipe,
> Or Poe without his opiate,
> Let each who swallows Groldor's salt
> Be stone-cold sober, never hyped,
> Untouched by the dope he ate,
> Nevermore to know the fault
> Of addict's craving. Never ripe
> Their dependence shall be. Overjoyed,
> They'll find addiction's null and void!"

He felt the magic field thicken about him, only a pale echo of the Merovencian phenomenon—but a counterforce sprang up to resist it almost immediately, and Matt found his whole body straining against it. As he finished the last couplet, he felt the whole field collapse, and staggered, leaning against the wall, gasping.

A hand touched his shoulder. "Are you well?" Callio asked, on the verge of panic.

"Just . . . peachy." Matt pushed himself away from the wall, still panting. "It . . . worked. Just fine."

"But nothing has happened," Callio protested.

"Maybe," Matt said. "Maybe not. We won't know until we meet the man we've come to find."

"How shall we find him, then?"

"I don't think we'll have to," Matt said slowly. "If I have him figured right, he'll find us—and fast, too. Before that happens, though, we've got some other things to do. Let's go."

He started out, Callio right on his heels, staying near the retaining wall in hopes of shadow. "Brace yourself for a lot of odd things . . ."

"Odder than that dragon that roared over our heads?"

"Yes, in their way. You're going to see carriages that look like giant beetles, and move without horses . . ."

"Magic!" Callio cried, eyes round.

"Hey, it's my hometown," Matt said. "And there're a lot of watchmen, only they wear light blue shirts and dark blue trousers, loose trousers, not tight like your leggings . . ."

"Ought we not to dress like them?"

"We should, but I didn't have the foresight to bring along a change of clothing," Matt said. "So if one of the watchmen stops you to ask about your funny clothes, you tell him . . . Callio? Callio, where are you!"

"Here, Lord Wizard." Callio materialized out of the darkness, holding up two shirts and two pairs of jeans. "Are these the clothes of which you speak?"

Matt stared. "Where did you find those?"

"I espied them hanging from a rope in a yard near this roadway. They may not fit too well, but these watchmen you speak of will find us less remarkable in them."

"You're right about that," Matt admitted. "I hate to take somebody else's clothes, but right now, I'm afraid we need them worse than they do." He pulled his purse out of his tights, drew out two large pieces of silver, and said, "Clip these to that rope where you got these clothes, okay?"

"Lord Wizard!" Callio exclaimed indignantly. "What proper thief . . ."

"The kind who has a conscience," Matt told him, "and the kind who wants to go with me. You want to come along or not?"

"I go." Callio snatched the silver and shot back over the fence.

Matt watched him narrowly, but the two pieces of silver were still winking under the streetlight as the thief came back, muttering and cursing every step of the way.

"Your talents could be invaluable," Matt told him, "but we have to use them ethically if we don't want to get into trouble. Come on, let's step into the angle of the railroad station while we change." He handed Callio the smaller set of clothes, not mentioning that they were a child's size. Callio would have fainted at the thought that children grew so big here.

They stepped out again ten minutes later with Matt's pack noticeably more full. Callio was still marveling over buttons and zippers. "Whoever would have thought to hold a garment shut with steel!"

"Yeah, it really is amazing," Matt agreed.

"They must be wealthy indeed, who owned these garments!"

"No, steel is just very cheap here. Be careful going into people's yards, okay? You were lucky you didn't run into a German shepherd."

Then Matt had to explain that the shepherd in question was a large dog, not a sheepherder from Allustria—but that became rather complicated, because the animals had originally been bred to herd sheep, and what's more, they were originally from Alsace, which Callio stubbornly refused to admit was one of the Germanies—turned out his father had been a native of the district, and had thought himself to be thoroughly a citizen of Merovence. By the time Matt straightened it out, they had reached Main Street.

There Callio stopped and stared. "It is as bright as day!"

"Fewer accidents that way," Matt told him.

A car came roaring by, and Callio leaped into Matt's arms with a yip of dismay.

"Oh, get down," Matt said in disgust, and dropped him.

The thief landed on his feet, eyes round. "Was that one of those carriages of which you spoke?"

"Horseless carriages, yes."

"Truly they could be dangerous!"

"So could the people," Matt told him. "Hands in pockets, okay? Your *own* pockets, Callio!"

"You spoil the whole adventure," the thief complained. "What is a 'pocket,' Lord Wizard?"

They were just getting that sorted out when the big black car pulled up to the curb in front of them. Matt turned to run, but he bumped into Callio, and by the time they'd sorted themselves out, the six-and-a-half-foot-tall heavyweight in the pin-striped suit had climbed out and opened the back door. He jerked his head at it and snapped, "Get in!"

The driver had climbed out, too, his hand inside his suit coat.

"Uh, couldn't we talk about this?" Matt hedged.

"You talk with the boss! Inside!"

The driver brought out his gun. Matt didn't like the way Callio was eyeing him, then thoughtfully studying the bulge under the armpit of the thug who was holding the door. He reminded himself that he had wanted to find Groldor anyway, but before he could give in, the thug snarled "Go on, get *in*!" and virtually tossed him into the backseat.

Matt rolled with the throw, tucking his head in, then crashed against the far door anyway as Callio jolted up against him. The thug got in beside Callio and slammed the door shut. Heavy clunking noises sounded from all four doors, and the car moved away from the curb. Experimentally, Matt tried the door latch, but sure enough, the panel didn't budge, and there weren't any lock releases in sight, electronic or mechanical.

"Why do you let them treat you so, Lord Wizard?" Callio asked, wide-eyed.

"Why not?" Matt said. "They're taking me where I want to go, anyway."

"But I cannot abide being in so small a space!" Callio turned on the thug, grabbing his lapels and yanking himself close. "You must let me out! I cannot stand to be so shut in! It is too much like gaol!"

"We all got that problem," the thug snarled, and jammed him back in his seat.

Matt protested, "Hey, you don't have to be so rough with . . ."

But Callio shot over the seat and next to the driver, grabbing *him* by the lapels. "You must let me out! I fear this monster will digest me whole! This is no coach, it is a ravening raptor!"

The driver swerved, narrowly missing a semi on his left, then swung the wheel too far to the right, almost colliding with a parked car, and jammed on the brakes. Callio slammed up against the windshield and bounced back into the seat, sobbing.

"The car won't hurt you, mac," the driver grunted, "but I will! Now get back in that seat and stay there!" He grabbed the little thief and shoved hard. Callio vaulted over the seatback and landed on the guard's lap. The man cursed and jammed him back between himself and Matt.

"Let up on the kid, will you?" Matt snapped.

"The boss said not to beat on you if we didn't have to," the man growled. "Do we have to?"

Matt opened his mouth for a sharp retort, but Callio looked up at him, still sobbing, and winked. The words evaporated on Matt's tongue as a chill of dread seized him. Just what was the little thief planning, anyway?

Papa walked through a village of hide tents and brush huts, laid out in neat circles with a common center. That was where he was going, escorted by a Percheron with a steel suit containing a man on its back.

Foot soldiers looked up from sharpening spears and polishing armor. More people boiled out of the tents and came running to see. Many of them wore only peasants' jerkins and leggings, but had the hard-bitten look of veterans nonetheless.

Papa was aware that, although the knight who rode the huge horse wasn't holding a lance or sword to his back, he was nonetheless alert to the slightest questionable movement. Papa had no doubt that his sword could be out and stabbing in a second.

"Here is far enough," the knight directed him.

Papa stopped about thirty feet from a silken pavilion—soiled and patched, but silken nonetheless. The guards saw, and one ducked inside. He came out a moment later and said, "The king will see you in a moment."

So this was how far the King of Ibile had fallen! But he was nonetheless a king, and perhaps his finest accomplishment was that he was still fighting. Certainly the presence of his troops spoke well of him, for they could have deserted easily at any time. They definitely seemed to care about their sovereign—Papa could see at least four drawn bows, and many naked swords, all with him as their targets. Apparently any stranger was a possible assassin.

Out he came, tall and handsome, but dressed in the leather and broadcloth of a hunter. Nonetheless, there was a nobility about him that left no doubt as to his station. Papa bowed. "Your Majesty!"

"You are well-mannered," King Rinaldo said with a smile. "I greet you, goodman. What is your name?"

"I am Ramón Rodrigo Mantrell, Majesty."

The king seemed to go still somehow. "I know that name Mantrell."

"It is not rare," Papa said, "but in this instance, it is the name you know indeed, for I am the father of Matthew Mantrell, Lord Wizard of Merovence."

"Are you indeed!" But the king was not convinced. "If you are indeed his father, and have come to seek me out, he will have told you something of our adventures together. Can you tell me what he might have to say that none others would know?"

"Yes, Majesty. He told me to ask if you were keeping an eye out for him."

King Rinaldo winced, remembering that, when he had met Matt, he had been locked by a wicked enchantment into the form of a dwarf cyclops; his other eye had been in a bottle on a shelf in King Gordogrosso's workroom. "Not exactly uncommon knowledge, but surely only Matthew would stoop so low as to give a watchword like that! How is it you are here, Master Mantrell? Your son told me he was very far from home!"

"He was, Your Majesty." The thought of just how far made Papa shiver. "But we ran into difficulties, my wife and I, so Matthew came back to fetch us here. He has gone back again, to fight an enemy who, he says, is an agent of the sorcerer who lies behind this war that troubles you so."

"What sorcerer?" Rinaldo lost his smile. "I know nothing of a sorcerer, only of an army of Moors who have swept over my land, led by a boy who calls himself the Mahdi!"

"Matthew has discovered that one man, a Nirobus by name, has caused the troubles that beset us both. He it is who excited a small group of sorcerers into inciting the Moors to conquer, and convincing a shepherd that he could lead them."

"Indeed!" King Rinaldo frowned. "He has learned much, our Matthew!"

"It is learning in which he is trained more than in anything else, Your Majesty." Papa couldn't quite stifle a smile of pride.

King Rinaldo grinned. "Now I know that you are his father, for only a proud papa would glisten so, simply because his son has learned how to learn. Come, enter my pavilion, Master Mantrell—but I pray you, keep your hands in plain sight, for my retainers are horribly suspicious."

"As they should be." Papa bowed, then followed King Rinaldo into the pavilion.

The king sat on a portable throne, rather ingeniously contrived. Everyone else stood, in accordance with protocol. Besides, that made it easier to draw their swords, or swing their halberds, in case Papa tried anything violent.

"I have fought and retreated with my army only once, Master Mantrell, and realized that we could not stand against the might of the Moorish army and the power of their magicians' magic." A shadow crossed his face. "I would say it was evil magic, but it seems to have wreaked no more suffering than any other form of war, and the Moors, by all my spies' reports, are as devoted to their faith as any Christian. I know their religion is untrue, but I cannot say it is evil."

"Nor would I, Your Majesty," Papa answered, "and although I think it contains many mistakes and allows many actions that I believe to be wrong, I must admit that the core of its beliefs is very much like our own."

"Save that they do not recognize Christ as God," said Rinaldo, frowning.

"That above all," Papa agreed, "but they do honor him as a prophet."

"They do. No, I could not call them evil."

"Nor can I," Papa agreed. "However, as with Christians, wicked men can lead them astray. Certainly evil sorcerers can use magic to gain the victories that might of arms alone could not."

"Even so," King Rinaldo agreed, "and because of that, I have bidden my people to leave their houses and farms and follow me into the hills. Fifty thousand of them have seen fit to obey. The others stayed to take their chances with Moorish mercy. I cannot say that I blame them, for to uproot one's whole life is no small thing. I have left a garrison in each city, putting up enough resistance to bog down the Moors' advance, but I fear that any citizens who trust too much in those soldiers will be horribly disappointed."

Papa frowned. "I had heard that the land was in the Mahdi's hands, but that many of the cities were still free."

"So my spies say, and I am amazed the invaders haven't sent parties to rout my garrisons and occupy the cities. Instead, I am told they have thrust straight through to the Pyrenees." King Rinaldo smiled bleakly. "Perhaps the citizens who chose to stay in their cities have chosen rightly after all."

"Perhaps, if the food and water last," Papa said. He frowned, thinking of typhus and cholera.

"I hope they will be well, my people," King Rinaldo sighed. "My spies say that the Mahdi keeps his soldiers on a tight rein; we have heard very little of looting or rapine, or any others of the sorts of random brutality that so often accompany an army on the march."

"He is a very devout man in his own religion, Your Majesty," Papa said.

King Rinaldo frowned. "Have you met him, then?"

Papa launched into an account of his and Matthew's visit with Tafas bin Daoud, leaving out only Lakshmi's contribution; he merely attributed their arrival and escape to magic, which was true enough as far as it went. King Rinaldo listened in complete silence, only nodding now and then or uttering an expletive at the Mahdi's complete and utter self-confidence. When Papa was done, the king said, "He is young and naive, then, but a man of good heart, and a genius in battle."

"He is," Papa agreed, "but the sorcerers behind him may be evil, and were most certainly persuaded to embark on this campaign of conquest by a man who posed as a sage, a holy hermit—but did not profess a religion."

"And you say the same man has upset your own homeland?"

Apparently Matt hadn't told the king about alternate universes. "He has, Majesty, as well as we can discover—and has addicted many of our young people to a drug that allows him to leach energy from them, to use for his magics."

King Rinaldo shuddered. "That is a most evil form of magic! Yes, I have done well to avoid outright battles."

"Very well indeed," Papa said, in pleased surprise. "How have you fought, then, Your Majesty?"

"By harassing the foe, Master Mantrell—cutting down their laggards, ambushing their food caravans, striking them hard and fast with raids that stampede their horses and slay a few soldiers, then disappearing into the night. We have slain only a few hundred, but the rest are beginning to live in fear that we may swoop down upon them at any moment." He forced a hard smile. "I had hoped for help from Merovence, but the queen has not even replied to my appeals."

"She has," Papa said, surprised. "Her messengers, then, have not reached you."

Rinaldo only stared at him for a minute, digesting the news, then said, "No, they have not. We were afraid there might have been couriers who were captured by the Mahdi's scourers. What does Her Majesty?"

"She has marched against the Moors," Papa said, "but the Mahdi awaits her on Ibile's side of the mountains. While he does, he has sent a quarter of his force by sea, to besiege her capital, Bordestang."

"So that is why the Moors have made only a token attack on the north country!" King Rinaldo cried.

"And will not do more, until they have fought Queen Alisande—after which, they may not be able to fight you," Papa said.

"I cannot let Queen Alisande fight my war for me!"

"Nor do you," Papa said evenly. "She fights to save her own country as much as yours, for the Mahdi is driving to conquer Bordestang and Merovence first. Then, when they are secure, he will turn back to finish the conquest of Ibile."

King Rinaldo frowned, puzzled. "A strange strategy."

"Only if you are fooled into believing that the Mahdi is the true enemy," Papa said.

"Who else could be?" King Rinaldo asked, frowning. "You mean this Nirobus fellow?"

"The same, Majesty. If he is truly a servant of Evil, trying to reconquer Ibile and Merovence for his master the Devil, he might well deem Merovence to be the worst danger."

"Yes, because I would not have regained my throne and expelled the evil sorcerer from my kingdom without the help of the queen and your son!" King Rinaldo cried. "Galling though it is to admit, they are a far greater danger to the Conquest of Evil than I am! I think you have hit upon it, Master Mantrell—or your son has! Explain to me the working of this campaign!"

CHAPTER 25

Papa explained about Groldor and the drug that was sweeping the cities of his home world, explained how that drug allowed Nirobus to steal energy for his magical conquests from young people.

"Merovence must be the greater danger because it has been ruled by good and godly kings during all the centuries that the lands around it were ruled by servants of evil," Papa guessed, "with only a year's lapse before Queen Alisande won back her throne."

"You are too modest, Master Mantrell," Rinaldo said, with a sardonic smile. "I doubt not it is the presence of your son beside a legitimate monarch devoted to Goodness and Righteousness that makes Merovence a greater threat than Ibile. We must prevent the fall of Queen Alisande at all costs! I shall ride to attack the Mahdi from the rear!"

"By your leave, Your Majesty, I doubt the wisdom of that course," Papa said quickly. "My son made it quite clear that Queen Alisande has turned back to defend Bordestang. If you wish to ride to her aid . . ."

"I must ride to Bordestang. Yes, I see that." King Rinaldo frowned. "Surely the Mahdi will already be marching to attack her there! But he will leave a force to harry these northern lands, so that I will not suspect he has taken the greater part of his army out of my kingdom."

"Then leave a small part of your own force," Papa counseled, "a garrison large enough to ride quickly here and there about the Northlands, to keep the illusion that the whole countryside is up in arms."

"An excellent device!" Rinaldo thumped the arm of his throne in delight. "While they scour the border, I shall take the bulk of my army to raise the siege of Bordestang!" Then he frowned. "It shall be perilous, though. I ride against a force buoyed by sorcerers, but I have no wizard to counter them!"

"You do now," Papa said.

Tafas was unhappy. Tafas was angry and scornful. "What, more of this nonsense?" he asked Sharif Haifaz. "Why should the men fret because of a dream?"

"No reason at all, if it only comes once, and to one man, my lord," Sharif answered, "but when it comes night after night to a hundred men at a time, and has always the same persons in that dream, men begin to whisper of witchcraft."

"Only for a dream?" Tafas scoffed. "Dreams can hurt no one! What cowards are they to be so frightened?"

"It is not that the knight in the dream is so frightful, my lord," Haifaz said carefully, "but that he is so ludicrous, so poorly armed, yet so fearless. He is ferocious in his enthusiasm, and strikes doubt in the hearts of our countrymen."

"Tell them to dream of our own valiant warriors, then," Tafas scolded. "Tell them to think of Tariq and Abu Bekr as they lie down! And give each man a little hashish before he goes to sleep. Now good night, Sharif!" He turned away, leaving the silken portal of his pavilion to stir in the wind.

"Good night, my lord," Sharif Haifaz said unhappily, and turned away to find a little hashish for himself.

"Aroint thee, dog of Morocco!"

Tafas leaped to his feet and saw the crazy, white-bearded old knight with the shaving basin on his head galloping straight toward him on a spavined, knock-kneed excuse for a horse. Off to the side sat a plump little man on a donkey, smiling placidly.

Tafas stared at the point of the lance in fascination. It had been broken and lashed back together, but was still sharp. He leaped aside, and the old idiot went charging by, then reined in and turned back. Tafas reached for his scimitar—but found only a pouch. Looking down, he saw with a shock that he wore only his shepherd's robe!

Impossible! A quick glance up and about showed a dry and barren plain with gyres of dust and clumps of weary grass. Where were the mountains? Where his army?

The old man rode down on him again, eyes glaring, mouth tight with anger. In spite of himself, Tafas felt fear, for how could the old fool be so brave unless he were mad?

"Go home, spawn of the desert!" the old knight cried. "Go home, or my lance shall send you to your Paradise!"

Tafas spun aside again. None of this was possible—and hard on the heels of that thought struck the realization that he must be in a dream.

Suddenly, the fear was gone. He could deal with a dream on its own terms. As the old knight thundered past, Tafas fumbled in his pouch and pulled out a shepherd's sling. Placing the rock in the cup, he whirled it about his head and, as the old knight turned his horse for another charge, the Moor let fly. The stone struck the knight square on his brazen helmet. He reeled in his saddle, then pulled himself back upright, crying, "The Golden Helmet of Mambrino makes me invulnerable! Do your worst, shepherd boy—I am invincible, for each time I fall, I shall rise again!"

Fear struck deep once more, and Tafas could not have said why. The old knight kicked his horse into motion, and it galloped straight toward Tafas the Shepherd.

Enough of this! Tafas stepped to the side, and the lance swung wide to follow him. At the last instant, the shepherd boy leaped back in close to the horse and, leaping high, seized the lance at its midpoint. As the horse thundered by, Tafas threw all his weight against the wood. The lance twisted out of the knight's hands; the butt sprang high, to catch him under the chin. The old man reeled, slipped, and fell.

His horse turned back with a neigh of despair. Tafas stalked over to the decrepit knight, lance lifted to strike—but the fellow's eyes were already sliding shut, even as he muttered, "What matter wounds . . . to the body of a knight . . ." Then his eyes closed, his head fell to the side, and his whole body went slack.

But the fear remained, burgeoning deep within Tafas, for he seemed to hear the echo of the old man's words: *For each time he falls, he shall rise again.* In panic, the Moor looked up at the knight's squire, but the plump little man seemed not at all distressed by his master's fall; he only met Tafas' eyes and nodded slowly, still smiling, still complacent.

Tafas roared, leveled the lance, and charged the little man, but the ground slipped from beneath his feet, the sky went dark, and he found himself falling, falling into endless depths, until his cushions pressed up against his back and he woke, sweating with fear.

The big black car stopped in front of a warehouse. The parking lot was dark. In the distance, one feeble streetlight tried to pierce the gloom, all the worse because a fog was rolling in from the river.

The guard opened the door, stepped through, and jerked his head. "Out."

"All right, all right," Matt grumbled. "Go on, Callio."

The thief clambered out, trembling, and loosed a long, shuddering sigh of relief. Matt followed, wondering if the little man really was that badly shaken, or if he was that good an actor.

The driver unlocked a personnel door to the side of the huge truck portal. "Inside," the guard ordered.

"You boys sure are talkative," Matt said.

"Go on, go on!" the guard snapped. "You make me sick!" He shoved Matt, hard.

Matt stumbled into the thief, heart leaping. The thug was already growing nervous. He must have been addicted to Groldor's drug. What better way to assure loyalty in your bodyguards?

"Come on, Callio, and don't worry—it'll be plenty big enough inside."

He glanced at the other guard, and saw drops of sweat on

the man's brow. He was staring, jaw clenched—another addict. At least, Matt could hope so.

Nonetheless, it bothered him. His verse shouldn't have just canceled the drug's effects—it should also have eliminated dependency, stopped the craving for the drug. Yes, the guards should no longer be high, but they also shouldn't be starting withdrawal. Matt had a nightmare vision of all the junkies on the East Coast being strung out, and unable to get a fix. What would they do, before they collapsed?

They stepped into gloom filled with huge crates. The driver and guard shoved them ahead down the loading bay and between avenues of packing cases.

"It's a castle," Callio said, awed.

The guard snorted. "You got a low idea of the high life." He turned to the driver. "Stuff shouldn't be wearing off so soon."

"Bad dose," the driver agreed. "The boss'll have more."

The avenue opened out into a huge dark space. Fifty feet away, a single light hung, illuminating a folding table with a man in a business suit sitting behind it, another thug to each side of him. Matt had to give Groldor credit—in its way, this was just as impressive as a great hall and a dais (and much more threatening).

"That's far enough," the guard grated, and Matt halted five feet from Groldor. But Callio began to tremble again. Matt ignored him long enough to study the boss—eyes alive with amusement under the hat brim, a cruel twist to the mouth, mustache and goatee beneath a grandfather of a nose, salt-and-pepper eyebrows. His complexion was sallow, his cheeks hollow. "Welcome home, Lord Wizard."

Then Callio lost it. "Let me out!" he howled, and sprang at Groldor's right-hand guard, catching his lapels to climb up and yell in his face, "I am no beast, to be caged in the dark with demons and ghosts! I am a . . ."

"You're a fool," the man snapped, and batted Callio away as if he were a fly.

"Leave him alone!" Matt yelled, and started for the guard. Callio landed, rolled, and leaped up on the left-hand guard, yammering, "Ghosts and goblins! All manner of things haunt the dark! Let me out, so that I may at least run away!"

"You ain't goin' nowhere." The guard pried Callio's hands off his lapels. "Ease up on the haberdashery, punk." He gave Callio a back-handed slap that sent him skidding to the feet of the driver, where he huddled in a miserable, sobbing bundle.

"No call to do that!" Matt swerved for the left-hand guard and launched a karate kick. The guard laughed, reaching to catch his foot—and Matt yanked it away, slamming a fist into his face.

It was like punching oak.

The guard snarled and waded in, slamming a left hook into Matt's belly, then a quick combination that Matt almost managed to block. He staggered back, but the right-hand guard caught him, spun him around, and swung a body blow that sent him staggering back against the car guard. The thug caught him, grinning, and the right-hand guard came for him, flexing his right hand.

"Enough," Groldor said quietly.

The right-hand guard snarled with disappointment and pivoted back to his station, folding his hands in front of him like an usher. Matt looked up at him and had the satisfaction of seeing staring eyes, beads of sweat. At a guess, all four guards were addicts.

In withdrawal. Maybe all the more dangerous because of that. His stomach hollowed with fear as he wondered if he was going to die that night.

"Hold him up," Groldor directed.

The car guard complied. "Boss, that last dose must have been milk sugar. I need . . ."

"You need to be silent and do as I tell you!" Groldor snapped.

The man stiffened, clamping his jaw shut. So did the other three—but they were shivering.

Matt managed to start breathing again.

"Sit down, Lord Wizard," Groldor said with a smile of cruel satisfaction. When Matt shook his head, the boss said, "I really must insist."

The car guard jammed Matt down on the folding chair in front of Groldor's card table.

"How . . ." Matt had to gasp for breath again; his stomach still wasn't working properly. "How'd you . . . find us?"

"Why, quite simply, lack-wit," Groldor sneered. "I set a needle afloat in a bowl and told it to seek he who had lately come from Merovence. The aura of that land clings about you, and attracts anything that has a trace of magic; like will to like." He gave Callio a contemptuous nod. "Since there were two of you, the needle swung that much more easily. Then I needed only scry to discover in what place you stood."

Matt nodded. "Thought it would be something like that." He glanced at the left-hand guard. "Better see to your men—they've got trouble."

"Yeah, boss," the right-hand guard whined. "I'm really gettin' strung out. Gimme another dose, please!"

"You need only one a day." Groldor stepped over to him, scowling. "I gave you the powder only an hour ago." He felt the thug's pulse, set a hand against his brow, slid up an eyelid, then drew down his own brows, eyes almost disappearing in shadow. "It is true—you have begun withdrawal." He slipped four foil envelopes out of his pocket. "Take one; give the others to your comrades."

"We ain't no commies," the car guard muttered, but the right-hand guard ripped fast and sprinkled the salt on his tongue. "Thanks, boss! That oughta fix me up in a few minutes." He tossed a packet to the left-hand guard, who grabbed it out of the air frantically, then took the other two to the car guard and driver.

"That won't do any good," Matt said quietly.

Groldor swung about, staring at him. The thugs swallowed their powders, then realized how quiet the boss had become, glanced at him, and followed his gaze to Matt.

"What have you done to the drug?" Groldor hissed.

"Only the reverse of what you did," Matt said.

"You've not had time! I've not seen you!"

"I recited the double verse as soon as I arrived at the station," Matt told him.

"Double?" Groldor's voice was menace itself. "Twofold?"

Matt nodded. "The first part took the kick out of the drug, the second killed the craving for it. Looks like Part Two didn't work."

"You bastard!" the right-hand guard howled, and leaped over to Matt, yanking him up high, fists pummeling. The other three ran to join in.

Matt blocked frantically, kicking and chopping, but he was only one against four very big and very experienced fighters. Punches hit his belly, his chest, his head; he saw one guard fall, another stagger, but the other two had triphammers for fists and were slamming blow after blow at his head, and he managed to block most of them and duck others, but every fifth punch exploded against his jaw, his eye, his ear, and the room dimmed . . .

A gunshot crashed through the warehouse.

The thugs spun, reaching for their revolvers—then groping, slapping, finally looking.

"What the hell happened to my piece?" the car guard howled.

"You were right, Lord Wizard!" Callio cried. "This little lever on the side prevents the longer lever from moving! I only needed to push it down!"

Matt stared. So did the thugs. Callio cradled three revolvers in his left arm and held the fourth pointed at them all.

The driver swore. "How the hell did you get my gat?"

"He's a thief," Matt said. "Remember when he went into a panic and jumped on you?"

The man swore again and started for Callio. The gun crashed in the thief's hand and the left-hand guard cried out, clapping a hand to his shoulder.

"He don't even know how to aim!" the driver shouted, and ran at Callio—but the thief's gun swiveled to center on him, and the thug skidded to a halt.

"Back," Callio said. "Get well back, all of you, back from the Lord Wizard. True, I do not know how to use these magical weapons, but if you come too close, I cannot miss. Get back!"

"Yes, get back," Groldor agreed, pulling out his own automatic. "He may not know how to shoot, but I do!"

Matt throttled a shout of anger and dove for Groldor in total silence—but the left-hand guard saw him and swung a ferocious backhand. Matt saw it coming, ducked, grabbed the arm and shoved it up behind the thug's back—and found himself staring down the barrel of Groldor's gun.

"Boss," the thug panted, "you wouldn't!"

"I have perfect aim," Groldor assured him. "You are in no danger."

Then the gun turned red in his fist. Groldor howled and dropped it, wringing his hand. The thugs shouted and started for it, but it glowed yellow and jumped on the pavement as a shot rang out. The barrel slid, ejecting the spent cartridge, and another fired, then another and another. The thugs cringed away from its muzzle; so did Callio and Matt.

But Groldor was busy sawing the air with his hands and chanting in Arabic—not that it did any good; the heated gun went on firing until the clip was empty. Two of the thugs howled, slumping, as bullets hit thigh and foot.

Finally it was silent. Everyone stared at the gun as though expecting it to reload itself. Then Groldor snarled, "How did you make it grow so hot, Lord Wizard?"

"He did not," said a hard but very feminine voice. "I did."

They all turned, to see a slender, voluptuous, but very stylish woman dressed in the height of fashion clacking toward them on stiletto heels, head high, every inch a princess.

Matt stared. "Lakshmi?"

The woman touched one guard; he slumped, unconscious, even as she turned to touch another. He slept, too, and she advanced on Groldor, who backed away in alarm, still gesturing and chanting.

"You rely on the magic of your homeland," Lakshmi said, "but it is weak here. My magic is within me."

"You are a djinna!"

"I am—and your fate is sealed." Lakshmi turned away from him contemptuously. "Take him with you, Lord Wizard—unless you wish to slay him here."

"It's tempting," Matt admitted, "but I think I'll take him back to Bordestang and let Mama decide what to do with him."

Lakshmi smiled. "It would be kinder to kill him quickly, while he sleeps."

"Yes," Matt agreed. "That's why I'm taking him to Mama." He looked into her eyes. "Thanks for yet another rescue, Your Highness."

"Thank your father," she said, her tone tart. "It was he who bade me follow and ward you—not that I have any greater hope of his gratitude than of yours."

"Someday there will be something I can do for you."

"There is now." For a moment, Lakshmi's smile grew lazy, and the full force of her allure blazed on Matt. It shook him to his core—in human form, and with the clothing of his own world covering her in modesty at the same time that it emphasized every aspect of an inhumanly voluptuous figure, she made him tremble with greater desire than ever.

Lakshmi sensed his reaction and moved in, eyelids growing heavy, lips curving and moistening in a sensuous smile. Matt backed away, fighting for control, and Lakshmi's smile turned bitter as she stopped. Her allure cut off abruptly, and she seemed to be only a woman again. "Not that you will do what you could to thank me. Perhaps someday you will discover some reward that you are willing to give."

Matt went limp with relief.

Then a howl of pain galvanized them both. They turned, to see Groldor writhing in Callio's grip—and staring down the barrel of one of the thief's recent acquisitions.

"He tried to creep away, Lord Wizard," Callio explained. "I did not think he should."

Matt stared. "How the hell did you learn that wrestling hold?"

"It came from inside," Callio said, bewildered, "came quite suddenly."

"I think you may be stealing more from my world than you know," Matt said. He knelt, pulling off Groldor's belt and tying his hands with it. "Put all the guns down, Callio. We don't want them coming back home."

"If you say so," the thief said, sulking. Three metallic objects clattered on the floor.

"All of them, Callio."

"You never let me keep anything," the thief pouted, but the fourth gun landed on the floor, too.

"Somebody gimme a fix!" one of the wounded guards howled. Then his eyes widened, and he gasped, "You did!"

"I guess my second spell just took longer to take effect," Matt said, relieved. Then he glanced up at Lakshmi. "Or did it?"

"It was a very weak spell," the djinna told him. "I have increased its power."

"Thanks again, Princess," Matt sighed. "There has to be something moral I can do for you someday."

"Releasing me from bondage was a great boon," she told him. "You have no idea how greatly you served me then!"

"Yeah, but I'm already past the traditional three-wish reward."

"No, you have only wished twice," Lakshmi told him. "The other requests were your father's, and I granted them only because it pleased me. All else I have done for you was again my own thought. It amused me."

"Best thing I ever did was telling you that you were free to do as you wished," Matt said. "I never guessed you'd want to be so helpful."

"I do hope for further reward," Lakshmi admitted. "Think long and hard, Wizard."

"As soon as I get this corrupted magus to justice." Matt hauled Groldor upright—and found the drug baron grinning. Matt frowned and demanded, "What's so funny?"

"Why, that you have come too late," Groldor told him. "Even now, that Mahdi comes to personal combat with your queen."

Matt stared at him for a long minute of horror.

Then he grabbed the man by the hair and the bound wrists,

ignoring his howl as he shouted, "Callio, hold tight! Princess, I'll see you back home!

> *"Lalinga wogreus marwold reiger*
> *Athelstrigen marx alupta*
> *Harleng krimorg barlow steiger."*

The warehouse wavered around them, then turned into formlessness as the dizziness struck.

Of course, to the two conscious thugs, it was Matt, Groldor, and Callio who had turned formless, then disappeared. The two men stared, their injuries forgotten for the moment. Voice taut with pain, the left-hand guard asked, "You think we oughta tell the cops when they get here?"

"Hey, why not?" his partner shrugged, then winced at the pain it caused. "They wouldn't believe us anyway."

CHAPTER 26

The fleet of fishing boats waited until the morning tide to sail into the mouth of the river, then coasted upstream all day. Late in the afternoon they anchored, a day's march from Bordestang. Rinaldo hoped the Moors wouldn't have thought to have sentries watch the river. Just in case they had, though, he waited until after sunset. Then, when his own scouts reported no trace of enemy troops, the king gave the order to land, and the long process of ferrying men and horses to shore began.

It was the middle of the night by the time the whole of the little army was landed. Then, without waiting for sunrise, King Rinaldo gave the order to march. Slowly and with muffled curses, his men picked their way through the dark until they found a river road. Then, with many glances over their shoulders, wary of ghosts and other night walkers, they marched on down the road in the moonlight.

King Rinaldo hoped nobody was watching.

The sentry skidded to a halt by Saul's chamber door, crying, "Witch Doctor, come quickly!"

"Why?" Saul bolted to his feet, leaving the ancient text he'd been trying to puzzle out. "What is it? More djinn?"

"No, my lord! It is the battlements themselves, the very stone! It has begun to flake and chip and fall away—and the mortar is loosening and trickling out!"

Saul gave an antiseptic curse and followed.

On the battlements, he found Mama already at work with a spell that was more of a song than a chant. As Saul came up, she finished and said, "I have bound their spells at least a little—the stone flakes more slowly. Can you think of a counterspell?"

"You stay with the competitive stuff," Saul told her. "I'm better at being constructive." He whipped a piece of string out of his pocket, tied the ends, and began to rig a cat's cradle while he chanted,

> "Weave the bonds about them tight,
> The molecules of silicates,
> The crystal lattice twisting light,
> Valences umbilicate,
> Edge to edge and plane to plane,
> Renew the bonds between the atoms,
> Strengthen them and let them gain,
> Like chains of reason binding datums,
> Countering spells and entropy.
> Let this wall of durance be,
> Blocks adamant and inchoate,
> Integral, inviolate!"

Sir Gilbert stared. "Why do you play a child's game as you cast your spell?"

"Because a cat's cradle is a model of a crystal lattice," Saul explained. "Each of the fingers is a molecule, see, and the string connecting them is an energy bond . . . Oh, never mind."

"I see again why I have not attempted to learn magic," Gilbert said, awed.

"You'd see it fast enough if I had time to start from the beginning." Saul was piqued at his failure as a teacher. "If I could tell you what a molecule of salt is, and how it can bond to several others, but only at angles . . ."

"When we have won this war, then," Sir Gilbert said hastily. "For now, it is enough to know that your strings hold the blocks of stone in place."

"Too bad they didn't do much for the cat," Saul said.

Sir Gilbert frowned. "Which cat, Witch Doctor?"

"The one that wasn't there," Saul explained, "but that wasn't the point, was it?"

Sir Gilbert asked, thoroughly confused, "Then what was?"

"That there was no cradle," Saul answered. "In fact, nothing really existed except the uncountable molecules in a handful of dust—all the rest was energy."

"Ah!" Sir Gilbert managed to get his chin above the depths long enough to catch a breath. "You mean that the Creator made everything from nothing, and made Man from dust! Moreover, that religion holds people together as with invisible bonds, to form a community!"

"That isn't quite what I had in mind," Saul said slowly, "but you've got the basic idea." He turned away to the stones of the ramparts, feeling the need of a change of topic. "How're we holding?"

"Quite well, now that you are done with your philosophical discourse," Mama said. Her brow was bedewed with perspiration. "But look you, the Moors march!"

Saul turned to stare out beyond the walls of the city and, sure enough, the enemy army was pressing in from every side. Sir Guy was down on the city wall with a handful of junior knights, directing the defense. As they watched, soldiers wound a small catapult—but half-cocked, it suddenly fell apart. A cry of distress went up from a company of archers.

"I'd better get down there fast and see what's going on," Saul said.

There was a horse waiting, and the citizens had the good sense to get out of his way—very far out; they were already running for their houses to take cover. Saul reined in at the foot of the stair up to the ramparts of the city wall, threw the reins to a waiting soldier, and ran up two steps at a time. He grabbed a sergeant and demanded, "What's going on?"

"This!" The sergeant lowered his pike and pointed to the head. It was freckled with spots of rust that multiplied even as Saul watched. "It spreads like rot in summer! The catapults fall apart as their fittings break; the arrows lose their heads!"

"I think I'll let that one pass," Saul muttered, then began to mime forging and dipping, chanting,

> "Rust must every smith beware,
> For moisture's in the very air.
> Since folks need water, can't be rainless,
> Chemists made a steel that's stainless."

A cheer went up from the archers. "I think you have succeeded, Witch Doctor," the sergeant said.

"I'll take what I can get," Saul told him. "Tell the artillerymen they can start lobbing rocks again."

Then a roar engulfed them, scaling ladders slammed against the wall, and the wave of Moors washed over them.

Saul, who never carried a sword, on general principles—the principle being that if he had one, he might use it—was very busy for a few minutes, repelling invaders with every karate technique he had ever learned and wishing he'd studied longer. He ducked a sword cut and winced as it hit another Moor, who howled and turned to slash at Saul.

"Hey, not me!" Saul cried. "Your buddy threw that cut!" He ducked another slash, then came up inside the Moor's guard to hit him hard and fast in the solar plexus. The chain mail hurt like the very devil, but the Moor doubled over in silent agony, and Saul turned to kick another assailant out of the way long enough to whirl back and chop at the first attacker's neck. The man fell, unconscious, and Saul yanked the light shield off his arm.

Someone struck him in the back.

He fell forward, struggling for breath and furious at the foul blow, then pushed himself over and up to swing the shield up just in time to deflect another sword cut, then caught his breath and pushed himself to his feet, shoving the edge of the shield into the attacker's belly. The man doubled over, eyes bulging, mouth gaping in a scream that was lost in the melee, and fell. Saul saw a broken spear on the pavement, scooped up the butt, and jabbed it into the belly of an on-coming Moor, then knocked him aside with the shield and stepped forward.

Suddenly, there was the edge of the wall, pitted and scarred, a scaling ladder leaning on it. Saul set his spear half against the top rung and pushed just as another conical helmet poked above the rim of the stone. The Moor's eyes were coming into sight as the ladder shot away from the wall, paused in balance a moment, then fell.

All along the wall, other defenders had managed to reach the ladders; they fell back one by one, with two or three Moorish soldiers on each, falling with howls and hideous curses—at least, Saul assumed they were hideous; he didn't speak Arabic or Berber. He had a notion he was going to learn, though, and fast.

The battlements were clearing quickly as groups of three and four defenders closed on single Moors. The attackers fought valiantly but fell with Frankish steel in their ribs, or fell unconscious, fit to be tied. Saul winced and turned away from the sight.

He was just in time to see the Black Knight come striding up to him, breathing like a blast furnace. He swung his visor up and called, "We have won, Witch Doctor!"

"This assault, yes." Saul turned to see the Moors regrouping beyond the walls. "They'll try again in a few minutes. How long can we last, Sir Guy?"

"As long as we must," the Black Knight grated.

But atop the castle wall, Mama was in her element, swaying as she chanted in Spanish. The world seemed not quite real as she told it how El Cid had led his men in defense of the city of Valencia. Tears ran from her eyes as she told of his death and his wife's sorrow, then of her great self-denial as she ordered his body to be tied to his horse.

It worked far better than she could ever have imagined, for as the Moorish army threw itself forward in the charge, King Rinaldo led his own army over the ridge and down at the rear of Beidizam's host. Beside him ran Papa, bawling in verse how El Cid led his army in capturing the city of Saragossa.

On the wall, though, a huge suckered tentacle suddenly shot up, waving, then slammed down, striking several soldiers aside and wrapping itself around another. A second tentacle joined it, and a third. They hoisted the body of the monster up; a yard-wide eye peered over the wall, and the soldiers howled in fear, backing away.

"What is it, Witch Doctor?" Sir Guy called.

"A devilfish!" Saul answered. "A giant squid! But how in blazes are they keeping it alive without water?"

"There are more!" a sergeant screamed. "One for each quarter of the wall!"

Then Saul realized that what mattered was that the devilfish was breathing air with no problems, and shrugged. If squids could breathe, whales could fly.

> "Up the food chain go we gaily:
> Every creature has its prey.
> Life yields life to raptors daily.
> Small mammals drained the dinos' day.
> The giant squid makes all turn pale,
> But even krakens fear the whale.
> Moby-Dick, arise and fly!
> Sperm whales, come! Your dinner's nigh!"

Shadows darkened the battlements, and Saul couldn't tell whether the defenders or the Moors were screaming louder. Huge forms shot down out of the sky; gaping jaws closed on the bodies of the giant squids. Ink jetted, and the huge tentacles let go of the wall to wrap about the sperm whales. The attacking Moors slowed, then retreated as the monsters rolled on the fields outside the town.

Saul winced at the plight of the fish out of water. The heck with breathing—that tonnage had to fall in on itself, without water to support it.

> "Embraced and beached, you'll both die stranded!
> Begone, get hence, to where no land is!
> You'd better fear the summer's sun,

And gravity's full fateful rages!
You your landward tasks have done—
Now get you gone, or death's your wages!
Whales and giant squids both ought ter,
As melting snowballs, turn to water!"

Sir Guy stared. "What was *that*?"

"Not my best," Saul said sheepishly, "but I was copying from somebody good. Did it work?"

Huge sucking sounds burst from beyond the walls. Soldiers ran, craning over the crenels, crying, "They fade! They shimmer! They're gone!"

"It worked," Saul sighed. "My friends back home would never have talked to me, if I'd left a whale to die on the beach."

"Still," Sir Guy said judiciously, "it would have given us oil for our lamps for quite a . . ."

"You'll have to use olives," Saul snapped. "What are the Moors doing?"

Sir Guy stepped up to the crenels and stared. "They turn to fight another foe! Witch Doctor! We are rescued!"

Saul ran to stare, and saw a phalanx of knights charging full-tilt into the rear of the Moorish army. The one in the lead wore a crown around his helmet, and beside him, in hauberk and helm, was Papa, singing for all he was worth—off-key and hoarse, but loudly! The Moors, taken by surprise, turned to fight the new foe, but many, still intent on reaching the city, fought their own men, and for a few minutes the army boiled in disarray while the men of Ibile took advantage of the opportunity, laying about them with sword and mace, pike and halberd.

"Sally forth!" Sir Guy roared. "We have an ally! We must join him in the fray!"

The soldiers answered with a shout of glee and ran toward the gatehouse.

The drawbridge lowered, the portcullis shot up, and the front-rank Moors, not yet knowing what was happening a quarter-mile behind them, shouted triumph and charged. They crashed headlong into a line of full-speed knights, and though the Moorish cavalry may have had it all over the heavily armored knights in maneuverability, they were no match for tons of galloping steel head to head. Sir Guy and his knights bowled them over and plowed them under, ramming deeply into the enemy army before their advance slowed. Behind them came a thousand soldiers, hewing and stabbing with halberd and pike. The Moors gave ground—but at a relayed signal from the Mahdi, the flanks suddenly stretched out and flowed forward, turning inward to engulf the defenders.

Then the gates of the city opened again, and Sir Gilbert came charging out with the reserves, to hit the Moorish line.

A few hundred Moors, thinking they saw a chance, galloped toward the open gate—but archers atop the wall rained arrows on them. Many fell, man or horse; the others turned to run, and took the opportunity to attack Sir Gilbert's force in the rear.

The archers aimed and loosed, flight after flight, until Sir Gilbert's rear was clear.

All of a sudden, the ground began to shake under Sir Guy's force and under King Rinaldo's, but not under the Mahdi's.

On the wall, Mama chanted in Spanish, and the ground stilled.

A dozen djinn appeared, reaching down to pluck individual soldiers one by one.

Mama's chant changed, and the soldiers fell from nerveless fingers. The djinn howled with anger and turned, streaming toward the lone, lithe figure atop the castle wall.

In the midst of the battle, Papa looked up, saw his wife's peril, and shouted out the verse his son had used on Lakshmi. The djinn shot upward, shouting in joy, then fell back to the battlements, shrinking to human size, and knelt in homage to Mama's beauty. She stared, taken aback for a moment—but only for a moment. Then she began to ask a few favors of the free djinn.

Finally, King Rinaldo hewed his way through to the pavilion, and the Moorish commander turned at bay—but Papa looked up, startled, hearing a malicious chant. Eyes narrowed, he turned his horse to ride down upon Beidizam, singing the verses of the death of the traitor Gamelon.

Halfway there, an invisible fist struck him off his horse.

With a cry of victory, Beidizam stepped up, swinging a scimitar—and the Genie of the Ring, freed by Papa's chant, boiled out of his confinement and struck his former master a blow that knocked him flat and senseless. Then the genie turned and bowed to Papa. "I have returned your kindness, O Wizard. Call upon me for a reward of three wishes, when you know them."

"The first is that you never slay or cause more pain than necessary, to any living creature!" Papa cried. "The second is that you make clear to these Moors that their battle is lost!"

The genie swelled, shooting up to tower twenty feet high. He surveyed the field from that vantage point, then turned his huge face down to grin at Papa. "There is no need to tell them that, honored sir, for they know it already."

That evening, Papa strolled the battlements with his arm around Mama, looking out over the field where defeated Moors huddled over thousands of campfires, penned inside invisible walls raised by genie-magic. "You have defended the castle and capital most excellently, my love."

"I thank you, *mi corazón,*" Mama said, "but I doubt we could have withstood this battle without your rescue."

"Oh, you would have found a way." Papa smiled down at her. "You always do."

They gazed into one another's eyes, mightily content after their celebration of their reunion. Slowly, Papa lowered his head for a long and lingering kiss.

Finally, Mama sighed and leaned her head against his shoulder. "Must you leave tomorrow with the king, then?"

"I must," Papa said, "for he says he cannot leave Queen Alisande to fight the Mahdi alone—and I am his wizard now, at least for this campaign. Besides, we cannot leave our new daughter-in-law to face her enemies without our help."

Mama looked up. " 'We'?"

"Yes, both of us, if you are willing. I have spoken with Saul, and he is confident of his ability to hold the castle without you, now that the Moors are beaten."

"Do you not fear having me ride into danger with you?"

"I do not think it will be so very dangerous now—at least, not if you are with me."

Mama smiled and gave him another lingering kiss. Then she said, "The Moors will still outnumber both armies by at least a third."

"Perhaps," Papa said, "but they will find they have much less strength than that to which they have become accustomed." He told her where the real power behind the throne had been coming from, and how Matt had gone to shut it off.

"We must go to save him!" Mama cried.

But Papa shook his head. "He must have won, or we would not have triumphed here."

"But so much more time passes here than there!"

"Yes," Papa said. "A whole night has passed, in this universe—weeks, since I left Matthew. Our son has either won or lost—and if he had lost, I doubt that we could have conquered the Moors' magic."

"There is sense in that," Mama said, frowning.

"Besides," Papa said, "he had the help of a good woman." And he told her about Lakshmi.

Mama eyed him sidelong. "Was Matthew the only one with whom this female of the djinn was infatuated?"

"She seemed to feel I would be an acceptable substitute," Papa admitted, "but I explained her error."

Mama had seen how Papa had made such explanations in the past. She smiled, feeling very smug, and turned to look out over the battlefield, leaning her head against his shoulder again. "It is amazing how many friends our son has made here. He was never so popular at home."

"He has found the world that is right for him, my dear," Papa said, "and perhaps right for us, too."

"So it would seem," Mama agreed, "and his friends are such excellent people."

"Most admirable," Papa agreed. He beamed down into Mama's eyes and added, "I think they like us, too."

The next day, they rode off between Sir Guy and Rinaldo. Back atop the city's wall, Saul eyed the thousands and thousands of Moorish prisoners roaming their invisible cage restlessly, and wished he hadn't been quite so cavalier about letting Mama go. "Well, it's up to you and me now, Sir Gilbert."

"Indeed it is, Witch Doctor." The Moncairean didn't seem at all distressed about it. "Can your magic bring food for this many?"

"Oh, sure," Saul said, then frowned in thought. "Might have a bad effect on market prices in Morocco, though."

In the shelter of a low, wide-spreading tree atop a hill, Alisande watched the Mahdi's troops file out of the mountain pass. She couldn't see individual people at that distance, of course—just a moving, multicolored stream that glittered in the sun. It would have seemed pretty if she hadn't known the glitter came from steel, polished by honing and use.

"How long, Majesty?" Lord Gautier asked.

"When their vanguard nears this mount, milord," Alisande answered. She turned her head a little, listening to horses stamping restlessly in the grove behind the hill. "Tell the squires to be sure their masters' horses do not neigh as the Moors come nigh."

Lord Gautier nodded at his own squire, who left to tell the others.

Alisande frowned, raising a hand to shade her eyes and squinting. "What is that flicker of white so high on the mountain above them?"

Ortho the Frank peered, then shrugged. "It could only be a sorcerer who stands ready to defend them, and I am loath to use magic that might make him aware of our presence."

"Then do not," Alisande directed. "Our only strength is in surprise."

They waited impatiently, suspense building as the Moorish column inched closer. Here and there in the fields, peasants bent double with mattock and hoe, but looked up at the invaders, or at the little hill, then turned back to their work again. A perceptive man might have noticed that there was a tremendous number of peasants tilling the earth in this region, but that person would have had to know both agriculture and this province very well, and the Mahdi had been a shepherd in semi-arid hill country. Besides, peasants were as much a part of the landscape as bushes or cattle—no one really noticed them except other peasants, and officers rarely listened to troopers.

On the Moors came, and when their vanguard was perhaps two hundred yards from the hill, Alisande snapped, "We ride!" She turned her warhorse to make its way down the back of the hill to her knights. A surge of yearning struck, yearning to have her husband beside her, protecting her with his magic, but she thrust it down.

She reined in before her troops and shouted, "Charge!," then waved her troops on in one circling movement that ended with spurring her horse. The Percheron turned and rumbled into faster motion, gathering speed as it moved from walk to trot to canter.

Behind her, the phalanx of knights followed, shushing each other.

Out from behind the hill Alisande burst, kicking her horse up to a gallop and leveling her lance.

"The queen rides out by herself!" Lord Gautier cried. "After her, quickly! She must not come to the Moors alone!"

The other knights answered with a shout and spurred their warhorses. They ran flat-out, lances level and unwavering, racing one another to catch up with the queen and protect her with their bodies.

In the fields, the peasants looked up and saw the rider in advance of the others with golden hair flying out from beneath her helmet. They dropped their mattocks and threw off their tunics, then caught up the pikes and halberds they had hidden in the furrows and charged the line of Moors in desperate silence, as their queen had ordered them.

The Moors saw the knights coming—and never thought to look at the peasants in the fields. They set up a wild ululation and kicked their horses into a charge.

CHAPTER 27

The Moors, in their lighter army and more agile horses, tried to swing wide to catch the knights from the sides—but the road fell into a ditch on one side and rose sharply into the hillside on the other. Funneled into staying on the road, lightly armored Moors rode against veritable human tanks, howling with rage at the trick, never thinking to flee or shrink.

Fifty feet from their leader, Alisande shouted her war cry, "For God, St. Moncaire, and St. Iago!"

"St. Moncaire!" the knights echoed.

The Moors called upon Allah to witness their valor and rode harder.

The two armies met with a crash. A few knights fell, but their comrades crushed hundreds of Moors in front of them, up against the hillsides, down into the ditch—where "peasants" coming up from the fields struck down hard with their pikes, and Moorish warriors died screaming with the Name on their lips. The peasants vaulted the ditch and struck into the Moorish army.

Too late, the Moors realized the trap and turned to repel the "peasants"—but they were packed too tightly to fight well; their scimitars needed room. The defenders, though, jabbed and stabbed with their pikes and halberds. Someone began to sing Sir Guy's war song, and the troopers who came running down the hillside joined in as they struck and struck again, hardened pikes ramming through boiled-leather armor and stabbing unarmored horses:

> *"Ran! Tan! Terre et ciel!*
> *Terre et ciel, et sang vermeil!*
> *Ran! Tan! Fer et feu!*
> *Fer et feu, et sang impure!*
> *Vive le vin Gaulois!"*

> "Ran! Tan! Earth and sky!
> Vermillion blood, and earth and sky!
> Ran! Tan! Iron and fire!
> Tainted blood, and iron and fire!
> Hail the wine of Gaul!"

Chanting, Alisande's army hewed its way through the wall of Moors.

At the head of the column, Alisande did the best she could to hew, too, but Lord Gautier and his knights were always there before her. The Moors, who could ordinarily dance rings around the "Franks," were packed too tightly to do more than try to render blow for blow. The heavier swords and axes of the knights cleaved through the lighter Moorish armor and left a wake of blood as they churned through to the center of the army, and the commander.

Suddenly they were there. Tafas bin Daoud sat waiting on his horse with buckler on one arm and scimitar in the other hand, a comely youth flanked by grizzled, grim veterans. The knights halted, awed by his self-possession, by the sheer charisma of the Mahdi.

Alisande rode out between her courtiers and reined in her horse, amazed by her opponent's youth. She swung up her visor out of courtesy to a gallant foe.

Tafas inclined his head in respect. "Your Majesty, our hour has come."

"It need not," Alisande returned, touched and stricken by the thought of having to strike down a man so young. "I am loath to smite you, boy."

Tafas' eyes flashed at the term, but he remained all courtesy. "And I am loath to strike a woman, especially one so fair—but it seems I must."

"Not at all," Alisande returned. "You may yet withdraw your armies to Morocco."

But Tafas shook his head and raised his blade in salute. "I am Tafas bin Daoud of the Rif, and I pray that you may surrender to Allah before the life leaves your body."

"I am Alisande of Merovence," the queen returned. "I commend my soul to Christ, and pray that He will grant you the grace to believe in Him and seek baptism ere you die, so that He may receive your soul into Heaven this day."

Tafas inclined his head again. "I thank you for your good wishes, Your Majesty. Now defend yourself!"

In the mountains behind them, the sorcerer in white gestured and chanted, then cried out in anger as the power he sought to command deserted him.

Tafas howled his ululating war cry and spurred his horse into a gallop, scimitar swinging high.

Someone pressed a lance into Alisande's hand. She kicked her horse into motion, crying, "For Merovence and Ibile!"

She charged at Tafas, lance level, a ton of force focused on that point—but the Moor danced aside at the last second, chopping down at her lance arm with a blade of Toledo steel. It glanced off the finest armor Merovence could boast and chopped into the lance itself instead. Tafas wrenched it out, almost pulled off his horse by Alisande's momentum, and the queen reined in. Moors scattered before her, but not one sought to interfere between Queen and Mahdi, nor did a single one of her knights. All understood that this must be a battle of the two commanders.

Tafas rode madly at Alisande's back, but she managed to turn her horse in time—as he had planned, for his stroke slashed down even as her gaze fell upon him. But Alisande had turned her horse counterclockwise, so that it was her shield at which he swung. The Moorish blade slid off it. Tafas recovered and swung his blade high again, but Alisande's own sword flashed out, and the Mahdi had to abort his own stroke to turn and take her blow on his buckler.

For a moment, they circled one another, swords raised, each seeking an opening. Then Alisande struck, and sword rang on sword, blows rained on shield and helmet. At last the two opponents drew back, both breathing heavily, both wary and watching for the slightest opening—but neither bleeding from even the slightest wound.

The knights and Moors shouted with joy. Slowly, the footmen stopped their slaughter, turning to watch.

Tafas slashed at Alisande's waist, and her shield moved too slowly; one hip plate fell, its thongs cut through. The Moors shouted at this sign of victory, and Tafas galloped around Alisande's horse with blinding speed. She tried to turn with him, to keep her shield between them, but he came up on her right, feinted high, then struck low, at the joint exposed by the lost plate. Alisande dropped her point as quickly as he slashed, though, parrying, then stabbing at him so quickly that he couldn't lean aside fast enough, and a trail of blood gleamed on his cheek.

The knights of Merovence roared approval; the cavalry of Morocco shouted in rage.

Tafas drew back, face darkening in anger, but he knew the score was even again—his cut was equal to Alisande's lost plate. Then he leaped his horse forward, blade slashing and circling too fast for eye to follow, until it stabbed straight at Alisande's eye-slits. But the queen ducked at the last moment and the scimitar glanced ringing off her helmet. She came up stabbing, and Tafas barely managed to drop his buckler in time to deflect her sword—but it scored a long groove in his breastplate.

Both sides were shouting so constantly now that neither Mahdi nor queen could hear their own strokes. They circled each other, gasping in hoarse gulps and wearying, each seeking an opening, neither finding any.

Then Tafas shouted, "O Nirobus! Grant me power now, I pray, that I may strike down this enemy of Islam!" He held his sword high, waiting.

Alisande stared, spellbound by the action, dread creeping over her as she waited for magic to strike. Then she recovered, realizing what an opportunity Tafas had given her, and struck at his undefended side.

Tafas swept his sword down with a cry of dismay, barely managing to parry. "Nirobus! Why do you desert me now?"

He was meat for her cleaving, Alisande realized, weakened by fatigue and now by despair—and if she could just summon the energy to strike, she could finish him with one blow.

She tried to lift her arm, but she was just too weary.

On the road half a mile away, Mama suddenly straightened in her saddle. "Ramón! She needs us!"

"Sir Guy!" Papa cried. "We must race!"

"No!" Mama held up her hand, then caught his. "We will come too late! It is energy she needs now, not an army!" Her eyes glazed and she chanted in Spanish, then went limp.

So did Papa. He felt suddenly weary. He hoped his strength had saved his daughter-in-law.

Energy suddenly gushed through her. Alisande swung her sword up with a cry of triumph and slashed at the Mahdi. The sword went flying from his hand.

The Moorish knights shouted in anger and started to move in—then froze as they saw the queen's sword, unwavering, fixed directly before the Mahdi's eyes.

"I charge you yield, my lord," Alisande panted, "and all your army with you."

"I cannot," Tafas said, pale and taut. "Strike."

A shout went up, Merovencian troopers pointing out across the fields. Alisande spared a quick glance and saw men in European livery running across the furrows toward the rear of the Moorish army.

"It is the King of Ibile!" Lord Gautier cried. "King Rinaldo rides!"

"Your army is half of what it was, my lord," Alisande panted, "between those you have sent to Bordestang, and those we have slain this day. Now another army charges down upon you, and they have little cause for chivalry. I charge you yield, not you alone or for yourself alone, but for all your men, that they may live!"

"Any soldier of Allah who dies in war wakes in Paradise," Tafas said through stiff lips.

Alisande could have screamed in frustration. How could she show mercy if the Moors would not surrender?

Then inspiration struck. "But who will defend Morocco, my lord? The knights of Ibile shall lead their army across the Strait, and Islam shall lose a province! I charge you yield, for the sake of your faith."

Tafas' glance was full of bitterness and anger, but he opened his mouth . . .

And a dust-devil boiled up between their horses, boiled up to the shoulders of their mounts, pulled in on itself, and was gone—but Matt stood there, dressed in strange loose clothing, looking about him in surprise with a strange little man, similarly dressed, clinging to him and moaning, and another fellow, even more outlandishly dressed, at his feet. For a split second, Alisande thought she saw a strangely dressed woman behind them, arms about their shoulders, but it must have been a trick of the light. In joy, she cried "Matthew!" even as she fought her horse, which tried to rear in panic.

So did Tafas' mount, but he reined it in, snatching his dagger from his belt and crying, "Islam!" But the dagger fell—he was too exhausted to hold it up.

Matt looked up, smiling in sympathy. "Tired? I'm afraid there won't be any extra energy flowing into you—I just closed off its source." Then he blew his wife a kiss, but instantly turned back to keep his eye on the enemy.

Alisande fought to keep her sword still—that one kiss threatened to turn her to jelly inside. Matthew was beside her after all!

"Lord Wizard," the little man said, "she brought Groldor with us!"

Matt looked down, then caught the fallen man by the collar with a cry of satisfaction. He scanned the line of Moors for a moment, then strode off purposefully toward a man in a purple turban, dragging Groldor behind him. Alisande cried out in alarm, but Matt only threw Groldor at the other's feet. "So you're the chief battle-sorcerer, huh? How's the magic working lately?"

The Moor stared at him in speechless fury.

"Not too well, huh?" Matt said sympathetically. "Recognize this one?"

The Moor looked down and his face went pale. "It is . . ." Then he clamped his jaw shut.

"It's Groldor, the sorcerer who was supposed to feed you the life energy of young men and young women he ensnared with his drug of enchanted salt," Matt snapped. "There won't be any more deliveries. I canceled his spell, and him with it."

The Moor raised his arm, trembling with anger and shouting a verse in Arabic, then snapped his forefinger down to point at Matt.

Nothing happened.

"A cockroach?" Tafas cried, astonished. "Why would you wish to turn him into a cockroach?"

"The easier to crush, my lord," Matt said, gaze still on the sorcerer.

Alisande fought down a surge of fear for her husband—after all, the danger had passed before she'd known what it was—and glared at Tafas, raising her sword again. "Once more I charge you yield, my lord, not out of fear or despair, but in the sure knowledge that your strength is gone."

"She's right," Matt said, "and it's because you're fighting against people who are devoted to goodness."

"We of Islam are even more certainly devoted to Good!"

"You are," Matt agreed, "and you thought you fought with the might of the Lord to strengthen your arm—but I have learned that you were deceived, my lord, most grievously deceived, and all your people with you."

"Deceived?" Tafas demanded warily, even as his heart leaped with hope that he might live. "How is this?"

"You thought you fought for Allah," Matt explained, "but you had been tricked into fighting for Shaitan's cause." He raised a hand to forestall the youth's objections. "Think of the results of your invasion—misery and suffering, and not many conversions. If you had conquered Ibile, the sorcerer who deceived you would have slain you by magic, then taken all your lands to rule them for Satan."

The Moorish captains cried out in indignation.

"Shaitan?"

"No!"

"Never!"

"Who else could be the source of magic that addicts young people, even children, to a drug that allows him to drain their life energy slowly in order to strengthen your forces?" Matt demanded. "And if your victories are bought with such stolen life, whose victories are they?"

"You lie!" Tafas cried, shaking with anger—and fear that Matt might be right. "I fought only for Allah!"

"But the man who talked you into fighting served a different master," Matt told him. He shook his head sadly. "Sorry, my lord. He used his magic to hunt up a shepherd boy who could convince men to follow him and had the genius to win battles, then bedazzled him with talk of the victory of Islam—when all along, he only cared about his own conquest, and manipulating you into conquering for him."

"You lie!" Tafas cried in despair. "You must! Nirobus is a holy man! He would never promote the cause of Shaitan!"

"But perhaps the cause of himself?" Matt shrugged. "Have you ever heard him call upon Allah, my lord? Oh, to speak of Allah, certainly, even to quote the Koran, for the devil can quote scripture to his purpose—but to actually pray? He is no muzzein or imam, my lord, nor a quadi, nor a clergyman of any sort."

"He is a holy hermit!"

Matt shrugged again. "Prove it, my lord. Go ask him— but take me along."

"Oh surely, lead my armies back to Morocco! Do you think me a fool?"

Matt's eyes lost focus; he turned slowly, gazing off toward the mountains. "I don't think we need to go that far."

Alisande looked up at the patch of white on the distant mountainside. She had thought it only a sorcerer! Could it really be the man who stood behind all this, come to see what he had expected to be a victory? But he had seen his own army vanquished! Why had he not fled? "My Lord Wizard," she said slowly, "I pray you, take care. Why would the genius who has wrought this all stand to await your coming, if he did not still expect victory?"

"Good point." Matt seemed to tense a little, to grow a trifle more bulky, but looked up to smile at the Mahdi. "I'm willing to take the chance, Lord Tafas. Are you?"

How could the Mahdi have refused the challenge, there in front of all his troops?

They climbed the trail to the cave, a dozen Moorish captains and a dozen knights of Merovence, with King Rinaldo and Sir Guy. Matt rode a captured Arabian stallion with Groldor slung over the pommel before him, bound, gagged, and gurgling with fury.

The white-robed man stood waiting for them—but as they came closer, they saw that his robes weren't really white, but a light gray, and the turban on his head was pinned with a blood-red ruby. Matt glanced at it narrowly as they approached; he didn't trust jewelry anymore.

He recognized the man, of course, though he did look a bit different without his gray three-piece suit and bowler hat.

They drew up in front of him. Nirobus was smiling at them, amused—even when Matt shoved Groldor off the horse to fall in front of his boss, red-faced and gabbling. "I thought I'd be a nice guy and return your minion," Matt told him. "No charge, no ransom."

"Why did you bother?" Nirobus didn't even look at Groldor. "He failed."

"So did you, Nirobus." Matt jerked his head downhill. "Your army has lost the war. Without your draining my world for energy, they can't win."

"They still outnumber you," Nirobus reminded, "and the Moors are ferocious fighters. They only need to change their tactics." Then he smiled, and the gentleness, even tenderness of that smile was even more chilling as he said, "Besides, there are other lands in your world—and other worlds. What

I have done once, I can do again." He turned to Tafas. "Be sure, you can still gain the victory."

"With energy drained from youths and maidens?" Tafas was a youth himself, or close enough to take it personally. "I will not lead an army with such a force!"

Nirobus shrugged. "You must take power where you can find it, Lord Tafas, or you will never truly be the Mahdi, never conquer Europe for Allah!"

"You do not deny that you strengthened my army with stolen lives!" Tafas cried, paling. "What if I did conquer Europe? What then?"

"Why, you would rule it under my guidance, and the wild horsemen from the steppe would conquer all of Asia and rule it."

"They are not Muslims!"

"They can become so," Nirobus said agreeably.

"Must we fight them, too?"

"No," Nirobus lectured, "for if you did, neither of you would win; you are both too strong, and would only chew one another to bits. You would rule Europe, and their khan would rule Asia."

"Under whose guidance?" Tafas demanded.

"Why, mine, of course," Nirobus said mildly.

"Then you do seek to conquer the world!"

"How else may all the world surrender to Allah?" Nirobus returned.

"There're an awful lot of souls in Africa," Matt reminded him. "You haven't started work there yet."

Nirobus turned to him, and his mild smile was chilling. "What makes you think that?"

For a moment, Matt's head reeled with the enormity of it. He wondered if the kingdom of Benin had mounted a campaign of conquest into the interior. He had a vision of warriors floating down the Congo River on barges, then coming ashore to burn villages and towns.

He forced himself to pay attention to the here and now—and found Nirobus gazing at him shrewdly. He shook himself, summoning a glare—the sorcerer could have slain him with a single spell while he was distracted.

"You care," Nirobus murmured, in tones of incredulity. "You actually care! You care about people whom you have never seen, of whom you have scarcely even heard!"

"Of course I care," Matt said, glowering to hide how the words had shaken him. "They're human, aren't they?"

"And you care for all who are human."

"Yes, I do!" Matt snapped. "Don't you?"

"Oh, I do, Lord Wizard," Nirobus said softly. "I definitely do—very much."

Matt stared. "Then why are you trying to conquer us all?"

"To keep you from fighting one another," Nirobus explained, "to establish a fair and rational system of laws that will restrain the strong and wealthy, protecting the poor and weak."

"You've brought down all this misery, all the bloodshed and pain of war, in the name of peace?" Matt cried.

"It is nothing compared to the centuries of security, happiness, and prosperity that a world order will bring," Nirobus returned.

The hell of it was that he very obviously believed what he was saying.

"And the junkies?" Matt asked. "The kids, even grade-school kids in New Jersey? Can the peace of your empire make up for leaching their lives away?"

"They were nothing," Nirobus said impatiently. "They had become slaves of the poppy already, and would have died young in any case. Why not put to use the life force they were squandering?"

"Because they might have been saved!" Matt snapped.

"Saved?" Finally Nirobus' lip curled in scorn. "I became a physician to save lives and alleviate suffering, then had to watch people die because my knowledge was not enough to save them. That, I could accept—but seeing people whose lives I had saved come to blows over a woman, a purse, a horse, to see them wound one another and come back to me to heal those wounds, to see them slay one another wasting the lives I had given back to them—it was enough to make me disgusted with all of humankind! I nearly despaired of our breed! But I finally did despair when I saved a young king from a flux that would have killed him, then saw him march off to make war upon his neighbor—and because I had healed him, a thousand peasants died, two thousand soldiers expired in agony!"

In spite of himself, Matt's heart twisted. "The guilt wasn't yours, Doctor."

"But it was! From that time forth I vowed to save only those who were worthy—then despaired of finding any way to detect them! Muslim, Christian, or Jew, there were good people and bad people of each religion, of every country! I thought that good people were weak and exploited, evil people wealthy and grasping—until I helped poor people become rich and gain power, then saw them turn on their weaker neighbors to gouge them of every penny they could find!"

"Didn't any of them give money to the poor?"

"Oh, yes, a few here and there!" Nirobus said angrily. "A few Muslims remembered their obligation to give alms, a few Christians remembered that their Savior had commanded them to feed the poor, a few Jews remembered that their Talmud told them to care for widows and orphans—but so few, so few, and for each of them, there was another who used those poor and defenseless as a woodcutter uses trees!"

"But that's why we have to try to persuade people to be good," Matt objected.

"I stopped believing in Good and Evil, Lord Wizard." Nirobus shook his head, eyes glittering. "You are an educated man who has read accounts telling how people have used one another and betrayed one another down through the centuries. You are a man who has traveled widely, you must have seen such abuse with your own eyes!" Nirobus shook his head slowly, gaze locked with Matt's. "I began to see that there is good in some people, evil in many, some good and some evil in most! I began to see that good and evil exist only within living beings, in people most of all! I saw that the

good often remain poor and oppressed and are rarely rewarded, the evil rarely punished and often prosperous!"

He gasped for breath, a little wild-eyed now, and Matt took
advantage of the pause to comment. "So you stopped believing in divine punishment or reward, and set out to dispense
both yourself."

"Who else would do it?" The question was a challenge as
well as a defense. "Mind you, at first I only exploited people
who were themselves exploiters, rewarded the virtuous a
little but not enough to make them able to hurt others—but
so few, so very few! I began to realize that I would never be
able to reward or punish on a scale that meant anything if I
were only myself, Nirobus the physician, a man alone. I saw
that to make any difference worth making, I would have to
have power, be able to govern a nation—and if I sought to
avoid war, I would have to govern many nations!"

"So to achieve peace, you declared war," Matt interpreted.

"Do not mock me, Lord Wizard! You shall discover my
meaning all too soon, if you live a few years longer and truly
watch the people around you! Yes, I delved through my
books and discovered a way to gain enough power to conquer; yes, I set up a channel for bringing that power from the
mean-spirited and doomed! Yes, I found a man who could
conquer the world, then found sorcerers so self-seeking as to
be completely predictable, sorcerers who would help my
Mahdi by channeling the energy I'd found into his troops,
his victories! But think how few people have died in this
war, how few atrocities Tafas has permitted! As to those
youths in your homeland, can you honestly say that even one
of them would not have bullied or beaten or raped or exploited his fellows, if he could have?"

Matt's mouth went dry. "I didn't know them all. Only a
handful."

"Judge by that handful, then! Can you honestly say that
even one of them was virtuous?"

"They could have been . . ."

"Could have been, but chose not to be! They sought their
own dooms, they deserved their own fates! I have been as

merciful as a conqueror may be, exploiting only those who deserved it, rewarding only those who did my work, turning human cruelty against itself in order to conquer the world and establish peace and order!"

"What about Papa and Mama?" Matt demanded.

"Ah!" Nirobus turned instantly from acid cynic to sympathetic mourner. "That, I regretted, and deeply, for they are scholars, and two of the very few really good people, whose happiness comes from helping those about them."

"Well, if you like them so much, how come you sidetracked Papa into buying the store, then drove him into bankruptcy?"

"Why, because it was the only way." Nirobus spread his hands. "You are their son, and I needed to lure you into the world of your birth so that I could trap you there. Besides, your father was blocking me from addicting more than a dozen young folk by making his store a haven. No, if my scheme was to succeed, your parents had to go." He glanced at Papa with a sardonic smile. "How could I have guessed that they themselves would prove to be wizards so powerful as to tip the balance, and send me sliding toward a temporary defeat?"

"Oh, surely not!" Mama protested. "Matthew would have triumphed without us!"

"Thanks, Mama, but I think he's right." Matt kept his gaze on Nirobus. "He was prepared for anything I might do, and watched me like a hawk. But he never thought to watch you two, until you'd already fouled up his plans good and proper."

"I fear it is so." Nirobus bowed to Mama and Papa. "Your pardon, lord and lady. I underestimated you severely."

"De nada," Mama said automatically, then blushed.

"I think we will be more happy here than in New Jersey," Papa said, "so it has all worked out for the best."

"Besides, here we have not only our son, but also his wife and child," Mama said with a happy smile.

"Yes, best for you." Nirobus still wore the sardonic smile. "But I? I shall have to flee to the barren lands and begin my plans anew."

"Oh, and come back with a small horde, to start killing

people and burning their means of livelihood?" Matt asked grimly. "Begin plans to leave people victims to the famine and plague that always follow war? Plans to slaughter a hundred thousand or so?"

"My warriors slay no more than they must, to conquer," Nirobus said, affronted. "Is this not so, Lord Tafas?"

"I have made sure that my soldiers treat all enemies with courtesy, even when defeated," the Mahdi admitted.

"Okay, so you're only going to slay fifty thousand," Matt said, "and let famine and plague finish off the other fifty."

"I have told you that the people I have hurt are only those who would willingly have injured others!"

"Interviewed each one of them personally, have you?"

"I have no need—I know the breed!" Nirobus snapped. "I have hurt only those who are too ignorant and too vicious to matter, Lord Wizard!"

"No," Matt said softly. "You have slain thousands of good people along with the wicked, Doctor. Even you have admitted that they exist, though they are rare. If you let people die wholesale, as they always do in war, you murder those few good ones along with the rest." He shook his head. "You have become the oppressor and exploiter you claim to despise. I'm sorry, but we can't let you go free to start this all over again."

"No," Alisande said, with total conviction. "We cannot."

King Rinaldo nodded.

"Fools, do you think you have any choice in the matter?" With a vindictive smile, Nirobus raised a hand to his forehead in salute—and rubbed the ruby in his turban.

CHAPTER 28

"Everyone back!" Matt shouted, and started his anti-genie chant—but too late. Smoke boiled from Nirobus' ruby and jetted high into the air, thickening and condensing into a gigantic human form. A genie with mammoth muscles and haughty, noble mien towered above them—and the women gasped, for he was so handsome as to freeze them in place.

"We are lost!" Tafas cried, staring upward, finally actually afraid. "He is a Marid, a veritable prince of the djinn! He wields power too great to comprehend!"

Papa started muttering.

The genie's huge voice rolled out, like a melody played on the deepest bells of a carillon. "What would you have me do . . ." His mouth twisted, and the last word came hard: ". . . master?"

"Clear this hillside for me, O Genie!" Nirobus waved a hand at the officers gathered before him. "Send them back to their troops, back to their homes!"

"To hear is to obey," the genie ground out, obviously hating every word he was saying. He raised huge hands, palms forward, fingers spread wide, chanting in Arabic.

Mama chanted just as firmly.

The genie made a circling gesture with each hand, ending by clenching his fists as his voice thundered out the last syllables of the spell. A gale blasted the line of officers.

Mama finished the rhyme and caught her breath.

The gale died on the instant.

The genie stared. "This cannot be!"

"What cannot be?" Nirobus asked in a tone of foreboding.

"Someone has countered my magic!" He glared down at the host, thundering, "Who has bound my spell?"

Nirobus' eyes widened. "The spellbinder!" He pointed at Mama. "It is she, O Genie! Remove her at once! Slay her, crush her!"

Papa finished his verse, then leaped in front of Mama, crying, "Do not dare!"

"Dare?" The genie roared laughter. "And who will stop me, little man?"

Dust boiled up in front of Papa, up and up till it was almost as tall as he, then thickened and coalesced into a beautiful woman, clad in her usual harem pants, bolero, slippers, and crown—and a very exasperated expression. "What now, mortal man?"

For answer, Papa only pointed upward.

Mama glanced at Papa, frowning.

Lakshmi turned, puzzled—then stared upward. "Prince Ranudin!"

The genie stared, too, eyes wide, then filling with fascination as a slow smile spread over his features. "Yes, I am Ranudin, Prince of the Djinn! But who are you, most beautiful creature?"

"I am Lakshmi, Princess of the Djinn!"

"Lakshmi?" Ranudin gawked. "But you were tiny, nearly a babe in arms when last I saw you!"

Lakshmi glanced at his chest and arms, and her face took on a look Matt knew only too well, a look that intensified as she looked up into Ranudin's face. "That was half a thousand years ago, Prince, and I was not a babe, but a girl on the verge of womanhood."

Now it was Matt who began muttering.

"You have crossed that verge indeed," Ranudin breathed, with a glance that virtually caressed every inch of her.

Lakshmi felt his appreciation, and smiled lazily as her eyelids drooped. A moan swept through the officers of both nations as the full extent of her allure manifested.

"But all of this, O Prince, was before you disappeared from

the sight of the djinn," Lakshmi said. "Now, at least, we know why—some foul mortal sorcerer captured you in that jewel!"

"There have I slept away the centuries, wakened only twice before this to perform irksome tasks for midget mortals— then to sleep again, though my dreams have been restless." Ranudin's voice went husky. "And you have the shape of my dreams! Some magic bore your image to my sleeping mind!"

"As you have always been vivid in mine," Lakshmi said from her throat.

Nirobus groaned.

"I have sought to amuse myself with lesser males, thinking you gone forever from the knowledge of the djinn." Lakshmi turned her head a little away, smiling coquettishly and looking up at him out of the corner of her eyes. "Need I continue to amuse myself with such, O Prince?"

"No, never!" Ranudin breathed.

"Yes, never shall you see him again!" Nirobus reached up to touch the ruby. "Back into the gem, Prince Ran . . ." He broke off with a howl of rage and frustration.

All eyes went to him—finally, for everyone had been watching the djinn—and saw that the cloth of his turban was empty, unadorned. Nirobus yanked it off and searched its folds frantically. "My ruby! It is gone! Where? How?"

Papa and Matt turned to stare at Callio.

The little thief held the huge gem up to the light, then grinned at Matt. "It is amazing what you can do when everyone is staring at something unusual."

"Yes, amazing," Papa agreed, his mouth dry.

Matt kept muttering.

"It is mine!" Nirobus cried, and came running at Callio.

But the little thief stepped up, holding the jewel high, crying, "Here, O Princess! A gift for your betrothal, if you choose that course!"

"I thank you, O Sleight of Hand." Lakshmi reached down to pluck the jewel from his fingers, a split second before Nirobus barreled into him. Callio cried out; Papa leaped to pull him free; Nirobus collapsed into a moaning heap.

Lakshmi turned back to Ranudin with a teasing smile,

weighing the jewel in her palm. "Must you now do whatever I desire, O Prince?"

"Princess," Ranudin said in his huskiest tones, "I do not doubt that I shall choose to fulfill your desires in every way."

Matt finished his chant and whispered to his parents, "He won't *have* to, though."

"I don't think the issue will arise," Mama told him.

"Then come," Lakshmi said, "and let us discover the truth of your boasts." She stepped into his arms, her own going up behind his neck, and he bent his head to kiss her. He was still kissing as dust boiled up about them, and their forms blurred to become one with the whirlwind—but just before Lakshmi's head disappeared, she turned her face to say, "Thank you, wizard. Once more am I beholden to you." Then even her features swam and blended with the motes about her. The whirlwind sprang high into the air and sailed away toward the south, and the desert.

"The Mediterranean coast always was a good place for a honeymoon," Mama said.

"I wonder if the djinn bother with weddings?" Papa asked.

Matt turned to Callio. "I thought you were a failure as a thief."

"Because I was always caught." Callio shrugged. "I could not help myself, Lord Wizard. I felt the need to boast of my exploits in every tavern."

Sir Guy stepped up to take Nirobus by the shoulder and pull him to his feet. "Come quietly, Doctor. Your magic can avail you nothing now."

"Unhand me!" Nirobus cried, and struck Sir Guy's hand away as he leaped back, leaped free. "Avail me nothing? Ignorant fools! Hearken to the song of doom!" He began to chant in Arabic, and Tafas cried out, doubling over in pain. His officers clustered around him with cries of concern, then screamed as he had and clutched their bellies.

Nirobus began to grow, his voice deepening, reverberating as he shifted into the language of Merovence.

Mama began to chant in Spanish.

"By cord, garrote, and pointed awl,"

Nirobus shouted,

"bind the tongues of women all!"

Mama's voice turned into a sort of cawing, consonants without any vowels.

"Blind their eyes and bind their limbs!"

Nirobus cried.

"Let all about me . . ."

A voice cried out in delight, a war cry, and an old knight in rusted armor came charging on a spavined old plowhorse, swelling to match Nirobus' giant size even as his mended lance centered on the sorcerer's heart. Nirobus cried out in rage, his fist swelling into a boulder as he swung a blow at the ancient cavalier—but the stone bounced off the brazen helmet, and the crooked lance struck squarely into Nirobus' chest. There was a crack of thunder, a blinding flash of light, and when the afterimages cleared, both knight and sorcerer were gone, leaving only a charred patch of stone behind.

"But I thought he was only a fiction!" Mama protested, wide-eyed.

"He is the incarnation of a spirit that is always abroad throughout the world, my love," Papa said, his arm around her, "but most particularly here."

"Then was Nirobus a spirit, too?" Matt wondered.

He was very glad when no one answered.

Tafas may have been horrified at seeing his "holy hermit" revealed as a cynical powermonger, and may have been chagrined at having let himself be hoodwinked and exploited, but he couldn't back away completely and keep the respect of his troops. "My men, too, have bled and died, King Rinaldo," he said, chin set stubbornly. "I cannot let those deaths be for nothing, cannot let my soldiers go home with no gain."

"But the land you have taken is not rightfully yours," Rinaldo said gently, "and if I do not take it back now, my descendants will."

He left unspoken that the price of that taking would be blood and death. Tafas glared at him, determined not to be overawed by age and experience.

They sat in an open-sided pavilion with Matt, Alisande, and Sir Guy—an open pavilion in an open field, with the Moorish army watching from one side and the combined forces of Merovence and Ibile from the other. Their chairs were folding hourglass-shapes standing on a Moorish carpet. Between them stood a low table with tiny cups of thick Moorish coffee and goblets of burgundy. Tafas had been pleasantly surprised when Matt had chosen the coffee with every sign of delight.

"Our forefathers' land, at least, you will not deny us!" Tafas snapped, "Not the province that Moors have held these five hundred years!"

"No, my lord, I never sought to push you back across the Straits," Rinaldo said mildly. "But the lands you yourself have taken belong to my people. Will you see them go homeless and poor for the sake of your pride?"

"For the sake of my people, you mean! And what of those folk of Ibile who have chosen to convert to Islam? I must protect them, must I not?"

"How many of them are there?" Rinaldo asked.

"I have bid my scribes keep careful count," Tafas snapped. "Four thousand three hundred fifty-seven of your subjects have embraced the True Faith!"

"Four thousand is enough to fill a small city," Matt pointed out. That was true, in medieval terms.

Rinaldo looked up with a smile. "Which small city did you have in mind?"

"Aldocer!" Tafas leaped on the notion with eagerness. "It is only a hundred miles from our Moorish province! Let us have Aldocer with the land between it and Gibraltar for our own!"

"All the Christians could leave if they wished," Alisande pointed out. "All the Muslims could go to Aldocer, or if they still wished to farm, to the lands the Christians have vacated."

"You would have to pay those expelled Christians for their land," Rinaldo said to Tafas.

The young man frowned. "We have already paid, in blood!"

"But gold is worth far less," Matt suggested. "Give them a little gold, too, Lord Tafas, or they will be beggars. Does not the Koran insist you give alms?"

"If it is alms . . ." Tafas mused.

"You would have to guarantee the safety of the Christians who wished to stay," Rinaldo stated, "and their freedom to worship as they pleased, and not be oppressed for it."

"We of the Faith have always given our protection to the People of the Book," Tafas told him.

"Then you won't mind giving him your pledge in writing, my lord," Matt said.

Tafas turned to him with a frown. "Why should you Christians be so generous?"

Matt didn't think it was the right time to explain saving face. "Ibile can reap huge benefits from your Moors, milord. The Arabian Empire is bringing fascinating new knowledge from India and Greece, is it not?"

"So my scholars say, yes." Tafas was wary of compliments.

"And fabulous tales, beautiful paintings and miniatures, breathtaking architecture." Matt turned to Rinaldo and Alisande. "They have brought a new system of numbers from India, have invented a new form of mathematics called *al gebr*, and have made a great number of advances in medicine. Besides, their merchants are sailing down the coasts of Africa and India and bringing back silks, pearls, and delectable spices, not to mention gold, ivory, and ebony!"

"Oh, mention them." Alisande smiled, amused. "Do mention them." She turned to Rinaldo. "So Moorish merchants in Ibile can trade with their counterparts from Arabia, Majesty, and trade again with merchants of your own."

"Yes, a most profitable trade, I doubt not!" Rinaldo said heartily. "I might even develop a taste for this 'coffee' of yours, Lord Tafas."

"I already have," Matt said emphatically. "I'm tempted to kidnap one of your officers, Lord Tafas, just so I can ransom him for his weight in coffee beans!"

Tafas smiled. "I shall see that twelve pounds are sent to you each month, Lord Wizard, in thanks for the service you have done me in unmasking Nirobus."

Matt groaned with pleasure.

Tafas turned to Rinaldo. "It is a good settlement, my lord, and might last as long as you and I live, but certainly no longer. Your armies will try to push my Moors back across the Straits someday—it is inevitable."

"That is the only major natural boundary, yes," Rinaldo agreed.

"Also, my descendants will wish to expand, and I will not be there to forbid it—nor, in loyalty to my faith, would I wish to."

Rinaldo scowled.

"I don't think your heirs will mind," Matt said quickly, "as long as the Moors expand by purchasing their land—and swear allegiance to the King of Ibile."

Rinaldo turned to him in astonishment, then began to smile.

Matt turned to Tafas. "Trade may take longer than conquest, my lord—but it's much cheaper, and far more profitable."

"You would not mind having Moors among your subjects?" Tafas asked in astonishment.

"Certainly not, if they will fight side by side with my Christians when Ibile is attacked." Rinaldo took fire at the idea. "They are doughty soldiers in war, and as the Lord Wizard says, they may enrich the land wonderfully in culture and commerce."

Tafas' face took on a cagey look. "Would you grant such

Moorish citizens the same rights and protections that you
have asked for Christians in my domain?"

"Of course," Rinaldo said instantly.

Tafas looked doubtful—but also very hopeful.

"Maybe the prosperity of Moorish trade can pay back your
people for their losses in this war," Matt said to Rinaldo. Privately, he hoped the people of Ibile might develop a vested
interest in having Moorish countrymen—literally vested, if
they had the good sense to invest in Moorish businesses.

"Conquest by gold instead of armies?" Tafas stared in
amazement. "What a splendid idea!"

Looking into his eyes, Matt felt a chill. The military genius was about to become an economic genius. The Japanese weren't supposed to develop that technique for another
five hundred years—or was it the American fruit compa-
nies? Well, come to think of it, the British East India Company came first . . . Matt felt a lot better. He was only jumping
history by four hundred years now.

Aloud, he said, "Yes, Lord Tafas. If all else fails and the
people of Ibile insist on getting their whole peninsula back,
maybe they can work out a gradual retreat and buy-back
plan."

Tafas grinned, and Rinaldo said, "Let us hope it will not
come to that, Lord Wizard. I think we may prove good
neighbors after all, Lord Tafas."

So the two armies parted with protestations of goodwill,
trying to forget the dead they had just buried. Tafas led his
Moors back to the south, Rinaldo bade his noblemen march
home and reclaim their castles, and Alisande's army marched
back to Bordestang.

Alisande was delighted to find her capital intact, even
though Mama had told her the whole tale of the siege. She
heaped gratitude and praises on the older woman, then rode
down to release the Moorish prisoners and send them marching to the coast under guard.

They entered the city and were pelted with flowers. The
people cheered the victors as they rode up to the castle,

where Saul stood grinning on the drawbridge with Angelique beside him. Alisande kissed them both, then insisted on knighting Saul no matter what he said—he had refused the honor before—then rode into her castle singing the joy of homecoming.

Matt lingered on the drawbridge to talk with Saul and his parents. "I have a little problem called Callio. We can't just turn him loose to end up in jail again."

"Amazing that he does," Papa said, "when he is such an accomplished thief—but he cannot help boasting of his successes."

Mama brightened. "So it is not the stealing that matters to him, only the acclaim?"

Matt nodded. "Starved for attention. You think he's a klepto?"

"No, a natural entertainer!" Mama declared. "He already knows sleight of hand—let him learn to be a conjurer!"

"And an escape artist!" Papa nodded, smiling. "We will help him invent vaudeville!"

"Why not?" Matt grinned. "I'm sure he can do it, with a little financial support from the castle." Then he grew serious. "But we have another problem. Can we all meet tomorrow morning in the middle of the courtyard at first light?"

Papa and Mama exchanged a glance. Mama said, "Of course, if need be."

"Sure," Saul said. "Why?"

"We need to close off the connection to our home universe," Matt explained.

"Well, you might leave a thread," Papa qualified.

Mama nodded. "Only between this castle and your post office box, Mateo. We do, after all, wish to send a few Christmas cards."

The next day, Mama entertained Alisande alone, in the chambers the queen had appointed for the use of Mama and Papa Mantrell. Mama poured and handed a demitasse to her daughter-in-law. "It is nowhere nearly as strong as the

Moors brew it, Majesty, and is well diluted with cream and sweetened with honey. Humor me by drinking of it."

"I will," Alisande said, "if you will call me 'Alisande' when we are alone."

Mama's smile was pure sunshine. "I shall be delighted, my dear."

Alisande tasted, and looked up in surprise. "Why, it is delicious when it is not so strong and muddy!"

"Is it not? But we must drink it only as a rare treat—too much of it can be bad for you."

"Too much of anything can be bad for a person," Alisande said wryly, "except possibly love." She looked up at Mama anxiously. "I hope you do not have to leave for your home too soon, Lady Mantrell."

"Jimena," Mama said firmly, "though I would be quite complimented if you called me 'Mama,' as Matt does."

Alisande tried to keep her smile in place while she dissolved inside. "As you wish . . . Mama! But you must make this a long visit, so that I will have time to practice!"

"Well, as to that . . ." Mama straightened in her chair a little, avoiding her eyes. "In our own world, my dear, Papa and I are quite ordinary folk; even though our educations should win us a fair amount of respect, they do not."

"You will have great respect here," Alisande said firmly, "even awe from the common folk."

"We have felt that," Mama said, smiling. "It is a very pleasant feeling. And our house in New Jersey, though pleasant enough, was not even as spacious as those of your merchants. Besides, Papa has no business now, and no job, nor have I."

"Then why not stay here?" Alisande said anxiously.

"That is exactly what Ramón and I were asking ourselves last night," Mama told her. "We could not think of a good answer."

Alisande stiffened. "Does that mean you wish to remain here? Forever?"

"Well, at least as long as we live," Mama said apologetically, "if you will have us."

"I would be delighted!" Alisande rose from her chair to throw her arms about her mother-in-law.

Surprised, Mama hugged her back, then tightened her embrace as she realized Alisande was shaking. "Why, poor child, you are weeping!" She held the Queen of Merovence in her arms for ten minutes, murmuring the sort of soothing inanities that come only to mothers.

At last Alisande straightened and stepped away, smiling and wiping her eyes. "You must forgive me, milady Mama. It must be the stress of this little war."

"A queen is always subject to great stress," Mama said, voice firm but sympathetic. "You must be able to weep with someone, my dear, or you will explode with your feelings."

"Yes. I thank you." Alisande smiled and sat again, taking another sip of the coffee. Its bite helped restore her. "Dare I hope, though, that your new grandchild has something to do with your decision to stay?"

"The child, and his mother," Mama told her, smiling gently. "Family is the true vocation of both Papa and myself, my dear, far more important to us than anything else—and since both my parents and Papa's have passed away, and Matt is our only child, and our new daughter-in-law is so *very* nice . . . Well, of course!" Then she stared, facts suddenly connecting. "The tears . . . It is not only the stress of the campaign that has brought you to weeping, is it?"

Alisande stared at her. "How did you know?"

"You forget, my dear, that I have been there before you! Come now, no hiding the truth! Out with it!"

"Well, yes." Alisande looked down into her coffee. "I cannot be sure yet, but I think that you shall have another grandchild before next summer's heat."

"And you went on campaign!" Mama cried, then seized a cushion and tucked it behind Alisande's head, pulled a hassock over and propped the queen's feet on it. "You must be sure to diné well now, though not too much—that old wives' tale about eating for two has caused many women to gain weight they could lose only with great difficulty! And no wine, or at least only a little! How foolish I was, to introduce you to coffee! And you must not worry, you must leave as much as possible to your ministers, and anything they cannot manage, you must assign to Papa and myself . . ."

Her voice flowed on, and her hands were very soothing as they massaged temples, touched wrist to measure pulse, tucked a lap robe about her—all completely unnecessary, of course, but Alisande leaned back and luxuriated in the attention, deciding that it really was very nice to have a mother again.

HER MAJESTY'S WIZARD

Book One of
A Wizard in Rhyme

by Christopher Stasheff

Matt's graduate research turned up a strange scrap of parchment; but when he tried to read the runes, they carried him away—straight into a sorcerer's dungeon. Teaming up with the dragon he met there, and with a lust witch and a priest who became a werewolf on occasion, Matt Mantrell set out to rescue the beautiful Princess Alisande and defeat the sorcerer and his dark magics.

Published by Del Rey Books.
Available at bookstores everywhere.

THE OATHBOUND WIZARD

Book Two of
A Wizard in Rhyme

by Christopher Stasheff

Matt vows to conquer a kingdom, if that's what it takes to win Queen Alisande's hand. But in this world of magic, his oath is literally binding: now he has to win a crown, or die in the attempt! Picking out a likely tyranny is easy, but even with a well-spoken cyclops, a surly dracogriff, and a chased damsel in his corner, overthrowing an evil genius was going to be tricky...

Published by Del Rey Books.
Available at bookstores everywhere.

THE WITCH DOCTOR

Book Three of
A Wizard in Rhyme

by Christopher Stasheff

First, Saul's best friend—Matt Mantrell, hero of *Her Majesty's Wizard*—mysteriously disappears, then a spider bite sends him to an alternate universe where poetry works magic. How Saul defeats an evil queen and finds Matt—with the help of the lovely ghost Angelique, a troll named Gruesome, the Spider King, and a host of other characters—makes for a story strong enough to trap a tyrant.

Published by Del Rey Books.
Available in bookstores everywhere.

THE SECULAR WIZARD

Book Four of
A Wizard in Rhyme

by Christopher Stasheff

Matt Mantrell, Lord Wizard of peaceful Merovence, hears that a neighboring king isn't committed to either Good or Evil. Aghast—that's not how things work in this world of magic—he sets out to investigate, dodging dastardly assassination attempts by the king's sinister prime minister. Aided and abetted by a collection of colorful characters, Matt gives the king an appreciation of humanist values—and the bad guys their just deserts.

Published by Del Rey Books.
Available in bookstores everywhere.

DEL REY® ONLINE!

The Del Rey Internet Newsletter...

A monthly electronic publication e-mailed to subscribers and posted on the rec.arts.sf.written Usenet newsgroup and on our Del Rey Books Web site (www.randomhouse.com/delrey/). It features hype-free descriptions of books that are new in the stores, a list of our upcoming books, special promotional programs and offers, announcements and news, a signing/reading/convention-attendance calendar for Del Rey authors and editors, "In Depth" essays in which professionals in the field (authors, artists, cover designers, salespeople, etc.) talk about their jobs in science fiction, a question-and-answer section, and more!

Subscribe to the DRIN: send a message reading "subscribe" in the subject or body to drin-dist@cruises.randomhouse.com

The Del Rey Books Web Site!

We make a lot of information available on our Web site at
www.randomhouse.com/delrey/

- all back issues and the current issue of the Del Rey Internet Newsletter
- sample chapters of almost every new book
- detailed interactive features of some of our books
- special features on various authors and SF/F worlds
- ordering information (and online ordering)
- reader reviews of upcoming books
- news and announcements
- our Works in Progress report, detailing the doings of our most popular authors
- bargain offers in our Del Rey Online Store
- manuscript transmission requirements
- and more!

If You're Not on the Web...

You can subscribe to the DRIN via e-mail (send a message reading "subscribe" in the subject or body to drin-dist@cruises.randomhouse.com), read it on the rec.arts.sf.written Usenet newsgroup the first few days of every month, or visit our gopher site (gopher.panix.com) for back issues of the DRIN and about a hundred sample chapters. We also have editors and other representatives who participate in America Online and CompuServe SF/F forums and rec.arts.sf.written, making contact and sharing information with SF/F readers.

Questions? E-mail us...

at delrey@randomhouse.com (though it sometimes takes us a little while to answer).

✒ FREE DRINKS ✒

Take the Del Rey® survey and get a free newsletter! Answer the questions below and we will send you complimentary copies of the DRINK (Del Rey® Ink) newsletter free for one year. Here's where you will find out all about upcoming books, read articles by top authors, artists, and editors, and get the inside scoop on your favorite books.

Age _____ Sex ❑ M ❑ F

Highest education level: ❑ high school ❑ college ❑ graduate degree

Annual income: ❑ $0-30,000 ❑ $30,001-60,000 ❑ over $60,000

Number of books you read per month: ❑ 0-2 ❑ 3-5 ❑ 6 or more

Preference: ❑ fantasy ❑ science fiction ❑ horror ❑ other fiction ❑ nonfiction

I buy books in hardcover: ❑ frequently ❑ sometimes ❑ rarely

I buy books at: ❑ superstores ❑ mall bookstores ❑ independent bookstores
  ❑ mail order

I read books by new authors: ❑ frequently ❑ sometimes ❑ rarely

I read comic books: ❑ frequently ❑ sometimes ❑ rarely

I watch the Sci-Fi cable TV channel: ❑ frequently ❑ sometimes ❑ rarely

I am interested in collector editions (signed by the author or illustrated):
  ❑ yes ❑ no ❑ maybe

I read Star Wars novels: ❑ frequently ❑ sometimes ❑ rarely

I read Star Trek novels: ❑ frequently ❑ sometimes ❑ rarely

I read the following newspapers and magazines:
❑ *Analog*	❑ *Locus*	❑ *Popular Science*
❑ *Asimov*	❑ *Wired*	❑ *USA Today*
❑ *SF Universe*	❑ *Realms of Fantasy*	❑ *The New York Times*

Check the box if you do not want your name and address shared with qualified vendors ❑

Name _____
Address _____
City/State/Zip _____
E-mail _____

stasheff

PLEASE SEND TO: DEL REY®/The DRINK
201 EAST 50TH STREET NEW YORK NY 10022
OR FAX TO THE ATTENTION OF DEL REY PUBLICITY 212/572-2676